DAUGHTERS OF THE RIVER HUONG

A Vietnamese royal concubine and her descendants

DAUGHTERS OF THE RIVER HUONG

A Vietnamese royal concubine and her descendants

Uyen Nicole Duong

RavensYard Publishing, Ltd.
Fairfax County, Virginia USA

ISBN 1-928928-16-1

Published by
RavensYard Publishing, Ltd.
P. O. Box 176
Oakton, Va. 22124 USA
www.ravensyard.com

To my family and the Vietnam I left behind

PETALS OF A BLACK ROSE

Of time itself in the room we would share
the rarest flowers
mingling aromas

. . .

And Eastern splendor on the walls
here all would whisper
to the soul in regret
her sweet mother tongue

All is order there, and elegance,
pleasure, peace, and opulence

. . .

And every color, even black,
became a lustrous prism
liquid turned to glowing glass
and what was crystal flowed

. . .

Now comes the time when swaying in its stem
Each flower offers incense to the night
phrases and fragrances circle in the dark
The violin trembles like a heart betrayed

. . .

The Sun will die in its sleep beneath its arch
like a mourning cloth trailing toward the East
listen, my dear, to the soft steps of our Night

from the translation of "Fleurs du Mal"
Charles Baudelaire (1821-1867)

CONTENTS

MAIN CHARACTERS' NAMES AND CONTEXT

First Generation

Huyen Phi (1895–1930) — the Paddle Girl from Hue's River Huong, who became the Mystique Concubine to the King of Annam 1900–1910

Thuan Thanh (1875–1945) — King of Annam, formerly Buu Linh, the Crowned Prince, who reigned as king 1889–1910.

Son La (1845–1935)— eunuch, servant to Huyen Phi, the Mystique Concubine

Mai (1895–1968) — chambermaid to the Mystique Concubine; nanny to Dew; later a rebel and spiritual medium

Sylvain Foucault (1865–1950) — Resident Superieur, State of Annam, French Indochina

Second Generation

The Children of the King of Annam and the Mystique Concubine:
Que Huong (1905–1976)— Princess Cinnamon, Grandma Que
Sam Huong (1905–1949) — Princess Ginseng, daughter of the Revolution
Que Lam (1910–?) — Prince Forest

Third Generation

Mi Suong (1934–) — Dew, daughter of Princess Cinnamon, mother of Simone

Tran Giang Son (1934–) — Hope, professor, husband of Dew, father of Simone

O-Lan—housekeeper for Princess Cinnamon, Hue noodle seller; daughter of Mai.

Andre Foucault (1935–1990) — lawyer, teacher, grandson of Sylvain Foucault

Dominique Clemenceau (1940–?) — wife of Andre Foucault

Christopher Sanders (1930–1985) — American reporter in Saigon, who married Simone

Fourth Generation

Simone Mi-Uyen (1955–) — first born daughter of Dew and Hope; singer, refugee, New York lawyer

Mimi Mi-chau (1958–)— second daughter of Dew and Hope, younger sister of Simone

Pierre (Pi) Phi-Long (1963 –) — son of Dew and Hope, younger brother of Simone and Mimi

DAUGHTERS OF THE RIVER HUONG

A Vietnamese royal concubine and her descendants

PART ONE

1. Christopher

Christopher must have sent Lucinda home for the weekend. The lacquered clock chimes six-thirty and I shut the apartment door behind me, my heels clicking and pivoting on the hardwood. I know he can hear my key turn out of the lock and then the hush down the hallway as I stand motionless in the vestibule. Through his library window, the sun must be paling to rose, the last trace lingering along the glass that separates him from Manhattan's skyline. I know he has been sitting there, waiting for the world to darken completely, his broad back humped in front of the long row of bookshelves.

He began his habit of shutting himself into the library when I began mine. Ever since I arrived, I would wake before he did. In the bleary early morning, I would turn away from him in bed to face a reproduction of Renoir's couple dancing arm in arm. Morning after morning I scrutinized the dancers hanging on the wall: the man's haggard face nestling against the woman's plump rosy cheeks, his uncombed raven hair against her swirling mass of chestnut brown strands. At some point in the formation of my routine, my husband caught on. He began sighing when I turned toward the wall. When that did nothing, he would rest his palm awkwardly on my shoulder, waiting for some kind of response. We would lie in silence waiting for the sun to rise, as if there were a chance it might not. Finally, he would get up, jab his arms into the arms of his robe, and head toward the dark library. I used to wait for his square-tipped fingers to start striking the electric keyboard.

Lucinda has put out a fresh arrangement of irises and stargazer lilies on the hallway table to welcome me home. He will hear me walk past the mirror, past the slim table legs, past the patina framed black-and-white photos of his grandparents, great-grandparents, cousins All his and not mine.

I will be pushing on the library door and then I will face him for the first time in months.

Our past life goes through my mind like clips from a slow movie.

It has been ten years since the fall of Saigon and the young girl from Vietnam that clung to him is a creature of the past. The fight between us was over nothing, but during the aftermath there was a major merger and acquisition closing in my firm of some two hundred lawyers. I announced that I needed to stay in the Hyatt Regency adjacent to the office rather than ride the subway back every night to our condo. Yesterday he called and asked me to come home, although he must have known I was only two days from the closing that could determine my career. Christopher has never interfered with my work schedule, no matter what the demand is. He never objected when I had to stay away from home during my three years of law school to participate in study groups, or when I first got hired and had to pull all-nighters to meet the partners' demands. He's always behaved like the perfect supportive husband of a modern career woman.

When he mentioned the jade phoenix and the two ivory plaques, I decided to cancel the rest of my hotel reservation. The phoenix and the plaques once belonged to my family's altar and have been locked in a safe deposit box at Chase Manhattan for almost ten years. The only other mention he ever made of them was to say they were there, at the bank. On the phone yesterday he had said casually that it was about time for him to return those items to me.

I went home at ten o'clock at night, the end of my work day, but he had locked the door to our bedroom, so I ended up sleeping in the guest bedroom. In the morning, I found a note he had written for me, reminding me of my follow-up appointment with my psychologist, Dr. Cookie D'Amico. When he did not show up for breakfast, Lucinda said that he had had an accident and had not been feeling well.

When I left for the subway in the morning, the yellow and red leaves blazed. I had not seen them like that since I began law school at Columbia and the frenetic pace of studying numbed everything. I was glad for the work then, since I did not have to think about my family who settled down in Houston, or about my husband pretending what he shared with my father in Vietnam did not exist. There was a time in my former Saigon when Christopher knew my father as Hope, the journalistic stringer who helped newsmen of the Associated Press interpret South Vietnam's culture and politics, and who passed on news tips about the complexity of the war.

Instead of working, I spent the entire morning in Dr. D'Amico's office talking about my recurring dream. I tried to describe the lush green rain forests of my dream turning swiftly into the low charcoal sky of the highlands, the sky brightened only by the wildflowers blooming beside the red dirt road. In the dream, topless *montagnard* women with dark brown torsoes climbed the winding slopes on bare feet. I could feel the sprinkling rain of the highlands and the ache in my knees when I tried to run uphill after them. I ran until the foliage and the cliffs telescoped into blackness and were replaced by the lithe bodies of the royal dancers of central Vietnam. They held buds of lotuses in their hands and their legs bent into a diamond shape while their lovely heads tilted beneath gold and jade headpieces. Then a fog swept through the dancers, clearing to reveal a procession of coffins floating on a silent river. In the dream, I could feel the intense heat rising off the coffins as they passed, heat that drowned my lungs and nostrils until I woke up choking.

A few days after I first told him about the dream, my husband gave me Dr. Cookie D'Amico's office number. Dr. D'Amico is Southeast Asian like me, and he thought she would be of some help. After a few months of regular sessions, Dr. D'Amico the psychologist had became Ms. Cookie my friend. I did not always take her seriously since I usually do not believe in psychologists' pep talks. It took months before I told her what I knew from my heart: that the dancers were the women of the extinct culture of Champa. She did some research and formed a theory about the connection between my central Vietnamese ancestry and the story of the Chams, an extinct race.

I am too headstrong for Western psychology, although in Ms. Cookie I have confided all of my fears. Since the fall of Saigon, I have dreaded any kind of separation — the anxiety of leaving a place knowing perhaps I will never see it again. Cookie said the anxiety naturally must have come from my traumatic departure from Vietnam. The whole circle of my husband's friends in New York City must have heard of my airlift escape from Vietnam in 1975 atop the U.S. Embassy, during the last hours before the Russian tanks rolled toward Saigon's Presidential Palace. I have heard enough comments made behind my back at cocktail receptions and Christmas parties. The story goes that I was my husband's under-aged mail bride ordered straight from a refugee camp. I have never bothered to correct the record: technically I was not a mail bride because we actually met in Saigon days before the change of guards.

Initially, I had gone to see Cookie only to please my husband because after all, he was paying her enough money to feed a whole Vietnamese village. Having a shrink was part of my becoming American, something considered trendy in my Manhattan life, like the fox coat he had bought me as a birthday present to protect my fragile frame from New York's harsh winters. So, when I first heard Cookie's interpretation of my dream, I had the urge to tell him. The check he sent to Cookie monthly had to bear its fruit. I mentioned the topic to him at dinner one day.

"You've heard of the Chams from central Vietnam?"

"Of course," Christopher answered. "I reported on the place."

"According to Cookie, I'm a descendant of the Chams and that's part of my problem."

"Huh. Actually, I could see the connection between you and the Chams." He leaned back in his chair. "The bridge of your nose is higher than the average Vietnamese nose and you're much taller than the average Vietnamese. If it had not been for your fair skin, I would say you look partly East Indian. And since I've got to know your disposition better, I would say you are not exactly the typical unexpressive Vietnamese woman."

I went on excitedly like a passionate lecturer before a class of wide-eyed students:

"My mother and maternal grandmother are from central Vietnam. Before the fifteenth century, central Vietnam used to be the Kingdom of Champa. Back then, the Chams fought the Vietnamese quite often, until the King of Vietnam married off his sister, some beautiful duchess, to a Cham king in exchange for land. So, the duchess was sold off into a loveless marriage for the sake of the nation. Later, she might have been burned to death in accordance with Cham custom when her older husband, the Cham king, passed away. It must be my cultural subconscious mind that created those dreams and all my nostalgia."

"Are you truly nostalgic, or just wistful and resentful?" Christopher asked casually.

"According to Cookie, I bear in me the collective subconsciousness of an extinct culture, with all its tragedy, which could trace back thousands of years, and that's why I am never truly happy, although I have all the reasons in the world to be happy."

I had been speaking more to myself than to him. He finished his glass of water, put down the linen napkin and got up from the dining table, heading toward the library:

"Really? That's interesting, but too complicated and completely unproven. I have a better explanation for your unhappiness, although I'm no psychologist."

He paused to meet my eyes:

"You've already hinted to me several times about the Vietnamese duchess who was sold off in exchange for the Chams' land. You're obssessed with the story. What's her name?"

"Huyen Tran. It was also the name of the street where my ancestral house was in Hue."

"But this isn't about the name of a street, is it, Simone? For years you kept singing a folk song about this self-sacrificing duchess in the shower."

"Did I?" I stopped eating. "I must have, but I didn't think you noticed."

"Oh yes, I did. I notice everything. In fact, I know the folk song. You forget too quickly that I lived in your former home for years. It was your father who taught it to me: *pity her, a lily-white rice grain, bathed in the disgrace of shameful stain, washed out in muddy water, burned in straw flame...*"

He took his eyes off me and was moving away from the dining table.

"I think you sang it deliberately for me to hear, Simone. If you could, you would sing it, too, in the middle of our love-making."

He stopped at the door to the hallway and abruptly turned toward me. I lowered my eyes to avoid his gaze.

"I married you, Simone, but I'm not the man you wanted to marry had it not been for the fall of Saigon. I'm not stupid. The simple truth is you're always unhappy because you are here with me, and I can't do anything about it but to send you to law school, and then to Cookie. But what was the alternative? Should I have left you in Vietnam with the Communists?"

I dropped my napkin and leaned over to pick it up from the floor.

When I looked up, he was gone.

That night, as he was reading in bed, I opened the closet to find the gift box that contained the unworn sequin dress he had given me for Valentine's Day. I knew what I wanted to do. I had been his faithful girl but despite our years together, I could not bring myself to tell him I loved him, knowing that the words were what he longed for to fortify our peace.

I held the dress up and asked him to get me a pair of scissors.

He was sitting on the bed, doing what I disliked most: smoking his cigar. I stood for a long time holding the black clingy material in my hands. I could put the dress back in the closet, come over and stretch myself down next to him so that the tension between us would quickly evaporate. Yet I stood still. Cigar smoke lingered on my skin, on every strand of my hair and along the nape of my neck. From the bed, he got up casually, too casually, in order to put on some jazz music. He returned to the bed and put on his reading glasses.

I repeated that I would like a pair of scissors.

When he did not move, I became overwhelmed with a titanic anger that made my hands shake. I tore at the sequin dress, scratching my own knuckles. He remained nonchalant, watching me the same way he watched a late night TV show. Then he slid open the nightstand drawer, took out a pair of scissors, sprang up and yanked the dress from me. He began cutting and sequins fell around us like confetti. I slumped down on the carpeted floor, terrified to see the sharp and swift blades shred the sparkling fabric. I began crying. He grimaced as he threw the scissors against the dresser mirror, crashing the glass into threaded shards. There, I saw our distorted faces. My tears must have moved him, and he leaned over and gathered me into his arms. I might have fought him, but he was twice my size. He put me down on the bed and collapsed next to me, as though the whole episode had become the unbearable weight of a building falling in an earthquake. We laid there, perhaps both feeling sorry for what we had done to each other, yet not knowing what to do or say. I wanted badly to climb over him and kiss his chest to seal the gap between us. Perhaps he would raise his head and catch my lips. For a long time, I listened to him breathe sadly next to me. Finally, with the constructed effort of a defeated soldier I curled up in a fetus posture. Slowly he moved to face me, entangling my limbs. I wanted to pull him to me so that the weight of his dense body would shield me from the cold that crept up in my chest.

In the cold came the flashback of what happened that day in April, 1975, when I first met him. Room two hundred and ten, in the historic Continental Hotel downtown Saigon. Then, his rhythm, no matter how ruthless and relentless, was, after all, the only thing I knew that could rid me of the cold seeping from the marble floor of the Continental Hotel onto my skin and limbs, the icy spread of a city's death. I knew, too, that in any passion he had for me, I would feel nothing but death spelling itself out, in coffins floating on the river of childhood.

I had not even told Cookie about the coffins during those couch sessions in her office. I had wanted a sacred place for them, a secret burial ground. The secret became my last bond to my childhood, and to the woman who had raised me. Her name was Cinnamon and she lived and died in the City of Hue.

The coffins disappeared when I heard my husband cry out: "Oh Simone, who did you love so much that you're still crying for him? Did he even exist or had he become all of Vietnam in your pretty head? I can always beat up a man, but how can I beat up a place that's already been beaten down in a war we lost?"

The following morning, I packed a few things and moved to the Hyatt uptown under the excuse of work. He helped me pack and even drove me there. There was no ultimatum, no discussion, as though we each had reached an implicit understanding of the future. I had a marketable degree, a career, and could survive without him. I had grown used to the fast pace of New York City. At 30, I still had my radiant youth, the beginning of a promising career with a prestigious Manhattan law firm, and a hefty starting salary.

I could have given up my key to our apartment, but he insisted that I keep it. He was so calm about it that I wondered whether he suffered at all from my decision, whether he had ever loved me, still loved me, or had stopped loving me.

I take my eyes off Lucinda's flower arrangement and walk down the hardwood hallway on careful footsteps. Behind the library door he must be listening with equal care, as though counting the rhythm of my heels to decipher my emotions. I reach the library door and the silence makes me quiver slightly. I draw a deep breath and push the door open.

The chair behind the mahongony desk is empty. The library is not well lit. I hear a slight cough and then the sound of the lighter. My eyes get adjusted to the dark, and I spot him near the bay window, lighting a cigar. His face is unusually haggard, as though he has not slept in days. It has been months since I last saw him, and somehow his face has changed. He nods at me. As he moves away from the window, I see the wheelchair.

"What's wrong with you?!"

He blows out a writhing stream of smoke.

"Right after you left, I fell and broke my knee; I couldn't get my balance anymore. They discovered bad cells in my bone marrow. After all the tests, they told me it had gotten to my brain. I decided not to have the surgery at first, but I'm going in tomorrow for the operation. That's why I called you."

"Why didn't you tell me?"

"Why? I've had symptoms for months and you didn't even notice."

I kneel down next to his wheelchair and he turns the wheel away to avoid me. I try to reach him with one hand, and he lets out a small cry of pain, which takes me aback. In what's left of the afternoon sun from the bay window, his face looks thin and pale, but his jawline is set with a stamp of resolution.

"Don't touch the knee. It hurts."

Quietly, he strokes my hair and raises my chin to look into my damp eyes.

"You should make it a goal in life to remarry, this time to someone you love."

Some thick, unseen curtain lies between us in the surrounding silence. Above us, the Swiss cookoo clock strikes its sounds. Seven of them. Clear, factual and precise like the polished furniture in his library. He tips over to pull me to him, but the wheelchair gets in the way. He sighs, but manages to hold my shoulders nonetheless. He unbuttons my silk blouse and caresses the curve of my flesh, but his touch is so light, and I feel almost nothing except for the dry skin of his fingertips.

He lets go of me, wheels himself away from me back toward the window.

"You don't understand, do you, that every man, bright or mediocre, rich or poor, cruel or kind, ugly or handsome, has his own fantasy: that he is loved unequivocally by some beautiful stranger who just happens to throw herself at him out of no reason. All these years since you arrived, I've kept on hoping that some day you would beam at me, tell me the fall of Saigon was a blessing in disguise, and that the day we met in the Continental Hotel was the day you accidentally found your prince charming who made your life right."

"You did make my life right. More than that, you kept your promise."

"That was all, wasn't it?"

I stand still. He is a proud man. A proud man does not reveal his vulnerability unless he is certain he is encountering death.

"You've always been too honest to lie, Simone. You kept telling me you were a refugee. All a refugee wants is a refuge."

I think of the mutated cells inside his bone. Fighting me must be his way of fighting them. He has paused to take a smoke, and a wry grin appears on his exhausted face.

"I thought a lot about how you would finally leave me. Some man from Columbia Law School, down Madison Avenue, in Central Park, or at that goddamned law firm of yours, would come along to take you away and there wouldn't be a damn thing I could do about it."

He signals for me to get closer. He puts his hand inside the robe's pocket and takes out a key.

"It goes to the safe deposit box, where I keep your family's heirlooms. In there, you'll also find an old tape. Remember when you came in to my hotel room, the tape recorder was on, and I was dictating. It's all there, what happened."

I place my head on his hand.

Again, he raises my chin and looks into my eyes: "Those eyes. I fell in love with them. Yet I don't think I even know you. How could that be true? For nine years I've watched you and I still can't see underneath it all."

I blink and a tear falls onto his wrist, like a crystal through which I can see part of my childhood. I begin to talk. It is the first time I talk to him about the little girl. More tears flow down like rain, onto the little girl's lotus ponds, all in an ancient city that exists no more in the time and space where we are. The image blurs amid my tears.

The year was 1965. The ancient city was Hue, central Vietnam. That year, the little girl had just turned ten.

2. Lotus Ponds

(Hue, the Republic of Vietnam, 1965) — Snow White and her blue Seven Dwarfs whirled against white along the hemline of my dress. When I walked, Snow White and her Seven Dwarfs walked with me. The dress had a spaghetti strap, hidden under a short-sleeved bolero jacket. I had just turned ten and the dress was a birthday gift from Grandma Que. That day we were going inside the Citadel to see Mey Mai, who would tell my fortune for the first time. We lived outside the Citadel that once separated commoners from the royal Violet City, situated in the center of the ancient capital, Hue. The Citadel, *Thanh Noi*, represented the King of Annam's abode and Hue's past glory.

Mai was her given name. "Mey," meaning "the old wise" in Vietnamese, was a courtesy title reserved for old women. As a young girl, Mai was a royal chambermaid in the Violet City, serving my great-grandmother, Huyen Phi, the Mystique Concubine of the King of Annam. When the King abdicated, Huyen Phi and Mai left the Violet City for a new life in the village. My Grandma Que, who was the daughter of the Mystique Concubine, was only five years old then, and Mai, the royal maid, became Grandma Que's nanny. Together, Huyen Phi and Mai learned how to raise silk worms. They supplied fine silk to all of Annam and beyond, even to French and Indian merchants off the coast.

I knew before I learned how to write my own name that we were descendants of the legendary Mystique Concubine. There was no picture of Huyen Phi in the house, although an ink-on-silk portrait of her hung behind the family altar. I stood for hours looking at her, scrutinizing her facial features. Her brows resembled two sword-like slanting ink strokes, the nose another vertical one, and her mouth consisted of two dots forming a little cherry. Huyen Phi did not look like a real person, let alone any of us.

Nor was there any picture of Mai. I was told that during the

Japanese occupation, the country was starving and Grandma Que had to let Mai go. Mai cried and cried and refused to leave. Grandma Que had to shove Mai onto the streets. No one in my family knew what happened to Mai since then, except that after the Japanese occupation and the end of the last Vietnamese monarch, Mai reemerged as a new woman. She rented a little house inside the Citadel and set up an altar to worship the female deities and goddesses of Vietnam. Before long, news spread past the small circle of the Citadel out to the green bamboo hamlets: the former royal chambermaid Mai had developed psychic ability to communicate with the dead, review the past and foretell the future. Mai never married. Before long, she became the respectable Mey Mai, the spiritual guide for the entire city of Hue.

Every other month, Grandma Que went to see Mey Mai to have her fortune told. Grandma Que had taken over the family's silk business and added to it the trading of cinnamon from Quang Ngai, the jungle province of central Vietnam. After all, her given name, Que, meant cinnamon. Her twin sister, Ms. Ginseng, had joined the revolution, been captured, tortured, and then released by the French. She returned to the ancestral house in Hue to die. There was no picture of her in the house, either, although she was supposed to be a mirror image of Grandma Que. At Ms. Ginseng's death, all the secondary schools in Hue flew a mourning flag, and the young schoolgirls wept for one of the first daughters of the revolution. Grandma Que believed her twin sister's spirit had blessed the family's trading business, which required her to purchase the best of cinnamon found deep in the jungles.

The war between the Republic and the Viet Cong was going on, night ambushes by the Viet Cong were regularly occurring, and Mey Mai's fortune telling helped Grandma Que pick safe routes for the transport of her merchandise along Highway One.

Don't travel that route on that day, her fortune said.

Sure enough, when that day came, dynamite would blow up a bus. Grandma Que would light an incense stick on the ancestral altar and reward the psychic with a handsome sum of money, jewelry, furniture, or medicine. No one knew what the psychic did with the money and nice gifts she had gathered from the inhabitants of Hue. Her fame grew. Mey Mai earned a reputation for her ability to talk to all deities and ghosts — she could predict the future with astounding accuracy.

Those days, Grandma Que frequently spoke to me of the mossy palaces and royal tombs of Hue. Our ancestors, the nine lords and thirteen Nguyen kings of Vietnam, reigned consecutively for almost two centuries, made Hue their Capital City, and built their tombs while they were still alive. The most ostentatious royal tomb was built after French colonists had arrived in Vietnam with their romanticism as well as their firing cannons and the best of sea-going ships. So in the outskirts of Hue, on a hill overlooking the greens of the ancient city and a miniature Versailles-look-alike garden bordered with lotus ponds at the bottom of the hill, the bronze statue of a pro-French Nguyen king sat among sombre walls studded with blue porcelain pieces and gold enameled bird and flower motifs.

Hue has the River Huong flowing through its heart. Huong means perfume or scent. So, the inhabitants of Hue call their city's heart vein the "River of Fragrance." The French and international tourist agencies call it the "Perfume River."

Hue was the kind of city that had a violet horizon. So, the kings' palaces were called the "Violet City," *Tu Cam Thanh*, where my great grandmother, Huyen Phi, once resided.

Hue was not just a city of kings and queens, but also of lovers and poets, dreaming always about a fragrance and a violet horizon that symbolized their romantic spirit. So, the river had to be called Perfume, sparkling green underneath the violet shade of cloud at sunset.

It was not just a city, or any city, but it was The City. Their City — those beautiful women speaking with the musical Hue accent, hiding their demure smiles beneath the cone hats that shaded their lacquer-like streams of long hair, moving their lithe bodies in their black silk trousers and white *ao dai's* — those silky, body-fitting tunics that split on both sides into fluttering wings.

That was how I should remember Hue, Grandma Que said.

Not how it was in the bloody 1800s, when the Mandarins' army — men who went barefoot and had no guns — started an uprising against French colonists, and thousands of Hue inhabitants died during a few days of fighting. The young king, Ham Nghi, was behind the short-lived coup, so he and what was left of his army had to abandon the Violet City and escape to the jungles of central Vietnam where he disguised himself as a montagnard. The French captured his teacher and took the old man with them to the jungle, in search of the young king. French troops went hunting like a safari, using the old Confucian teacher as bait. French gunmen immediately arrested the first montagnard who recognized the old man and knelt down.

It was a clever trick, but in Grandma Que's opinion, French colonists were not astute enough to know that his parents and his teacher were the only people to whom the king would kneel down. The trick had to be the work of those Vietnamese traitors — the *Viet Gian* — who, for materialistic rewards, would broker their culture, sell their own roots, and betray their king.

I thought it was dumb of the young king to kneel down like that. If it had been me, I would have escaped deep into the jungle. Maybe I would have disguised myself as a rabbit. Better still, as a bird. I would grow wings to fly away from those Frenchmen with guns.

The French spared the young king's life and exiled him. For a Vietnamese king, exile, according to Grandma Que, was the equivalent of death. At times, Grandma Que said, death was better than life because death ennobled and immortalized. I thought of those dragonflies hovering over blooms of honeysuckles and birds of paradise in the ancestral house's back yard. Days later, I would find them lying on the front porch, flying no more. I picked one up and stared at its corpse. Grandma Que said too much summer heat and flower fragrance had killed the dragonflies. I did not see any ennobling in their death.

Exile. Exile. Exile. I remembered the Vietnamese word Grandma Que had used that day when she told me of Ham Nghi, her great grandfather, the young king. The word sounded mysterious. I liked the way it was spoken. Starting with the high ascending pitch, the *accent aigu*, and ending with no pitch. *Kiep tha-huong. Kiep vien-phuong.* The destiny of those who had to live away from their homeland.

Every little girl of Hue roots was destined to have a poetic soul, Grandma Que said. If my younger sister Mi-Chau and I ever had to live away from Hue, I should always find ways to grow a big, tall tree, a longan tree, for example, making a shade under which I could recite poetry to nurture my poetic soul. She told me to wait patiently, even if it would take years for the tree to grow, bear fruits, and provide a shade large enough to cover a swinging hammock. I watched her as she described the tree to me. Her soulful eyes shone on me, those black pupils reminding me of lacquer-like, perfectly round longan nuts.

"Wait patiently," she said.

I will, I murmured to myself, and to a pair of moving longan nuts that could see my soul.

On that memorable day in 1965, Grandma Que and I boarded a cyclo, a vehicle made up of a bicycle, the front of which was connected to a sedan chair. We sat in the sedan chair, grandmother and granddaughter, and the driver biked behind us. I loved riding the cyclo, enjoying the wind that caressed my face and blew my hair backward. When the cyclo came to a slope, the driver got off his bike and pushed the sedan up the slope. I turned around to find his sweaty face hidden beneath the old, frayed cone hat. I understood the hardship of a cyclo driver's life. Grandma Que always gave him a big tip and told me to address him as "Uncle Cyclo."

Lotus ponds appeared before me and filled up one side of the road as we approached the Citadel. Greyish green and mossy, the ancient wall blocked the other side of the bumpy road. We moved along the Citadel, bumped up and down in the sedan chair with Uncle Cyclo biking and breathing heavily behind us. As we approached the main gate of the Citadel, with its carved dragons and curved roof, I saw a row of rusty cannons lined up in a vestibule pointing away from the Citadel. Grandma Que called them the bodyguards of the king, now useless, but once representing a golden era, respected by China and admired by Siam.

The cyclo moved slowly through the front gate to reach the other side of the mossy Citadel, and my eyes were filled once again with lotus ponds. Lotuses floated over wide leaves covering up the surface of the water like a peaceful, soothing plate of mauve, lavender and dull green. When the Snow White dress got old, I would ask Grandma Que to make me a lotus pond dress. The hemline would have drawings of mauve lotuses among beds of jade leaves floating on the dark, mossy water. When I walked, my lotus ponds would go with me, dancing around my knees against the clear white background of floating clouds. The wind would blow freely on my shoulders down to my lotus ponds.

3. Mey Mai's Séance

"Good morning, Princess," Mey Mai said to Grandma Que as we entered.

Mey Mai was the only person in Hue who still called Grandma Que princess. The term always brought a smile to Grandma Que's solemn face and brightened her dark, inscrutable eyes. An energic and plump woman, Mey Mai stood in stark contrast to Grandma Que. Energy emerged from the old woman's animated bird-like eyes and rosy round face, and almost wiped away any sign of sagging muscles associated with her seventy years of life. The face was so round and plump that the wrinkles on her skin appeared insignificant and undetectable. She stood with her back straight: too tall, imposing, and exuberant for an old Vietnamese woman, full of animation and warmth. There she stood to greet us, the cheerful Mey Mai, almost filling up the narrow entrance, and I squeezed in between her satin-clad body and the wooden door-frame, just in time for her to hug me tightly. I smelled cedar incense on her satin sleeves.

The visitors situated themselves on colorful cod mats, circling an altar which emanated a fog of burnt incense. Grandma Que took her usual place, right across from the altar. Behind the altar was the painting of a woman with sharp slanting eyes and leafing eyebrows, whom Grandma Que explained was the Goddess Lieu Hanh, deity of womanhood. Mey Mai sat in the middle of the cod mat, dressed in a loose, seven-color satin *ao dai*. The horizontal blocks of colors and the shine of the fabric made her body appear stockier. Incense smoke filled the air as she placed her palms together in the middle of her chest, closing her eyes in concentration. Her lips pulled into a broad, euphoric smile.

A group of women dressed in green satin gathered in front of the altar and started chanting. I could not figure out their words. One of them stepped forward to place a piece of red silk cloth over Mey Mai's head, covering up her grayish bun of hair.

Mey Mai began to shake her head, gently and slowly at first and then faster and faster, picking up the rhythm of the drum beat. Sitting directly behind her, the drummer wore a purple turban and a loose *ao dai* designed for a man, worn over purple trousers that matched his turban.

Mey Mai stood up and swayed. She raised one leg and turned around on the supporting leg, her body tilting and rising as she tried to balance herself. She swayed to the hypnotic, eerie chorale. And then she spun. Her head shook and swirled underneath the red silk cloth, straining and quivering like a shapeless animal yearning to escape its cage.

I held my breath and stared.

The thickened incense smoke made me cough. The coughing tore at my itchy and burnt throat and I could not stop. Grandma Que placed her hand over my mouth, smoothing my chest with her other hand. Under the cloth I caught a glimpse of Mey Mai's white eyes. Her pupils had tugged behind her swollen, wrinkled eyelids. For a moment, I thought my lips had frozen. Just at the point when my ears were starting to go numb, the drum beats stopped and Mey Mai convulsed and fell backward. The red silk cloth fell off her head. Two woman chanters immediately stepped forward to catch her before she hit the floor.

A thick silence followed as Mey Mai lowered herself down to the floor, her legs crossed in Buddhist meditation, her face grimacing in pain. Someone had opened the door and a cold air swept through my limbs. I hung onto the flap of Grandma Que's *ao dai*.

When Mey Mai spoke, her voice was someone else's voice, now deep and solemn, now light and clear. The words came in garbled strands, with complicated nouns and verbs of the adults' world. But I recognized one word — that mysterious and melodious word I had heard from Grandma Que. *Exile. Exile. Exile.*

Grandma Que was shifting her body slightly, and I could feel her pulsing breathing at the top of my head. I nervously pulled the flap of her *ao dai*. Squeezing my hand, she bent over and whispered into my ears.

"There is nothing to fear. This place is full of ancestors."

I looked around. No one in that smoke-filled room looked like the set of black-and-white photographs that lined up on the altar at the house. Nor did anyone resemble the translucent Huyen Phi in her silk-and-black-ink portrait. No one looked anything remotely like Grandma Que. My feet were trembling against my will. I grabbed them and tugged them underneath the hem of my Snow White dress. One of the chanting women had struck a bell, giving a sharp, jingling sound, and Mey Mai bent down as though struck with pain. She started hissing. Her back leaped forward in a pleading gesture, as she broke out crying. My cough had returned, although I tried in vain to suppress it. I could hear Mey Mai's sobs in unison with my cough and the racy pumping of my heart. All that time, people around us were bowing their heads all the way down, their forehead touching the cod mat.

When Mey Mai's sobbing and convulsion stopped, my coughing automatically ceased. She turned her head upward to the ceiling, but her eyes dashed around the room. Again, she spoke. This time I understood her words.

"Soon, during a Lunar New Year celebration, after almost a hundred years, this City will undergo another massacre....Hell on earth will be waiting."

The steady beats of the drummer were lost in the audience's rising whispers. Oblivious to her audience's reaction, Mey Mai was parading and my eyes followed her footsteps. She stopped in the middle of the red-and-ivory cod mat that dented under her naked heels, tugging her fingers inside her colorful sleeves. She closed her arms into a circle and then swung them rhythmically forward at the space up front, murmuring strings of sounds, which at times were swallowed into her heavy breathing. Mey Mai made a couple of rounds in front of the altar before she fell backward as though pulled by a powerful force coming at her from behind her back, her neck slightly swollen, her pupils rolled up and the whiteness of her eyes expanding.

She was strangling herself, rolling on the cod mat, and the audience stirred in chaos. The chanting women stepped forward and gathered around her, pulling the hair around her temples.

Someone announced across the room that a spirit had entered the room and got into Mey Mai.

I swallowed with difficulty and my stomach began to hurt as though the unknown force that tortured Mey Mai had gone over to me. I squeezed Grandma Que's hand for assurance, hearing her prayer to the Compassionate Buddha, "Nam-Mo-A-Di-Da-Phat..." I concentrated on her words to calm myself, closing my eyes to avoid the irritating incense smoke.

"Little one, open your eyes!"

I opened my eyes and saw Mey Mai's euphoric face. She was speaking in a young woman's melodious voice—a stranger's voice.

"You, my dear, will escape the massacre."

I turned away from her and squeezed the corner of the flap of Grandma Que's *ao dai*, wet and wrinkled from my unconscious nibbling on it.

"I will always protect you," Mey Mai said, in the voice of the stranger. She reached out for my hands, but I avoided her touch. The incense smoke confused my eyes. I rubbed them with my knuckles.

"Hush, hush, calm down," she half-sang. *"Your fate, my dear little one, will be in faraway places."*

I turned to Grandma Que. "Is she talking to me?" I asked.

Grandma Que said nothing and the stranger's voice continued to emerge from Mey Mai's lips.

"Yes, I am speaking to you, and don't be afraid, my child."

4. Spirit of the River Huong

I felt light and exposed, as though a thousand beams of light were traveling through me, and in this streak of focused brightness I began to see things. I no longer smelled burning incense. Instead, the fragrance of blossoming lotuses filled my nostrils.

I saw shapes of stone, brick pyramids and towers, their reds and grays mingling with the dull green of moss. The pyramids dwindled into cone shapes situated solemnly on the coifed heads of silent women moving among the ruins of old temples. The women held flickering candles burning over lotus buds growing from the middle of their palms. Their bare feet quickened over moss and brick, then floated over an expanse of lotus ponds. I heard the tiny splash of frogs jumping around the banks mixed with the clink of the dancers' copper anklets. The women danced in smooth, slow, and deliberate movements, their curved fingers closing and opening to the chanting human voices coming from so far away — a thin echo that cut through the stuffy air. The sounds rose, and the dance formed. The women joined hands. With their bodies and fingers they formed shapes and circles, pyramids and half-moon fans. They moved stoically, surrounding me, at times hovering over my head. I blinked. The women were lining up in front of me, with candles burning in their hands. Slowly, their palms opened and the wax from their candles turned into blood dripping onto their wrists, the thick redness permeating through the yellow, mauve, and pastel green of blooming lotuses underneath their naked feet.

Someone must have lifted me up and I felt the sensation of flying through that stuffy air. I was being laid down on floating lotuses, then moved to the top of a gigantic tower. Grave eyes looked down onto me. The dancers' candles were spilling into me and I felt the heat of a dark fire. The horizon had turned reddish and I felt the presence of some being, powerful and absorbing, suspended in the air, bearing down onto the women's limbs as they slowly turned to a display of frozen silhouettes. I alone was flying high in the heat of a fire.

Then the tantalizing presence merged into me and I felt free.

I flickered my eyelids and the dancing women disappeared, replaced by Mey Mai's jovial face. I held my spinning head, curled up in Grandma Que's lap and wanted badly to cry. Strings of whispers kept emerging from Mey Mai's wrinkled lips.

The voice asked me to look up and meet the Spirit of the River Huong.

I looked up and saw only Mey Mai.

As the sugared voice poured words into my ears in the fog of incense smoke, I saw on Mey Mai's face Grandma Que's black longan eyes.

Part One

The eyes grew larger and larger until they filled up the myopic horizon of my mind, looking at me through Mey Mai's wrinkled eyelids. And then they dwindled into two small dots, and Mey Mai's face was replaced with the face of a woman I had never seen before, her silhouette edged against the translucent horizon that met a sparkling river. All turned dark except for a moving spot of light.

In the spot, I saw the woman. Her dark hair was tucked behind her ears below a gold turban, her black lashes moving like flickering shadows under the long, slanting, painted brows of a queen. The lashes cast shadows of small pointed arrows onto her fine and translucent cheekbones. Her earrings sparkled into a thousand stars. Her thick, curvy lips moved slightly as she mimed the words I read from her mouth.

"*My child,*" the stranger's voice said, "*wait patiently.*"

She was repeating Grandma Que's favorite phrase.

That was how the Spirit of the River Huong first spoke to me in 1965, through Mey Mai's wrinkled mouth and eyes, in the clear voice of a young woman. The spirit told me that she resided in the river and would wait for me there. She went on to tell me her life story as the Mystique Concubine of the Violet City.

"*Wait, and wait patiently…*"

We were on the way back from the séance and the cyclo passed by the lotus ponds again. I immersed myself in the mass of twinkling pastels and fell into a full, heavy sleep. Among the lotuses, I saw the edge of brilliant green jade in the shape of a phoenix, standing against the flying golden dragon. The phoenix sat on the chest of a woman who looked like Grandma Que. With her eyes closed, she floated on a mossy green river sparkling under silver lights. Her red brocade smock opened up, floated on the water like a parachute, and gradually turned into a slender boat. And then the boat changed into the shape of a coffin. A floating red coffin.

"*The Mystique Concubine, Her Royal Highness, please wake up and talk to me,*" I whispered, imitating the voice of Mey Mai. I watched her dark lashes until they moved and her eyes opened.

"*Wait patiently,*" she intoned.

I woke up as the cyclo came to a sudden stop at the familiar white colonial villa under the shade of the magnolia tree. Grandma Que lifted me off the sedan and led me into the house, passing by the row of orchid baskets hanging in front of the French bay window.

"Home!" Grandma Que called. "Look how beautiful; and built by the Mystique Concubine herself!"

After dinner, Grandma Que retired to her quarters on the other side of the courtyard, and I knocked on my parents' bedroom door. The door swung open and I announced immediately that I had met the Spirit of the River Huong. I repeated Mey Mai's words: there would be another massacre in Hue during a Lunar New Year celebration, and I would escape from it.

Dew, my mother, the only daughter of Grandma Que, was sitting on a sofa before a fruit bowl, peeling a guava. She dropped the knife.

My father, who had opened the door for me, frowned. "You'll be escaping all right, young lady, from all this nonsense started by your superstitious grandmother."

Ignoring the hurt look on my face, he turned to my mother.

"Your mother took the girl to a séance inside the Citadel."

He darted out and I stayed on with my mother. Standing by my parents' bedroom window, I looked out to the interior courtyard and saw my father walking across. Grandma Que's quarters lit up, and I saw her meeting my father on the porch. I opened the bedroom window and craned my neck out to listen better. It was obvious my father was not giving any deference to the Spirit of the River Huong. He accused Grandma Que of spoiling my mind with superstition and she accused him of acting like a Western man who paid no respect to ancestors. After a while, they were both talking at the same time.

I rushed into my bedroom and shut the door. I went to bed seeing small ripples of a river under the clear, bluish moonlight. I was walking alongside the river, inhaling the freshness of rain water and the clean scent of red soil. I sniffed into my lungs the pungent odor of betel juice and dried *bo ket* nuts when their bean shells were broken. I stared into the calming water, its darkness becoming a velvet cloak stretching across to the other side of the river, where I saw the almond shape of a paddle boat moving slowly and silently in the hot air of a tropical autumn night.

That summer, I spent most of my time wandering in the garden, chasing butterflies and reading folk stories underneath longan trees. I devoured plenty of longan fruits; my hair and shirt smelled like syrup and my face and hands felt perpetually sticky. In between feasts, I thought of the woman lying in the red coffin, and I whispered alone under the patchwork shade of trees.

"*Mystique Concubine, I want to see you again,*" I said.

Occasionally, she would appear in that floating coffin and speak to me. A few times, she even stepped out of the coffin as it turned back into a boat. She took my hands and led me on board. The boat carried bundles of sparkling silk threads. Two little girls sat among the bundles of silk. They were about my size and looked identical in their black silk trousers and pink blouses, with matching pink bows on their hair.

"*Meet Ginseng and Cinnamon,*" she smiled.

But before I could say hello, one of them fell into the water and disappeared.

"*It was Ginseng who fell. She was always the careless one,*" she sighed.

My mother caught me crying one day under the longan tree and asked me why. I shook my head and she took me inside the house and wiped my face with a steamed cloth. She told me it was about time I should be acting like a big sister to set an example for my younger siblings, Mi-Chau and Pi. The steamed cloth sent heat through the pores of my face. I leaned my back against my mother's lap for her to wipe my neck.

"Cinnamon is Grandma Que, but where is Ginseng?" I asked. "I think she fell into the River Huong and died."

"Who gave you that idea?" My mother sounded alarmed. She dropped the steamed cloth.

"What happened to her?" I asked in my tiny voice.

My mother sighed and said nothing. She picked up the steamed cloth from the floor and fiddled with the corners. A moment of silence passed before she took my hands. She led me to her bedroom and we both lay down. One of her arms became my pillow. With her other hand she waved a straw fan slowly over my swollen face as she talked.

"I was named Dew—Beautiful Dew, Mi-Suong, the purest kind that clings to flowers at night and in the early morning before sunrise. Aunt Ginseng picked the name for me before I was born, before she was sent to *Hoa Lo*, the death-row prison in the north for revolutionaries and patriots of Vietnam. I only saw her twice; the last time was right before she died."

That night, I learned about the death of my mother's only aunt, Princess Ginseng.

And I, too, believed that her soul had blessed the magnolia tree.

PART TWO

1. The Wait of a Royal Concubine

"Wait patiently!"

I once heard this phrase from a popular drum song. It was about the legend of the waiting wife.

When the king sent out his messengers to announce the royal decree across the land, calling for the people to defend the country, noblemen responded and left their home to traverse jungles, climb mountains, and assemble under the king's torch. Flags were flown, horses galloped, and the royal sword was passed on to the commander general. Noblemen wore their gunsmoke-filled cloaks in battlefields. They tore out a piece of their cloak, wrote the message of victory on it, and let the singing bird carry it home, to the villages.

In the villages their wives held small babies, waiting for the return of their husbands, for that glorious day when victory would be declared over invaders and the national territory restored under one Heaven-chosen king. Daily the women cooked their rice, casting their sorrowful eyes upon the smoke that came out of their rice pots. The silver smoke traveled past the treetops and through layers of clouds. The women waited for the singing bird who carried messages of victory from the battles afar. The wait could be forever.

Or, the singing bird might just carry home the news of death.

Dead noblemen turned into gods through the flow of their blood. Gods that protected the royal sword as it made its way home to the king's throne. Heaven mourned their deaths, and their widows wilted away in loneliness, still waiting for warrior husbands who never returned. The singing birds all turned sentimental. Their sad songs echoed over oceans and forests.

One young wife refused to believe her husband would not return. She kept hearing songs of victory, seeing flags flying home, longing for the galloping sounds of her husband's horse. Leaves in the forest budded and fell and seasons changed, and she kept waiting. One day, carrying her baby, she climbed to the top of a cliff overlooking the ocean so she could see her warrior husband ride his horse home, when the singing bird would sing the joyful song of reunion.

She stood there day after day, night after night, forgetting time.

"Wait patiently," she kept murmuring to the harsh wind, and the singing bird repeated her call. She was alone on top of the cliff. Her baby had fallen asleep.

And the legend goes, the woman eventually turned into a limestone statue, holding her baby, waiting for her warrior husband. The wait was eternity.

For hundreds of years, the limestone statue watches over the South China Sea, guarding the coast of Vietnam. The waiting wife becomes the sorrow of the Vietnamese woman in wartime. She becomes the culture itself.

2. The Face of Brutality

I have heard the legend and know what it feels like to wait for my husband, although he is not at war.

I lean on the half-moon window frame carved into coiling dragon shapes, looking out at the night. The lanterns in the courtyard flicker against the silver threads of an elusive moon.

I see it. The face.

Its contours merge with the night, so the face no longer has shape. Yet I know it snarls at me, since the beam from the pair of beastly eyes follows my movements. I see the red pupils moving in the dark.

For years I have stood here looking at the night, sensing the presence and seeing the face. I call it the Face of Brutality. It mocks me every night, telling me to stop waiting. But I wait and wait. One night passes. Another night comes.

Tonight my senses are sharper than usual. This is my last night in the Violet City.

I go back inside to look after my daughters, Cinnamon and Ginseng. The twin girls are holding hands in their sleep, their tiny, rosy fingers intertwining, the tips fragile and pinkish like young roots. The girls' joined hands rest in the hollow between their bodies, their black fuzzy heads leaning against each other. The twins seek comfort from each other's warmth. Occasionally they stir gently, their hands separating and rejoining as they breathe steadily.

I sit by the edge of the lacquer divan where they sleep, running my fingers through the mother-of-pearl inlays and shining black paint. We will be taking the lacquer divan with us tomorrow. The entourage will consist of my chambermaid, Mai, my eunuch, Son La, my twin daughters, and myself. We will depart in the morning to a village approximately two hundred kilometers away from the Violet City, in the outskirts of Hue, on the way to the Port of Thuan An. By this same time tomorrow night, the half-moon window will be closed behind me, and my life in the Violet City will be the past.

But I know the Face of Brutality will still be out there. It goes where I go.

The lacquer divan was a special gift from my husband before the girls were born. The wood came from the forests near the foothills of the Truong Son, The Elongated Mountains, in the province of Thanh Hoa, known for its cinnamon and cedar wood. He had the divan made and delivered to me during my seventh month of pregnancy, in anticipation of the arrival of a son.

I, too, had expected a baby boy. The day the court's physician confirmed my pregnancy, I ran to my window and stared triumphantly at the Face of Brutality, right into the eyes of that secret animal who had been watching me and haunting my life. I sneered at it. My son could become the future King of Annam. Heaven had answered my prayers.

It was my maid, Mai, who first discovered my pregnancy. The round-faced and dove-eyed Mai is the only daughter of an herb doctor and has more talents than the average maid. She claims knowledge of astrology and astronomy, as well as principles of herbal medicine, passed to her by her learned father. She also boasts to me about her sixth sense and psychic ability.

I remember so well the night when, in helping me change for bed, Mai began examining my eyebrows. The eyebrows of a pregnant woman, in the early stage of her pregnancy, would stand up a certain way. Mai nodded quietly as she brushed my brows backward with her thumbs. And then she left my boudoir to fetch her medicine box. When she returned, she removed from the box a small piece of dark green jade. She tied a red silk thread to my left wrist and connected it to the piece of jade. She pressed her thumb against the soft skin on the inside of my elbow. She bent her head over my wrist, and listened attentively to my pulse.

"My lady, you are very, very pregnant," she announced.

She asked to examine my belly. Quietly I took off my tunic. I had noticed the change in my body for weeks so Mai's excitement did not surprise me. Mai told me to lie on my side and examined my lower abdomen from a side view.

"I hear a very strong heartbeat, as though there are two of them. Strong kicks, strong turns. I have no doubt it will be a boy, my lady."

She held me up and took both of my hands in hers. "Your life will be different. You will be the mother of a prince. No more waiting." Before I could react, she placed a finger on my lips. "There is so much jealousy among the royal concubines, so you must keep this a secret, until the baby is stronger and more mature. That way, no one can harm you and the baby. Only then will we summon the court physician."

It was a difficult pregnancy. I was sick quite often, and by my seventh month of pregnancy, I had become so big that at times I could no longer move. When I looked down, I could no longer see the hemline of my smock, or the green phoenix wings at the tip of my velvet slippers.

Even the court's physician had expected a healthy, huge baby boy.

I felt a sharp pain in my chest and womb when I saw my husband, standing behind the red-and-gold brocade curtain, turn and walk away after the midwife announced the birth of two princesses. My husband left as the maids put the crying infants into my arms, one on each side of me. So I kissed my daughters and named them Cinnamon and Ginseng, in memory of the forests of central Vietnam, where my ancestors came from.

3. That Paddle Girl

I remember it was a cool night like this when he first met me on the River Huong, a meeting that ended my life as a poor orphan, a Champa girl making a living by paddling passengers across the river.

We, the Chams, are the disappearing Hindu minorities of central Vietnam. The Kingdom of Champa was officially annexed into Vietnam during the fifteenth century, and by the start of the sixteenth century, most Chams had taken on Vietnamese last names.

My family, too, took on Vietnamese last names. Only in our minds do we hold on to what is left of those ancient, abandoned mossy temples, stone towers, wood and rock carvings, and the sad candle dances of central Vietnam dating back to our Hindu heritage.

We are the Chams: the conquered, the extinct.

My extended family made their living by chopping wood and searching for ginseng and cinnamon in the forests until the French came, imposed high taxes, and controlled the trade. My family then moved away from the foothills of the Truong Son mountains and concentrated instead alongside the various rivers of central Vietnam. We needed to learn a new trade. We began making a living by paddling passengers across these rivers, as though paddling away our pain, resentment, and nostalgia for our lost kingdom. My folks settled in Kim Long, a boat dock area in the outskirts of Hue. Typhoid fever claimed the lives of several, the same way malaria had claimed the lives of generations of Cham cinnamon and ginseng traders. Only my parents survived. I was their only child.

The surviving Chams of the defeated, extinct kingdom of Champa had always rotated their trade between the jungles and the water. Paddling along rivers to us was a sacred art. It was told to Cham children that after the last battle, the Viets captured the queen of Champa and transported her by boat back to the north. The exodus began in the rivers of our kingdom. Under a full moon, the captured queen, crying for the defeated, jumped into the river and drowned herself. The surviving Chams called out after her, Mee-Ey, Mee-Ey, meaning "that noble woman." The sound Mee-Ey entered history and was mistaken as the name of the Champa queen.

After centuries, the mourning sound of Mee-Ey worked its way into the folk tunes of central Vietnam, or what was left of the Champa Kingdom. I knew these tunes very well, from the Nam Ai tune, (mourning for the southern land), to the Nam Binh (peace for the south), and the Mai Day tune, (mourning of the paddle). The wailing sounds of the pentatonic scale were always heartbreakingly sad. The Chams believed Mee-Ey's soul never left the water. So when we paddled along our rivers, we hoped to catch her spirit. It was believed that the spirit came alive particularly in moonlit nights.

By my generation, the Chams' resentment toward the Viets had dwindled. I grew up knowing I was Cham and part of the heritage of Mee-Ey. I accepted, too, that I was part of Annam, regardless of who claimed ownership to the land.

My father died when I was five. From my mother, I learned to paddle our boat, carrying on the family trade. We stayed in Kim Long, upstream from the River Huong that separates Hue in half. After my father's death, my mother took me further down to the banks of the River Huong in the heart of Hue. We moved there to attract a more exclusive clientele and to avoid the fierce competition in commercial Kim Long. I grew up on our boat, learning the art of paddling against the wind, in heat as well as in cold. I also learned the art of cooking a clay pot of rice on burned logs in the middle of the river, amidst whirling wind and sparkling waves.

When I turned twelve, my mother also died, leaving me to paddle alone on the River Huong. I did not think of her as being dead. Her spirit had soared high to join the star-filled sky of Hue and reunite with the spirit of Mee Ey. She reappeared each night, shining above me and watching over me, keeping me company as I kept on paddling. I got the strength to carry on my existence that way.

None of my passengers knew where I came from. No one asked. To the inhabitants of Hue, I became the sound and sight of the River Huong itself. To disperse the loneliness, I sang into the sky. Singing kept me going, even in the coldest night.

I also learned poetry from mandarin scholars who crossed the river. I could recognize those learned men immediately: white trousers, black tunics and turbans, and in their arms cloth bags stuffed with Chinese books, chess games, and baked clay teapots. They spoke in poems and conversed in verses. These poems, they told me, depicted the sufferings of the people of Annam under French rule. They wanted the King of Annam inside the Citadel to hear them. The French, I was told, suppressed the mandarin scholars and the people, but could not extinguish their poetry. Sing on, they told me, sing for the King of Annam and the whole city of Hue.

So I sang. To the rhythm of my paddles, I sang.

I grew up without noting the passage of time. One day, in the radiant sunshine, I leaned over the edge of my boat, which was also my only home. My skin was dark, my brows bushy, my legs long and muscular. These characteristics of my Cham blood had become more distinctive from the long days and nights of paddling, which helped accent my small waist against my full hips. With my paddles and strong arms, I learned to guard against the roving eyes and hands of male passengers. But the mandarins were always respectful, telling me they were students of Confucian thoughts. In their poems I found my solace, even if I did not understand the words. I pushed my chest forward, inhaling air into my lungs, and words burst from my mouth. The paddle cutting through that stoic water became my beat. I felt full singing their words. I felt alive.

I kept on paddling and singing until I met him. I had turned fifteen that year.

4. The King of Annam

On the night of our meeting, as a fifteen-year-old paddle girl who had never encountered an aristocrat, I did not see in him the image of the King of Annam. Rather, I saw him as a lean young man, extraordinarily handsome in his turban and black organza tunic. The dressing style — that combination of black and white — identified him as a mandarin or a student of Confucius' thoughts.

But there was something different about this young mandarin. It was in the proud way he carried himself. He looked at no one and carried no cloth bag. He had no books or chess game or clay teapot with him. He looked not more than twenty five years old, perhaps a little too slender and frail despite the healthy shine of his dark skin. His frailty contrasted vividly with the fierceness of his face — he had that serious, sullen, and cocky countenance of a lion. I had seen the painting of a lion's face in a banner carried by an opera troupe who once boarded my boat. If I were to transform that holy animal on the poster into the image of a man, it would be him.

He boarded the boat. I paddled across, but when the passengers disembarked, he stayed on. He crossed the river again, back to the other side and, again, stayed on with the boat while the others disembarked. By the third time we went back and forth, I had noticed his heated eyes shining. My body felt heavy under the gaze of his dark, probing pupils. I sang to calm myself and he listened attentively, his eyes never leaving my belly and waist. By the fourth time we crossed the river, he paid all the other customers a silver coin each for them to stay onshore. As we took off, he told me he wanted to take over the paddling and that was how we crossed the River Huong, bathed in the soothing breeze of the wind and the illuminating glow of the moon, intoxicated by each other's presence.

Then he gave me a gold coin. Far too much. He was touching my hands and looking into my eyes. Embarrassed, I tried to remove my hands. And then he asked me:

"How would you like being married to a king?"

I giggled and said I would love to marry a king, but no king ever took a boat across this river in the middle of the night. He told me his given name. "Buu Linh," he said. It meant a holy animal, a royal one, he explained.

"A lion, perhaps?" I asked, giggling.

He did not reply. He gazed, instead, deep into my eyes. Before he left my boat, he said he would send somebody to fetch me soon, and then I would be with my husband king.

Of course, I did not believe him.

Before she passed away, my mother told me it would be better for me to marry a Cham man, someone robust enough to help me with the paddling trade. My mother hinted that I should stay away from Vietnamese men, who would never accept a Cham girl like me and would treat me like a second-class citizen.

I never thought much of my mother's advice until my unexpected wedding day, chosen and planned for me by people I had never met.

My mother had not warned me of the magic of the River Huong and its moonlight, which could turn life into dreams, even if they were sad dreams that would ultimately imprison a woman with muscular arms and legs, whose eyes were accustomed to looking through the black sky to find her guiding star for paddling a lonely boat. I found out the meaning of dream on the day the royal guards appeared all around the riverbank to take me away. Those guards paraded in yellow and red uniforms, their slanting eyes hidden under cone hats embroidered with gleaming gold threads. They lined up along with the royal musicians dressed in blue satin and violet raw silk.

That was how a royal bride was taken to her husband: by royal guards and royal musicians. I was told this later, after five women got on the boat and started to dress me. For the first time in my life I wore a silk *ao dai* and felt its softness caressing my skin. The women put a red brocade smock over the golden silk *ao dai*, topped my head with a green turban, put heavy gold earrings on my earlobes, which, together with bracelets, pendants and anklets, felt like bondage and shackles on both sides of my face and all of my limbs. They gave me a perfumed fan to hold, and told me I was being costumed to become the chosen royal bride.

I was in a daze. All I could remember was the sight of the main road leading to the Citadel circling around the royal palaces. As I peeped from behind the red curtains of my rickshaw, I saw the amazing sight of lotus ponds. Thousands of lotuses bloomed under sharp sunlight. I looked behind me and saw the progression of women dressed in green satin carrying golden boxes, followed by the fleet of musicians and guards. I tried to imagine my new life, but I could envision nothing. I closed my eyes and felt in my palm the shape of the gold coin given to me by the young man whose face reminded me of a lion. I had kept the coin with me all this time for good luck.

When the bouncy movements of the rickshaw stopped, the curtains were raised and my eyes were blinded with blazing lights. In bewilderment and confusion, I could not tell whether they were beams of sunlight or lanterns. The women who had dressed me quickly gathered around my rickshaw. Two of them raised my arms and literally lifted me off the carriage. From there on, they carried me along and I was placed on a red satin mat. A hand gently pushed my head down and a voice whispered to me that I should not look up. I kept my head bowed, but my eyes discretely rolled upward and I saw the lower body of a tall, trim man. I focused my attention on his gold boots, the gold hemline of his shimmering *ao dai*, and the sharp, pointed end of a gold-carved scabbard dangling on his right side.

I had never seen a man carrying a gold sword before.

He made three steps forward toward me and I trembled. The women had pressed my head down so low that my forehead and all that oiled, coifed hair underneath the green turban almost touched the satin mat. I could not see his face. His boots and sword made a swift turn and he walked slowly away from me. I saw the boots

Part Two

climbing up a stage, on steps that were bordered with carved gold dragons. The man had sat down, his boots resting firmly on the last step of the pedestal above my head. The same whispering voice told me to keep kneeling and bowing.

I heard the salute shouted by men. "Le Nap Phi." The offering ceremony for a royal concubine to enter the palace.

The shouting continued. "Long live Heaven's son. A thousand years of life and happiness."

The music began. The whispering voice told me to kowtow and bring my head to the floor numerous times. I was supposed to worship my husband-to-be, formerly Crowned Prince Buu Linh, now the King of Annam presiding under the dynasty name, Thuan Thanh.

So this was the man, I thought to myself, to whom I should sing the mandarins' songs depicting the sufferings of the people of Annam. I was not singing any song. I was bowing endlessly to a pair of golden boots.

This whispering voice and dozens of female hands guided me along, telling me I was already in the grandiose West Palace inside the Violet City. Through all the rituals I was to keep my head low, my forehead pointing toward the floor, never to lift my eyes up. So I moved along in my sleepwalk, thinking of the lion face on display in an opera troupe and wondering where that royal husband of mine had gone and how in the world I could recognize him in this crowd. I kept looking for the familiar pair of gold boots and the pointed tip of the gold carved scabbard. After a while, gold boots and scabbards seemed to be everywhere.

I caught glimpses of carved dragons, phoenixes, lions. I lifted my eyes once and saw the solemn faces of men, so many men, together with the rosy cheeks and curious, surreptitious glances of women all dressed alike, their head bowed like mine, yet their eyes met mine, proving that they, too, were peeping at me, the royal bride. It was my wedding, a joyous occasion, yet no one was smiling. I kept moving in a trance, unable to decipher whether I was happy or sad.

When the fanfare died out, I found myself in a perfumed tub. The heavy clothes and jewelry had been removed, piece by piece, by unknown hands. The bath was elaborate and numerous fingers ran through every muscle group, every fold in my body. When the bath was over, they draped me in loose pantaloons and a camisole, topped with colorful outer garments. I was moved along a narrow corridor where several men lined up on both sides, their head bowing. At the sight of these men, I jerked backward out of reflex, conscious of my naked flesh underneath the loose layers of sheer silk. Instinctively I reached out for the familiar feel of my paddle. My hand hung empty in the air.

Someone pressed upon my back for me to march on. The whispering voice told me not to be afraid, as those solemn-faced men were all eunuchs. Eunuchs were men who were no longer men, the voice explained. The women kept moving me along the corridors, a walking puppet covered in layers of silk.

5. The Eunuch Son La

A fanfare of stringed instruments and jingling bells started, paused, and restarted. When the music died out, I found myself sitting alone between shiny wood pillars circled by carved dragons, on a lacquer bed. The sudden silence intimidated me, so I wiggled my hanging feet, and the velvet slippers dropped to the floor. Cold air brushed my naked heels.

I heard a crisp knock at the door. The curtains were raised, and in the smoky red lantern light, a diminutive old man entered the room, followed by two women carrying a porcelain sink. The man approached the bed, knelt down before me and introduced himself as my servant, the Eunuch Son La. The two young women knelt docilely with him, their face expressionless and their eyelids lowered.

A moment passed and the women took hold of my dangling feet. I jerked back and the old man looked up with kindness in his eyes.

"My lady, please relax. We are here to wait on you."

I looked down at the man kowtowing before me and found

the attentive and dehydrated face of an old man with the grin and gaze of an earnest child. The women dipped both my feet into the hot water and the eunuch's hands were firmly grabbing my heels. I shuddered, struggled to escape, and he murmured:

"My lady, do not fear me. I am not a man and I am here to serve."

I looked again at the old man, puzzled by his direct statement that he was not a man. His soft, skilled palms pressed upon my skin and his fingers adroitly made their way through the cracks between my nervous toes. He must have felt the calluses of my paddling life and sighed sympathetically. He rubbed and lotioned my feet, again and again, with the attentiveness of an artisan.

"Pay no attention to me, my dear lady. I am an old eunuch. A eunuch is a man, but he is not a man. Take notice only of what I can do for you, my Lady."

I drifted in and out of senseless, indecipherable dreams and my skin burned. The eunuch was drying my feet and rubbing them against some soft, fuzzy fabric, but just at the point when I thought the massage was over, I felt the coolness of lotion upon my skin again, and the rubbing recommenced.

Finally, the two women raised my feet and gently pushed me back against the pile of pillows. I lay on my back with my eyes closed, panting. I felt the gentle touch of probing fingers on my body again and the women were slowly peeling off my camisole and pantaloons. Startled, I opened my eyes and found the two young women undressing me, handling each piece of garment expertly. The eunuch remained kneeling on the floor, his head bowing, on the other side of the curtains that separated us.

All of my modesty was gone when I observed the wax-like, emotionless face of the women, their chin pressed down to the hollow of their neck. The women's mechanical act spoke for the impersonal nature of the occasion. They were just preparing me like a statue ready to be displayed. They oiled and powdered my body with soft cotton balls and silky brushes, and then they wrapped me again in layers of soft white silk. All this time I had managed to clutch on to my gold coin but finally one of two women undid my fist and removed that good luck charm. I uttered a feeble sound of protest.

"This is a necessity, my lady," the old man said to me from the other side of the curtains.

"You are being presented to Heaven's son, wrapped in perfumed silk. That way, no weapon can ever be carried by a royal concubine."

The eunuch Son La got up and, with a quick, almost imperceptible hand gesture, signaled to the pair of women and they backed away toward the door, carrying the porcelain sink and bowing their head, as usual. I thought he would leave too, but he knelt down by the bed and spoke softly.

"Those maids, my lady, they may or may not be your friends, but I am. You see, I have one-fourth Cham blood in me."

I stirred slightly in the bed and caught sight of his dark face and fierce brows on the other side of the curtains, and all of a sudden I felt less lonely.

"You have been part of an unusual occurrence, my lady, a historic event. Never before has a woman like you been admitted to the palace this way. You were brought here in a formal wedding, the same way daughters of cabinet ministers — the *thuong thu* — were married to Heaven's son. You were already given a place in the West Palace, among the highest honors accorded a concubine. Normally, commoners are admitted as dressers or maids, never in a formal wedding."

He kept his head bowed to the floor, and I had to lean forward to hear him more clearly.

"His Highness must have been smitten by you. He has broken all traditions, making you into an object of envy and curiosity. But this is a very difficult time for Annam and we will all be affected. Things are changing and you must be prepared for your fate."

I heard footsteps outside and saw shades of flickering lanterns passing by the half-moon window. The old man immediately changed his speech pattern. He was wishing me a thousand years of happiness and a hundred children.

A hundred children? I did not want a hundred children.

"Close your eyes and pray," he continued. "In fact, all you need is one child: a son. Keep his Royal Highness with you as long as you can, and Heaven will grant you a son.

6. Conjugal Bliss

Behind brocade drapes and muslin curtains, I leaned against the satin pillows and listened to my own effusive heartbeat and the shuffling of fabric as my body shifted slightly in the bundle of silk. I wondered whether the moon had ascended yet. I missed my boat and my river. An immense loneliness had just come over me when, again, I heard footsteps.

The double door swung wide-open and there entered the entourage, headed by that wealthy passenger who, on that fated night on the River Huong, had insisted on paddling my boat. His steps were forceful and his gaze direct. I recognized the familiar pair of golden boots, but no longer saw the golden sword. He was approaching me steadily and when I lifted my eyes, I saw the face of a lion.

"Buu Linh," I whispered to myself. That holy animal.

I no longer had the gold coin he had given me to hold on to, so I clenched my fist to calm myself. My heart sank when I saw a dozen women following him in pairs. They were dressed in blue and white satin and gathered around him, helping him undress. First, his turban was removed. Then one by one the buttons of his gold *ao dai* were undone by the women's adroit hands, traveling across his costumed body like little birds wavering over a landscape. His eyes were fixed upon me when each garment was peeled off. He became a silhouette in a dream, a blurred figure who moved his limbs deliberately and slowly to facilitate the women's undressing of him as though he were performing a dance. All the golden and multi-colored garments were eventually gone and he displayed a brown torso over a pair of white silk slacks and the dream dance came to a stop.

He raised the curtains and we looked at each other face to face. I quietly registered in my mind the facial features that had become curiously familiar to me, since I had memorized them and envisioned them every night since our encounter on the River Huong. Yet the face remained that of a stranger.

He sat down on the edge of the bed and leaned forward. His breath was heavy and hot on my cheek and I felt the same magnet I had felt when he touched my palm and gave me the gold coin on the boat. Self-conscious, I glanced toward the women, who had all lined up and knelt down around the bed. I raised my eyes to meet his with an unspoken question.

"They are trained to surround us," he whispered into my hair and nibbled my earlobe.

My embarrassment lingered on, and I stiffened when his hands reached underneath my armpit to undo the silk wrapping. He was skilled at unwrapping me, suggesting to me he had done this many times. He withdrew his hand.

He left the bed and stood in the middle of the room, the red lanterns flickering onto his naked back. The women rose, acknowledged his hand gesture, and left the room quietly like ghosts. He came back to the bed and this time, he slipped his hands underneath my silk wrapping while pulling on the string of his silk pantaloons. I shuddered as his fingers traveled underneath the silk. My cheeks felt hot as my eyes followed the wave of the soft fabric that rolled down and gathered around his thighs. My skin was burning when he kissed me once, twice, and then too many times to count. His musky body smell reminded me of the night he had crossed and recrossed the river with me and it seemed as though we were paddling against the waves there behind the curtains, the boat rocking and rocking.

Instinctively my muscular arms and legs wrapped around my dream, and I became my River Huong, watery and flowing, heated and cooling at the same time. I let go of the security associated with the familiar feel of the damp, wooden paddles that smelled of moss. I let go of all those hidden tears blended into those Hue rivers upon which my ancestors paddled away the sorrow of the defeated Cham race, forever wanting to recapture the spirit of Mee-Ey mourning her lost kingdom, towers, temples and tombs. I let go, too, of my mother's monotonous words uttered before her death, advising me not to fall in love with a Vietnamese man.

I had become a river that merged with the flesh of a Vietnamese man.

I let go of myself. My teeth bit down on his shoulders when I felt him piercing through me. Like an arrow he travelled until he reached the shooting star once presiding over the River Huong and guiding me in my paddling pattern. The arrow he had become cut a silky path on which I arched my back to touch my new rainbow and find that excruciating pain and tantalizing delight of knowledge.

I turned sixteen that year, the age of a ripened moon.

The morning after my wedding, he must have left while I was still sleeping. The royal decree came and was read to me when I was still dreamily resting in the mess of wrapping silk. I had wanted to see and feel his face next to me when the sun hit those muslin curtains. Yet I was only greeted with his official words read to me by eunuchs.

Words of a king, not a lover.

The decree said he had given me my permanent quarters in the West Palace. He also gave me my royal title. I was to be called Huyen Phi, "the Mystique Concubine."

He was back the following night, his gaze raptured and locked with mine while a dozen women took off his royal clothes before my eyes. I became my River Huong and he became my shooting star, again and again, travelling up where a cooling river met sun and sun melted into cooling river and I created my own universe.

He explained to me the meaning of my royal title. He considered our encounter on the River Huong mystical, and my royal title was to memorialize that mystique. No Nguyen king had ever picked his bride the way he did, my lover said. And so I would enter history as the myth of Hue, as the woman who brought the tunes of the common people to the heart of the King of Annam. But the Nguyen kings honored their founding father's tradition of not crowning a queen. So every consort could only be titled as a royal concubine. Only one would be chosen as queen and so crowned if her son became the crowned prince. The fact I was given a royal title immediately and allowed to take my place in the West Palace was the testament of his adoration.

I did not know then, that adoration, by nature, was short-lived.

Once again, he was gone before dawn. I got up alone, facing my panic, isolation, and the terrible feeling that this could be my fate.

Later on, I gave that terrible sixth sense a name. I called it the Face of Brutality.

7. The Luxury of Words

After a month or so of intense passion, the routines of my conjugal life with the King of Annam began to form. It was a relationship where body movements substituted for the luxury of words. During the day, I patrolled the courtyard nervously, missing the sparkling waves of the River Huong and the silver moon to which I used to sing the folk tunes of central Vietnam and the poems of my mandarin passengers.

At night, his hunger for me shut off all opportunities for songs, poems, or conversations, and I responded to him as a lioness who moaned and screamed but did not speak. I knew all about his body and nothing about his mind. I became acquainted intimately with every cell of his skin and the raising and calming of his flesh and hair roots, but nothing of his thoughts.

In the peak of my delight, discovery, and curiosity, I was already haunted with the fear of abandonment and tragedy. Lying in his arms, I could not help remembering the words of Son La, and those warnings of his became the torture chamber of my mind. I hung on to my king, hoping I would bear a son, as the old eunuch had advised. I tore up the silk wrapping at the clicking sound of my king's golden boots outside the double door. My fierceness and passion became our bondage. The more I despaired at the thought of him leaving me the next day, the more fiercely I loved him like a wounded, starved lioness.

Yet the inevitable could not be avoided. Like all concubines, I was doomed to a wait.

He was with me night after night for a while, joining and meeting my fierceness with his own urgency. And then he would disappear for days, or at times, months. He would return as a surprise, only for a while, and then he would again depart. In between his visits, I waited and waited, concocting all the words I would like to speak to him when he returned.

When he did return, the hunger took over and I had no occasion to deliver my words. And then the waiting began again as his visits became more sporadic. One day, Son La told me that it was about time for me to wait, not just for the return of the King of Annam, but also for a pregnancy that could solidify my place in the Violet City. Under Son La's encouragement, I began counting days and nights.

I no longer needed the protection of my wooden paddles against the roving eyes and hands of men, as there were no men. My world consisted of chambermaids and my Eunuch Son La. I could no longer sing, as there was neither sky nor river to sing to. The isolation caused me to lose my head.

Some time during the process of waiting, I started screaming at night, but my heart-wrenching screams were swallowed by the four walls of my boudoir, muffled by the thickness of those brocade curtains. When my throat got hoarse, I stopped screaming and listened to the stillness of the night. The only person who knew was my eunuch Son La. The old man often looked at me with bewilderment, murmuring to himself that in his forty years servicing the Royal Palace he had never seen a concubine express herself this way. I would mourn and call out my lover's name, "Buu Linh, Buu Linh," and Son La would frantically and nervously try to silence me, cautioning me I was not supposed to call the King of Annam by his given name. I should be addressing my husband by his dynasty name, the Royal Highness Thuan Thanh. In response to the stern warning, I would disdainfully pout my lips, beat on my chest, and utter vicious words. Son La would be kneeling by my bed, despaired and confused, fearful that the guards would hear my blasphemous curses and whining.

"What can you expect, Son La?" I sobbed. "I'm a common paddle girl!"

Every time I passed a night without Buu Linh, I cursed both

Heaven and Earth. I even ripped a down pillow into pieces, having wetted it first with my tears. When my king did not show up for months, I hated him and wanted him dead. I shut my eyes and imagined him loving a dozen women whose fingers travelled across his brown skin when they undressed him. I pulled on my hair until the hairline around my forehead became red, raw and blistered.

In my moments of rage, Son La would massage my feet and kiss my toes to calm me down. "Hush, hush. You cannot say those bad words about Heaven's son. It's the most hideous crime. You can be sentenced to death, and three generations of your family can be beheaded as well."

"But I have no family," I sobbed. "I am an orphan. They can kill me but I have no relatives for them to behead. In any event, it is better to die than to love a man who leaves me like this. I am imprisoned here. I can't go anywhere."

"But he loves you," Son La said rapidly.

I stopped sobbing, looking at Son La with disbelief.

"How do you know?"

"He must love you. He has not been with anyone as much as you. He has some fifty wives, mostly daughters of the ministers, who show no zest for life. You're different. Look at you, you are full of life. After all, he found you by the River Huong."

The old man rubbed my toe. "Perhaps this will make you feel better," he said, raising my toe to his mouth and closing his lips over it.

I did calm down. I looked at the old man's face and felt tremendous affection for him. But he was not Buu Linh and I was alone.

I tumbled into the courtyard one day and found Son La moving slowly in the courtyard, his limbs like branches in a slight wind.

"What are you doing Son La?

"Tai Chi. An ancient art to balance your body, soul, and spirit." Son La stopped midway and bowed respectfully. "Move with me, my Lady, it will help you," he urged.

I mimicked his watery circles in air.

"It's like a dance," I said.

"It is the freeing of the soul from the body. Breathe, my Lady, breathe."

"Tell me more about freeing the soul," I told Son La one night.

"Good, my Lady, I will teach you Himalayan Buddhist meditation. Again, it will help you."

He sat down on a rug in my boudoir and I sat with him, imitating his posture. The exercise went on and I lost track of time. I was surprised by the old man's dexterity and suppleness.

"How did you learn all of this?" I asked him.

"I am a eunuch, my Lady." He was pressing his palms together over his head. "We have only our minds to develop. It is my greatest resource; otherwise I would have wasted away, living inside the Palace."

I pressed my palms together too, day after day. I pressed my heels into the ground. As I pushed myself further and further into the center of the earth, my spirit began to roar, as thoigh a strong wind had lifted the core of my body. Soon, Son La no longer had to suck my toes to keep me from screaming. I had learned the art of gathering my energy and dispersing it at the same time.

My husband's conjugal visits had become fewer and fewer. His absence, rather than his presence, became my way of life. I accepted my circumstances while waiting for the unknown. When my screaming at night fully stopped, I concluded that God had sent Son La to me to compensate for my misery inside the Palace.

8. Servants and Confidants

Son La was the oldest son of a low-level mandarin and his concubine, an opera actress. His mother, the illegitimate child of a Vietnamese man and a Cham woman, gave Son La his one-fourth Cham blood. When the French occupied Annam, Son La's father joined the mandarins' army and was killed during the king's uprising against the French in Hue. Son La was only eleven then, the oldest of ten children.

Opera performers and artists were classless citizens, forbidden from sitting for the mandarins' exam, and occupied the bottom of society. As such, they were free from Confucian protocols, although they frequently portrayed characters that epitomized Confucian ethics. Outside her stage, Son La's mother was the outcast of society, a woman of Cham descent, concubine and widow of a poor man, a washed-out actress who had prematurely aged because of poverty and childbirth. After his father was murdered, Son La's mother no longer had the health and look to carry on the life of a performer. She became a curtain drawer for small opera troupes performing in faraway villages, and her ten children were dragged around with her to do odd jobs. During rice harvests, they learned to pick up scattered rice dropped onto the dirt road from farmers' baskets for dinner. Son La passed his early childhood in hunger and yearning for a decent meal with plenty of rice and meat. As a child, he had already devised his own method to conquer hunger. He let his mind drift to the sky, and immersed himself in thoughts that he imagined as filling the cavern of his belly.

When Son La turned twelve, he was castrated so he could begin a career with the royal court. Manhood went in exchange for better subsistence and a means to feed the many mouths of an extended family, all sharing the last name of a poor mandarin. Son La insisted on telling me that becoming a eunuch was his personal choice, for he knew he could gain Confucian knowledge living among the aristocracy. On the day of his castration, his family gathered at the ceremony, where a specialist summoned for the occasion numbed Son La's flesh with herbs. After the procedure two men carried him and ran around in a circle fifty times to help stop the bleeding and ease the pain. The ceremony was considered an ennobling act.

The plan went well and Son La's goals were achieved. Son La soon became the sole supporter of the extended family, feeding not only his nine siblings and aging mother, but also his father's first and second wives and their children. When he was assigned to me, Son La was already 55 years old, an eager, attentive old man with the innocent grin of a young boy. As a eunuch, he was wise, careful, and loyal. A genuine noble quality existed in him, which was lacking among the petty personnel inside the royal court. I did not fully recognize this quality until much later, after my chambermaid, Mai, had joined me in the West Palace and, together, my pair of servants introduced me to the wonders of learning.

It was Son La who brought Mai into royal life.

"Let me present to you, my Lady, this very smart young girl," Son La said to me one day, pointing toward the dove-eyed girl about fourteen years of age, who had followed him into my boudoir. She was a chubby girl, quite tall for her age, and swift. Dressed as a royal maid, she smirked at me and immediately lowered her head, as they had all been taught to do.

"She is not your ordinary maid. She is the only daughter of an herb doctor and teacher in my village. The scholar failed the Confucian exam only because he rebelled against the examiners' rules. This fourteen-year-old girl knows how to read and compose poetry better than a mandarin."

"Poetry?" I asked, arching my eyebrows. Secretly my heart lifted as I remembered my favorite mandarin passengers on the River Huong.

"Yes, my Lady, poetry," the girl said. And then she began to speak in verses.

"Did you learn those words from the mandarins who travel the River Huong?" I asked, unable to conceal my excitement.

"No, my Lady. I learned them from my father's books," she responded, wrinkling her forehead in confusion.

"Books?"

I did not know a woman could learn from books.

"You, too, my Lady, could learn to read." She raised her eyes to meet mine. She was no longer bowing her head.

For the rest of my life, I would always remember Mai as I first saw her that day in my boudoir. I could never forget the surreptitious glance and mischievous smile of the young girl who did not always bow her head as she was taught to do, and who introduced me to my first Confucian book. Son La had brought Mai into my secluded life, another blessing. Together they uncovered my thirst for learning, and took turns teaching me how to read "Chu Han," Chinese characters. It was a slow, elaborate and frustrating process, but I eventually succeeded, having dedicated to ancient characters and calligraphy the same passion I had dedicated to paddling.

9. The Pregnancy

In this last night of my life in the Violet City, I tuck my twin daughters underneath the cotton blanket and move toward the half-moon window to take a last look. The Face of Brutality is still out there. I glare at it and recall the night my twin daughters were conceived.

Inside the Citadel it was the Chief Eunuch who announced nightly where His Royal Highness had decided to spend the night. The Chief Eunuch was an old man, as old as the walls of the concubines' courtyards. He walked with his back stooping, eyes to the ground. He talked to us, the women of the Violet City, without looking at us. Slow and thrifty with words, he never said more than what he needed to say. When the sun went to sleep behind the elongated shape of the Truong Son range that separated Hue from Laos, we, the lonely women of the Violet City leaned against the carved pillars under our curved roofs, looking out to our respective courtyard. We waited for the lantern that signaled the arrival of the Chief Eunuch, who always took time with his announcement, as though to tease us. Yet he delivered his words with a stern face, and there was no teasing in the pair of eyes so dry and dull they reminded me of cracked earth.

It was an autumn night and the lotuses must have blossomed fully all around the Violet City when the Head Eunuch announced the arrival of the King of Annam in my courtyard. As in the old days, my royal husband entered my boudoir with his entourage, dismissed the woman dressers, and reached for me with the same hunger as during our first night as husband and wife. But it had been a long time, so I reclined placidly in my bed, watching him disrobed, observing the same lover in a different light, as a different woman.

That night, the lioness in me cooled and transformed into hissing steam. I savored him in the steam of my soul, one that had known sorrow and the impermanent nature of things. In many ways, I had been reborn and reformed. The young teen lioness had matured into a calm, poised woman who, like all women of the Violet City, learned in her desolate life that she could love and belong to one man, yet share him with hundreds of other young, beautiful, and obedient women. Every night there was a happy, blossoming woman and many weeping ones. Some of us kept waiting and others gave up, as our youth and beauty faded away, along with our capacity for anguish.

I had long discovered that the women of the Violet City immediately disliked me due to my Cham blood and common background, and they cheered when the King of Annam stopped returning to my boudoir. My lack of sophistication had helped me survive the vicious comments of my peers. Quite often, I did not even understand their mockery. And I was lucky to have a protective eunuch and a clever chambermaid, who both helped shield me from misfortunes and the trap of royal protocols.

That night when the Head Eunuch's announcement was heard over all concubines' courtyards — that his Royal Highness would soon arrive in my boudoir, I knew the surge of jealousy would be revived among my competitors in the Violet City. The comfort of his arms that night did not soothe away my knowledge of possible danger, even though my skin cells danced under his fingertips.

He had shuddered himself into a long-lasting rest, our fingers having yarned together and his perspiring face buried into the stream of my hair, when I gathered all of my courage and spoke. I casually talked of the sufferings of the warrior's wife who turned into a limestone statue because of her wait, and the King raised his head to look at my face. Panic appeared in his eyes.

"What are you suggesting, woman?"

I instinctively covered my lips with my hand and began whispering, not knowing why the secretive manner was called for. I recited to him the poetry of the mandarins who had traveled my river, wanting me to convey to the King of Annam the sufferings of his people. With Son La's and Mai's help, I had learned the meanings of those words. They described the responsibility of Heaven's son to stop the sufferings of his populace, including the wait of those longing individuals, which could harden human flesh into stone. I was thinking solely of myself, my own longing and despair. I was not sophisticated enough then to think of Annam.

But he must have construed the poetic words more profoundly, as the mandarins had intended. He sat up in bed and arranged the sheets around his waist. He said he was a powerless king, that it was just a matter of time before the monarchy would end, that to be a citizen of freedom was better than being a king in slavery and bondage. He dropped his head to his chin and I might have seen tears in the corners of his eyes. Something broke inside me to see tears on a lion's face.

That night, I became pregnant.

10. *Monsieur* Sylvain Foucault, the French Resident Superieur

Despite the good news of my pregnancy, I continued to be saddened by the knowledge that to me, the King of Annam remained a total stranger while my womb bore his seed. I wanted to travel within his mind the same way he had traveled within my body. I wanted to understand his fear.

I turned to Son La for help, as usual, telling him one day that perhaps I had seen the king's tears. The eunuch's wrinkled face immediately turned grave and somber. He pondered a long time and looked at me with profound sadness.

"A son, my lady, is important to you. To him, there is also the State of Annam."

"What about the State of Annam?"

"We are not free, my Lady. What happened to the Chams a long time ago is happening to the Viets. Annam is under French protectorate now. Our King is...just a king."

Son La finished his sentence with a touch of irony. I gave him a blank look. Sighing again, he took out a small book and showed it to me. It was completely different from the books from which I had learned to read and write. For one thing, there were no characters.

Son La opened the book and pointed to the painting of a skinny bearded man, scantily dressed, stretching his limbs on a cross, his head dropping to one side:

"This man is called Jesus Christ. Many people, including the Vietnamese, believe he is the son of God, a different God; one worshipped by French priests."

"Why is he hanging there?"

"According to the French priests, he sacrificed himself for all mankind."

Son La went on to explain to me how Catholicism had brought the French to Vietnam and how our King, the son of Heaven, had become jealous and fearful of Jesus Christ, the son of a Western God. The result of the conflict was the colonization of Vietnam by the French, who then devided Vietnam into three states: Tonkin, Annam, and Cochinchina. The Emperor of Vietnam became the King of Annam, controlled by a French Resident Superieur. This led to the King's uprising and the massacre of Hue, which had killed Son La's father. All of these occurred before my Buu Linh occupied the throne.

Son La concluded that no one could predict what would happen to the Annamese monarchy.

"The *Can Vuong*, the King's anti-French Loyalists' Movement, headed by the mandarins, is now gradually changing to the *Cach Mang*, the Revolution."

Son La closed the book of Jesus Christ. His voice was tight and quick when he mentioned *Cach Mang*.

"What does that mean, *Cach Mang*?"

"It means changing Heaven's mandate. There are Confucian scholars who no longer believe in Heaven's son. They are seeking other ways to gain independence for Vietnam. One scholar advocates following the Japanese model. Another scholar advocates the demolition of the monarchy. The King, controlled by the French Resident Superieur, is seen by them as a puppet."

A puppet? I thought of myself on my wedding day, dragged through the bathing routines, then along the corridors that led to the conjugal bed where I was wrapped in silk.

"Who is this French Resident Superieur?" I asked.

"A Frenchman by the name of Sylvain Foucault. We call him

Monsieur Foucault and your royal husband resents him with all his heart."

11. The Opera Network

Through Son La, I learned more about my husband. Several kings of Annam and their royal concubines had a passion for the opera and various troupes were allowed to perform inside the Citadel. Son La had been serving on the King's opera-viewing committee for years. He and other court personnel liaised with the various opera troupes to set up royal performances and to research the art. Occasionally, he was even allowed to leave the Violet City and tour Hue as part of this opera recruitment and research mission. The mission enabled Son La to reach out to old friends of his actress mother, who became the resourceful eunuch's network of spies. Son La loved the job, as it allowed him the opportunity to see and listen to the outside world. Without Son La and his opera network, I would have been just one of those longing concubines of the Violet City, shut off from the world, idle and unconcerned even if hurricanes had reached the Port of Thuan An and swept away half of the capital. Son La became my eyes and ears for political events and underground news, and he helped me understand the chaos of my time.

From Son La, I learned that armed resistance and anti-French literary movements led by the mandarins had filled the nation with tension. Inside the Citadel, my royal husband and Monsieur Foucault carried on their silent battle and bitter cold war. In between the two of them, the Royal Cabinet, *Co Mat Vien*, administered the bureaucracy plagued with power struggles and petty politics, while the real power over the country rested with the French.

That was how the Annam court moved into the twentieth century.

My husband and I had become myths. The manner in which I entered the palace had made me a symbol of the king's connection to commoners. My arrival in the West Palace also added to my husband's image as the unconventional, anti-French king, almost a cult figure searching for the deeper roots of Annam — its Cham heritage.

The anecdotes fed to me by Son La through his opera network described my husband as a stubborn teenager who came to the throne at 14 years of age, and who, in his young adulthood, had turned into a serious scholar of Confucian philosophy and ancient literature. To keep up with his time, he also learned French.

From the beginning, my husband disappointed the French Resident Superieur. After the young king's coronation, the Resident Superieur built a bridge inside the Citadel and honored the young king by naming it after his dynasty. The 14-year-old was not at all pleased. He felt it was an insult to bestow the dynasty name on a bridge frequently walked upon by French protectorates. During the ribbon-cutting ceremony, the Resident Superieur jokingly told my husband:

"If and when this bridge collapses, you will have your country all to yourself and the protectorates will respectfully withdraw."

My husband, according to Son La, said nothing in reply, but the young man remembered Foucault's boastful promise.

Foucault did more than just naming a bridge after the King of Annam. During the coronation of the 14-year-old king, Foucault also had photographs taken of the teenager sitting awkwardly on the throne. The Foucault family owned several commercial enterprises in Vietnam, including a publishing house in Tonkin and a tourist agency. The Foucault family made the photograph of the young king into a postcard and marketed it in Europe and Africa to attract tourists to Indochina. The postcard also travelled among anti-French patriots who wrote the word puppet across the face of the photograph. The young King of Annam had become a commercial commodity for French colonists and an object of ridicule among Vietnamese dissident poets and freedom fighters.

It was not until my husband turned sixteen when he discovered that he had appeared on a postcard for commercial gain. Humiliated, he issued a decree ordering the discontinuation and destruction of all such postcards. The unwritten norm of royal protocols in Annam allowed all royal decrees to be reviewed and vetoed by the French

Resident Superieur. It was alleged that when Foucault saw the decree, he laughed and dropped it in the trash basket.

My husband heard the news. He did not touch his meals for two days, and then left for a hunting trip to the jungles of central Vietnam. He allegedly fired at trees and then broke out crying in the jungle.

During the same year, the bridge named after my husband was damaged during a monsoon hurricane. My husband went to see Foucault.

"Now that the bridge has collapsed, will Monsieur Resident Superieur keep his promise and give independence to Vietnam?"

Foucault was stunned.

"Your Royal Highness, if I ever made such a promise, it was made in jest."

"Just when did you learn to make statements in jest regarding the affairs of Vietnam?" the young king angrily retorted.

It was then that Foucault fully realized the crowning of the insolent teenager had been a mistake. The relationship between the colonist-bureaucrat and the young Vietnamese king was openly hostile thereafter.

A free spirit, my husband grew up into a young man with a passion for the opera. He played the drum with royal opera troupes, and frequently escaped the palace at night to travel outside the Citadel in civilian clothes.

But rumors continued to spread about my husband's bizarre behavior, including the story of how he had found me and brought me to the palace. His manner of picking and choosing a bride and sexual appetite became the topic of incessant gossip in the Violet City and among the citizens of Hue.

King Thuan Thanh was tempestuously infatuated with jungle hunting just as much as with the opera. His hunting, a dangerous hobby, quite often put the lives of his domestic staff at risk, as he relentlessly pursued man-eaters like leopards and tigers. News travelled to the countryside that once the king fired a pistol shot at the booted feet of one of his cabinet ministers to test how the mandarin would react. The king missed the target, but the shot was shocking enough for the poor old man to jump ten feet high before he collapsed in tears. His Royal Highness' excursions outside the

Citadel became more and more frequent, almost always ending up with beautiful women being brought to the palace.

The rumors went on and on, portraying less his concern for state affairs and more his insane behaviors, incessant demands, and bizarre habits. Foucault was reportedly quite concerned with the young king's lavish spending and the growing budget needed to support the royal entourage, including the king's women.

There was other news as well. Certain mandarin scholars believed Thuan Thanh faked insanity only to bypass French surveillance. Stories traveled about how the king frequently sent back to Foucault and the Royal Cabinet documents left unsigned, or marked with changes. He questioned French authority by citing, in the margins of the documents he was asked to sign, previously executed treaties that were violated. Outside the Citadel, his citizens whispered tales about his secret trips to Tonkin to make contacts with anti-French resistance forces, and how the French Resident Superieur likewise gave secret orders to isolate the King of Annam inside the Violet City as a form of house arrest.

In such a climate, I quietly prepared for the birth of my son.

12. Hatred and Independence

By the fifth month of my pregnancy, the entire Violet City knew the good news and anticipated the arrival of my son. My husband already had several sons born to other concubines, but none had been made a crowned prince, and never before in the history of the Nguyen dynasty had a son been conceived by a concubine of Cham descent.

Those were the happy and hopeful days of my life in the Violet City, despite the fact that during my pregnancy, my husband stopped coming to my boudoir. He would soon return, when his son was born. I delighted myself at the thought.

It was a clear, moonlit night when I decided to dismiss all chambermaids. I wanted an evening all to myself. Mai had asked to retire early and I was left to walk the courtyard alone. I returned to my boudoir and decided to prepare my own bath.

The chambermaids had prepared perfumed water in a porcelain sink. I started to pour water from the sink into the tub. At the bottom of the porcelain sink, I saw numerous dots of brown and black dirt. The water was full of them. I paused, took another look and the dirt appeared to move. I looked again. The dirt spots were indeed moving. I rubbed my eyes and then stared without blinking. The dirt spots appeared larger, this time wiggling and swimming vigorously.

I dropped the porcelain sink and screamed.

Only Son La heard me and he rushed in, finding myself struggling in the mess of water, with dirt spots moving and swimming at my feet. He took me into his arms and rubbed off the dirt spots.

"Oh, Heaven," he blurted out.

I saw his face turn green and then everything around it began to turn black.

When I opened my eyes, I saw Mai's and Son La's faces staring down at me.

"They were leeches, my Lady," Son La said. I saw anger in his eyes.

"Leeches?" I cried.

Having grown up around water, I knew about those slimy, stubborn creatures. They sucked upon flesh and engorged themselves with human blood. They clung to the skin and did not let go. Farmers often got bitten by them, and only a heavy application of raw limestone liquid directly upon the parasite could disconnect their hungry mouth from human flesh. They traveled swiftly in water and could invade orifices of the human body. They were nearly impossible to kill. To incapacitate the creature, one had to nail it on a surface and dry it under direct sun so it became dehydrated and dysfunctional. But the moment it hit water, the creature could revitalize. Chop one in half, and each half would turn into a new leech.

I could have been sitting in a tub full of young leeches, which could invade my body and destroy the baby inside my womb. Who could have done such a thing inside the West Palace? It could be anyone. Mai knelt down by my bed, kissed my feet, cried, and told me how sorry she was to have left me alone.

I told them I was once the paddle girl on a wild river, and was not afraid of leeches. Together Son La and Mai cleaned up the leeches in my washroom. They talked among themselves. They had a plan to deal with the situation. It needed my approval and cooperation, they said.

We did not report the incident, and in the following days, I participated in all rituals and protocols of the West Palace as though nothing had happened. Yet I could tell from the glancing of eyes and the whispering of mouths and lips that the royal community had heard of the terrible mischief. The whole Violet City was wondering how I could have survived the ordeal. I noticed eyes glancing up and down my tummy with blatant curiosity.

The rumor had begun — spread by Son La and Mai — that I was well protected by the spirit of Mee-Ey, the ancient queen of Champa watching over her land and descendants. I was so strong and so well-guarded by the spirit that when the leeches hit my skin, they immediately deteriorated and became dirt.

And the rumor went on, my unborn son was also protected by Champa's queenly spirit demanding her land back from the Vietnamese. My son would become the best warrior of Annam. After such a rumor, Mai whispered into my ears one night, perhaps my unknown enemies in the Violet City — those jealous concubines and their loyal eunuchs who resented the forthcoming arrival of my son — should surely leave me alone. Who wanted to be cursed by the fierce and powerful spirit of Mee-Ey?

I was not harmed by the leeches, but fate played another cruel trick on me.

After the birth of my twin daughters, the King of Annam

stopped coming to my boudoir all together. I became the lonely Mystique Concubine who no longer carried her mystique.

Still, the women of the Nguyen Dynasty lived on. I did, too, carrying a placid death in the heart. We, the royal concubines of King Thuan Thanh, survived by turning our energy to some mundane purpose: the fifty or so royal dishes at every meal, prepared in the special Hue way, food that was artfully made into shapes of flowers and leaves, arranged so expertly on tiny translucent blue and white porcelain plates. And then we performed the myriad tasks routinely planned around the Queen Mother, a diminutive old woman whose fragile frame was buried under layers of cloth, whose eyes had lost focus, and who was perpetually afraid of sunshine. In the ceremonial hall, when the eunuchs placed her on the pedestal for a court ceremony, she would clutch her shoulders, bringing her limbs together into a fetal position to escape the light. Perhaps at one time, before the arrival of French protectorates, the Queen Mother was a figure of authority inside the Citadel. But those days were over, and in my time, my husband's mother lived like a ghost and a reminder of all the bad time when the throne changed hands. It was known all over the royal courtyards that her husband, the late king Dai Duc, the father-in-law I never met, was placed on the throne while the French were shooting at our port. Three days later he was poisoned, and his cousin succeeded to the throne. After his death, his favorite concubine, the beautiful Lady Tu Minh, escaped the palace with her baby son, Prince Buu Linh. Tu Minh and her son Buu Linh spent fourteen years living as commoners in the villages of central Vietnam. My husband was raised in the countryside and got his taste for commoners' life that way.

On the day the French protectorates announced the selection of Prince Buu Linh as the new King of Annam, troops had to go to the countryside to fetch mother and son. The mother had tried to hide her son in the rice field. When they found him, she cried and blurted out that Heaven had once more betrayed her. The troops had to drag her back to the palace and she put up a fierce fight, murmuring all the way that the throne was the source of death.

At my husband's coronation, his mother was crowned as *Hoang Thai Hau Tu Minh* (Tu Minh, the Queen Mother of Annam), the highest royal title accorded a woman of the Violet City. At the

Part Two

ceremony, the poor woman, once beautiful, cheerful, and kind, talked to the blank space in front of her, looking diminutive and terrified on the ostentatious throne carved with images of flying phoenixes. Afterwards, she turned into a mute. The fanciful clothes the ladies put on her and the salutes of the young women who bowed to her could not shake the silence. At official ceremonies, I watched the royal concubines moving around their mother-in-law, never understanding what she wanted. Nobody cared. The direction for our daily lives came from the Head Eunuch. But the royal rituals went on, and at every occasion the Queen Mother was treated like the ink painting of Confucius, which we worshipped and bowed to without thought. Yet her dull eyes, jerking limbs, and trembling lips all rubbed fear onto our skin. We became afraid of our own tomorrow. We all knew kings and queens could be killed, or if they survived, they went insane.

Other than fear, our lives became stagnant, surrounded by inanimate objects. We waited for the monthly cycles of our menses, and news, any kind of news.

And that was how I acquired the habit of standing by the window frame, looking into the night, deeper and deeper until my pupils could meet the moonlit River Huong of my past. Since childhood, my eyes had been accustomed to piercing through darkness. For years I had made my way across the river at night that way. In the Violet City, I had to train and retrain my eyes to regain a sense of control over my fate.

But then something happened in the process.

In my effort of regaining the sharpness of my vision, I began to see the Face of Brutality, identified by a pair of beastly eyes with no sockets. Just the bright red, moving pupils staring at me, wanting me to make a mistake so it could laugh.

I survived a difficult childbirth and the disappointment of an abandoned wife, and began to concentrate, instead, on raising my twin daughters.

When the twins were one-month old, my husband sent a

royal decree giving them their official titles. My older daughter, Cinnamon Fragrance, was ordained *Nam Tran Cong Chua* (the Princess of the South Sea Pearl), and my younger daughter, Ginseng Fragrance, was given the title *Nam Binh Cong Chua* (the Princess for Peace of the South.) I did not like the pompous titles. I called my little girls Cinnamon and Ginseng — symbolic of the jungles of central Vietnam where my ancestors had come from.

As Son La fed me with more gossip about the Revolution and the changing of Heaven's mandates, I began to think more about the State of Annam. In my boudoir, I asked Son La one day:

"The state affairs, the welfare and independence of Annam, aren't they the duties of everyone?"

Son La was preparing an ink plate for his calligraphy:

"Yes my Lady. It is the duty of everyone who inhabits this land, Cham and Viet alike."

"If that's the case, that everyone shares in this duty, then what happens to Heaven's daughters? Why should everything be centered around Heaven's son?"

Son La jumped up, almost dropping his ink plate, his worried eyes failing to meet mine:

"Because a daughter gets married, bears the last name of her husband, and becomes property of the husband's family."

I became upset, as though months of practiced self-control had amounted to nothing. Those days, I had picked up knitting and embroidery to pass time, and on that particular day, after Son La had cavalierly yet factually described my fate, I caught myself repeatedly stabbing my forefinger with the needle. A tiny drip of blood stained the front of my silk gown, yet I was oblivious to the pain. My whole life rushed through my head and I realized how the Violet City had turned me into a piece of property belonging to my husband inside his Citadel. But even the King could not completely control my fate. My love for Buu Linh and my daughters had not helped ease my sense of worthlessness. When I was still paddling my boat for a living, life was hard, but I belonged to no one.

"Who said so, Heaven?" I asked contemptuously.

Son La, seeing the drip of blood, was speechless.

"I haven't heard a word from Heaven. It sounds more like the saying of Confucius, a man," I added sarcastically.

I put the basket of yarns aside and began to recite: "The pious woman has as guidance the rule of the Three Obediences, according to which she is to obey three masters of her life: father, husband, and son. Her subjugation is due to her inferior nature: she is weak, ignorant, and prone to mistakes, and thus must depend on men's wisdom to conduct herself. To reflect favorably on the honor of these men, she is most of all expected to uphold the ultimate value of chastity. Chastity in the unmarried girl means virginity. In the married woman, it refers to her unconditional faithfulness to her husband, alive or dead. To play her designated role, she is reminded to cultivate the Four Virtues: diligence in housework, attractiveness in person, reticence in speech, and modesty and politeness in behavior."

I paused to breathe and continued:

"We Cham women do not take on the husband's last name, do we?"

Son La was still eyeing me, concerned and probing:

"No, Cham societies are matriarchal, my Lady. The Cham woman takes control of her household."

He paused and darted his eyes around the four walls of my boudoir. Casting his eyes toward the floor, he covered his mouth with his sleeves and lowered his voice:

"You don't have to stay here. You can escape. I can make it happen."

Neither of us was able to speak. My head began to spin. I had never once considered the option. Son La rushed out of the room, even forgetting to kowtow and bid farewell.

He had suggested the ultimate taboo.

That night I could not sleep, thinking of the future of Cinnamon and Ginseng. I thought, too, of my husband's calming and rising flesh. Somehow my heart told me the magnet only happened once in a lifetime. But how could I know? I had never known any other man. I was doomed to the fate of a pious concubine. I rushed to the half-moon window and stared at the night. The Face of Brutality was staring back at me.

I collapsed onto the muffling silk of the bed and wept. I could not give up waiting for him. I could not leave since I kept hanging on to the scintilla of hope that he would return to my boudoir, one of these days. The longing for him that had been suppressed burnt inside me again. I tossed and turned and the deepest part of me longed for the warmth of his, his alone, and no one else's. In terror, I realized I had been imprisoned, not by the teaching of Confucius and his virtues, nor by the courtyards of the Citadel, but instead by my own heart.

13. The Exodus

That Face of Brutality took forms more vividly when Son La continued to feed me with rumors on the deteriorating relationship between my husband and *Monsieur* Foucault. According to Son La, the rumors were so widespread they reached the countryside, circulated among the green-bamboo hamlets near the port of Thuan An and traveled up and down the coast, north to Tonkin and south to Cochinchina.

The latest rumors related to my husband's all-female military troupe. The beautiful women he brought to the Violet City were ordered to practice combat skills, ride horses and use weapons. These women, including his old and new loves, dressers, and chambermaids, wore royal guard uniforms. His all-female troupe grew to consist of some 300 young women, consuming a sizable part of the court's budget. The rumor also portrayed him as a psychotic and sadistic king who abused the throne: he allegedly whipped or cut off the breasts of those women who refused to obey orders.

If there were such a female troupe, he had kept it away from his ordained royal concubines.

Gossips about the insane, uncontrolled king crossed the land, igniting the anti-French fume among subversive resistance movements, and setting the stage for more and more piecemeal guerrilla uprisings. The royal concubines of the Violet City waited and waited for another night with his Royal Highness, who all the more isolated himself from all of his consorts.

I waited like the rest of his concubines, until one day when Son La rushed in, kowtowed, and whispered into my ears the most shocking news.

Foucault had received a telegraph, the official words of the Minister of Colonies, *Monsieur* Bernard Bronti. Due to overspending and budget mismanagement, neglect of the affairs of the State, and deteriorating mental health, the King of Annam, His Royal Highness Thuan Thanh, had been requested by the protectorate government to abdicate. His temporary new home would be *Cap St. Jacques*, a resort beach in Cochinchina, until final arrangements could be made for him to settle permanently on the island of Reunion, Africa — another French colony off the coast of Madagascar.

I was luckier than most royal concubines. The tragedy that befell my husband became my tragedy, but it also occasioned our last night together.

The abdicated king did return to my boudoir, for the last union, before the final change of guards. Seven years had passed and I had just turned twenty three.

As the Head Eunuch announced his Royal Highness' arrival, I sadly realized too much pain and waiting had killed off the palpitation of young love and infatuation in my heart. I calmly received him, again with the muscular tone of my belly, arms and legs. I was the same robust paddle girl.

Son La had told me my husband would be taking two of his concubines with him. They were both in their teens. I was over twenty and, hence, was not chosen for the exodus to the island of Reunion. He did not want me to be his consort for the forthcoming life in exile and old age.

In the early morning, he left me in bed and went to my half-moon window. There he stood, for hours. Looking at his elegant back from the bed, I wondered if he, too, saw the Face of Brutality and its beastly eyes. As the sun appeared and the first morning rays hit the courtyard, he began reciting a poem. I knew it was not dedicated to me. He was simply reading to himself. He must have viewed me as an uneducated woman, as in our time together, never once did he try to discuss anything literary, artistic, or political.

Son La's and Mai's teaching had paid off. I understood what the poem was about. As he spoke, I memorized every word:

Literary men, military men, all lining up before my velvet cloak
A lonely king, I bear my cross
Three times a royal toast, like the people's blood
My sorrow, my tears, or Heaven's flood?

I had not sung since my entrance to the palace. The loss of the River Huong and the rhythm of my paddles had robbed me of my melodies. All of a sudden at the inspiration of his words I had the urge to sing my husband's poem in the wailing melodies of my Cham heritage. So I did just that. I sang. I repeated every word he had spoken in the stream of melodies dormant in my blood veins. Each word became some fifty notes of music, vibrating across the land to the bottom depth of my River Huong.

When I stopped, I caught his eyes. They stared at me the same way they focused on my belly and waist the night we met on the River Huong. He no longer looked like a lion. He had the countenance of an exhausted prisoner folding up at the hour of persecution.

"I've always known you were special," he said.

For me, that was enough for a farewell moment. I was his Mystique Concubine. In the thin space between us, I felt two souls reach out for each other because they were the same. We looked at each other, a polygamous husband and a monogamous wife, for a long time.

Then he asked to see the twins.

He watched the identical girls for a while and attempted to embrace them, but they resisted, rubbing their eyes with their lotus root fingers before settling down to sit on both sides of him, pulling on his robe. He stroked their hair and they warmed up to him, little by little. Ginseng eventually climbed up and sat in his lap, while Cinnamon unsuccessfully competed for the same space. Cinnamon rushed over to me, her big, dark eyes looking back at him with curiosity. He signaled to her, and she carefully approached him, finally placing her face in his lap.

They were together, father and daughters.

He turned to me: "I'll go, but you must stay with Annam. It is your land."

I nodded. He kissed the girls' foreheads.

"You will tell them of the River Huong."

I nodded.

"You will teach them to sing my poem."

I nodded. And then he left.

I found on the pillow something he had left for me. It was a jade phoenix, intricately carved and imprinted against a plaque of gold, bearing the dragon and royal seal of the Nguyen dynasty. The phoenix was a symbol reserved only for the Nguyen Dynasty's Crowned Queen, seen in public only at two occasions: her coronation and her death.

He must have taken it away from his prematurely old and non-communicative Queen Mother Tu Minh, and passed it on to me, his Mystique Concubine. My tears fell onto the cool stone. I lifted my tunic, wiped off the tears on the radiant jade, clutched the phoenix and placed it against my bare belly, feeling the cold texture of gem against my sensitive skin. I knew something was taking form inside my womb after our last night together. This time I knew with certainty it would be a boy.

I even knew what to name my son: Que Lam, meaning the Forest of Cinnamon.

14. The Encounter

Things were hatefully normal the following week. According to Son La, my husband had left for *Cap St. Jacques*, Cochinchina, but his entourage from the Violet City, including the two chosen concubines, had not departed. Foucault had ordered that they be held up inside the Violet City until further instructions, leaving the entire royal court bewildered and wondering. Tension filled the Violet City. The Royal Cabinet, as well as all female inhabitants of the Violet City, were holding their breath, waiting for Foucault's words or telegraphs from his government in France. No one knew for sure what would come next, or what would happen to the concubines and children of King Thuan Thanh.

I waited, as usual, with the rest of the concubines.

It was a bright morning and I was watching Cinnamon and Ginseng play in the main courtyard of the West Palace when I heard noises and bells. The Head Eunuch and his entourage were rushing through, asking all of us to clear the way. Mai helped me pick up the twins and we retreated.

I stopped a eunuch and asked. "What is the fuss?"

"The Resident Superieur is coming, my Lady."

"What?" I could not believe the words. "The Frenchman is coming here?"

"There will be a photo session. The Resident Superieur has so requested."

"A photo session?!"

"Yes, my Lady. Please clear the way. It is an emergency request."

The eunuch turned and walked away, his mind obviously focused on carrying out the Frenchman's order. The eunuchs began to stage the courtyard like an opera stage. I went back to my boudoir and pondered. The taking of photographs! I had never seen such a thing. But I had heard of the postcard incident and how it had angered my husband. I called for Son La and Mai, and they arrived together a while later, a look of concern shadowing both faces.

"The Foucault Enterprise has organized tourist attractions for European subjects to come and visit Annam, my Lady," Son La said. "The project has been going on for a while. They've been taking photographs of the lotus ponds, the dragon gate, the Thai Hoa cabinet meeting hall, the throne, the grand altars honoring the Nguyen Founding Lords, everything. Now they are moving inside the West Palace."

"It is very inappropriate, my Lady," Mai added, her eyes reddening. "It is good that His Royal Highness is gone. Otherwise, imagine the humiliation. For almost two hundred years, no outsider has been able to have an audience with the royal concubines of Hue."

I had been told the rules since my first day of residence in the Violet City. The West Palace was off limits to men, except Court personnel — the eunuchs — and the King of Annam.

"Today, a number of royal concubines have been asked to pose for the photographers. Not even with the courtesy of a warning, my Lady." Mai wiped her eyes with her sleeves.

I thought of the Confucian rules of the Three Obediences— absolute submission to father, husband, and son. Under the French protectorate authority, it appeared to me that my husband's concubines had to obey an additional boss, that French Resident Superieur, *Monsieur* Foucault. I sighed and told Son La and Mai I did not wish to see what was going on in the main courtyard.

"Close all curtains and shut the entrance," I instructed.

Much to my dismay, both stood still with their head bowed.

"What are you waiting for?" I was irritated.

"I think the Head Eunuch would be coming here soon to speak to you."

"About what?"

Mai broke out crying. When Son La began to speak, his voice was weak and remote:

"The Resident Superieur has asked to see you. I heard it is something about a special postcard."

The Head Eunuch arrived shortly thereafter. The stooping old man did most of the talking. I sat at my tea table while he stayed closer to the entrance, his eyes fixated to the floor and never once lifted past the rosewood footstool — a barricade that adjoined the entrance connecting my boudoir to the courtyard. The footstool had always been there. I just took it for granted.

To enter my boudoir from the courtyard, one had to lift the flap of one's long dress and step over the footstool. The barricade kept people from rushing in. For the first time in my life inside the Violet City, I focused my attention on the barricade, as I listened to the Head Eunuch describing the wish of Sylvain Foucault.

No real man except King Thuan Thanh had set foot in my boudoir. The Head Eunuch and Son La, of course, were not real men. During my pregnancy, the court physician, who was sixty-five years old, had to be lifted by Eunuchs when he stepped over the footstool to reach my bed. I lay behind brocade curtains, and the old man felt my silk-clad belly by extending his one arm in between the curtain folds, without ever laying eyes on me. To feel my pulse, he placed his ears and thumb over a silk thread that had been tied to my wrist. There was never any direct skin-to-skin contact.

The Head Eunuch had finished his speech and was still kow-towing near the entrance when I left the tea table to walk around my boudoir. For the first time, I became keenly aware of every piece of furniture, every carving, every fold of the curtains surrounding the bed. I felt the shiny wood pillars that accented the room and divided it into quarters. I moved my palm along the edge of the lacquer divan and felt the smoothness of the mother of pearls.

I began to see the brown torso of my husband, the silky slacks that draped the columns of his thighs, and those long fingers of his that once molded my flesh. I saw traces of my husband everywhere on the impersonal and familiar furniture that made up my existence. The emotions overwhelmed me and I had to place one hand over my heart, almost losing my balance. The Head Eunuch, who, all this time, had kept his head bowed and his eyes toward the floor, failed to notice my shift of emotion.

My king was not here, yet I could feel him. I turned to the Head Eunuch:

"I will not comply with the *Monsieur's* wish."

The Head Eunuch remained kneeling, his eyes glancing toward the footstool barricade, obviously looking forward to the time when he could step over it to return to the main courtyard. For once, I had the urge to see the barricade grow higher and higher so no one would be able to step into my world.

Years ago, after my husband stopped coming to me, I once harbored the desire to escape the West Palace so I could roam Hue at my whim. But the days kept passing by and gradually I grew accustomed to my fate, losing all desire to escape the confines of my boudoir. To seek the freedom of my River Huong, I simply stood by my half-moon window looking out. The sudden recognition of the gradual change made me want badly to weep.

The Head Eunuch had started a new speech. He told me of the time predating my birth, when French gunmen first entered the Violet City. The head of the French army, one Lieutenant Mahee, dug up the mausoleum of the late emperor Tu Duc to search for treasure. Too bad for him, he could not find the late emperor's coffin. To this day, the French had never been able to decipher where the emperor was actually buried.

"The Frenchman wanted to excavate the late emperor's tomb, and he did, my Lady," the Head Eunuch droned.

"I am sure there were people who objected," I replied.

"The Minister of Protocols and Culture, my Lady. He spent the rest of his life objecting, yet the digging was done."

I moved toward the window and raised the curtain. I could see part of what was going on in the main courtyard. Never had the West Palace been so animated. I recognized the royal concubines who were preparing themselves for the photo session, among whom were the two young women, both sixteen years old, who had been chosen to accompany my husband in exile and were awaiting departure. Some of the children, the young princes and princesses of Annam, had also been dressed up in royal attires for the photo shoot. The participants were shy, yet beaming in a festive atmosphere. The day must have been the highlight of their dull existence, ironically brought on by the departure of their husband and father. No one expressed sadness or anger. Beautiful furniture was being moved to stage the scene. The eunuchs scurried around like ants. Among those little people, a black box seemed towering high, situated on a three-legged stand, and I saw the silhouette of a tall man bending over it.

"Is that a camera?" I asked, pointing.

"Yes, my Lady," the Head Eunuch had leaped to his feet, standing behind me. "It has a lens, through which you can see yourself upside down."

"Upside down?"

"Yes, the size of a bee. The equipment makes a noise and your image is captured on paper. The West can do many a splendid thing."

"And the man who stands behind it?"

"The photographer, my Lady, a Western man."

I had never seen a camera before. Nor had I seen a Western man, although I had studied the painting of Jesus Christ inside Son La's book. To me, the man on the cross and his dark beard and long hair represented the image of a Western male.

"I want to walk the main courtyard," I told the Head Eunuch.

We stepped over the footstool barricade, passed the double-door entrance of my boudoir, and he followed me toward the gleaming central courtyard, full of sunshine.

I took my time scrutinizing the machine called the camera and the face of the tall Western man who bowed before me. The camera was exactly what the Head Eunuch had described. I even peeped inside the black box and saw the bee-sized image of the posing concubines and their children. As to the Western man standing behind the machine, he could not take his eyes off me, and I had to remind him to bow his head. I could not tell his age. In many ways, he looked very old, his pores extremely large, his golden hair growing every-where on his uncombed head, at the top of his lips, along his square jaw, and even on his hands. His arms were awkwardly long. He reminded me of an old, golden ape. On the other hand, he exuded all the characteristics of youth. His gait was straight, like a bamboo tree, his movements swift, and his cheeks rosy, bumpy, and shiny, a sharp contrast to the smooth, olive complexion of my husband or the dehydrated wrinkles of the old eunuchs. Most fascinating was the light blue of his eyes, as though the sky had reflected itself in the clear pupils. I had never seen such blue eyes before, yet I could not stare at him very long for fear he would lose respect for me. I suspected he must have dyed his pupils with eye drops, perhaps to perform Western witchcraft or magic. He did not look anything like the grim darkness and melancholy of the sacrificing Jesus Christ.

My curiosity was satisfied and I told the Head Eunuch what I wanted done. Sylvain Foucault did not want any picture of me and my daughters wearing royal attires and posing in the courtyard. Other concubines of the exiled King Thuan Thanh could easily do that task. Foucault desired a special scene for a special postcard. There could be no other convenient time to stage the scene than after my husband had been dragged off his throne, leaving a bunch of dependents and descendants unattended and uncared for, disposable at the mercy of the protectorate authorities.

I could read Foucault's mind. He must have congratulated himself on the availability of the Mystique Concubine, the orphan paddle girl. I lifted my chin to the sky and thought of the mysterious Heaven who had arranged my life onto courses I could never predict. Once and for all, I wanted some control over my fate. I told the Head Eunuch I wanted a personal audience with the Frenchman who had sent my husband away. I wanted to move the lacquer divan to the open courtyard. A chair should be placed in front of the divan, far enough to create a noticeable distance, but close enough for conversation. I would be sitting on the divan, dressed in ceremonial attire. If Foucault wanted to change me into a postcard, he had to do it my way.

Dressed in the best of costumes made out of thick, heavy, crispy satin and brocade that completely hid my body shape, I sat on the divan in the middle of the courtyard from dawn until sunset to wait for Foucault. My burning rage intensified as the hours passed slowly, and he was nowhere to be seen.

I had told Mai and Son La to come and get me when the sun died out, and if Foucault had not come by then, we would repeat the waiting game the following day.

I knew that from those half-moon windows overlooking the courtyard, the curious eyes of the concubines, their maids and eunuchs were peeping out to watch my movements. Foucault's intention to use me in a postcard was known to Son La and Mai. It must equally have been known to the petty gossipers of the Violet City, who were all dying to know my reaction.

Whether my exiled husband could be humiliated rested entirely in my hands.

When beams of sunlight turned yellow, signaling the end of the day, I cast my eyes across the tiled courtyard toward the half-moon window of my boudoir, where Mai would be raising the curtains and nodding her head. Before I could adjust my posture to remove myself from the divan, I heard footsteps.

An imposing figure appeared before me in a fitted gray outfit, a crispy white collar protruding from underneath, with an accenting red bow in the middle. The man who was walking toward my lacquer divan wore high boots and a hat. I saw strands of brown hair protruding from the hat, and a pair of chestnut eyes. Like a cat's eyes.

The man resembled neither the golden-ape photographer nor the bearded Jesus Christ. He moved his stocky frame with the combined grace of a crawling python and a hungry leopard, and his fierce face, with its high-bridged, dominant nose and thick whiskers, exuded an intimidating, animalistic quality. Under the brocade gown, my shoulders felt weak. I moved my perfumed fan lightly and took my eyes off him to maintain my composure. I did not want him to think I was afraid.

I had expected to see an interpreter, but Foucault was alone.

"So this is the famous Mystique Concubine," he said in Vietnamese, his voice deep and throaty, with a perfect Tonkinese accent. He stopped by the chair I had set up for him, sat down and crossed the muscular columns of his legs, his coarse and bulky hands resting on the chair's arms. He shifted his gigantic body as though the chair was too small for him, unbuttoned his sleeves and rolled them up. I noticed the fuzzy brown hair on his arms. Another ape. He was everything my husband was not.

"I expect you to say the proper greetings, now that I know you speak our language so well," I said.

"D'accord," he said as he stepped out of his chair and bowed. "Thua Ba, My Lady."

As he sat back down, his eyes were fixed on me as though they were grabbing my limbs.

"What are you doing sitting on that silly divan, wearing those bulky clothes?"

"What makes you think I would allow a Western man inside my boudoir? Especially the man who has just helped exile my husband!"

"Suppose my photographer and myself had come to your boat on the River Huong?"

He was crude and uncultured, and did not speak to me with the refined and humble manners like the mandarins or the eunuchs. I did not know what to say or how to act.

"*Thua ba*, right now you look incredibly beautiful because you are offended. But I wish you would get off that divan and move around. You must realize the Annamese protocols do not become you."

I snapped the fan shut in rage.

"I saw you getting out of your bridal rickshaw when you first came. I said to myself, what a fine woman, built like a Westerner, with hips and height and dark rosy skin like us swarthy Mediterraneans. What a waste to have you in Buu Linh's possession. Your husband is a fool."

The fan flew across the courtyard, hit his face, and dropped to the floor. For a moment, I thought I heard ooh's and aah's from my secret observers behind those half-moon windows overlooking and circling the main courtyard. The whiskered ape bent to pick up my fan. I was trembling. I had shown my temper. Despite hours of thought and preparation, I had not done the right thing. Would he kill me, as he had my husband's father, the late King Dai Duc, or would he exile me elsewhere off the coast of Vietnam?

The whiskered ape did not seem in the least offended. In fact, the whiskers rose and his thick lips pulled into a smile. He stretched his body in the chair and scrutinized the fan.

"Dainty little thing. Like all things that belong to poor Buu Linh and his dynasty. I wished he had not acted up so badly. The three of us, Buu Linh, yourself, and I share one thing in common. We all have a bad temper."

"Stop talking that way about my husband and live up to the refinement of the French empire," I said sternly, thinking of how Son La had educated me on the Empire of France and all those missionaries who had come to our land and befriended the earlier Nguyen Lords.

"The refinement of the Empire is not my concern. My ancestors, like you paddle people, used to fish in the Mediterranean Sea and around the island of Corse before they moved to their castles in Loire."

He was mentioning places I did not know and, again, my sense of power collapsed.

"Don't turn down my photographer's lens too quickly. See first what photography can do for you."

He reached inside his gray trouser pockets and handed me

some glossy cardboards. My curiosity took over and I examined the pictures he showed: from the sceneries portrayed, I imagined an array of vast sapphire seas and pink or white castles — the type of majestic grandeur completely different from my River Huong and the West Palace.

"You are an enticing belle, but I have no interest in Buu Linh's women, twittering Annamese birds. I'm almost twice your age, old enough to be your father. I have a purely commercial interest in mind."

His accent was that of a native.

"A wealthy European acquaintance of mine had expressed an interest in making postcards of the royal concubines inside the palace." He waved his arm as if shooing a fly away. "He's fascinated with the Annamese camisole, cai yem, so different from the Victorian lace corset, but it's got to be worn by a genuine royal concubine. The legend will say Bath of a Royal Concubine."

As he announced this, he painted the words in an imaginary line across the sky in front of him in a sweeping gesture. I remained silent. He went on:

"…Some say perversion. Some say art. Some say a taste for the exotic. I say my patron would be paying lots of money to the Foucault gallery. A snap of you in this royal setting would be perfect. As a former paddle girl, you're most likely not too prudish."

I was correct. He picked me because of my past.

"Nothing complicated, nothing too out of line," he raised my fan to his nose, inhaled, and closed his eyes. He looked like a monster in repose. "Just a picture of your naked back, the profile of your face and hair next to a royal porcelain sink of sparkling water, maybe among a gaggle of little maids or eunuchs. Have your photograph taken in a second or so, and you will be well fed for the rest of your life."

He handed me my fan and I turned away. The fan dropped onto my divan. I would not touch what he had touched. I smoothed the corner of my costume.

"Very well, then, if the refinement of your Empire is not your concern, neither is the state of Annam my concern. After all, I am Cham."

I paused to let this sink in.

"Above all, I want to live. Disobeying you, I suppose I can be killed. So here I am. In the open courtyard. If you want your postcard, take my picture this way. You know the whole Violet City is watching right now. Go get your photographer. Send your men and women and set up your scene. But I will sit here, dressed like this. It will be a struggle to get all this fabric off me. You will have to drag me around to get the kind of picture you want. Capture my image and you will see on paper the scene of a woman dragged against her will. This is the only way you can have my picture taken."

In the clear brown of his eyes I could see the flame I had ignited. I saw also the reflection of the bright redness of my gown. I threw his pictures back at him.

"If you had come to me on the River Huong, I would have knocked you off my boat with my paddles."

His pupils seized mine in rage. I did not move.

"Your predecessors came in here and dug up the late emperor's tomb for treasure. Now you come in here and want a wife to undress and smear the honor of her husband. These are acts of spoiled children, barbarians who carry weapons. I was just a paddle girl, but I can tell you when an act is a barbaric act."

His brown eyes had turned glacial and they were affixed on mine still, his whiskers vibrating furiously over his tightened lips. I watched the Western man rise and walk away as the last ray of the afternoon sun died out on his grey suit. I shivered.

His face had become the Face of Brutality.

15. Conquering the Face of Brutality

The following month, the Head Eunuch made a special announcement. The eight-year-old Prince Vinh Quang, son of Bang Phi, The Concubine of Egality, would soon be crowned the new King of Annam. The selection of Vinh Quang had already been endorsed by the French protectorate government. Prince Vinh Quang was the youngest of my husband's twenty-eight sons, believed to be the most docile. For the coronation, the troops had to fetch him. He was crawling under a table.

The French Resident Superieur had also made the decision to cut the royal budget. Because Thuan Thanh had abdicated, certain of his concubines and children would have to leave the Violet City. My name was at the top of the list.

The Head Eunuch had a meeting with me to deliver a short and impersonal message. I could keep all of my jewelry. I could take the lacquer divan as a token from my husband. Under Mai's advice, I had hidden the jade phoenix beneath my undergarment.

No allowance would be coming from the court or the protectorate government. I would have to find a means to support myself and my daughters. In preparation for my departure, the Head Eunuch had asked me to choose a new place of abode. He showed me a map of the outskirts of Hue.

In those few seconds, I reflected on the life I wanted for my daughters. The River Huong was my home, but my daughters would not paddle passengers across rivers.

I looked at the names listed on the map. The name Quynh Anh caught my attention. Since I had learned to read, I knew Quynh Anh was a fancy name with its roots in ancient Chinese, meaning the crystallized essence of a flower that blossomed at night. I thought of my encounter with my husband under a full moon on the River Huong, and how I had stood by the window frame, night after night, hoping to find the same moon hovering over the Violet City. I asked the Head Eunuch about the village of Quynh Anh. He said the villagers raised silk worms and produced silk of the finest kind in central Vietnam. Quynh Anh was also the birthplace of several scholars and officers of the court, among whom were a mandarin of the first rank, *Hong Lo Tu Khanh*, who served as my husband's astronomer, and Nguyen Tung, the Admiral of the Vietnamese Royal Fleet, which guarded the Port of Thuan An.

I asked the Head Eunuch for details about the job of these two officials. Despite the French presence, the Nguyen kings had continued their tradition of *Te Nam Giao*, an annual ceremony that took place in the outskirts of Hue, in which the king would pray to Heaven for the good of his people. The king's astronomist was responsible for organizing the ceremony in accordance with the configuration of stars. The Vietnamese Royal Fleet existed in name only, although Admiral Nguyen Tung was still in command. The French, with their cannons, gunpowder, sea-going vessels and navy force, controlled the Port.

These two court officials had a reputation for their integrity and loyalty to the monarchy. They had made their birthplace, the village of Quynh Anh, famous. They could become the teachers and father figures for my two daughters. And my son.

So I told the Head Eunuch I would like to move to Quynh Anh, and I would trade my jewelry for gold taels, enough to buy myself a small silk farm.

It is my last night in the Violet City.

I stand by my half-moon window to take one last look.

I can not forget the whiskered face of Sylvain Foucault, and his chestnut eyes.

I know outside, the Fact of Brutality is still waiting.

PART THREE

Dew's Memoir (Hue, 1949)

1. Aunt Ginseng, Daughter of the Revolution

The first beautiful woman I met in my life was my own mother. The villagers of Quynh Anh called her Princess Cinnamon. The silk merchants called her Madame Que. I called her Ma.

The silk traders and villagers of Quynh Anh who came to the house to take orders from Ma and helped her prepare festivities for ancestors' worships said the porcelain skin of her cheeks was like lotus petals. They said the stream of her black hair was shinier than polished lacquer, and compared her slender frame to the best of willow trees that bent graciously in the strong wind without breaking. They alleged that as a young girl, Ma once took a nap under a magnolia tree, her stream of black hair spreading around her head, emanating the fragrance of cinnamon oil, which she loved. A snake was enticed by the fragrance, and crawled onto the stream of her hair. Struck by the beauty of Ma's face, the snake became spellbound, frozen as though it had seen a goddess. When Ma woke up and moved her head, the snake silently crawled away. Even the meanest of creatures would be awed by Ma's beauty, they said.

I was the ugly daughter of a beauty queen. The silk traders and villagers said I was a cute and nice little girl, but no one described me in terms of lotuses, lacquer and willow trees. My nose was too flat, my mouth too full, my skin so pale it almost reflected a bluish shade. Only my eyes resembled Ma's, which the traders and villagers compared to longan nuts in autumn ponds.

Ours was a household full of women and no men. Ma had all kinds of domestic help, all coordinated by Nanny Mai. Like a fortress of humans, they surrounded Ma, catered to her needs, and supposedly protected her. Yet, unknown to Ma, the servants gossiped, feeding me with information about certain things. For example, the servants disputed the traders' overblown ideas about Ma's beauty. Even Nanny Mai would join in and agree that Ma was not anywhere as pretty as the Mystique Concubine herself. Or Ma's twin sister, my Aunt Ginseng.

Ma told me the Mystique Concubine had died at the height of her beauty, falling into a deep slumber from which she never emerged. Her soul just simply flew away, escorted by nightingales. Ma was twenty-five years old when the Mystique Concubine passed on. Aunt Ginseng had already left home, too busy fighting in the jungles of north Vietnam to return home for her mother's funeral. Like Lady Trieu of ancient Vietnam fighting the Wu's from China, Auntie Ginseng wore her golden armor, pointing a sword to the sky, riding an elephant. Every little girl born in Vietnam (even a product of French elementary school like me) knew the legend of Lady Trieu, who pledged she would ride the wind to save her people from drowning in slavery. The enemies were looking for Aunt Ginseng all the time, so, I had to keep a secret. I was never to mention Auntie Ginseng to anyone, except within the household.

"I don't understand why your mother had to tell these tales," Nanny Mai said one day.

"Your grandmother died in a fire in the middle of a war, and your Auntie has been in a French jail up north for having spied for Ho Chi Minh troops. There's no such thing as a young woman riding elephants nowadays."

When I repeated Nanny Mai's words to Ma, she went after Nanny Mai and slapped the poor woman in the face.

"How can you betray me so?" Ma clenched her teeth.

Nanny Mai teared and apologized over and over again. Seeing the red marks on Nanny Mai's cheeks, Ma knelt down on the floor and begged for the Nanny's forgiveness, apologizing to the woman who had helped raise both her and me. Shocked to see Ma on the floor, Nanny Mai asked me to ignore the bad stories she told me earlier, saying she was very sorry to have confused me, confirming that indeed my aunt was a woman warrior riding elephants like Lady Trieu. I watched the two grown-ups with amazement and amusement. I knew, instinctively then, that not only did Ma have beauty, but she also had a genuine, fierce flare for the dramatic.

Despite the number of female servants, Ma insisted on doing certain things herself. Like taking care of the altar room.

It was in the altar room that my father, the black-and-white photograph of an Annamese mandarin, lived together with his father, the *Hong Lo Tu Khanh*, first rank literary officer and astronomer of the Nguyen court, and Admiral Nguyen Tung, who adopted Ma. They all lived in an array of black-and-white photographs framed in rosewood carvings, which Ma polished everyday with fresh lemon juice to make the rosewood shine.

All photographs and silk paintings were placed lower than the picture of my emperor grandfather, King Thuan Thanh of Annam, taken at his coronation. Later on, I discovered the same picture had made its way to history books. My grandfather had become the legend in Vietnamese history as an exiled, anti-French king, admired by generations of Vietnamese patriots. But in the picture sitting in that smoky altar room, my emperor grandfather looked like a boy and did not seem much older than I. He was not even all that handsome or smart, just a dazed boy dressed up in fancy clothes. At least he was a real person. His wife, the dead Mystique Concubine, on the other hand, was preserved in a silk portrait. There were no photographs of her anywhere. In the silk painting, she looked surreal, and I could not imagine her face.

Much later, there was a time when I turned sixteen and I was about to leave home to study at the French convent in the highlands. This was a costly and complex arrangement that Ma painstakingly accomplished, since the Convent was not just for any girl. Before I left, I asked Ma whether she loved my father. She looked at me as though the question was totally inappropriate, as if love was a concept meant to remain unspoken forever.

Part Three

I couldn't remember exactly when Ma first took me to the altar and made me learn those names and faces of those dead men, including my father's. When the children I played with asked me where my father was, I would say automatically that he was on the altar. Ma would burn incense everyday and place plenty of fresh fruits there. The spirits could only consume those fruits symbolically, so I got to eat them all, getting all the blessings of my ancestors by devouring their leftovers, each time Ma rearranged her tray.

Three items on the altar received Ma's special attention. She polished them with cinnamon-scented oil and covered them with a satin red silk cloth. I often watched her handle them with utmost deference. Occasionally she let me touch them. Just a light touch. The bright green jade phoenix that shone under candle light, and the two ivory plaques, each bearing carved red Chinese characters, spoke of Ma's royal and mandarin heritage. The jade, as well as the elephant tusks from which these plaques were made, must have been thousands of years old, Ma said. The older they were, the prettier they got. The phoenix, a gift from King Thuan Thanh to his Mystique Concubine, identified my grandmother as the uncrowned Queen of Annam. The two ivory plaques were like ID cards, held by my two grandfathers, commemorating their lifetime career and loyalty to the Nguyen Court.

When I touched the items, the coldness of jade and ivory sent chills along my spinal cord. To reach them, I would have to stand on the lacquer divan, studded with mother-of-pearl inlay, imposingly situated in front of the altar table.

On the altar, there were two rosewood frames that remained blank. Ma reserved them for Aunt Ginseng and Uncle Forest. She polished the empty frames the same way she polished the dead men's photographs. She said her sister and brother had left home. Either they would return one day, or they would become spirits to join the ancestral altar.

"Why did they leave home?" I asked.

Ma pulled me into her lap and whispered the stories to me. There was an airplane circling the air over the village Quynh Anh once, and a young village girl, friend of Auntie Ginseng, had taken out a hand-held mirror she always carried in her blouse pocket. French soldiers thought she was trying to send a signal to anti-French rebels who could shoot down the plane. So French soldiers shot the young village girl. Aunt Ginseng saw this. She became mad. So she left home to make sure no innocent young girls would ever get shot again.

Uncle Forest, on the other hand, left for an entirely different reason. He had been raised, not only by his mother, the Mystique Concubine, but also by his adoptive father, Admiral Nguyen Tung. The Admiral died when Uncle Forest was eight years old. Years later, after a devastating flood swept through the village of Quynh Anh, the family had to move the Admiral's skeleton to a new burial ground. The Admiral's remains were uncovered, and the young Forest got to hold the skull of his adoptive father in his hands. Something touched the core of his soul during the experience. He made his decision then. He left a note for both the Mystique Concubine and Ma bidding farewell, announcing that he'd be joining Auntie Ginseng somewhere in the north. He even wanted to go to Japan to study the Japanese experience of industrialization. That was what both his biological father and adoptive father would have wanted him to do, he wrote in his note.

The year was 1925. My Uncle Forest was fifteen.

"What do they look like?" I asked Ma.

"Like Lady Trieu and Thai Hoc the Patriot."

It was easy for a young girl to get a notion of Lady Trieu, because even the maids who couldn't read a newspaper would talk about the gold-armored woman. It was not as easy to get acquainted with Thai Hoc the Patriot.

"Did he look anything like Napoleon?" I asked once.

"No, no, no, no," Ma's voice shrilled. "Not at all! Napoleon was French!"

I was disappointed. Napoleon was the conqueror, the patriot, the greatest man of all men.

Something must have clicked in Ma's head after my question that day. She abruptly withdrew me from French Catholic elementary school to enroll me at Lycée Dong Khanh. I had to sit through an examination first, and to the best of my recollection, I did very poorly. The maids in the house gossiped that when one was the daughter of the richest woman in Hue, one got admitted to wherever one wanted to be! There, on the steps of the red brick schoolhouse called Lycée Dong Khanh, a group of older students showed me a leaflet with Thai Hoc the Patriot's face on it. I formed my first notion of Uncle Forest then. On the leaflet appeared a short-haired, square-faced man with a trim moustache and bushy brows, looking on grimly. He was no Napoleon, but he had his own appeal.

The students told me Thai Hoc the Patriot led a revolution and died at 26 years of age on a French guillotine before I was born. Before he died, he said something like this: "If a man does not achieve success, at least he achieves a legend." Thai Hoc the Patriot died, so he became a legend. Legend meant death. Death was what happened to a man who led a revolution and achieved no success. Those who succeeded lived.

At least my matriculation to Lycée Dong Khanh helped me understand why Ma left those two frames blank. Auntie Ginseng and Uncle Forest left home to become legends. They could be dead at any time. Then, they would join the spirits that became my roots, my home. Meanwhile, I was to keep another secret. I was not supposed to mention Uncle Forest to anyone, except within the household. I did not want Uncle Forest to be guillotined like Thai Hoc the Patriot. I pledged to myself I would keep my lips sealed.

2. White Magnolia

Growing up with Ma in her ancestral house on the slope of Nam Giao also meant getting to know her magnolia tree in the front yard. It was Ma who had made it grow so tall and spread its leaf-heavy branches over the red tiled roof, sprinkling petals all over the front yard. The tree became the benchmark of how far I could go back to my earliest memory of living with Ma.

Ma said white magnolias reminded her of Ginseng. As a young girl, Auntie Ginseng often picked a magnolia bloom and placed it next to her face. She would cock her head and pretend she was being photographed like a silver screen star of the West. The translucent white petal shone onto her young skin. And then Auntie Ginseng would take the bloom and place it next to the Mystique Concubine's face to compare. Mother and daugher would laugh, and Ginseng would throw the bloom at Ma, asking Ma to do the same thing. Ma would refuse, just to irk Ginseng. Ma called Ginseng the magnolia thrower of the house. At times, Ma said, the magnolia thrower would lick off the fresh drops of dew on the white petals.

"Sweet, sweet, sweet," she would claim, licking her lips.

Ginseng said when she grew up, she would get married and have a baby girl, whom she would name Dew. Not just any Dew, but the best of Dew. Mi-Suong. Beautiful Dew. That was the origin of my name.

Of course, as a grown woman, Ginseng had no time for a baby because she was busy wearing golden armor, even wooden shoes like Joan of Arc. My aunt pointed her sword at the sky and rode giant elephants in the misty jungles of north Vietnam.

I was grateful for the absentee Auntie Ginseng for having given me such a beautiful name, and I was equally fascinated with her riding elephants. But I could never understand how she could throw those dainty magnolia blooms around like table tennis balls. Ginseng must have had a mean streak in her to treat magnolia blooms that harshly.

The big blooms rested tender in my hand; those whitish, ivory petals, large enough to fill up a porcelain winter melon soup bowl that could feed five adults. Ma would place the blue and white translucent bowl out on the mossy porch to collect rainwater. Every day, she would pick a fresh bloom, severing it from its grainy, long stem with a pair of scissors. She would float the cut bloom inside the bowl and place it on the rosewood altar table. The floral scent filled up the room, lingering upon the ivory lace curtains and the edges of the dark furniture that shone with lemon juice.

Much later, I fell in love and married a philosophy student at Sorbonne whose *nom de guerre* was *L'Espoir*, the French word for "Hope." When he brought home to me my first bottle of Christian Dior perfume from Paris, I sat dumbstruck until I could recall what the scent reminded me of: the cut magnolia blooms that permeated Ma's altar room.

I imagined, too, the flowers would turn into a woman's face, smooth and white like magnolia, with painted brows like two slanting ink strokes, just like in the silk painting that supposedly captured her in the altar room. The woman became my notion of my grandmother, the Mystique Concubine of the Violet City and the matriarch of my family, a household consisting of women and no living men. Through generations, Ma said, we the women and young girls of the ancestral house would be bound together by that absentee woman, who became the spirit of th River Huong.

I imagined she would evaporate into a tiny stream of air, traveling so lightly from her silk portrait to the porcelain bowl, and eventually becoming the bloom of magnolia floating in the rainwater that smelled like the early morning dew of the perspiring glass window behind curtains. And then like smoke, she would curl herself out of the bowl, her long black hair floating behind her back. Like Ma, she wore white silk pajamas, the soft fabric reminding me of the rich, smooth texture of the white bloom petals that covered the ground of our front yard.

In that dark altar room, I imagined my grandmother would float through the dark space, her naked feet suspended slightly above the tiled floor. At times, my three dead grandfathers would also come alive, walking out of their black-and-white frames. The emperor boy would pull my sleeves, making me bow. The two old men — a paternal grandfather and an adoptive maternal one — would approach me, placing their dehydrated hands onto my forehead, their long, curled fingernails dragging across my temples like the touch of a dry bamboo branch.

And I would faint.

Of course, Ma knew nothing about my fantasy. She would think I was impious.

The fear and excitement combined made me regard the altar room with both love and awe. Most of the time, I avoided the altar room by spending my days in the front yard, drunk in the sweet smell of waxy blooms. They were mine and not just Auntie Ginseng's little table tennis balls.

But soon, I discovered that just like Auntie Ginseng, I had my own mean streak.

When the white blooms fell like rain onto the damp ground, I picked them up and placed them in a bamboo basket. I had a little shovel, and one morning, I tried to replant those blooms into a flower bed that followed the shape of my bedroom window, directly underneath it.

I wanted to create my own magnolia tree.

In the process, I never expected to see those pitiful earthworms. At the sight of them, I threw the shovel and ran back to the house. The reddish brown creatures were shaped like chopsticks, yet grotesquely soft and wriggling. They could crawl through the cracks between my fingers. My shovel had stabbed them in half, each half still corkscrewing through the dirt as though gasping for life.

I had seen earthworms living and dying. I held my dirty hands together and stared at my palms. A tear fell into the middle of my joined hands. In my joined palms, I saw a clear little pond in which I could still imagine shadows of the reddish creatures wriggling in despair. Even in death, they still moved. I cried into the pond of my palms because I knew I had killed them.

Yet I would do it again, trying to plant my tree. I had become obsessed with the idea even though I knew the planting of my dream tree had killed, and would continue to kill.

In the only two times I met Aunt Ginseng, I never got a chance to ask the thrower of magnolia blooms why she did such a thing. What was so compelling that she had to pull a petal apart, the same way I had to stab earthworms to get to my version of a dream?

The first time I met Aunt Ginseng, it was in the middle of an autumn night, yet the air outside was full of fog. It was the day of the August Moon festival. We were supposed to get a clear, full moon.

I had eaten lots of greasy sesame cakes during the day and woke up in the chill of the night, my eyes catching the stream of August moon from the open window. I was busy listening to the rumbling noises in my stomach, concentrating all of my attention on my belly button.

In the stillness of the night, I realized that the window was wide open. It was the fog that had gotten inside and made me sick. It had got into my belly button and given me a stomachache. I turned over on my stomach and hid my face into the pillow. From the corners of my eyes, I raised my eyelids and glanced upward at the window frame.

Ma was standing outside the window, holding the lantern, staring back at me. Ma, standing still, behaving oddly and strangely dressed. She had on dark cotton pajamas and a funny-looking, unattractive green hunter's hat. Her eyes were fixated onto my face, intensely like a stranger. Her hair was divided and tightly woven into two Chinese braids, hanging on both sides of her face, protruding from under the hat rim. The lantern flickered in her hand. I noticed she was not wearing the green jade bangle and the gold carved bracelet, which had been blessed with Quan Yin's holy water by a monk.

Something was not right. Ma wore that jewelry all the time, even in sleep. The intensity of her glare was so haunting I could not continue looking at her. I had to close my eyes again.

And then the terror struck.

It was not Ma at all at the window frame. It was a stranger I had never met. She had Ma's face.

I must have fainted for a few minutes. When I regained consciousness, I caught myself still frozen in fear. I opened my eyes again and the first thing I saw was the empty window frame. The woman was gone.

I heard voices, coming out of the altar room, racy and competing. I listened and listened. Ma was speaking to another woman.

"She betrayed all of us," the stranger said.

"Don't say that about your own mother," Ma was pleading. It was strange to hear her voice choked and weak.

"You and your bourgeois life! Think of the sufferings of this country!"

"But I am your flesh and blood!"

I got out of bed and left my room. The voices became clear and clearer. I was approaching the altar room. I pushed lightly on the door, already ajar. I peeped in. The room was well lit. All lights had been turned on, and all lanterns and candles were burning.

There were two of Ma in the room. But no, there was only one Ma. My Ma in her ivory silk pajamas, her dark long hair falling to one side, the jade bangle and gold carved bracelet circling her wrists, the velvet slippers enclosing her feet. The other woman, a replica of Ma, was everything I did not want Ma to be. If Ma was a willow tree, the other woman was a bamboo shoot. In the black pajamas and rubber sandals, she looked and acted like a foul peasant, almost too robust, too monstrous. And she was yelling at my Ma.

"Face up to reality, your revered mother slept with the enemy for wealth and security...People are dying every day, and you are well fed! Why?"

Ma's hands covered her face.

"You know what the irony was, sister?" the replica continued.

"It was Foucault who secured my release. Without him they

would have executed me along with Nguyen Thi Minh Khai, the first Vietnamese woman to join the Party in Moscow!"

I pushed on the door and stepped in.

"Stop yelling at my mother, you monster, you scared me at the window!" I screamed hate at her.

The two versions of Ma turned toward me simultaneously, both standing awkwardly in front of me, as though they were caught stealing.

I burst out crying. The two versions of Ma stood there and watched.

"Dew, meet your Aunt Ginseng," Ma said softly, brushing her long fingers through my entangled hair.

I looked at the woman who was supposed to be Auntie Ginseng. There was no gold armor. No wooden sabots. No pointed sword. Just a dark-skinned version of Ma in coarse peasant's pajamas and an ugly hat.

"Come here, Dew," she extended her arms, her eyes softened and her voice soothing.

"No."

"Don't be sullen, Dew. Your aunt has come back home for a few minutes. Just a few minutes. She is fighting a war for the good of all of us, remember, like Lady Trieu," Ma said desperately.

The unwelcomed auntie was approaching me. I could smell her peasant smell, like dirt and rainwater and wild cookoos and roosters. I turned away, but she got me just in time.

I struggled against her embrace, but finally yielded to her warm hand and amazingly soft touch.

"Hello, Dew. I saw you sleeping from the window," she said, her voice sturdy and friendly.

"Where's your gold armor?" I asked.

Aunt Ginseng chuckled.

"In here, my gold armor is in here," she said, pointing to the middle of her chest.

I looked at her face and acknowledged the resemblance. In close proximity, she was indeed my Ma. The exact same face, except the skin was coarser and darker — a shade between amber and brown sugar.

"I'll give you something to replace the gold armor," she said, reaching inside her blouse pocket and displaying in her palm a pebble. "I found it in a stream near the Chinese border. I saved it for you".

I stared at the tiny pebble, the size of a huge peanut. It was a very pretty pebble, multi-colored and smooth.

"Look closely at it. It gives off golden light, see?" she said.

I looked and she was right. I saw the golden spark. Maybe she was right. Maybe the pebble had Lady Trieu's gold armor in it. Maybe it was magic.

"I love you very much. I have to go before sunrise."

And then she let go of me.

So that was how I met my only aunt. Aunt Ginseng came and went like a ghost, a dream, a wind, between the midnight moon and dawn, in all that fog. I could not decide whether to love or dislike her. For one thing, she made Ma plead. I knew, however, the servants were right. Auntie Ginseng was very beautiful, even in those dirty looking, ill-smelling black pajamas and funny hat of hers. The amber-brown-sugar skin shone like the color of light from the lantern she held in her hand the moment she left us. Yet, she could not be as beautiful as my Ma. She was never graceful like a willow tree. Ma said wherever Ginseng went, in that long journey of her's, her fate was probably with the goddesses of Vietnam.

I kept Aunt Ginseng's pebble in a little satin bag that used to hold Ma's pearl strand, and from that day on, I thought of Aunt Ginseng in a different light. She was no longer the elephant rider but instead, a lone traveler who chopped down bamboo logs and walked through muddy ponds, in humid whirling winds, across winding streams which held golden frogs and silver trouts. There, she collected golden pebbles for me. Lady Trieu's golden armor had shattered into pieces that sank into the bottom of those streams and turned into smooth pebbles. The woman warrior with braided hair, clad in black pajamas, jumped from tall trees like leopards and crawled through marshes like crocodiles.

3. A Way Homeward

In a way, I wished Aunt Ginseng had never come home the second time, so that I could continue dreaming about her as the black-clad tigress whose fate belonged to the Vietnamese goddesses.

But she did return home the second time. And the last.

The years past and I reached my teens, eventually celebrating my sixteenth birthday in 1949. The news of Aunt Ginseng's return arrived in the summer of 1949 in a telegraph. Ma started crying after reading it, almost hysterically, and then the household was suddenly animated because Ma ordered the servants to make preparations. Weeks of preparation, anticipation, and celebration ensued. Ma announced to everyone in the house that although Aunt Ginseng had been captured again and imprisoned for years at Hoa Lo—that infamous prison in the north—with the intervention of the progressive liberal socialist Albert Sarrault, formerly Governor General of Indochina, Auntie Ginseng had just been pardoned by the protectorate government.

The female warrior would return home to rest.

And since Aunt Ginseng would be returning home soon, Ma joyfully announced, perhaps we would soon be hearing from Uncle Forest. Her eyes sparkled, her voice became an octave higher, and all her words started running together with the excitement of an earnest child. Prospect of a reunion between the three children of the Mystique Concubine became the rejuvenating potion that made Ma a new woman.

The hopes were high and the preparation lavishing. Ma hired teams of seamstresses to cut, sew, and embroider silk and linen for Aunt Ginseng. A new bed was built by the carpenters out of rosewood. New lace curtains were made. And birds' nest soups were prepared daily in anticipation of her homecoming.

I was still going to school daily. The students of Lycée Dong Khanh talked about my aunt's release, confirming to me my aunt was indeed legendarily famous. Everyday after school I came home to Ma's joyful eyes and the house's bubbling spirit of festivity. Her laughs rang in the air as she paraded around, supervising the teams of cooks and seamstresses. She wanted everything to be perfect. Weeks went by and Ma's happiness was almost too full and her animation too high.

I came home from school one day to an abnormal silence. No light had been lit, and the house was absolutely quiet as though the heat of the desert had brushed through the air.

I went into the new quarter set up for Aunt Ginseng and found Ma sitting alone in the dark. All the servants had retreated to their own quarters. The door to the bedroom reserved for Aunt Ginseng was left ajar.

"Don't go in there, Dew. Your aunt has come home and needs to rest," Ma said quietly as though she had no energy left.

I dashed my eyes around, knowing something had gone wrong. Very wrong.

I pushed the bedroom door open. The room, decorated with hanging silk scrolls, lace curtains and satin blankets, was empty. I stood in the middle of the room, bewildered and upset. And then I heard someone speaking, out in the interior courtyard, together with the sound of uneven footsteps.

I rushed to the courtyard and found her, the shadow of the woman who had come home. Ma had followed me, trying to catch up.

"Dew, your aunt is very ill."

The shadow turned around and I had to jerk back. I found not the young vivacious woman in black pajamas who had yelled at Ma and had given me a pebble. Instead, I found a stooping, limping old woman with dead eyes and a scarred face. Parts of her brows were missing. She stared at me, yet not seeing me

"Do you have a womb and a pair of breasts?" she asked.

I approached her and grabbed her hands. The wrists, too, were full of scars. One little finger was missing.

"Do you have a womb and a pair of breasts?" she repeated.

"Don't listen to her, Dew, she is not herself," Ma said.

I felt her face. No longer that amber-sugar-brown skin. The scar tissues rubbed against my fingers. She smiled. The mouth was crooked. I noticed, too, part of her upper lip was missing.

I let go of her and stood dazed, while Ma tried to catch the disfigured woman and brought her inside. She faintly resisted, and managed to push Ma aside.

Limping on her foot, the old woman ripped off her blouse. Under the dying twilight, I saw scar tissues on her breasts. The nipples were missing. I covered my eyes.

The topless woman was singing senselessly in gibberish. "Do you have a womb and a pair of breasts?" she sang the question like a chorus.

Ma had forbidden the servants to come in. That night, I helped Ma feed Aunt Ginseng her bird's nest soup, and then we washed her together in the porcelain tub, rubbing a hot towel over her scarred and nippleless breasts. I felt her rough scar tissues, thinking of the smoothness of white magnolias. My tears dropped onto her shoulders, and I could not make a sound. Ma was biting her lips all the time. She did not cry.

That night I sat by my bedroom window looking out at the magnolia tree. Aunt Ginseng was singing her question like an imbecile.

"Do you have a womb and a pair of breasts?"

I saw Ma walking the front yard under all that moonlight. She circled the magnolia tree several times, bent to pick up blooms from the ground and placed them next to her face. And then she threw them at the tall tree. She repeated the gesture several times and I watched the white petals scattering around her.

I called out to her and she turned toward the window where I sat. I could see her face under that moonlight. It was full of tears.

"I will not take this, Dew, I will not," she yelled, competing with the sound of Aunt Ginseng's gibberish.

"You and I, Dew, we will write Albert Sarraut. We will write Sylvain Foucault in Paris," she kept yelling.

I saw Ma springing forward and then falling to the ground, among all those white petals. I climbed onto the window and grabbed the iron rods, my hand reaching out to her.

From the bed of white magnolias covering the damp ground,

Ma looked up at me:

"They've butchered my beautiful sister. They've destroyed her brain."

In the following weeks and months, Ma prohibited most of the servants from entering my aunt's quarters. Caring for Aunt Ginseng became the exclusive task of Nanny Mai. Ma and I wrote letter after letter, and Ma started making trips to Saigon and Hanoi to appeal my aunt's case. She contacted newspapers and hired translators to prepare papers to be sent to Paris. I had never seen Ma so feverish.

While Ma was away for her trips, I cut magnolia blooms and floated them in the porcelain bowl. I cleaned the rosewood frames with lemon juice and burned incense sticks. Aunt Ginseng would limp around the house singing her favorite line. She took off her shirt at least once a day, displaying her disfigured torso and smiling her crooked smile.

I no longer dreamed about Lady Trieu's golden armor or the black-pajama tigress. My aunt had come home, but my perfect notion of an unbeatable female warrior had tarnished. As it turned out, the former Governor General Albert Sarrault did not respond to Ma's plea for justice, and my Uncle Forest never came home to join his sisters.

The return and disfigurement of my aunt in 1949 imprinted tragedy onto my otherwise peaceful, well-protected life. Understanding the tragedy became my entree to the turbulence of Vietnamese history. That summer, I learned that in 1945, when I celebrated my twelfth birthday safe and secure in Ma's big house in Hue, the Viet Minh occupied Tonkin up north and declared independence for the country. But France returned to Indochina shortly thereafter, and the Viet Minh fought the French. My aunt Ginseng and my absentee Uncle Forest became legends in that war. They were among the famous sons and daughters of the Vietnamese revolution. But to me, my aunt Ginseng became my notion of tragedy, and my Uncle Forest remained just a name. Their pictures never filled the empty frames in Ma's well-polished altar room.

After the summer of 1949, I lived through the revolution and greeted my young adulthood in the false sense of protection offered by Ma's beautiful house and its beautiful garden. In my growing ambivalence about my sheltered existence, I watched the dying days of French colonialism. In 1954, the Viet Minh won the war, at last. Defeated in the battle of Dien Bien Phu, France let go of Indochina, leaving space for the Americans, the Chinese and the Russians.

And another war ensued, allegedly against the Americans, making Vietnam famous.

During the summer of 1949 when Aunt Ginseng stayed with us, no one in the house spoke very much. But in all that sadness, fate had a way to make me believe, again, in the mystical relationship between me, my aunt and Ma's magnolia tree. It happened one night when Ma was away from home, somewhere in Cochinchina or Tonkin, searching in vain for justice and for a forum to prosecute the colonists' crime committed against her twin sister.

I woke up in the middle of a summer night, feeling the heat coming from outside. I saw the window open, framing imbecile Ginseng's scared and crooked face. The moon was hanging behind her. Apparently she had wandered into the front yard and had pushed my window open. She was staring at me, with a lantern in her hand, just like the first time we met.

"Come inside, Auntie, you are letting in the heat," I said.

She did not respond, the lantern flickering in her hand.

I reached out for the satin bag underneath my pillow, where I had stored her pebble, and showed her the stone: "Remember this?"

She was still staring. I approached the window, holding the pebble against her lantern, the iron rods of the window frame separating us.

"See this? The golden shine. It's a piece of your golden armor, Auntie."

She grabbed onto the iron rods to scrutinize the stone in my hand.

"It's yours, Dew," she said.

Oh Heaven, she had just called me Dew.

"I am Dew, you remember?"

I was overjoyed. My aunt was lucid. "You named me, remember?"

"Of course I remember. You are Dew, my niece. I am in Hoa Lo, behind bars, and you've come to visit me."

My aunt had regained her memory. I wished Ma were here to see for herself.

"You are no longer in prison, Auntie, you are home now," I said, and she nodded.

I rushed to the front yard and took her to her bedroom. She began taking off her shirt.

"Don't, Auntie," I took her hands and led her to the mirror.

"You are a lady. Don't take off your shirt."

I sat her down in front of the mirror and combed her coarse, prematurely gray hair. I divided her hair into halves and made two braids.

"Remember how you came home the first time? You had braided hair like this. You were very beautiful then."

She stared at herself in the mirror, motionless.

"You are still very beautiful, Auntie," I hurried on, wanting her to feel good. She looked at me with the gaze that exposed my lies. I looked down to the floor in shame.

"Can you keep a secret for me, Dew?" she said, dreamily.

"Yes, I would do anything for you, Auntie," I responded without thinking.

She reached out for my shirt pocket and removed the pebble. Very swiftly she put it on her tongue and swallowed. She was quick and determined and I was too stunned to react. Then, her eyes dilated while she choked and coughed vehemently. I screamed out, but the door to Aunt Ginseng's bedroom was tightly closed, and the servants, including Nanny Mai, were all soundly sleeping in their own quarters separated by the interior courtyard. My aunt put one hand over my mouth and the other hand over my throat. For a moment, I could not breathe. She was smothering me. We struggled for a while until she cooled down, and we collapsed together.

But the pebble was just the size of a huge peanut and it had not hurt my aunt, although I knew she would eventually get sick. Lying next to me, the invalid woman began to talk.

"Dew, that's the secret. I just swallowed the secret. You promised you would keep a secret."

"You are ill, Auntie. I need to tell someone. You need to go to the hospital. That pebble..."

"No I won't, I won't go anywhere. I am home, remember? This is where I grew up. I won't be sick anymore. I just swallowed Lady Trieu's armor and it stayed with me."

I stared at the tissues around my aunt's crooked lips. The tissues vibrated together with her speech. My aunt was not crazy. Not at the moment. She knew what she was doing.

"To get this secret, Dew, they would have to cut open my stomach, and I won't let them. They already pierced my womb and cut my breasts, Dew."

"Auntie, please." I winced. "Don't talk about it."

"But I have to, Dew, I have to talk. I have to…"

I got up and rushed out. I went to my room and locked the door. I left my aunt alone.

I heard noises from her quarters all night. Strange noises. Like the moving of furniture, the dragging of chairs, and the tearing of cloth. I did nothing. Nothing. I just sat by the window and stared out at the magnolia tree under all that silver moonlight. Hours passed and then I saw my aunt limping out to the front yard. Just as I had seen Ma the night of Ginseng's homecoming. The servants were all in their quarters and nothing could stop Ginseng.

"Where is your gold armor, Auntie Ginseng?" I whispered from the window.

My very ill Aunt Ginseng all of a sudden became very strong, and she was dragging and moving chairs to the yard all by herself. She tried to pile them up underneath the magnolia tree. She struggled. She failed. She fell. She got up again. She limped herself around until she achieved what she set out to do. Overall, she was very skillful and determined. After all, she was the female warrior who pursued Lady Trieu's dream and picked up the golden pebble for me from a stream and she kept going until they pierced her womb and cut her breasts. And then she swallowed the secret and made me join her.

So I joined her by watching from my bedroom window. She dragged the lace curtains into the yard with her and then she climbed on the pile of chairs and reached out for a strong branch. She knew how to pick the strongest of all branches like an expert. No matter what, she had come home.

The lace curtains Ma's seamstresses had sewn for Ginseng's homecoming flew around the disfigured woman who reached out for the magnolia tree. And then she became the falling bloom herself, dangling in the air, forever, until the moonlight caught her and off she flew. I knew it was too late. And I, her beautiful dew, sat by the window and watched. The same way I had watched the earthworms die.

The air was still and cool, as though my aunt had brought back the fog.

I left my aunt fluttering in the night and went to the mirror and took off my shirt. I saw a skinny girl, so pale her skin was almost tinted blue. I was no female warrior and could only hold a shovel. My world was confined to Ma's front yard and the steps of the red brick schoolhouse called Lycée Dong Khanh.

I imagined myself without nipples and a pair of stabbed breasts and wondered how it felt like to have darts of hatred pierce through my womb. When streams of blood flowed, they would permeate the ground and become alive as reddish earthworms. I whispered to Auntie Ginseng that I wanted neither the footsteps of Lady Trieu nor the solitude of Ma, who was always waiting. I whispered that for the rest of my life I would just plant, plant, and plant. I promised Auntie Ginseng that I would give her the best of magnolia trees bearing the smoothest petals so the young cheerful girl could pick them and throw them around like table tennis balls, in ripples of laughter surrounding a peaceful childhood.

I brought my palms together and formed a little pond, in which I could see the wriggling helpless earthworms stabbed to death, their blood smearing all the lace curtains that circled and strangled my aunt. I went to bed while white magnolias danced around my aunt, drops of dew gathering on her damp skin, healing scars and softening rough tissues to make her beautiful like the past. I had let her be.

I placed my head onto the pillow and realized I had never asked my aunt why she loved throwing magnolia blooms. Out there, I knew she would find a way to tell me, somehow, some time, and she would not blame me for sitting and watching. After all, it mattered very little why she did what she did. To me, in the end, she had chosen to return home. To her magnolia tree.

PART FOUR

1. The Child Performer and Her Nightingale

Like most young girls growing up in Vietnam, I learned the ancient country's golden era through fables and myths. In the beginning of history, before the Hans' arrival in the plateaus of the Red River, Vietnam was a tribal society ruled consecutively by the eighteen Hung Kings. This went on for two thousand years; a long time of peace, harmony, and tranquillity before border wars erupted and the Hans took over the Viet peninsula, commencing the age-old border conflict between China and Vietnam.

Back then, as early as 2000 B.C., the daughters of Hung Kings were called Mi Nuong. The word "Mi" symbolizes the beauty of a princess from the peaceful Hung era. Grandma Que took great pains to instill in me the pride that we were all descendants of Huyen Phi, the Mystique Concubine of the Nguyen Dynasty. She made sure that in memory of our ancestors, her female descendants would all have compound first names beginning with "Mi". My mother was Mi-Suong, Beautiful Dew. She married a commoner, so her two daughters bore a last name that was not royal. Yet we both inherited the "Mi" in our first name — symbol of a Vietnamese princess. I was named Mi-Uyen, Beautiful Lovebird, and my younger sister Mi-Chau, Beautiful Gem. Grandma Que frequently talked of the kind of inner beauty "Mi" signified — the aesthetics that was so far from being skin-deep it transcended the physical world and lasted into eternity. At a minimum, the first name beginning with "Mi" would always remind us to conduct ourselves with the kind of class associated with the inner soul.

As a young girl, I did not find the need to learn the Mi origin of my name. It did not help solidify my sense of beauty, nor my understanding of class or the inner soul. I thought, instead, of a note on my piano. Mi Mi Mi Mi. Together they sounded like the name of a cat. I equated the "Mi" sound with pure vibrations of the lips. When the lips were gently brought together and then opened upon a breath, the air brushed slightly outward, and the sound was delivered with the softness of a caress.

Right from the beginning of my existence, I was already a child in love with sounds.

In the summer of 1990, my mother called me in Manhattan to wish me Happy Birthday.

"You know I won't sing Happy Birthday to you," she said.

My mother was musically deaf.

"You, on the other hand, have both Truong Chi's soulful voice and Mi Nuong's beautiful face," she added ruefully.

I had turned thirty-five and tiny lines had appeared underneath my eyes, yet my mother still thought of me as the twenty year-old former beauty queen of Saigon's College of Law, a maiden who once practiced singing. Mi-Nuong was the daughter of the eighteenth Hung King. Mi-Nuong fell in love with the singing voice of Truong Chi, a fisherman she had never met. He lived by the river across from her palace, and sang every day at sunset. The voice mesmerized the princess, who became lovesick to the point of being bedridden. King Hung summoned the man with the beautiful singing voice to the palace, in hopes of saving his daughter. But Truong Chi was so physically ugly that upon seeing the face that trapped his beautiful voice, the princess quickly recovered.

I thought perhaps Mi-Nuong never fully recovered. Disappointment and death wish must have remained with her. One could never recover from facing the contradiction between life and dream, between ugliness and beauty, between our need to live and our dark desire to perish. The poor man's ugly face must have mirrored certain ugly part of the princess' soul, and she must have lived on with that discovery. The unfulfilled love story between a Vietnamese princess and her Quasimodo always invoked in me the urge to sing.

I thought of the soprano voice as a nightingale flying into a limitless sky, surpassing the stilted confines of a human life. I wanted to wing with the nightingale toward that brand-new horizon created every time my voice stretched beyond the next note on the right-hand side of my piano keyboard.

In childhood, my voice once lingered around the high DO, the C on the piano keyboard, and then I managed to reach the high E, the MI note, spelled like the beginning of my first name. At some point, I was prepared to go all the way to the high A, the LA. La, la, la, la, la, la, la, la, the sound often associated with a song. Repeated nine times to trace the scale, up and down. DO RE MI FA SOL FA MI RE DO. The tip of the tongue curling up to touch the palate. The breath pushing through to find a space outward. The tongue softening, giving up its security, hanging and relaxing in the middle of the open mouth. And the sound traveling like a stream shooting through the curvy lips to reach the sky.

By my thirty-fifth birthday, I knew I would never become an opera singer, a diva, and I would never reach a perfect "A," the high LA, on the right-hand side of my piano keyboard. It would always be a struggle to reach that high note, never with the level of ease and perfection necessary for me to feel the soaring nightingale was still part of me. In Vietnam, I was once a young girl practicing the scale. In America, I became a lawyer instead. The nightingale I once knew had left.

The nightingale came to me quite early in life when I started singing after the radio at five years of age. We were living in Hue at the time. Then, the stretching of the voice seemed so natural and effortless, and I was free to follow my nightingale, when its pair of wings lifted the heaviness from my chest and flapped air into my lungs. My mother said I sounded like a clear bell. She was not surprised and, instead, encouraged me when I climbed on a chair, holding a handkerchief in one hand, gesturing with the other hand, singing about someone who lost his love on the blueberry fields during the Indochina War. The name of the song was "The Blueberry Fields," *Nhung Doi Hoa Sim*, based on a famous Vietnamese poem.

The song had created the career of an eighteen year-old singer in Saigon, who had taken on the stage name "The Sparrow of Go Cong," commemorating a province in South Vietnam and the singer's birthplace. I had memorized the words by simply listening to the radio. After my performance, my mother whispered to me that she would call me the "Sparrow of Hue." Although I preferred the nightingale, I found the stage name acceptable. In fact, in my mind then, I hardly distinguished nightingales from sparrows or lovebirds. They were all beautiful birds who twittered those clear sounds and flapped those wings.

Those days, my mother took delight in training me on my stage gestures after "The Sparrow of Go Cong," whom I had never seen because she only performed in nightclubs, and there was no television in Hue back then. My mother supplied me with the handkerchief, telling me how to hold it with one hand while swaying my little body. I was to raise the other hand in mid-air, and then to press it against my heart. At times, I would tilt my head to one side and place my cheek on my palm while waving the handkerchief to my mother. "Slower, slower, there you go," she would tell me.

We made a good team, combining the natural instinct of a five-year-old and the creativity of a young mother. By age five, I was already performing for my mother and her guests from Lycée Dong Khanh, where she taught literature. Everybody at her tea parties told her what a precious child I was.

To prepare for my celebrity status, my mother took me to the best photography studio in Hue, the Tan Tan shop. She placed me on a staircase, and then the bright light blinded my eyes. The background wall behind the staircase was full of posters and black-and-white pictures of beautiful women in coifed hairdos. Later, I found out they were photographs of Elizabeth Taylor, Barbara Stanwich, Ava Gardner, Jeanne Tierney, and Sophia Loren. My mother made me hold a doll, a flower, a leaf, or a little stuffed rabbit. I was either to sit down demurely on the steps with my hands together under my chin, or to pose in a dance, bringing my knees and feet together a certain dainty way so they could form the shape of leaves underneath a rosebud.

I learned to stand and sit like a flower.

My mother was not surprised that I sang so early in life. She had always said the gene ran in the family, yet my mother could not sing. So, where did my voice come from? No one in the family or her circle of friends bothered to ask. Everyone took it for granted. A theory was implicitly shared among my relatives and the women of Hue that the fabulous voice would reappear and someone along the bloodline would be destined to sing. It was just a matter of time before that bell-like voice resonated again, linking the past to the present.

Everybody in Hue knew that my great-grandmother, the legendary Paddle Girl of the River Huong who later became the renowned Mystique Concubine of the Nguyen Dynasty, had sung all her teenage life on the River Huong, which divided the ancient city of Hue in half. Huong was Vietnam's river of romance. It had its own fragrance.

The adults said Hue was the only city in Vietnam with a true violet horizon, *Chan Troi Tim*. A shade of mauve at sunrise, lavender in the early afternoon, which deepened into royal purple at dusk. Purple turned into the darkness of coal at night time. That was why the royal palaces of Hue were called the Violet City, *Tu Cam Thanh*. I began to imagine my royal great-grandmother as a shadow in lavender, purple blue, and rich violet. When violet became the sparkling pure blackness of coal, she became the night.

I could not remember exactly how it began, except that by the time I turned ten, I already knew the story about my great-grandmother's death. In one version of her life story, the storytellers of Hue maintained that my great-grandmother's fabulous voice attracted the young King of Annam, who came to her boat and took her to the other side of the River Huong, where she became a royal concubine at fifteen years of age. But the French protectorates exiled the King to Africa, and my great-grandmother—that legendary singing queen of Hue—stayed in Hue and died in loneliness. Since his exile, she was a queen without a throne, a singer who did not sing, and a beautiful woman without a lover. This was a concept I never understood until much later in life, after I had married Christopher Sanders, Hue had been replaced with New York City, and my River Huong had changed into the Hudson River, where I no longer dreamt of a soprano's voice echoing her pentatonic scale across the waves.

The day my great-grandmother died in Hue, I was told, nightingales gathered all around her bedroom window. Her eyes were still cast forlornly toward the horizon beyond the window, in hopes of her husband's return, when her heart stopped beating. The nightingales all mourned the voice they shared with her. Death forever silenced it.

I was told, too, that on the day her spirit departed, the waves of the River Huong awakened and sparkled into tingling sounds. Someone even said the moon dropped tears onto those sparkling waves. The moon's teardrops hit the surface of the River Huong, creating a vibrating chord. In the symphony of nature, my great-grandmother's spirit went away, but the inhabitants of Hue predicted that her spirit would return. Her voice was destined to come back one day, and one of her descendants would sing in her place.

That descendent was supposed to be me, the wide-eyed child who sat on the steps of a miniature stage in the Tan Tan portrait studio, with a silk bow on her hair, doll-like, yet serene and self-composed. The inhabitants of Hue rumored that at five years of age, I was already acting like a queen.

Tales were told to me consistently all throughout my childhood in Hue, and by the time I reached my teens, I had turned into a hopelessly romantic young girl, naive of course, and melancholic. When I sang Vietnamese folk tunes, I thought of the moon, the waves, the River Huong on the best nights and days, and the image of my beautiful great-grandmother lying motionless in death, while nightingales gathered around the frame of her half-moon bedroom window.

In 1960, the radio also played the twist and rock-and-roll, imported to South Vietnam from America. At five years of age, I already instinctively wanted to sway to the wild music. With the help of my teenage aunt, Y-Van, my father's younger sister who was living with us at the time, I began to perform the twist for families in the neighborhood. We were living in the only apartment building in Hue, the two-story Phu Cam complex on Nguyen Truong To street, the main thoroughfare that connected the Phu Cam Church across the Ben Ngu River to Hue University, where my father taught.

I remembered the Phu Cam Church by its stark orange color and spiky domes that combined a touch of European gothic with the antiquity of East Asian architecture. To my eyes those days, at sunset, the Church turned bright orange, edging its spikes against the low sky of sleepy Hue. The brown bridge that swung across the dark green Ben Ngu River resembled a pathway that flowed right into the Church, which appeared still and stagnant like a painting of primitive colors and minimum strokes. The Phu Cam complex housed Hue's middle-class families, including officers in the South Vietnamese army and teachers at various high schools or the University. Everyone there at Phu Cam was pretty much up to date on Western culture — primarily French and American, communicated to us in the popular French magazine *Paris Match*.

All youths at Phu Cam welcomed the arrival of the twist. The girls especially idolized beautiful Jackie Bouvier Kennedy with her square jaw, distinctive chin, deeply set brown eyes that were too far apart, quite often hidden behind those world-famous signature sunglasses. Auntie Y-Van trained me well on the twist as well as on how to recognize Jackie in *Paris Match*.

My twist performances started with Aunt Y-Van's network of boyfriends. Y-Van loved to hang around college students and senior high school boys, and there were plenty of them at the Phu Cam complex. Somehow she managed to brag about my talent to their families, who all loved to watch the cutest little girl of the Phu Cam complex wiggling her body. A typical performance consisted of the following steps: First, Aunt Y-Van would bring me into a family's living room, and all family members arranged to sit in a circle. Then, someone in the family would put an Elvis Presley record on a turntable, and I would do the twist. I earned money doing it, at the suggestion of Aunt Y-Van, who collected a piaster from each member of the audience, acting as my agent, promoter and manager. My performances were always in the afternoon, after my nursery school. Aunt Y-Van was supposed to babysit me until my mother got home from Lycée Dong Khanh.

The pop culture of America reached Vietnam through the radio in the early sixties and helped create me as a legitimate professional child performer, one who earned money as well as applause. Yet all this time, my mother had thought I was only singing popular Vietnamese love ballads and the folk tunes of Hue—a testament for the reincarnation of my great-grandmother's eternal voice.

2. Love Between Generations

I could never forget a Vietnamese twist song named "Love Between Generations," *Tinh yeu giua hai the he.* The lyric went like this:

When you were 20 years old,
I was just born,
and you turned 40,
I reached my glorious 20...

Aunt Y-Van taught me the lyric for special performances, when my childish voice took over and the turntable was closed, and I sang and danced at the same time, without accompaniment, except for Aunt Y-Van's clapping hands and her boyfriends' whistling. They even snapped their fingers, expertly smashing their thumb and middle finger together, to create a drum beat for me. For these special performances, my earnings for the song were increased from one piaster per audience member to two piasters. Aunt Y-Van kept the money, promising to deposit all those bills into a clay pig so that when I grew up, I could have money for my first *ao dai*—that silk, bodice-fitting Vietnamese tunic worn by young women, slit high on both sides such that the lank flaps seemed to hug the girl's legs. Serious singers, Aunt Y-Van said, wore silk *ao dai* over white pantaloons when they sang love songs in Saigon's nightclubs, in contrast to twist and rock-and-roll singers who wore black miniskirts, with mid-thigh hemlines, and *escapin* shoes upon which they pressed their pointed toes to the floor to do their twist. That was how I should dress when I was old enough to sing in nightclubs.

Needless to say, I never saw the money. Before my sixth birthday, Aunt Y-Van was sent to a boarding school in Dalat called "Couvent des Oiseaux." She kissed my cheeks, teared a little, gave me my clay pig, and told me not to tell anyone about our twist performances. I cracked the clay pig one day and found only a few coins inside. I saw none of those green-paper piasters I had earned by yelling at the top of my lungs while swaying my hips.

After we had left Hue, I once asked Aunt Y-Van what had happened to my clay-pig money those days in Hue, and she looked baffled, not knowing what I was referring to, although she remembered how cute I was doing the twist in front of her neighborhood boyfriends and their families. I asked my mother, too, whether she ever discovered I was doing the twist for money those days, and she laughed and gave me no direct answer, saying instead that Phu Cam was a close-knit community in sleepy Hue, and people always talked about how cute and talented her daughter was. She also gently and casually reminded me how Aunt Y-Van had been shipped immediately to a boarding school in the highlands in the summer of 1960, so that the Catholic nuns could reform her into a proper *Couvent* girl, one who should repent for having spent little nieces' clay-pig money on silver fingernail polish. To the best of my knowledge, Aunt Y-Van never got reformed. She kept wearing silver finger nail polish even when the dotted freckles of old age had appeared on the top of her bony hands.

Later on, in America, at get-together parties of alumni of the boarding school, Auntie Y-Van always talked proudly of her brief stint at Dalat's *Couvent des Oiseaux*, how she played tricks on those devoted, stern-faced French nuns dedicated to the reform of wild, rose-cheeked Vietnamese girls. For example, Aunt Y-Van once put a Paris Match clipping inside the Bible and placed it on the desk of *La Mere Superieure*. The clipping was of a voluptuous and topless Brigitte Bardot, covering her breasts with her crossed arms and puffy hair. "Et Dieu creat La Femme" (And God created Women), the precocious Vietnamese teenager wrote the name of Bardot's film across the chest of the sensuous French star.

3. The French Villa on Nam Giao Slope

After my Aunt Y-Van was gone, my father — a bookworm professor at Hue University — decided to divert his attention from his
books to the role of a father, which he had long delegated to my
mother and Grandma Que. He decided it was time I stopped singing Vietnamese love ballads, since the pop love songs were ruining
my mind as well as my voice. I needed to learn classical music — real
music. Efforts were instantly made to enroll me in a French Catholic
school, the Jeanne D'Arc Institute. At Jeanne D'Arc, I was given the
name Simone.

The nickname "Si" replaced my Vietnamese name Mi-Uyen
since then.

Much later came weekly piano lessons given by an old French
nun called *Soeur* Josephine. During those morning practice sessions,
after *Soeur* Josephine had taught me some fingering techniques
and heard me play, I would be left in a small practice room with
the upright piano and my piano music book: "La Methode Rose."
My mind and fingers often wandered away from the scores of "Au
Claire de La Lune" and "La Valse de Venice" to the familiar tunes of
Vietnamese love ballads.

The year I turned six, we moved from the Phu Cam complex
to Grandma Que's old villa in Nam Giao, away from the heart of
Hue and its River Huong. My earliest memory of Grandma Que
consisted of her dark eyes, heart-shaped lips painted with deep red
lipstick, and the quiet silhouette of a slender woman, with long hair
rolled up into a bun, dressed in black silk and satin, smelling like the
cinnamon fragrance that came out of her potpourri. In her beautiful
villa, she walked around on velvet slippers without making a sound,
as though she simply glided among muslin curtains, carved wood
pillars, delicate bamboo screens, rosewood chairs and divans, and
bowls of cut lotuses floating in water, which graced the top of her
shining lacquer tables and cabinets. Before we moved in, Grandma

Que lived alone in the villa with two maids, a couple of canaries dancing in a gold matted cage, a parrot who called her princess, and two rabbits.

The highlight of Grandma Que's altar room was her huge, dark brown, sorrowful-looking cinnamon log, sitting in a porcelain pot and emanating the spicy and pungent scent that characterized, according to her, the mystical ambiance of central Vietnam. The hunters from the Quynh Anh hamlet, where she was raised, had given the cinnamon log to her as a gift of longevity, since her given name, Que, meant Cinnamon. Allegedly, the hunters had searched out the oldest cinnamon tree in the deep jungles of the Quang Tri province. The tree was hundreds of years old, paralleling the development of the region. Grandma Que believed that magic originated in the deepest part of the jungle, where old trees took on holy and powerful spirits. Destiny could be cruel, she said. She called cruel destiny the Face of Brutality. To her, the cinnamon log gave her a sense of power over that Face of Brutality.

Nam Giao was a hilly area glutted with green. The villa, located on Princess Huyen Tran Street, had a front yard with beautiful tall trees, including an old magnolia tree giving off white flowers, whose sweet fragrance filled my nostrils and lungs when I woke up from my afternoon nap. The front yard merged in with the luscious green grass surrounding the villa. The open green area studded with flowers and fruit trees circled the white colonial structure, keeping it in shade. There was a river across the street, not as large as the River Huong, more like a stream, a body of calming, dark mossy green water that sparkled under the moon and stars at night. Although the river was literally across from the villa, the water looked so far away to my six-year-old eyes staring out from my bedroom window. I thought, then, that the river had to belong to another, slower world that slipped in and out of existence.

Immediately after we moved into the ancestral house, my mother began to landscape our front and backyard. Grandma Que said my mother loved gardening ever since she was a child my age, and the shovel had always been her best friend. My mother read books on horticulture late at night, and I often hopped in her lap, peeping at colorful pictures of flowers, leaves, and plants on those glossy pages. On the weekends, I was used to seeing my mother's slender back and her cotton hat rising and moving among those beds of soil she had built with her shovel. She hired an old man to assist her and he usually followed her as she moved along the soil beds. She wore rubber gloves and stopped whenever she saw earthworms. Those poor creatures wriggled, fighting desperately for life against the emotionless shovel that stabbed. The old man would stoop between the flower beds to remove them. I often sat by my bedroom window to watch my mother and the old man until my eyes grew tired and then my head would drop on the table. Quite often when I got up and rubbed my eyes, the two of them were still moving around in the garden while the sun slowly died out, its rays turning yellow-brown on my mother's slender back. It took six months before our front and backyard blossomed with beds of flowers. By the time the flowers bloomed, I overheard my mother tell the old man that soon the butterflies would come to land. She wanted to plant the violet French *pensees* and the blue Forget-me-nots, and it would be a difficult task because those species of flowers needed the cooler climate of the highlands.

"Those tiny flowers will be nice for Si when she grows up. She can put them inside her scrapbook. It's the kind of things girls want to do," my mother said. The old man nodded.

At night, I dreamt of chasing butterflies and picking violet and blue flowers out of my mother's flower beds. I ran wild in my mother's garden even in the middle of dream.

During weekdays I often took an afternoon nap after school, and when I got up, Grandma Que would feed me an afternoon snack, usually a French *flanc* floating in dark, caramelized syrup, and then I would ride my bike and Grandma Que would walk along to accompany me. Together we traveled slowly down one of those slopes of Nam Giao, on Princess Huyen Tran Street, along the bank of that dark green river. We passed quiet green areas and solemn-looking villas until Grandma Que signaled it was time to go back. On the way back to the house, we had to go up the slope, so she would push my bike, and I would put my feet up on the bike frame, almost to the steering wheel, no longer pedaling, laughing my six-year-old laughs. The first thing I smelled as we approached the villa was the fragrance of white magnolias. Grandma Que said white magnolias often housed the spirits of beautiful women. The soft white blooms resembled a beautiful woman's face. The spirit of the matriarch of my family, my great-grandmother the Mystique Concubine, and that of my grandaunt Ginseng, daughter of the revolution, had gone into the magnolia tree, watching over the ancestral house. I had nothing to fear, Grandma Que assured me, since the spirits would always be my protectors.

Grandma Que spoke big words to me that early on in my life. All those exotic phrases sounded so fascinating simply because they came from her heart-shaped lips.

"*Oan chi nhung khach tieu phong, ma xui phan bac nam trong ma dao,*" she said. *It is no use to lament, those rose-cheeked, ill-fated women of the East.* That was why the Mystique Concubine was so unhappy about her life as a royal concubine, and encouraged her children to join the revolution to challenge Heaven's mandate, Grandma Que explained.

"Concubine...what's a concubine? Revolution...what is a revolution?" I kept asking and she kept telling me to wait until I grew up a little more. Meanwhile, she pushed the saddle of my bike, up the slope, against the wind. Before we entered the house we would stand on the riverside watching sunset. A breeze of cool air caressed my limbs when the reddish color of the late afternoon extinguished over the tiled rooftop, and darkness gradually spread upon the river and on top of all those green trees. And in that changing color of the end of day, Grandma Que would tell me stories of the Vietnamese princesses from ancient times. Five hundred years ago, Princess Huyen Tran went south to marry the Champa King so Vietnam could gain two provinces, in which lay the city of Hue. And that was why they named the street of our house after the princess, *Cong Chua Huyen Tran.* Two thousand years ago, Princess Mi Nuong loved the singing voice of an ugly fisherman and could not marry him. When he died of lovesickness, his heart crystallized into a piece of jade. The villagers carved it into a teacup and presented it to the princess as a gift. Saddened, she shed her tears into the teacup. At the bottom of the teacup appeared the lonely fisherman, singing his heart to her. When her tears fell into the teacup, it shattered into a thousand pieces.

"Why? " I asked.

Grandma Que explained that the teacup was the broken heart of the fisherman who loved so much and received so little in return. I did not understand the message, but instead of insisting on a better answer, I usually became dazed watching Grandma Que's serene facial expression. I saw how her eyes had become so remote. She was looking straight into the sun, telling me the sun had died and a day had ended. When the sun died, its reddish color faded, and one could look into the sun without hurting one's eyes. She said she became acquainted with the perfect sun that way. When I pulled on the corner of her blouse, she shrugged slightly, removed her eyes from that very violet horizon, and squeezed my hand. She told me Princess Mi Nuong was sad because she had loved perfection — that beautiful singing voice of a man she could never marry. Grandma Que patted my head and said I had the voice and thus, unlike the unlucky princess, I would never have to look elsewhere for perfection because the voice was already within me.

4. Andre Foucault and His Baudelaire

When you were 20 years old,
I was just born,
and you turned 40,
I reached my glorious 20.

I never thought the twist song of my childhood could have fore-warned Andre's arrival the summer of 1961 in Hue.

Andre Foucault materialized for me the image of an angel. An angel to me was the product of wild imagination combined with the bits and pieces I learned about God and Jesus Christ from Catholic prep school. I learned the contours of an angel the same way I learned the lovely French language — with the paradoxical mixture of fascination and detachment I usually held toward any Western product thrust into my life in Vietnam.

At school, the nuns made it clear that angels came from the sky. I was reminded of a nightingale that flapped her wings every time I sang — an image so pure, so far-reaching, so ethereal, so beautiful it could not exist for very long in mundane life, like that fleeting moment when my voice reached the high note, then cracked or faltered. Angels and Andre fell under the same category as the nightingale that represented the fleeting possession of beauty in my singing. These precious things came into my life to deposit silts of memory and when I blinked my eyes, they were gone for good.

The day after my thirty fifth birthday, I woke up in my Manhattan apartment alone in my bed, the urge to sing bursting my lungs, yet I was unable to make the sound. Andre and Hue and those childhood performances and singing lessons all seemed so far away. My mind became my own River Huong. On this side of the riverbank were America, Manhattan, law, and a jailhouse of memory. On the other side of the riverbank were Vietnam, Hue, Andre, and my urge to sing.

I got out of bed that day and celebrated my birthday with the malaise of an aging dame. I tumbled to the bathroom, looked into the mirror, and found nostalgia in a pair of forlorn, ebony eyes. I saw a stranger's mouth that ceased to laugh and pulled into a forced smile, lost to any illusive radiance of youth.

I bent my head over the sink, seeing the rich brown eyes of Andre and hearing the words of Baudelaire. *Ma douleur, donne-moi la main...Et, comme un long linceul trainant a l'Orient, entends, ma chere, entends la douce nuit qui marche...*

I saw my-six-year-old self lying on my back with one arm crossing my forehead, one leg up and my toes wiggling, drawing circles onto the misty air. The circles formed words of Baudelaire: *Douleur* for pain; *L'Orient* for my home; *La Douce Nuit* for my night; *Linceul* for my mourning cloth for the angel who had departed. At the dawn of a Manhattan day I could hear the traffic on Fifth Avenue. *Pain, give me your hand. And, like a mourning cloth training toward the Orient, listen, my dear, listen to the footsteps of the Lady Night.*

In broad New York City daylight I was listening to my Night, to the quietude that carried its own sound. Oh my Night. Her sweet scent fell all over me. The Night spread and carried with her the words I had written onto the air with my wiggling toe when I was a child. Andre's words. Those words were blossomed into Baudelaire's flowers of pain, his *Fleurs du Mal*. Decades later, I folded and unfolded corners of my soul and filled them with those same words. I had to see you again, my memory. Childhood turned into dreams, with symbols of beauty stuck in a surreal corner of the mind, becoming spots of pain. Andre and Baudelaire, inseparable in my memory of Vietnam, taught me the meaning of pain. Oh my my my. I could stop breathing right at that moment and still heard words.

I started to think of myself as a woman who housed in her soul the anecdotes of Indochina. Stories told by elderly women connected to me in blood ties thicker than fate. Up, up the ladder of the blood ties, and their stories told to me became myths. Their mysteries crystal-lized in my heart and made me into the keeper of memory.

At thirty five years of age, I had become thousands of years old.

Wrapping a wool shawl over my shoulders, I rode the elevator down to the building lobby and walked the streets, my head flooded with memories of those hot summer nights in Vietnam and images of a beautiful man separated from me, not only by an ocean, but also by twenty years of age. A man who had viewed my mother's tropical flowers in Vietnam as Baudelaire's *Fleurs du Mal*.

I stopped at a coffeehouse, smelling fresh bagels and blueberry muffins. I heard from the radio's classical station Beethoven's *Elegischer Gesang, Op. 118.*

"Sanft wie du lebtest hast du vollendet, zu heilig, für den Schmerz! Kein Auge wein' ob des himmlischen Geistes Heimkehr. Sanft, sanft wie du lebtest hast du vollendet." *As gently as you lived, have you ended, too holy for grieving! No eye weeps, while your heavenly spirit returns home. Gently, gently as you lived, have you finished.*

The sounds of Beethoven became the mourning for the departure of a noble spirit. I mimed the German lyric but could not sing although the sound continued in my head. The sound chilled and made me bend. I held my stomach in pain. Oh Andre.

5. Birthday in Hue

In the summer of 1961, all my mother's work in the yard was completed in time for my sixth birthday party, thrown for me in her newly landscaped garden. The kids at my French school, together with my former friends from the Phu Cam complex and children of our neighbors on Princess Huyen Tran Street were all invited. I had never had a party like that before. My mother placed chairs and benches all over the front yard and arranged freshly cut summer flowers on a serving table full of my favorite food: sticky rice, syrup drinks, and all kinds of Vietnamese rice flour cakes and French sweets like *gateaux au rum, bonbons, petits beurres* and *choux à la creme*.

My father had tied colorful balloons to all the trees. I was busy blowing a balloon. When I looked up, I saw a tall, brown-haired man walking through the front gate toward me. He was one of those Frenchmen from *Paris Match*, walking out of the magazine. He moved underneath the shade of the magnolia tree, his shoulders slightly tilting to one side to avoid the drooping branches. Like Santa Claus, he carried a doll and a big bag. For a moment I thought the French nuns' angel was descending upon my life, bringing with him lots of toys, including French dolls with golden hair, who could sing and speak small French phases in a whisper.

He came into the front yard where the kids were playing, the only European, lost yet standing out, towering tall amidst a bunch of Vietnamese children and adults, a lean, muscular frame and broad shoulders under an ivory cotton shirt. Even with the tan, he was lighter than we were. I noticed those deeply set eyes and the delicate bone structure that defined the high bridge of his nose, bony cheeks, and square jaw. From a corner, I ran up to him, craning my neck to look up at his face. I noticed, too, a dimple on his bluish chin, which, I found out much later on, was the trademark of a well-shaved man. At that tender age, I knew he was beautiful. Like pictures of men wearing trench coats in Aunt Y-Van's *Paris Match.*

"*Je m'appelle Si,*" I said, proudly introducing myself. Cute Si, poupee Si, six-year-old coquettish Si, as everyone in my family had described me. Si. Si. Si. Like the French name for a note on the piano.

"*Enchante, Mademoiselle,*" he said with a smile and a twinkling sparkle in his brown eyes. "*Je m'appelle Andre.*" He had just called me "Miss," as though I were an adult.

"You are...so tall," I added, in what I thought was perfect French.

He bent and looked down closely at me, a look of surprise as though he had not expected to see me so close to him. His pupils were pure chocolate. They smiled at me under thick lashes.

There was something else in his eyes, I thought. A sense of recognition. Much, much later on, in Paris, he told me it was the recognition of a treasure long lost: he saw in me that day the eyes of *L'Indochine.*

My tall angel put down the bag of toys, picked me up and kissed me on both cheeks. He handed me the doll, telling me there were more in the bag. I touched his face, its cool smoothness reminding me of an orange with the finest of peel, silky to my fingertips. He smelled so nice, like soap, candies, lemon, a slight touch of cough syrup, and something else, too. It was a scent I couldn't identify, so different from the cinnamon scent emanating from the mandarin collar of Grandma Que, so distinctive from the fragrance of white magnolias that permeated the air. Only much later, well into womanhood, did I discover it was the smell of a freshly bathed, well-shaved man.

"*Elle est tres jolie,*" he turned to my father. Of course I was beautiful, I thought. Unlike my baby sister Mi-Chau, who was almost bald, I was Si, a child with thick, long, black hair like a woman. Grandma Que went through great length to make sure my hair was beautiful. She sprinkled cinnamon essence on me. She boiled the nut *boket,* and dipped my hair in its broth every day. (She had been using the same shampooing method on her own hair all her life, and at her age, her salt-and-pepper hair was still shining, falling to her knee caps.) Whatever the broth did to my hair, it grew so long and thick my mother was afraid I would trip over it. Every one in the family, except Grandma Que, was concerned I would not grow and would remain a midget because my hair had gotten too heavy for my body weight. Every day I had to get up at least one hour ahead of school bus time so Grandma Que could braid my hair and tie it with a bow.

My mother had moved the party to the backyard garden and had put some cod mats down on the grass. Andre volunteered to be my pony. All of the kids lined up, including my sister Mi-Chau. But I got most of the rides. Everybody else was jealous.

There was a moment in the pony game when Andre, my pony, turned over on his back to take a rest. I was climbing onto him. I sat on his chest, laughing and laughing. I spread my legs, wiggled myself down to his stomach, and laughed some more. The next thing I remembered was a tremendous sense of affection when I was looking down onto his face. His hands were resting on my waist, and he was smiling at me. I could see the rose tip of his tongue and his shiny white row of teeth. Instinctively, I bent down to kiss the curvy corner of his mouth. When I looked up, his moving eyelashes reminded me of the evening butterflies hovering over my mother's flowers in the twilight of sunset. The day butterflies were colorful, but the evening butterflies were usually larger, of somber brown or black. They gathered in the garden only at sunset or at night.

Trying to catch the butterflies, I touched his lashes, and he closed his eyes.

"Your lashes are curly, unlike mine." I touched my own lashes.

For a moment, Andre opened his eyes, and the evening butterflies fluttered their wings.

"*Oui, c'est ca, ma cherie. C'est la difference entre l'Est et l'Ouest.*" Where was East and where was West and why did they have to be different? I toppled down off him and began to arrange my newly acquired dolls on his torso. I put my tiny hand underneath his cotton shirt, feeling the light brown fuzzy hair on his chest, his firm stomach muscle and warm skin.

And then I remembered my old doll. The old doll looked like a miniature version of Andre.

Before Andre arrived with his selection of dolls, I had only one Western doll, given to me by Grandma Que's French physician. So, I rushed inside the house to fetch my old doll, eager to return for fear Andre would disappear. I wanted to show Andre my old doll.

It was a boy doll, with short brown hair, dressed in a dark blue shirt and matching shorts. His plastic lashes could not move like Andre's. He carried a water bottle on a strap, and I often filled it with water, so his shirt was perpetually wet. I had had him for so long. I told Andre even though the new dolls were prettier, the boy would always be my favorite.

"Il te ressemble, un garcon," I said, pointing at Andre, who was a boy like my doll, addressing him with the informal pronoun.

"Oui, moi, je suis un garcon," he said, acknowledging he was a boy.

"Et moi, je suis une fille, avec les cheveux longues," I pointed at my long hair. Boys, like my old doll, had short hair and wore shorts. Girls, like me, wore dresses or silky pantaloons and had long hair.

"Et toi, une fille tres jolie," he stroked my long hair, confirming I was a beautiful girl.

The tender moment evaporated when Grandma Que appeared at the door opening to the garden holding a fan, her silhouette edging against the bamboo curtain that dangled in the wind. Her arrival meant it was time to blow the candles and cut the cake. I would be singing a solo, "Au Claire de la Lune."

In the last sun ray before dusk, Grandma Que stood still, staring down at one reclining Andre, who was trying to curl himself upward as I was still holding him down with my two hands, attempting to climb on him.

Grandma Que's hair was always rolled into a bun in the back of her neck, held in place with an ivory comb connected to a black silk net. When she took the comb off, her long hair fell to her side, almost touching her knees. When she moved, the stream of hair shook behind her like a holy animal. She wrapped the stream of hair around her palm, rolled it up, and held it back in place with the comb.

I had known her well to realize the sign of her suppressed anger. Her manipulation of the stream of hair became her expression of emotion. When she was mad, she would let her hair down and then roll it up again, this time tighter than before as though she was determined to hold her emotions in place.

"*Vous etes le grandfils de Monsieur Sylvain Foucault?*" Grandma Que asked.

"*Oui, Madame, le plus jeune,*" he finally sprang to his feet, and the dolls began to fall in a cascade. To Grandma Que he bowed, nodding, confirming that he was the youngest grandson of one *Monsieur* Sylvain Foucault.

Who was *Monsieur* Sylvain Foucault? I kept asking since that day.

It was a long, long time, years later, before my father took me seriously and explained the web between Andre's family and mine.

Andre was the youngest grandson of a French colonist, Sylvain Foucault, formerly French Resident Superieur of Annam, the top French administrator to watch over the *Annamite* Imperial Court seated in Hue. Monsieur Foucault disliked a young Vietnamese king, His Royal Highness Thuan Thanh, and arranged for the king's exile to the Island of Reunion in Africa.

The unfortunate King of Annam, I was told, was my maternal great-grandfather. One of his royal concubines was that Paddle Girl whose singing voice echoed all over the River Huong and whose spirit allegedly became the nightingale that helped my voice soar to the sky when I tried to reach the high notes. When the King was exiled, one of his daughters, a baby girl named after the fragrance of cinnamon in central Vietnam, was only five years old. The baby grew up and grew old, had a daughter named Dew who loved to plant flowers and a granddaughter named Simone who loved to sing, and they all lived happily in a villa in Nam Giao.

I knew who the King's daughter was. The villagers of Quynh Anh who came to our house to offer gifts on New Year's Day knew her as "Princess Cinnamon." I knew her as Grandma Que, the old woman who raised me, and whose sad eyes looked pensively into the dying sun when the day ended.

She was the woman who told me all those Hue anecdotes that became my soul.

I grew up learning about Andre in bits and pieces by listening to adults at lunches, tea parties, and dinners. Andre and his good looks were the favorite topic of discussion for my mother's friends, the women of Lycée Dong Khanh who congregated in Grandma Que's living room. I remembered the details about Andre's life even if I didn't fully understand them then. An international lawyer who took care of the adoption of Vietnamese orphans and represented the European shipping industry, those days in Hue, Andre taught part-time at Hue University and spent his leisure time researching the ancient capital. He had sought out my father's help at the University. My sixth birthday was the occasion for my father to introduce him to the family. Born and raised in wealth, Andre left Paris and the Foucault clan and moved to New York City with his American mother when she decided to divorce his French father. When America began to send troops to Vietnam, Andre had just graduated from Columbia Law School. He took a job with a shipping company controlled by his estranged French father for an opportunity to go to Vietnam. Andre was in Hue to understand his paternal family's ties to Indochina, and to make peace with us. To demonstrate his goodwill, he had presented Grandma Que with the Vietnamese antiques acquired by the Foucault family. Grandma Que received those treasures nonchalantly, for she had long made up her mind to dislike anyone whose last name was Foucault.

After my birthday was over, when all my friends had gone home, I fell asleep on the cod mat until a cold breeze awakened me. I opened my eyes and found my father and Andre talking.

"You will find your Indochina," I heard my father say as I caught sight of his raised brows over his teacup.

"Where is Indochina?" I asked Andre, in my sleepy voice.

I felt a strong, warm arm drawing me in, and smelled the familiar scent of candies, soap, and lemon.

"Here, Indochina is here," Andre said.

I looked up and found his brown eyes looking down at my face. "I have found my Indochina," he said, smiling at me.

I, on the other hand, knew I had found my playmate.

Since my sixth birthday, every Sunday, Andre came to our house to learn Vietnamese from my father. My father, who taught French literature, became Andre's good friend. After their lesson, they would move to my mother's garden. Andre, my sister Mi-Chau, and I all played pony rides. I, of course, always got most of the rides, and Andre always made me laugh. When the pony game came to a close, my pony would get up from the ground, brushing the grass off his clothes and joining my father at tea. The conversation was often dominated by my father's long-winding speech, full of words I could not understand.

"*La France et L'Indochine*. The love and hate between the cruel, arrogant, exploitive colonial master and his beautiful, complex, intelligent, and resentful slave," my father said ardently. I listened, with fascination, grappling with my father's string of adjectives. "And America. All those shiny GE refrigerators, Coca Cola tin cans, Salem cigarettes, nicely stocked supermarkets with wrapped fruits and vegetables, long, big cars manufactured in Detroit, and New York skyscrapers, all of those nice things topped with the catchy phrase Democracy-for-the-Third-World, a notion existing only in the naiveté of a well-intentioned *nouveau riche*."

"What is a supermarket?" I asked my mother.

"A market that is super," she answered. "Food is frozen to last for months." My mother gave her simplistic explanation, ignoring the fact that I was pouting.

As my father continued to preach, Andre's face would change expression, taking on an air of seriousness that set him apart from me, into a different world much above my head. And then I realized he was no longer my pony or playmate, but rather my father's counterpart. The two men drank lotus tea, and talked for hours while my mother attended to her beds of flowers, and I was forgotten.

I found excuses to hang around, listening to the conversations, quite often in a combination of French, Vietnamese, and English. I guessed at the meaning, not understanding all, yet completely mesmerized by the adults' use of words and the sounds of three very different languages. I often jumped into Andre's lap and put my little hand underneath his shirt, feeling his chest and stomach muscles and the fuzzy hair on his warm skin. Quite often he caught my hand, either tapped on it, or raised it to his mouth, turning it over to kiss my palm. I would laugh. At times I would pull his shirt out of his slacks and attempted to crawl under his shirt, scratching his belly, pulling his buttons apart, rubbing my cheek against his chest. He would pick me up, place me on the table, tickle me and kiss my stomach, his shirt flying open. My mother would shout across the yard that I needed to be spanked and Andre was indulging me too much. All this time, my father was too absorbed in his talk to notice my childish prank.

I never had enough of Andre. He supplied all of the horseplay that my father, a skinny, bespectacled professor and a stern, aloof Asian daddy, never provided.

All was well and good until Andre announced to my family that he would soon return to France to get married.

6. Dominique Clemenceau

Grandma Que once told me that to marry meant to live with someone, to love and cook for that person. I assumed Andre would be returning to France to live with and cook for his someone.

Andre's someone turned out to be a woman, blond-headed, lying on the beach, wearing a two-piece bathing suit and dark sunglasses. Like the women in *Paris Match*.

It was an afternoon English high-tea party and several friends of my parents had come over to visit. Andre was showing them her picture, and I took a peep. The picture was in color, very rare in Vietnam those days, where the norm of photography was black and white.

Andre said her name was Dominique Clemenceau. She was French.

I memorized her name and studied her picture, the way she lay on her side, with one leg bent. I also noticed her red lips.

"*C'est une jeunne fille que tu vas epouser. Je suis une jeunne fille, aussi,*" I said. Andre was marrying a girl, like me, except for the golden hair, the legs, and the lips. And she had to be much bigger.

Nobody heard me. The adults were talking and laughing. Andre was describing something called "la lune de miel." The honeymoon. He kept talking about the vacation at *La Cote d'Azur.*

"*Qu'est ce que c'est que la lune de miel?*" I pulled his sleeve. What is a honeymoon? Nobody paid attention.

"*Je voudrais aller à la Cote d'Azur avec toi,*" I said with a pout. I wanted to go to *La Cote d'Azur* with Andre.

Again, nobody paid attention. The focus was on the woman in the bathing suit.

Thoughts rushed through my head. I loved Grandma Que and wanted to cook for her. And I lived with her. So naturally I would want to marry Grandma Que, except that somehow I understood intuitively one could not marry her own Grandmother, the way my mother was married to my father. Further, Grandma Que said she was already married, to my grandfather who wore a green turban and sat in the picture on the family altar, and she would not marry another person.

I did not mind living with Andre. I would be willing to cook for Andre, so long as I stood on a chair to reach the stove. And I loved Andre as much as I loved Grandma Que. So, perhaps I should marry Andre.

"I want to marry you, Andre," I said, about to break out in tears.

Still, nobody paid any attention. I ran into my mother's bedroom and sat alone. I wished either Andre or Grandma Que would come and comfort me. No one did. I thought of the woman in the picture. Andre would be living with her in France and would not be returning to Vietnam to play pony rides. He must have loved her and wanted to cook for her. If he married her, could I still marry him?

I went to my mother's vanity table and looked at myself. I could look like the French woman. I took off my shirt and my skirt and wore only my dotted panties. I took my mother's red lipstick and applied it on myself. I found her Jackie Kennedy sunglasses and wore them. They kept falling over the bridge of my tiny nose, but I pressed them all the way in and managed.

Something was missing. I went to my mother's armoire and found a brassiere. I tried to wear it and the thing was far too big so I had to hold on to it. Something was still missing. The golden hair. So I looked for my mother's gold scarf and tied it around my head. I also stood on her escapin high heels. I was complete. I checked myself in the mirror again and I was pleased. I could definitely go to *La Cote d'Azur* with Andre like this.

And then I came back to the living room. I stood in the middle of the room, on my mother's heels, holding on to the loose brassiere around my chest with one hand, and the golden scarf around my head with the other hand. The grown-ups were still looking at the pictures.

"I want to marry Andre," I said timidly. Still nobody noticed me.

"Andre, I want to marry you. " I yelled at the top of my lungs.

The room fell silent. I never forgot my mother's face, her dropped jaw, the O shape of her mouth, and her wide eyes.

"Oh Good Lord!" she said, jumping out toward me, while they started roaring, all of my parents' friends. Andre was also laughing at my efforts to please him.

Like the rest of Southeast Asia, Hue had its monsoon rain season. It was a rainy night when my father took Andre to the airport. I stayed in my room and cried. Andre had left for Paris to marry Dominique. Andre said he would return, soon, to his lawyering job and teaching position in Hue, as well as the mission he undertook for the children of Vietnam. With Dominique, of course, he told my parents.

My mother did not believe him.

"Vietnam is just a fad for him. He is young and he'll stay on in Paris with his wife," she said.

The following days and months were gloomy as the rainy season continued. My father purchased a piano for me and Mi-Chau, and I no longer had to go to the practice room at the Jeanne d'Arc

Institute for practice.

Instead of pony rides with Andre, my Sunday afternoons were now reserved for piano practice, "Au Claire de la Lune" and "Carnivale de Venice." Over-simplified versions of Schumann's "Melodie" and Chopin's "Berceuse." I was learning so fast *Soeur* Josephine stated I should audition for the national conservatory soon.

The days went by and I kept on working at the keyboard. Every Sunday afternoon I sat by my piano, near the window, looking out at the garden. My boy doll, who looked like Andre, sat on top of the piano, together with my music sheets. No more pony rides but I kept hoping.

The rainy season ended and the calendar year was almost over. Christmas was about to arrive and I was chosen to play a shepherd in "That Winter Night," a Christmas musical composed and produced by *Soeur* Josephine. The Catholic nun tested the range of my voice and decided she would write a short aria for the shepherd. So I sang her music, four lines to be exact: an uplifting C Major score, with lofty words celebrating the birth of Jesus Christ.

That was the first time I sang on stage. *Soeur* Josephine told my parents I should definitely be enrolled in the national conservatory.

The week before Christmas, my parents threw a party for their friends. Grandma Que made her specialty dish: shrimp balls on a kumquat tree. She created little mandarin oranges out of shirmp paste, wrapped them in clear cellophane, and attached them to the branches of a real *kumquat* tree. The guests picked the oranges from the tree and ate them, surprised to find out the oranges were made out of fresh ground shrimp. It was a royal dish. All the Western expatriates in Hue were invited. My parents wanted me to play my piano for their guests. Wearing a velvet dress, I played the simplified version of Schumann's "Romance" perfectly, without a mistake. My mother's almond eyes lit up with joy and pride. The guests shouted out, "bisse, bisse," the French word for an encore. I stood on the piano bench, beamed, and curtsied as my mother had trained me to do.

From my piano bench, I saw Andre walking in, beautiful as

always, with a woman. I instinctively recognized her. She was statuesquely tall, almost as tall as Andre, and much more imposing than in her picture. Her golden hair was tied up in a pony tail, with a multi-color scarf. She wore a bias-cut flowery Western dress and red lipstick. Her eyes were pale blue. She did not smile.

I stared at the beautiful couple. My broad grin faded. Andre approached and picked me up, kissing me.

"Tres bien!" he said, referring to my "Romance" performance. The adults were embracing, shaking hands. French and English were spoken. I remained in Andre's arms, yet feeling lost and neglected.

"Un gros baiser pour Tata Dominique, Simone," my mother said. She wanted me to give a big welcome kiss for Aunt Dominique.

I reluctantly went from Andre's arms to the blond woman's arms. She smelled nice, too, like fresh flowers and cosmetic powder, but still she did not smile.

"Elle est si drole," she looked at my face curiously.

Drole? I was not pleased. Comic? Quaint? Funny? Like a comedienne? No, I was supposed to be beautiful. Not "drole."

"Elle est magnifique," Andre said defensively. To him, I was magnificent.

"Vous etes...comme Sylvie Vartan," I said to her, carefully using the formal form of address. To me, she was like the blond French pop singer, Sylvie Vartan, whose record was played in my house, and whose picture I had seen in Aunt Y-Van's *Paris Match.* I could not think of anybody else who was blond. "Tata" Dominique started to smirk.

"Comment? Elle s'appelle Simone?" She turned to Andre with a question mark in her glassy blue eyes, her thin, shapely brows coming together, forming lines between them.

"It's just a cute French name, for school. Her real name is Mi-Uyen," my mother said defensively. "Her sister does not have a French name, because she's not in school yet."

My mother pointed to my sister Mi-Chau, who was always dirty from eating too much food too hastily. Mi-Chau was standing in the corner, behind the lamp, eating a cream puff. Her favorite "choux a la creme. "

"Ah oui," Dominique said coldly. Mi-Chau had finished her cream puff and was ready to kiss Aunt Dominique, but Dominique turned away.

"*Il est tres chaud, ici!*" Dominique complained about the heat.

"*Tres chaud, mais pas trop cher!*" My mother tried to make a joke, a pun on words, reversing "tres chaud" into "trop cher." It might be too hot here, but not too expensive! Dominique did not respond. I ran from Dominique to my mother.

"Show *Tata* Dominique your drawings and poems," my mother said. She wanted Dominique to see proof of my talents.

I stood still, buried my face in my mother's lap. I did not want to show *Tata* Dominique anything. This blond woman in a flowery dress did not like us. I could tell. I longed to be with Andre, but Dominique was sitting with him all the time, her hand resting on his.

I listened in as all of the guests were talking. Andre had been back in Hue for months and had been traveling with his new bride through central Vietnam. The highlands; spectacular green hills, valleys, and waterfalls. The famous Pass of Cloud, *Le Col De Nuage*, connecting Hue to DaNang, the military base of the Americans, where the famous American entertainer, Bob Hope, would be doing a Christmas show for soldiers. The white beaches of Cam Ranh and Dai Lanh, where American troops were disembarked from their fleet.

Anger filled my heart. I fought the tears. Andre had been back for months and he did not stop by for our Sunday afternoon pony rides. He had not missed me. He spent all his time with her. He left me waiting.

I ran to Grandma Que. Back to where I belonged.

All during the party, Grandma Que sat quietly on a rosewood chair, casting her eyes away from the guests, who raved about her shrimp balls. She did not speak. Something was about to happen. I just knew. I had learned to read the mood of the dignified woman who helped raise me.

7. Farewell to Hue

Toward the end of the party, my father made an important announcement to all of his friends. This was not just a Christmas party. It was a celebration. Also a farewell party.

My father had accepted a tenured position with the Faculty of Letters, University of Saigon. Andre, too, would be leaving Hue to return to France to practice law. Dominique could not stand the heat and humidity of Vietnam. My mother was right. Vietnam to Andre was just a fad.

My fate was decided, too. *Soeur* Josephine had written a letter of recommendations. In Saigon, I would audition for *Truong Quoc Gia Am Nhac*, The National Institute of Music and Drama. I would also be taking private singing lessons with a French Italian singer, Madame Misticelli, the only opera teacher in Vietnam, and a personal friend of *Soeur* Josephine.

It meant we were all moving to Saigon. My father announced his teaching would start in January of the new calendar year. So we would be packing right after Christmas.

People were still talking, congratulating my father for his new teaching appointment. Grandma Que stood up from her rosewood chair. She did her usual thing — letting go of her hair and rolling it up again, in one definite motion. But nobody noticed her. She left the room. I stood alone.

My temples began to hurt and the headache came on as a result of overwhelming emotions. I recognized years later that the painful moment must have been the first time I experienced, as an innocent child, the nostalgia of loss. The entire evening and its events had all been too much for me: the arrival of Dominique, our forthcoming departure from Hue, and my separation from Grandma Que.

I ran after Grandma Que into the garden. Of course, nobody noticed our absence from the party. In the clear starry night the moon had come out, and Grandma Que stood looking at its bluish shape.

I heard footsteps and turned around. Andre had noticed our leaving the party, and had followed us.

I reached out for him, and he took me in his arms. I began to cry, relieved to let out all those tears that had been suppressed since Schumann's *Romance*.

Holding me, Andre spoke to Grandma Que in his French-accented Vietnamese:

"It is a beautiful moon, isn't it?"

"Yes."

"Reminds me of the River Huong."

"What do you know about the River Huong?"

"I used to walk along the banks almost daily... Your mother once paddled a boat across the River Huong and met her prince charming that way. I study the lives of your ancestors."

"You mean, the life of my mother?" Grandma Que's face was lit with rage. "From what I can remember of Mr. Sylvain Foucault, you don't look like him."

"I look like my mother, an Italian American. My grandfather said I had his passion, even though we didn't look alike," Andre said slowly, his voice cautious and sad. "Madame, I would like to talk to you."

I looked up at his face and, under the moonlight, recognized the serious expression that characterized those moments when he drifted into a different world and ceased to be my playmate. He kept on talking with a tone of urgency, despite Grandma Que's apparent irritation. His French accent and choppy Vietnamese made it hard for me to follow him.

"You see, as a child, I spent time with my grandfather in his old age, during his dying days, listening to him talk, at a time when he no longer had any interest in life but to reflect upon his deeds in Indochina..."

"How noble of him, and what did you find out, may I ask?"

"You have a twin sister. When your father was exiled, your mother was with child, so you also have a brother, Madame."

Grandma Que's twin sister and baby brother? My mother's Auntie Ginseng and Uncle Forest? Grandma Que never talked about them, but she must have loved them, like I love my sister Mi-Chau and my infant brother Phi-Long. I was keenly interested. I looked toward Grandma Que. She was gazing at the moon.

"I don't need you to tell me what I have, *Monsieur* Foucault," she said coldly.

"But you must understand why your mother did what she did. About the postcards..."

"Please stop, *Monsieur* Foucault. You have no right to talk about the postcards."

Postcards? What postcards? I was getting confused. When Andre had left for France, he had promised to send me a postcard— scenery of the beautiful cafés of Paris, the river Seine, and the garden of Luxembourg. I tapped on Andre's arms, but he earnestly continued on. I noticed he was unconsciously making a fist.

"Forgive me, but I can't stop, Madame. If you didn't know, then I must let you know. Your sister and brother both left home and joined *Cach Mang*, ultimately Ho Chi Minh's revolution, the Viet Minh, at an early age."

The revolution? I had heard the big word, *Cach Mang*, from Grandma Que herself. I grabbed Andre's hand and tried to interrupt him to ask questions, but he was oblivious.

"My grandfather was not just an enemy, or just a business partner of your mother, Madame," he said, his brows coming together. "Your mother wanted to secure the repatriation of your father and the restoration of the monarchy. She knew that my grandfather, the Resident Superieur of Annam, could protect your twin sister and younger brother, the young revolutionists jailed in Hoa Lo. My grandfather could set them free. And he did just that, Madame; he secured their safety, the best he could, a very dangerous task, an act of treason against France. You should know, too, that back in France, he died a lonely and unhappy man, and I hope that after so many years, you can find the compassion in your heart to forgive."

"At least your grandfather died of old age, having lived his long and comfortable life. I won't tell you how I had to bury my loved ones, *Monsieur* Foucault. Untimely deaths. Without proper burials, without coffins," Grandma Que said. "I was not even able to procure some of the bodies to bring them home."

"It was a very long war, Madame. My grandfather and your parents were all extraordinary individuals. They had to do what they had to do. Can you at least try to understand what your mother had to do when she was alive?"

Grandma Que raised her arms and removed the ivory comb, her hair cascading down her side:

"Who are you to tell me? You understand nothing about my mother."

"Perhaps I don't, but Madame, I do understand how you feel. Things must have been very hard for you, and I'm terribly sorry."

Grandma Que was staring at him steadily. I thought I saw the firing reflection of stars in her eyes.

"Why are you, a Foucault, saying sorry? What for? About understanding how I feel, you are not part of my family, and as a Foucault, you are not entitled to feel what I feel."

After all the guests had left, my father began discussing the move. Grandma Que sat silently in the rosewood chair all throughout the discussion.

"I just want to know one thing, Master." Grandma Que always addressed my father formally as *ong giao* as school teacher and master of the house. "Will the girls have a piano?"

"They will share one, yes." My father removed his glasses to clean them, acting disturbed.

"Will there be a housekeeper?"

"Not on my teaching salary."

"Will the children go to French or Vietnamese school?"

"I will decide that later, Mother," my father replied, raising his voice.

"Will my daughter and grandchildren come back to this ancestral house, one day? Your wife is my only child."

"My job is in Saigon and I doubt if we will come back to Hue, Mother."

I was scared. No one had spoken to Grandma Que in that tone of voice. My mother, unhappy wife and daughter, looked pleadingly at one unhappy husband and one unhappy mother-in-law. I sat in a corner twisting a strand of hair, never feeling this sad before.

Grandma Que got up to leave.

"I'll leave so you can discuss your move with your wife." She let go of her hair and rolled it up again. "I would like my cinnamon log to go with Si and Mi-Chau," she said decidedly.

"That won't be necessary, Mother. Si and Mi-Chau are children.

They have no use for your cinnamon log," my father protested.

"The cinnamon log is meant to protect my granddaughters. They should take it with them wherever they go." Grandma Que sat down again. She was just about to turn her hair loose, again, from the ivory comb.

"If we need cinnamon for cooking, we'll go to the store," my father retorted.

"You don't understand, Master, this is a very very old tree..."

"Then it needs to stay with you all the more," my father interrupted her.

I grew sadder and sadder in my little corner.

"The tree belongs to the girls, and they need it," Grandma Que said firmly.

"I'll decide what they need. They are my daughters!"

"And may I remind you, *ong giao*, they are also my granddaughters." Grandma Que stood up. She closed her lips, rerolled her hair, and then left the room.

8. Saigon

In the years to come, I thought of life in Saigon as transient, expecting the day we would all be returning to Hue. My mother shared my thoughts, although we never openly discussed our longing.

In 1966, Saigon to me was just a bee-hive. A noisy city packed with little men slouching in their cotton shirts, little women swaying in their colorful *ao dai's* or cotton print pajamas, and little children twisting their rubber sandals on paved sidewalks, swinging their plastic briefcases containing their violet ink bottles and scrap books with pre-printed lines. I saw none of the elegant image of French "Cochinchine," that "gem of the Far East," or "Paris of Asia" as the adults had referred to their capital city.

The only thing impressive about Saigon was its magnificent downtown. It overwhelmed me. My mother explained that the French colonists who built *Cochinchine* must have attempted to incorporate certain features of central Paris into Saigon. But the hot and humid Asian city, bathed all year round either in dust particles dancing in burning sunshine or unexpected tropical monsoon rain, did not exactly turn out to be a miniature Paris, even though the French touch permeated the ambiance of various districts of Saigon, most notably the *Rue* Catinat downtown district. A giant clock highlighted the facade of the Ben Thanh market, a two storied shopping galleria stretching itself through several blocks of downtown Saigon. The landmark clock watched over the weaving traffic on the multi-laned *Rue* Catinat, bordered by tall trees and rooftop nightclubs bearing fancy French names, from the Rex, the *Au Chalet*, the Crystal Palace, to most notably, the ice-cream parlor *Pole Nord*, the North Pole, a favorite hangout of Saigonese youth. Once in a while, either my father or Andre would bring me and Mi-Chau there for ice cream.

A white, French-domed opera house occupied one end of *Rue* Catinat, used by the South Vietnamese government as its parliament house. At the other end of *Rue* Catinat was Saigon's *Hotel de Ville*, City Hall, an ornate, canary yellow structure decorated with distinctive white moldings, seahorse and angel motifs. To the left of the Opera House was the almost-one-hundred-year-old Continental Hotel — a square, white, elegant structure with its ornate French facade, glass windows, and long marble corridor. The multi-laned traffic *Rue* Catinat, separated by a median on which were situated dozens of souvenir shops and busy little kiosques, reminded the French-speaking Saigonese and nostalgic French colonists of the Champs Elysees. But the colonists and the Saigonese fashion-conscious crowd were all dreaming, since at best *Rue* Catinat would only be an Asia substitute. The small scale of the shops, the lack of glitz, not to mention the Asian-styled noise and petty unkemptness took away from Saigon any illusion of Parisian grandeur or romanticism.

My glimpses of glamorous downtown Saigon were infrequent and short-lived. I only accompanied my mother on those rare shopping sprees for special occasions such as New Year, or birthday celebration dinners where the children were given filet mignons, French onion soups, buttery gateaux studded with raisins, and crispy apples and pears that were imported and wrapped in soft white tissue papers. Unlike Mi-Chau and Phi-Long, I did not care much for filet mignons or apples, and would rather trade them for *com tam*, crushed white rice sprinkled with fish sauce and garnished with Vietnamese bacon bits.

In the early days of our lives in Saigon, my mother talked incessantly to me and Mi-Chau about Grandma Que's villa in Hue and its garden. In Saigon, we lived in a barren townhouse in the back of a small alley. Saigon eroded her dreams, my mother said. It had taken away her only hobby, gardening.

"Why do you like gardening so much, mother?" I frequently asked her.

Most of the time, she did not answer. Once, only once, she dreamily said, "*Comme les fleurs de lys que j'ai cueillies dans le jardin de mes pensees*. My flower beds became the gardens of my thoughts."

In those moments, my mother and I became the best of friends, and I would gently place my head onto her arms, listening to her talk. My mother talked of the checkerboard marble floor of Grandma Que's villa, its high ceilings with molded corners and green French shutters. She talked of the beautiful shapes and colors of roses, daisies, lilies, sunflowers. She talked of the chimes that decked the front and back porches, dangling in the wind, making their clear, reedy music.

Every night, before bedtime, my mother wrote letters to her woman friends in Hue, the female teachers of Lycée Dong Khanh. She read her letters out loud for me to hear, as though she were delivering a monologue before an audience, describing the beautiful time of her life in Hue and her longing to go home.

"I am so afraid I will never see flowers or a garden again in these filthy alleys of Saigon. To escape, I turn to poetry and pretend to garden with words. *Les fleurs de lys que j'ai cueillies dans le jardin de mes pensees*. Picking lilies from the garden of my thoughts."

When my father entered the room, she would stop the monologue and pretend to read a newspaper.

My mother considered life in Saigon too tough for her leisurely style, and complained that the power of the American dollar was uprooting traditions and the identity of the Vietnamese middle class.

I was too young then to understand the political role of the Americans, yet old enough to get a picture of our economic life in Saigon, painted vividly by my frustrated mother. She constantly stressed the need to be frugal. At lunches and dinners, she complained to my father, and I quietly listened. Our family, as well as other civil servants, school teachers, and families of combat soldiers had to struggle hard to survive the skyrocketing inflation of Saigon on meager monthly salaries. The cyclo drivers and maids who rushed into the city from war zones occupied the bottom of the wage-earning chart. On the other hand, if one worked for or did business with the Americans, salaries were much higher and, therefore, life was better. Landlords preferred leasing properties to American tenants. Taxi drivers preferred picking up American passengers. A new type of money maker appeared on the scene of Saigon's commerce: the contractors and auctioneers who transacted with the Americans. Young girls from the countryside poured into nightclubs, bars, and dancing parlors serving American GI's. A new occupation appeared on the scene of the Vietnamese social classes: the GI wives and girlfriends, not highly respected, according to my mother, but pleasantly well-fed.

I saw them, the GI's, occasionally, on Saigon streets, in their army uniforms, those black and white men, all too tall to fit the low sky and small alleys of Saigon. Either rosy under the sun, or glisteningly dark like the night, the GI's were all towering, hairy figures obviously out of place. Occasionally, I found a soft, dark-featured one who looked a bit like Andre.

"They are not French. They are Americans. They are supposed to be our friends," my mother would explain.

"As my children, you stay away from the GI's, you hear?" my mother would tell me and Mi-Chau, pointing her fingers at the hord of children who followed the GI's. Once I challenged my mother's contradiction:

"If the GI's are our friends, why aren't we allowed to follow them like the children of the streets?"

"Those children were the *bui doi*, dust of life. They are orphans, shoeshiners and errand boys. You are not the *bui doi*," my mother exclaimed.

I enviously watched the *bui doi* roaming in their free-spirited way, even if they looked dusty and dirty. Circling or following the GI's, the children shouted in rhythm, "OK Salem, Coca Cola, and chewing gum," and those towering figures in army uniforms would smile broadly, distributing items to the children who fought among themselves for the largest share of the goodies. The *bui doi* got all the things they asked for in their broken English, from cigarettes to milk cartons and, most of the time, Coke cans and fruity chewing gums. We got none because we were children of respected schoolteachers and civil servants. In addition to his tenured position at Saigon University, my father taught private night schools — those classes that prepared the young men of South Vietnam for their college entrance examinations, which they had to pass to avoid the draft.

My father's moonlighting, I was told, was his effort to earn extra money to pay for my private French school. So, despite the hardship of life in Saigon, I continued having my ears filled with lyrical French, my eyes filled with pictures of French countryside, and my thoughts inundated with details about the daily lives of French boys and girls described in the beautiful prose of the best of French writers like Alphonse Daudet and Anatole France. The French education did little to change my Vietnamese soul. I still preferred crushed rice and fried tufu dipped in peanut sauce over fancy filet mignon and the "laughing cow" cheese, *la vache qui rit,* which my mother forced me to eat to gain weight.

Mi-Chau, on the other hand, suffered a different fate. Citing patriotic reasons, my father withdrew her from the French curriculum and put her in public Vietnamese school instead. Behind his back, my mother whispered to me that the real reason for Mi-Chau's Vietnamese schooling was the lack of money. She taught me to be frugal that way.

To return to sleepy Hue, under the protection of Grandma Que, was my mother's version of a dream. One day we would all be returning to the old colonial house where her children would be raised among tropical flowers and in the musical sound of jingling chimes. She never accepted our departure from Hue as a one-way trip. She had a special suitcase, packed with sweaters and finer clothing. Hue was colder than Saigon, and the suitcase was for that one day when she would be returning to Grandma Que's villa.

Yet, during the Lunar New Year of 1968, the Year of the Monkey, my father announced we would never return to Hue. My mother's brows came together over her red, sullen eyes. As usual, she did not protest the decision. The special suitcase, however, was never unpacked. She kept it under my bed. Only I knew where it was.

9. The *Tet* Offensive — Madame Cinnamon and the Communist Spy

Time passed. My mother had not even returned to Hue for a visit when the next catastrophe arrived. As it turned out, my father's decision to leave Hue was a good one. The celebration of the Lunar New Year, *Tet Mau Than*, in February of 1968, entered history as a tragic event. The *Tet* Offensive. The massacre of Hue. As a thirteen-year-old, I was mature enough to grasp the tragedies of the *Tet* Offensive as my personal tragedy as well.

First, Grandma Que was in Hue with the Viet Cong. Growing up in non-communist South Vietnam, I was conditioned to think of the Viet Cong as boogie men and enemies, a mean and dangerous species like snakes, tigers, or cannibals. On the day the radio announed Hue had been seized by the Viet Cong, I wrapped myself in a blanket, thinking of Mey Mai's words — there would be another massacre in the City of Hue, from which I would escape. It was happening. The Spirit of the River Huong was correct. I thought of Grandma Que living alone in the old colonial house. Would the magnolia tree protect her against flying rockets? Or would she die buried under white magnolias blooms?

Second, the Violet City — representing memories of that guardian angel of mine, the Mystique Concubine — became the celebrated battlefield. American marines were helicoptered into battle to help recover the imperial city. TV broadcasts of scenes from Hue were available for Saigon inhabitants to view what had happened to their beloved imperial city. The mourning of Hue citizens filled the evening news. It was reported that when the Viet Cong withdrew their troops, thousands of civilians were buried alive or executed.

My mother, Mi-Chau, and I prayed to the compassionate Buddha every night while the fighting for the imperial city continued. We would all cry together watching television; corpses of soldiers were shipped out of the Citadel surrounding the Violet City, from the skinny Viet Cong guerilla fighters in their black pajamas, to the equally skinny South Vietnamese soldiers in their green army uniforms, to the American marines, the gigantic men of the West.

In the end, the South Vietnamese Army and U.S. marines declared their victory — the Viet Cong were completely ousted from the imperial city. Hue, once more, belonged to the American-backed Republic of Vietnam. The broadcast news said the Violet City was badly damaged. My father sighed one evening at dinner and claimed that vestige of a culture and past glory was almost wiped out. Excavation was conducted for Hue citizens to find traces of their loved ones. Bodies of Hue citizens were uncovered in all shapes or forms, parts missing, limbs chained together, arms tied behind the back. It was also reported that among the dead were Western civilians — Germans, French, Americans, British, who had come to Hue for research, medical, academic, or humanitarian services.

"Lucky Andre and Dominique," my father said, "leaving just in time."

Finally, we got a telegram from Grandma Que. The ancestral house was damaged, but she was all right, thanks to the cinnamon log sitting in the altar room, she said. The cinnamon log contained magic from the jungles of central Vietnam and protected her against havoc or tragedies. Apparently, the log was not powerful enough to keep our surviving relatives in Hue after the *Tet* Offensive. Several of them left Hue to resettle in Saigon, and told us of what had happened to our ancestral house on Princess Huyen Tran Street. The Viet Cong had chosen the villa as a place for political meetings. Hue citizens were summoned to hear propaganda talks on American crimes, and Grandma Que was chosen to preside over these meetings. The Viet Cong called her Mother of the Revolution.

Gathering coals and wood logs, she cooked barrels of rice to feed Viet Cong troops, with the same calmness as she had prepared gourmet shrimp balls on a kumquat tree for Western expatriates at the Christmas party. Later we heard that prior to withdrawal, the Viet Cong were about to loot her house and destroy her antiques. Grandma Que, twin sister of the heroine Ginseng, daughter of the revolution, stood in front of the altar and demanded to see the political commissar:

"Take whatever you want in the house before you go back to

the jungle. But do not touch these artifacts. They don't belong to me. They belong to the culture of Vietnam. Destroying these and you would be committing the same crime as the Americans. You would be guilty before the dragon and the fairy that represent the country's roots. Even the French had to give these items back, and I am just the keeper. Uncle Ho would agree with me, I am positive. If your men do this, I will write to Uncle Ho and General Vo Nguyen Giap myself. Or you can kill this old woman."

I imagined the slender silhouette of Grandma Que in front of the family altar, dainty like a willow. She repeated her hair-rolling routine as she delivered her stern speech to men wearing cone hat and black pajamas, with their AK 47's pointing at her. The Spirit of the River Huong must have been lurking behind Grandma Que, circling the altar in the smoke of incense, while the omnipresent cinnamon log emanated its mystical power to protect her. Finally, the men in black pajamas had to lower their head and bow, pointing their threatening AK 47's to the ground.

Even the Commissar had to lower his eyes and ordered his men to leave the house. The antiques and musical instruments once belonging to the Hue Imperial Court remained intact.

Our Hue relatives added a postscript to the story. The well-known medium of the Inner Citadel, Mey Mai, had disappeared after the *Tet* Offensive. It was alleged she had joined Viet Cong troops in their withdrawal into the jungle, back to the Ho Chi Minh Trail. Mey Mai, the psychic, the prophet, the wise one, the Mystique Concubine's loyal chambermaid, Grandma Que's endeared nanny, had always been a communist spy. In 1968, she served as colonel in charge of information warfare for Ho Chi Minh's National Liberation Front and its communist cause. The money and gifts she earned through fortune telling had always gone to the Front. She had always been one of the celebrated daughters of the Revolution, following the footsteps of my Grand Aunt Ginseng.

So, Mey Mai was a Viet Cong! And a famous one, with a long revolutionary communist and intelligence career. But I never thought of her as a bad person. She used to embrace me and hold me in her lap. And she spoke to me the words of the singing Paddle Girl — that powerful Spirit of the River Huong.

We learned that when the *Tet* Offensive was over, Grandma Que had to repair the exterior damage the war had done to the ancestral house. In her letters, she stated what I already knew: that the Spirit of the River Huong, the magnolia tree and her mystical cinnamon log had protected our ancestral abode.

But my father had a different story to tell. He said it had to be Mey Mai, the communist spy, who secured Grandma Que's safety and protected our property. Even a dangerous, deceiving communist spy had loyalty and a heart. Further, the old villa, isolated underneath rows of tall trees and sitting on the slope of hilly Nam Giao, was not situated on the Viet Cong's incoming or exiting route. The location made it strategically safe from the war. And no, my father continued, Grandma Que would never have written Uncle Ho or General Giap about the matter of her antiques. If she had, the letters would have been ignored. They could have got her into trouble with the South Vietnamese government. Imagine a South Vietnamese writing to Uncle Ho and General Giap in the north?

I did not believe my father. When Grandma Que said she would do something, she meant it. The Spirit of the River Huong, the magnolia tree, and the cinnamon log would never allow Grandma Que to be harmed in any way.

In the summer of 1968, my mother wrote to Grandma Que, begging her to leave Hue for Saigon, for fear there might be another *Tet* Offensive. Mey Mai had disappeared and if another *Tet* Offensive were to occur, there would not be anyone to protect Grandma Que against the Viet Cong, who condemned members of the royal family and descendants of the Nguyen Dynasty.

Grandma Que refused. She had decided to live and die as the keeper of memories.

That summer, when life got back to normal, we also got a telegram from Andre in *Cote D'Azur*: "Heard of *Tet* Offensive. Please telegram. Anxiously waiting. Andre."

So, Andre had not forgotten me, in spite of Dominique.

The inhabitants of Vietnam learned to insulate themselves from bad memory. The *Tet* Offensive was soon forgotten, and the war could seem deceptively far away. In many ways our lives before and after the *Tet* Offensive remained unaffected.

By the beginning of 1969, I had auditioned for and enrolled at the National Institute of Music and Drama. That same year, I began taking private singing lessons from Madame Misticelli at her villa on Rue Tu Duc, a small, tree-filled street representing the best neighborhood of Saigon, with rows of red brick French villas and yellow and grey stucco estate houses. For regular academic work, I attended Lycée Marie Curie, a French secondary school in the heart of Saigon.

After the *Tet* Offensive, my mother stopped talking about returning to her ancestral house in Hue. Instead, she wanted to resume her hobby in tropical horticulture, but the townhouse in District Eight had no spare land.

In the beginning, my mother remained quiet and sad. Then she became more and more irritated. The silence broke, and she began complaining to my father incessantly about her needs to have flowers around her. My father finally gave in. Since the townhouse had no front or back yard, he had to knock down a bedroom, open the roof, and build a patio for potted plants and flowers. She would never again have an old man to assist her and to remove earthworms, nor the green grass of a circling yard.

In the patio, my father had built a small fountain made out of cement, greyish and dull, to catch rainwater. My mother eventually made peace with potting plants, and arranged her flower pots and crawling ferns and vines around the ugly cement structure. She also put lawn chairs around it. When she was finished, the grey cement fountain appeared bright and cheerful, and the townhome was no longer barren.

By the time my mother's flower pots all blossomed, we got another telegram from Paris. Andre and Dominique were returning to Vietnam to live.

"Call me crazy, *mon professeur*," the telegram said, "especially after the Tet Offensive, but I just can't stay away from L'Indochine. My bride will have to understand."

My Sunday afternoon routines with Andre were resumed that same year, in a different form. Andre no longer came to our house alone. Dominique drove a *Deux Chevaux*, dropped him off at our house, came in for the courtesy formality, and then left. She would come back to pick him up a couple of hours later. Every Sunday afternoon, I looked out from the living room window and saw them together in the *Deux Chevaux*, approaching our house and stopping by the curb. Husband and wife sat quietly and separately from each other, staring ahead. I asked my mother whether they were mad at each other. She said I was too young to inquire into such a thing.

Dominique was a dainty and aloof white lily lost in the tropics, her blue eyes and straight blond hair cool and sophisticated, her flowery Western dresses, silk scarf, and sling sandals all making a striking fashion statement in the dust of Saigon among the polyester clad and cone-hatted street vendors. She would kiss me on my cheeks but would never smile. I could hardly feel the contact with her thin lips. I was told she taught French and English at Lycée Marie Curie, and when I was old enough to attend the eleventh grade, *La Seconde*, she would become my teacher. I dreaded the day.

My world in Saigon those days centered around the smiling and overweight Madame Misticelli, the school girls and professors at Lycée Marie Curie, the National Institute of Music and Dramatic Arts, the patio where my mother spent her leisure time, occasional outings for ice cream at the *Pole Nord*, and my Sunday visits with Andre. The Sunday meetings continued, but the pony games between us belonged exclusively to my memory of my mother's garden in Hue, those butterflies fluttering their wings over violet petals in the yellow twilight of a dying summer day. Andre's Vietnamese language lessons taken from my father had gradually advanced to discussions of Vietnamese literature, which included Vietnamese modern poetry modeled after French literary romanticism of the late nineteenth and early twentieth centuries — those images and sentiments of Verlaine, Rimbaux, Baudelaire, and Appollinaire. I doubted if Andre's Vietnamese had really improved, because during these literary sessions, my father did most of the talking.

Days rolled by and I became a slender teenager, attached to Andre still, yet afraid of Dominique. Andre told my parents he would like to be my play uncle. According to him, Dominique did not object to the concept of becoming my French play aunt.

10. Yellow Roses and Baudelaire

In 1969, I turned fourteen. In a moody teenage temper, I had told my mother I absolutely did not want a birthday party with friends my age. I requested that my sibilings, Mi-Chau and Pi, be sent away for the day.

It had rained all afternoon, and when the rain stopped, I sat by the window looking onto the cemented alley, fresh, clean, and wet with the recent tropical shower. Andre's *Deux Chevaux* appeared and parked at the curb. Obviously he was coming for his Vietnamese lessons with my father. This time he was driving the *Deux Chevaux* himself, and Dominique was not accompanying him. The norm was broken and I rushed out to the door.

Andre was carrying a bouquet of yellow tea roses in his hand and he bent over to kiss me on my cheek.

"Surprise!"

My mother entered the living room from the kitchen, carrying a cake with thick, white buttercream frosting and fourteen candles on its surface. She announced there would be no Vietnamese lessons that day, as Uncle Andre would be celebrating my fourteenth birthday with us in the patio.

Andre also produced a vase, announcing solemnly that the best of roses should always be presented in French crystal. He also had a wrapped present with him, claiming it was from Aunt Dominique. I tore up the gold wrapping and glistening matching bow, running my fingers on the fine silk of a colorful scarf bearing the signature of Christian Dior. I had never had anything that beautiful in my school girl's wardrobe, yet I folded the scarf nonchalantly and placed it back inside the bundle of wrinkled and torn wrapping paper, feeling no real emotion. It looked too much like something Dominique would wear. My attention was on the bouquet of yellow roses.

Andre said the flowers, twenty-four buds, had been ordered especially from the highlands, the resort City of Dalat, where the fresh and cool air of a milder climate produced better roses. I filled the crystal vase with rainwater from the patio's fountain, and sprinkled water on the rosebuds.

It was a quiet, adult-like birthday party, just as I had wanted it. My mother had honored my wish and sent both Mi-Chau and Pi Long to the beach in Vung Tau. The beach was formerly the French resort of *Cap St. Jacques*, where my great-grandfather, King Thuan Thanh of Annam, had been placed under house arrest prior to his exile. Before sunset, I blew out the fourteen candles on the cream cake, *banh bong lan*, and we sat in lounge chairs, listening to Andre recite Baudelaire:

Mon enfant, ma seur,...

Sa douce langue natale...

Aimer á loisir
Aimer et mourir
Au pays qui te ressemble

I wanted to sing those words:

My child, my sister,...

Your sweet native tongue...

Loving in leisure
Loving and dying
In the country resembling you.

I felt a vague sense of sadness. Why did loving have to go with dying? When I looked at Andre, he met my eyes. His thick lashes moved, and I saw again the nocturnal butterflies of Hue.

It was then that Andre began talking about himself. I had never seen him in such an agitated, passionate state. His brows came together over those beautiful brown eyes, his cheek muscles tensed up, and an expression of pain swept through his face. He told us how he had always been a lover of Baudelaire. He had studied comparative literature at Yale and then Sorbonne, and wanted to become a writer. But the Foucault family objected and he became a solicitor instead.

He turned to my mother and thanked her for all those beautiful flowers that, throughout the years of his friendship with our family, had provided him with the paradoxical images of Baudelaire's "Fleurs du Mal" in the Far East. My mother smiled and said her flowers were not meant to be the image of pain or the darkness of Baudelaire, nor the *chanson de sanglots* that inspired poets. She was planting them out of necessity, for herself and in memory of her own childhood.

Andre went on and on about the burden of being a romantic and an idealist in a world full of ugliness, and his eyes, slightly red, were wandering toward me although he had begun to address my father.

"*Professeur*, I feel at home in Vietnam. It is terrible, the damage done by war to a land so devastatingly beautiful. You know, I would even turn down the Foucault's inheritance to remain forever in Indochina if I had to, and even if it meant losing Dominique."

My father cut him off and gave him a schoolteacher's speech.

"Whether you give up your inheritance, Vietnam is still poor and the hundred years of colonialism and a continuing war have already taken place," my father said reproachfully.

I was old enough then to understand every word, yet did not fully grasp the meaning of the complex issues — why Andre looked so stricken with guilt and my father appeared so exasperated. When I looked over to Andre, his eyes were still fixed on me and he continued speaking, almost monotonously. I might not have understood everything, but as usual, I memorized his words.

"My family made a fortune out of Indochina. My grandfather was involved in tortures and the beheading of the Vietnamese patriots. There was also the oppression of Vietnamese peasants and laborers on railroads, in rubber and coffee plantations and dangerous coal mines. I happen to know all about those things from my family's living room and my grandfather's study. But I would not call my feelings guilt or shame. I know I should not make myself responsible for French exploitation and oppression of her colony. After all I was not even born then. But *Professeur*, do you believe in myticism — the unexplained things that happen to us? Why do I love this land so much? How can one explain why one loves a certain color or shape?

I never want to leave here," Andre said. He turned over to face my father.

"Then why did you marry Dominique, who doesn't want to live in Vietnam?" My father asked. I immediately perked up.

But Andre said nothing in response. He mentioned, instead, that I was growing up very fast, and he would like to take pictures of me dressed in traditional Vietnamese costumes of the 1920s. He talked of the collection of black-and-white photographs that his grandfather, Sylvain Foucault, had taken of women in the Violet City. The photograph collection became part of the Foucault library in France. Andre described how, as a boy growing up in Paris, he had stared at these photographs displayed in his father's study and had studied them. Old pictures of Indochina and the Violet City had been part of his childhood before he set foot in Vietnam. He mentioned again and again how, with each day, I was looking more and more like the beauty featured in those old photographs.

"What beauty?" I asked, and he gave no answer.

The afternoon sun was about to die out, when Andre asked:

"How is Madame Cinnamon these days, living alone in Hue? She has always been alone, hasn't she?"

"It is my mother's fate," my mother said.

"My only wish after so many years is to have Madame Cinnamon's forgiveness so my grandfather's soul can rest in peace. I guess she never forgives. I can't blame her."

"You're forgiven, Andre, if it means that much to you," my mother said gently. "You have it from me. My mother is very stubborn."

The party ended as quietly as it had started and Andre's lips barely touched my cheekbone as he headed for the door. After he was gone, my father sat alone in the patio for a long time.

"Poor Andre," my father said. "He wanted to write a book— an epic— on France, America, and Indochina. But it's been years and he hasn't completed it."

That night, I stood in front of the mirror and wrapped the Christian Dior silk scarf around my shoulders, letting the silk caress my bare skin. My instinct told me the scarf was Andre's idea, not Dominique's. I took one of Andre's roses, smashed it against my chest and let the crushed rose petals fall down along my side.

I woke up in the middle of the night to the fragrance of Andre's roses, their yellow petals dancing in my head. I repeated those words of Baudelaire. *Au pays qui te ressemble.* Like a drunk, I got out of bed, swayed my fourteen-year-old body back and forth in an imaginary dance, and drifted in and out of romantic dreams. And then I stood still, watching twenty-three yellow roses bloom in a French crystal vase. The crushed petals of the twenty-fourth rose were still lingering on my skin.

A notion entered my head the day after my fourteenth birthday that I would become an international lawyer, writer, poet, traveler of the world, seeker of beauty, and lover of Baudelaire. Like Andre. I would do all this and sing at the same time. If my mother had to plant flowers, I, too, had to sing, no matter what.

11. The Maiden Who Practiced Singing

The day after my thirty fifth birthday, I walked into my Fifth Avenue office and from my glass wall, stared at a bubbling Manhattan below. Somewhere in front of the glass was America and behind it a blurred Saigon of the seventies, all before the fall of a regime broke my life as a young woman in half. I could still hear the helicopter sound on top of the U.S. embassy in central Saigon. I could still see myself, twenty years of age, boarding the helicopter alone. When the machine had lifted itself into the hot air, I was still craning my head to look down at the U.S. Embassy building, at all those panic-stricken faces below.

Fifteen years had passed since then.

I mindlessly arranged the papers on my desk, knowing America had welcomed me with all my ardor and aspiration. The papers on my desk spoke of my successful law career. I had done well for myself.

Yet, in this land of dreams and opportunities, I had let go of my childhood dream. I had not taken up singing as a serious pursuit. I had become a Mahattan lawyer and spent the money I earned on trivial things like Chanel goods. To fool myself with a sense of noblesse oblige, in my days as a young associate in my law firm, I spent 900 hours a year on pro bono work, in addition to my normal load of 2,000 billable hours a year.

All throughout the seventies and eighties, boat people rushed out to sea to escape communist Vietnam. One of these boat people was from the village of Quynh Anh. He brought us the news of Grandma Que's death. No details were given.

So, for a decade, I continuously sent money to friends and relatives in my former Vietnam, fooling myself that I was helping those young women who might be trying to reach their own high note, in memory of Princess Cinnamon.

But that was all I did. There was deliberate, self-constructed amnesia somewhere in my brain to cope with the pain. My years went by like a long sleepwalk.

Sitting among stacks of legal documents, I decided to take up singing again. I would seek the best coaches among the voice teachers and music professors in the vibrant artistic community of New York City. I would repeat the arduous struggle to reach DO, RE, MI, FA, SOL, and then my ultimate high LA.

I leaned back in the comfort of my leather chair, yet feeling the pain of knowing that in pushing the limit of my voice, I would give up, start again and then give up. In between, I would cry into my pillow, for something so beyond my reach...the regaining of my childhood.

Constance, the high-cheek boned, black-haired German Italian choir director, had reminded me of the need to imagine someone—anyone — reigning in the round dome of the wood paneled theater. To this someone, said Constance, I should attempt to deliver the heartbeat of a muse.

During rehearsal, she would shout "Flat, flat, I can't stand it," and automatically I would imagine that special person as my sole audience. And then the notes emanating from my lips would become dark, light, opaque, translucent legato, pulsating vibrato, and the voice would cut through the space like a shooting star.

Nothing stood between the streamlined darting of the voice from my lips to the heart of that special someone.

After dress rehearsal I went home and wrote down in my choir notebook, *Cher Andre, je veux emprunter ton ame, encore une fois.* Dear Andre, it's time to borrow your heart, again.

Throughout the choir practice of Haydn's Salve Regina, I kept with me an orange, velvet-covered hardbound notebook, where occasionally I recorded the beautiful sayings I had read.

"*C'est l'heure, O Poete, de decliner ton nom, ta naissance, et ta race.* It's time, Poet, to decline your name, birth and race." — Leger.

"But where is what I started for so long ago? And why is it yet unfound?"—Whitman.

"I am thinking of aurochs and angels, the secret of durable pigments, prophetic sonnets, the refuge of art. And this is the only immortality you and I may share."— Nabokov.

I also wrote down the seven notes of the chromatic scale, from A to G. Each time my voice reached a note, I blacked out the corresponding letter with a marker, the harsh, black ink permeating through the pages and smearing the handwritings that made up my favorite literary quotes. Up half a tone on the diatonic scale. And half a tone more. Breathe out on each word slowly without the chest frame collapsing. Let the voice soar high. Higher and higher. Hold the note and the vibrato would linger forever, past the point where the sound itself ripples out, dissolving in space. Onto the search for freedom. To where the Statue of Liberty holds out her fingertips. And even higher, to the limitless sky.

All letters became blackened except for the ultimate high A. Andre's name began with an A, the infinitely crisp and clear stroke. In singing, I felt a pulse within me and I silently called it my "Art," starting with a capital "A" like Andre's name. To reach the high note, my "Art" had to spill out of me. My body became the container of my "Art," and I had to break that confine.

Grandma Que used to talk to me about the silkworm who wanted to shed itself into beautiful fabric until all that was left was the naked body of a helpless insect. She said the Mystique Concubine's spirit had blessed the silk worms of her silk farm, enabling the production of the best of silk. The beauty the silk worm gave belonged to others. All threads were peeled off to expose the soft, pulsing worm inside. The silkworm struggled against the web of threads, among the fragrant cocoon of green leaves. When the threads were removed, the flesh was displayed, and the silk worm perished. To reach freedom, the silk worm had to encounter death.

My mind went back to the singing lessons of the past, to the sweet time in Vietnam, before that fatal day of April 1975, the fall of Saigon. Before all the chaos began...

In 1970 Andre and Dominique lived in a villa on *Rue* Tu Duc, a few blocks from Madame Misticelli's house in Saigon. On the way to my private music lessons, I biked slowly under rows of soaring tall trees bordering the narrow street, singing to myself. Occasionally, I saw Andre walking alone, wearing glasses, holding a book in his hand. He rarely said anything to me, except nodding to acknowledge my presence, as though he deliberately kept a distance, or was preoccupied with other things. I would hurry to pass him, conscious that perhaps he wanted to avoid me. I missed seeing his beautiful brown eyes underneath those wire-rimmed glasses. I grew sad as though the butterflies of Hue had finally flown away, beyond my reach.

But those fluttering butterflies came back to me, one day. I was practicing the scale in the living room, next to my piano, attempting to reach the high C note, a DO, and then working myself up to the high E note. I was pushing my breasts forward, drawing a long, deep breath from beneath my diaphragm muscle, lower and lower, deeper and deeper into my abdomen, in order to support the heightened pitch. Yet I simply could not stretch my voice to reach a comfort zone. Frustrated, I stopped singing and looked out at the window.

I caught his gaze. Andre was watching me. My cheeks were heated, my body inflamed. I thought for a moment I had stopped breathing.

Outside the window, the butterfly lashes fluttered. My heart fluttered, too, with them.

It was not a Sunday when he was supposed to come over for his Vietnamese lessons. Yet Andre stopped by unexpectedly to let us know Dominique had won the battle. The couple would be going back to Paris, and Andre's Indochina would soon be a closed chapter in the book he still had to write.

That year, 1970, I had turned fifteen, still a flat-chested, long-haired melancholy girl who stood five feet tall, weighed eighty five pounds and looked barely twelve years old. I had become skinnier. My long hair had lost its lusciousness due to lack of care and the humidity and dust of one busy, polluted Saigon. Worst of all, the hardship of life in Saigon had made me into an ill-tempered teenager.

The war had escalated, paralleling the skyrocketed cost of living in Saigon. My mother had to take on a teaching job at a secondary school. In overpopulated and entrepreneurial Saigon, my parents' salaries could not afford a nanny for my brother Phi-Long, nicknamed Pi, or any kind of domestic help then quite common in middle-class Vietnamese households. Houses rented to Americans generated revenues about five times higher than rentals to locals. Contractors doing work for Americans made millions, while civil servants and school teachers — the impoverished middle class— could not afford red meat at daily meals. After the *Tet* Offensive, it became common knowledge that domestic maids and cyclo drivers could be Viet Cong agents or sentries. Poor people joined Viet Cong underground operations at Cu Chi or retreated into the jungles or Ho Chi Minh Trails, hoping the Communist Liberation Army would eventually prevail and bring about better lives, closing the gap between the poor and the rich.

Naturally, I became the household help my mother could not otherwise afford. She taught in the afternoon. I attended Lycée Marie Curie in the morning. When my mother was teaching, I took care of Pi. Late in the afternoon, my sister Mi-Chau would stay with Pi for an hour so that I could cook the evening meal. I did everything else in the house, including washing clothes by hand, hanging them over wires that criss-crossed our patio and destroyed the aesthetic look of my mother's potted flowers.

"You have to hold on to Pi. You cannot move or let him go until I return," I told Mi-Chau one time.

When I returned after cooking the evening meal, Pi was crying and struggling, as Mi-Chau was holding him down. When I took him from Mi-Chau, I realized the bed was stained, and that Pi had wetted his pants.

"You said not to let him go. I couldn't take him to the bathroom," she cried.

I cried, too, feeling sorry for myself. Like my mother, I had fantasized about returning to Hue, to the comfort and luxury of Grandma Que's lifestyle.

I struggled on to keep up with my singing practice. Once a week, I had to go to piano lesson at the Institute, and then singing lesson with Madame Misticelli. I put Pi on the front, and Mi-Chau on the back of my bicycle, and biked to the Institute. When I was taking lessons, Mi-Chau would stand outside the classroom with my bike and Pi. One day, she wandered off, after tying Pi to the bike with the bicycle rope. After one hour of practice, I came out of the classroom, catching her untying Pi. The child's wrists were bruised and red. I slapped Mi-Chau and she screamed.

I slipped down and squatted onto the floor, exhausted and defeated, my vision blurred because of the shock. I started seeing the front yard of Grandma Que's villa in Hue, the sweet and peaceful time I had lost. My father and Saigon had failed me. He, with all his education in Paris, and Saigon, with its glamorous downtown, could not provide me the comfort and caring given me by Grandma Que and her city of dream.

Life went on as a struggle until an accident happened. I was standing on a wooden stool and was just about to light the kerosene stove to cook rice when the stool gave way under me. I lost my balance and fell. Mi-Chau had fallen asleep, and Pi had gone into the kitchen. He pulled on the stool. I fell on top of him, together with the kerosene stove. Luckily, the stove was not lighted. But sister and brother were bruised, bathed in kerosene. We had no evening meal that day.

That night, my mother wrote Grandma Que:

"I am sorry to bother you again, mother, but your grandchildren need your help. We are living in substandard conditions because my husband's teaching salary and mine are not enough to keep up with the cost of living here. Si handles Pi and the household while I am at work. Today, the kerosene stove fell on them..."

She read me the letter and I began to hope, although it would take a lot for Grandma Que to leave the ancestral house after my parents had abandoned her in Hue.

In despair, I thought of Andre. I had written to Paris, sending Andre my sketches, poems, water color paintings, and passages of prose I wrote about Hue in Vietnamese and French. I described how I could not practice singing because of household chores and babysitting responsibilities.

That summer, my parents received two letters on the same day. The first letter was from Grandma Que. She would be departing for Saigon soon to help my mother take care of Pi and the household. The ancestral house would be looked after by a villager from the Quynh Anh hamlet working for wages.

My parents did not show me the second letter stamped in Paris. After dinner, my parents locked their bedroom door and stayed inside for about an hour. I could hear their voices, rapid and intense, but could not make out what they were saying. When they emerged behind the door, they told me I could finish the rest of the school year in the prestigious neighborhood of St. Germain des Pres, Paris, upon one condition.

Andre wanted to have Grandma Que's approval. He wanted the matter to constitute a gesture of trust from the woman who did not forgive.

I never envisioned Grandma Que in that filthy alley of Saigon's District Eight. Yet, as I was carrying Pi in my arms after his afternoon bath, exhausted, ill-tempered, with his weight bearing down on my side, I looked up and saw her face. Those black eyes and heart-shaped lips that spelled beauty even in a sixty year-old woman.

Later I found out she had arrived in Saigon unexpectedly and had taken a cab from Tan Son Nhat airport. Her hair had thinned out some, the grey more pronouned around her temples. Other than that, she was the same as I remembered her, the royal grandmother who always conducted herself with the dignity of a princess.

She showed no reaction toward the congested traffic of Saigon, the barren alley of District Eight, or the modesty of our townhouse. She acted as though she had been there for quite some time. Immediately, she started to reorganize the kitchen, getting rid of the hazardous old kerosene stove.

Pi was dressed everyday in crispy linen, and I had time to take a nap after school.

I could tell, however, that she had become older and more pensive. It was the first time she ever left the ancestral house of Nam Giao. She had brought with her to Saigon only three items from the family altar in Hue: the jade phoenix affixed to a gold plate bearing the seal of the Nguyen dynasty, which the King of Annam had given to his Mystique Concubine before his exile, and the two ivory plaques that respectively identified Grandma Que's father-in-law, the *Hong Lo Tu Khanh*, and her adoptive father, Admiral Nguyen Tung. The day after her arrival in Saigon, she set up a modest altar table and placed these three items on a small pedestal, behind a glass jar full of incense sticks. It was not the same intricate altar in the Nam Giao villa, but it enabled her to resume the habit of burning incense. For the first time, our home in Saigon had an altar and burning incense, just like the old days in Hue.

About a week later, the fourth item arrived, the lacquer divan given to the Mystique Concubine by the King of Annam. The divan was delivered intact, packed perfectly between layers of foam. Grandma Que had had it transported from Hue to our townhome. The shipping had cost her a fortune.

For the rest of my time with her in Saigon until I saw her last, Grandma Que slept on this divan.

It was obvious to me that when she decided to leave the ancestral house, she had also decided that she could not part from the four symbols of her heritage: the jade phoenix, the two ivory plaques, and the lacquer divan. In Saigon, she resumed the habit of polishing them everyday.

It also meant that she had decided to stay with us for a long time.

But Saigon forced her to change, as it had changed me and my mother. It was not long before Grandma Que integrated herself into the urban life of the small alleys of Saigon. She no longer wore silk pajamas or a brocade *ao dai* or an ivory comb on her hair. Instead, she was dressed in polyester blouses and black pantaloons like the rest of the old women of the neighborhood. In many ways she managed to fit in like a glove. She was a natural at haggling over the price of fresh fish and crawling blue crabs at the wet market, or walking home with her plastic basket full of spinach and green herbs in one hand, her other hand holding the folds of her black trousers as she hopped over little ponds of sewage water in the alley. No one in the neighborhood could distinguish her from the old women of urban Saigon whose full-time job was to do household chores and take care of small children. For social activities, they squatted and congregated on the narrow front porches of townhomes and duplexes, and occasionally, Grandma Que would join them.

The Anamese princess in her had given way to the nanny she had become. No one could imagine that not too long ago, she was the old dainty woman dressed in silk pajamas or brocade *ao dai's*, wearing dark red lipstick, the heavy gold bracelets carved with dragon shapes dangling on her two wrists. Not too long ago, she was the stern woman who lived alone in a high-ceiling, marble floored villa, with her parrot, white rabbits, and a cinnamon log emanating its spicy scent all over her antiques, even onto an array of photographs on a family altar perpetually covered with the smoke of incense.

"You want to go to Paris to be with Andre Foucault and his wife, don't you?" Grandma Que asked me soon after her arrival in Saigon.

I told her "yes, yes, yes." Silently, my eyes pleaded: Grandma, please approve.

"You think this French couple would be kind to you?"

I told her "yes, yes, yes." My eyes silently told her: it doesn't matter; please, understand, I want to go.

"Of course, you will go. There, the Westerners can teach you how to sing like a diva of the Italian stage. When Huyen Phi was still alive, she once traveled to Europe to sell silk, and she often told me about the Italian stage. How grand it was. Not like here. Ours is a poor country, and performing artists, those Vietnamese leading stars of the southern opera, *dao cai luong*, are not well-educated or well-respected. It isn't the place for a true first-class lady," she pondered, talking to herself.

My eyes told her again, yes, I agreed with her every word.

"The more I think about it, the more I feel you must go," she said. "But if you are not happy there, rush home."

Grandma Que sighed, nodded her head and went on to prepare for Pi's bath. She did not act overjoyed, but the nod meant the matter of my departure for Paris had had her blessings.

12. My Secret and Paris, 1970

The decision was made. I would be sent to France, entrusted to the care of Andre and Dominique at least until I finished high school, and perhaps even beyond that point to include my college years if I could attend Sorbonne. Paris and exposure to the Francophone culture had great educational value; no one in my family would argue with that.

To me, going to Paris meant having the life of *Paris Match* with *Tonton* Andre who resembled the romantic French actor Alain Delon and had the personality of Santa Claus. I frowned at the thought of having *Tata* Dominique around all the time, but overcame the unpleasantness with the image of a smiling and attentive Andre. I could not think of any woman or child who would not like being around *Tonton* Andre, with all of his dolls and toys and piano music books ordered from Paris. At night, I saw myself appearing in *Paris Match*, no longer as a skinny little girl in cotton Vietnamese pajamas or a plain pleated skirt, but a fashionable young woman, wearing dark glasses, dancing on platform heels in a grey wool coat with a fur lapel.

My excitement for the forthcoming trip was tempered only by the thought that I would be away from Grandma Que, so soon after she had just arrived in Saigon. At one point, I solemnly claimed I could not eat French food, things such as beefsteak and *fromage*, so I would like Grandma Que to come along and cook for me; otherwise I might be starved in Paris. Of course, my request was quickly disregarded. My mother, in particular, was very much annoyed. It was impious for a granddaughter to make such a suggestion. She reminded me that Grandma Que was one of the thirty six children of a Nguyen king, even if he abdicated and was exiled. If there hadn't been a war, and if history had been different, Grandma Que would have visited Paris on state affairs, accompanied by her own staff of interpreters and domestic help, never as a cook. And, of course, Grandma Que would never go at the courtesy of a Foucault, I should have known.

I arrived in Paris in time to see the change of seasons. Andre and Dominique lived in the fashionable neighborhood of St. Germain des Pres in the heart of the Left Bank. Paris held images of a cold and smoky *La Seine* and pairs of adults strolling hand in hand. Paris greeted me with the beauty of a grey sky stooping over rows of quaint, old red brick townhomes, narrow paved streets and sleek branches bursting with red and yellow leaves in the cool air.

In all my excitement and desire, I never once expected that there could be another side to Paris — how awful the City of Light could make me feel.

The first problem manifested itself during school enrollment.

"She can't be more than twelve years old, this little girl," the French nun exclaimed when I was presented for enrollment.

Her sentiment was confirmed by almost every Parisian I met thereafter. The disappointment I felt inside was greater than I could show. I had wanted to go to Paris as a young woman, not as a child. Yet every Parisian I met thought of me as a child. Naturally they could not see my old soul.

The second problem was even more severe than the first. Contrary to my expectation, Andre was routinely away in Marseille for his shipping business. Quite often, I was surrounded by *les enfants terribles* of St. Germain des Pres: those French teenagers who looked and talked so differently, they could not be my friends. To avoid them, I had to spend time with Dominique, who was cold and aloof and not at all accustomed to befriending a melancholy Vietnamese teenager.

Joy did not come so naturally, and I had to train myself to be happy. I learned restraint and solitude in living with Dominique, giving her embraces without feeling the warmth, eating her *petits beurres* out of politeness without tasting the sweet, speaking a foreign language while afraid of being made fun of.

Life got better only when Andre was back in Paris in between his business trips to the coastal cities. Andre opened for me a life full of wonders, puttling little limit on what was appropriate or inappropriate for a young teenager to absorb. We went south to the coast to find sunshine when Paris got cold. There, Antibe and its museums left me with images of peach and yellow villas facing cobble stoned, winding alleys bordered with flowering bushes. I stared at Picasso paintings, fascinated by his lines and shapes, ignorant of the meaning. Aix-en-Provence offered me not only its tranquil beauty, but also the Far-Eastern center where Andre showed me black-and-white pictures of a Nguyen king and his Annamite entourage when they visited Paris. Vestige of my maternal extended family, he claimed.

Finally, *La Cite*. We strolled the city, took l'autobus, climbed the steps of *Sacre Coeur*, walked through the narrow streets of Montmartre, and toured the outskirts of Paris in his *Citroen*. In the boutiques of glamorous Champs Elysees, Andre bought me a Dior hat, an extravaganza for a teenager accustomed to wearing cotton pajamas to run around the alleys of Saigon. I proudly wore my Dior hat even in the evening hours to accompany him, thinking of myself as his companion and not just a child. My fifteen years of life lit up when the night sparkled and the stream of traffic passing *L'Arc de Triomphe* became diamond necklaces that graced the City of Light with spark.

It was in Roma, not Paris, that I truly viewed myself as the young girl who practiced singing. In Roma I first heard Haydn's *Salve Regina* sung in a church, where Andre arranged for an Italian singer who had appeared at *La Scala* to test the range of my voice.

"*Salve Regina, mater misericordiae; vita dulcedo, et spes nostra, salve. Hail, O Queen, Mother of Mercy, our life, our sweetness, and our hope. Hail!*"

The music was so beautiful it made me cry. Crying because of beautiful music was as easy as crying for love, Andre murmured to himself. I, as usual, attempted to memorize his words. I memorized, too, *Salve Regina's* sacred Latin. I needed no understanding nor translation, just the sheer beauty of sound.

"*Ad te suspiramus, gementes et flentes, in hac lacrimprum valle. To thee we send up our sighs, weeping in the valley of tears.*"

The image of Virgin Mary, pure and good, reminded me of Quan Yin the female Buddha in her white robe, standing on a lotus blossom floating over the South China Sea. When I told Andre of my comparison, he nodded, but went on to tell me that the tortuous lines of *Salve Regina* reminded him of his soul, yet its lofty sound resembled my noble face, and I blushed in joy.

"*Eja ergo, advocata nostra...O clemens, O pia, O dulcis Virgo Maria. Hasten theretofore, our Advocate...O merciful, o pious, sweet Virgin Mary.*"

So Andre adored my face, the way he adored the face of a grown-up beauty, although the Italian voice coach, like the Parisians, thought I was a twelve year-old child.

But the happiness of Roma was short-lived. Back to Paris, to the Gare de Lyon with its bright yellow lights on a snowy night. Back to the St. Germain des Pres townhouse, where he kissed Dominique on the doorsteps and I rushed off to my schoolgirl bedroom, wishing we had never come back.

The sweet moments of my stay in Europe were overshadowed and tarnished by episodes of intense arguments between Andre and Dominique. I walked the neighborhood aimlessly for hours, or isolated myself in the living room or the attic, away from the bedroom where harsh and rapid French was spoken. I could not understand all.

And then he was gone again.

Fall and winter time in Paris passed so slowly. There was no picture of me appearing in *Paris Match*. I learned to eat fromage, including Camembert, and actually liked it. I frequently cut classes and wandered along the streets of *Quartier Latin* with its abundance of used bookstores and record shops. I hopped on City buses, down to the banks of *La Seine*, back to St. Germain des Pres with its cafés and *magazins*, where I peeped at expensive boutiques and looked up at barren trees.

Somewhere along the sidewalks, I would hear the sounds of Chopin. Chopin became my best friend. I followed his sound from one draped window to another, along rows of brownstones, until I reached home. Dominique's home. Every day was a wandering journey. Off I went in my little short coat and patent leather shoes. When asked about school, I learned to make up a bunch of lies.

No one in Saigon was supposed to know my sorrow, fear, and homesickness. In letters sent home, I only spoke of the melancholic beauty of Chopin's music, the house intricately decorated with oil paintings and velvet curtains, Dominique's buttery biscuits, *petits beurres*, and *soupe d'oignon*, the svelte mannequins of Galerie LaFayette where Dominique bought me a wool Scottish dress, and the tree-filled neighborhood of *St. Germain des Pres*. Trees that towered over rooftops and chimneys, drawing smoke out of the Parisians' mouth and nostrils when they walked the streets. "*Ca va, ca va bien,*" the men in trench coats and hats and the women in mini-skirts and high boots stopped momentarily to greet each other in their Parisian French, underneath those trees.

No one was supposed to know the bitter lessons Paris had taught me — that reality could never match the beauty of a dream. I was too proud to tell anyone, especially Grandma Que, about the haunting solitude of a young girl removed from her home. For months, I cried every night, badly wanting to return to the filthy alleys of Saigon's District Eight.

My school record was a disaster, although my French got better and I did learn new things — improved piano fingering techniques, operatic singing, oil painting, and a bunch of other impractical niceties that did not require much language proficiency, including an undying taste for French baguettes, butter, escargots, bouillabaisse, and

The only consistently nice thing about those days in Paris was the fact that I was always free to practice singing.

No one knew Paris also housed my secret.

"Non, non nous ne sommes pas amoureux, c'est impossible, c'est formidable."
He had broken down in tears.

Something happened, something broke, and I did not stay the
full year. I would return to Saigon before springtime. So Paris to
me meant summer, fall and winter. Just a little radiant sunshine and
then long months of falling red leaves, white snow, and skeleton
branches.

Nineteen seventy-one. How happy I was to be hit with the
heat and humidity and the dirt of Saigon as the door of the Air
France plane opened at Tan Son Nhat airport, and I knew at once I
was home. Back to Grandma Que. The load of hidden sorrow that
persisted through my time in Paris was lifted from me, like a leaf
twirling off an autumn branch.

I stepped out of the plane and looked back for the last time. The
Air France stewardess smiled at me and said: *"Au Revoir."*

In her clear chestnut eyes, I recalled the sceneries of Paris
circling around Andre, who knelt down, his hands pressing upon
his stomach, his chest heaving.

Oh Lord what have I done to the little girl I once held in my arms?

His hands took hold of his anguished face. I tried to catch his
arm and he avoided my touch.

*But what difference does it make, Lord, even if I kneel down before you and
put upon you the weight of my sins, while for years I already consumed her with
my eyes?*

I resented Paris for making me remember Andre this way. Stop
crying, Andre, I told him and he kept shaking his head.

No, no, no, you will never understand the pain of Baudelaire.

Of course, I understood. Only Andre did not understand. There
was nothing he could have done to me that I would not have done
to myself.

According to Grandma Que, I was already on the verge of developing into a young woman. So she began to have dozens of classic *ao dai's* made for me, with darts around the bustline, nipped at the waist line — the form-fitting style designed only for young women.

All the good food, leisurely lifestyle, and the constant walking around the streets of Paris had done me wonder. I sprang up wonderfully to five feet five, impressively tall for a Vietnamese girl of my generation. Paris had changed me from a skinny young girl to a beautiful lady, everyone in the District Eight neighborhood commented. Paris had also confirmed me as a hopeless romantic, with my newly acquired repertoire of French poems, classical music, and European movies starring Brigitte Bardot, Catherine Deneuve, Alain Delon, Claudia Cardinale, Gina Lolobrigia, and Jean Paul Belmondo.

I kept writing Andre and he kept writing back, but only to my parents, always referring to me as the niece or daughter he would like to have.

I finished high school at Lycée Marie Curie, passed the *Tu Tai* College Entrance Examination, and was dying to return to Paris to see Andre and attend Sorbonne. But my father talked to Andre separately and preferred for me to attend graduate school in America. To prepare for that course of life, I enrolled at the Faculty of Law in Saigon, while waiting for the right graduate scholarship to the United States.

Sadly and bitterly, I blamed Andre for not wanting me to return to Paris. How else could my father get the crazy idea that I was better off at an American college?

Constance gave a hand signal, and the music began.

"*Lacrimosa son io, perduto ho l'idol mio. I am melancholy. I have lost my idol.*"

Six months after my thirty fifth birthday, boxed in a severe velvet black long dress and standing in the first row of a 140-member choir, I sang the gorgeous sound of Wolfgang Amadeus Mozart. Sometime in the program, a lyric soprano would be singing Schumann's *Traumerei.*

In moments of *Traumerei*, I saw the past. The sound took me back to Rome. I saw again the black-haired, skinny young girl resting her head on Andre's shoulders. In Paris and Rome, she was supposed to be twelve years old, since she was not big enough for her fifteen years of life.

"My feet are too sore for me to walk," she had complained, so he carried her on his back, one early autumn day, down the foggy street of Rome to her first singing lesson, in a city where the great art of operatic singing originated. He had promised to show her how the human voice could become the instrument in competition with an orchestra. The voice could stand alone in its own time and space, with all its nuances, colors, and texture.

They went inside a grandiose old church and he put her down and asked her to walk through a set of tall, mahogony double doors. At the other end of a corridor, a real Italian opera singer would soon confirm the girl was a lyric soprano, a real honor for a sullen Vietnamese girl who loved to sing. The young girl would be singing Schumann's *Traumerei*.

The vibrato on the last note of Mozart's *Lacrimosa* quivered and extinguished. Constance gave another hand gesture to prepare the choir for Haydn's *Salve Regina in G*.

"*Ad te suspiramus, exules filii Avae. Ad te suspiramus, gementes et flentes, in hac lacrimarum valle. To thee we cry, poor banished children of Eve. To thee we send up our sighs, groaning and weeping in this valley of tears.*"

From the corner of my eyes, I thought I saw fog. He emerged from all that fog, a surreal figure, at the end of the music hall. His gorgeous self, in a trench coat, like that day in Rome. I kept on singing and he leaned against the set of closed doors, beautiful and youthful as ever. No one saw him except me. For a moment, time seemed to hold still, until he started to speak.

"*Bonjours, c'est magnifique. Tout ce que tu as fait. Je t'adore, eternellement,*" he said, one hand in his coat's pocket. "*Put your mind at rest. You made the right decision not to return to Paris with me in 1975. You have found your place in America, on your own, singing,*" he said.

We were having our private conversation across the music hall, above the heads of a bunch of New Yorkers sitting stiff and still, staring at a stage. In my mind, they froze, leaving the world to me and him, alone. We talked in the middle of Haydn's choral music.

"*Ad te suspiramus*," I sang my solo line. More eyes were on me, yet my eyes were on him. No more tears. He stood so beautifully and cheerfully at the end of the corridor.

Could you have saved me from my Fleurs du Mal? No, no, no.

I stayed with the high LA. Forever on the A note, which spelled his name. There was no gap between me and him, on that high A. The audience was clapping, and he clapped, too.

Brava, brava, he said, disappearing gradually, together with the fog.

Bravo for a man, Brava for a woman, he had told me that day in Rome.

13. Requiem in the Garden of Luxembourg

It must have been in the tree-filled neighborhood of St. Germain des Pres and the Garden of Luxembourg in Paris that I first recognized, at the tender age of fifteen, that the difference between Southeast Asia and Europe. The difference manifested itself in the colors and shapes of leaves.

In Southeast Asia, tall trees gave off dark green leaves that shone like wax, forming enormous shades. The wide, luscious surface of a tropical leaf sucked up plenty of early morning dews, drank and bathed itself always in generous dosage of sunshine. Huge trunks of trees challenged the arms of children, and I could still see the little girl running around the front yard of Grandma Que's villa, seeking an enorrmous shade under which to lie down, or attempting to embrace a tall magnolia tree. Grandma Que said the tropical climate did wonders for vegetation. In the wealth of sunshine, a tree had no other way to grow but tall and big, and leaves had no other way but to turn into wide, flat surfaces of luscious green.

The same slender young girl was standing underneath rows of trees, not the thick and tall trees of the tropics, but those thin branches giving off red leaves that crumbled under a grayish low sky. Here in Parisian autumn, there was no need for a shade of leaves to protect the girl against a burning sun. Instead, leaves turned red and fell, covering the ground, and then they dried up and broke under human footsteps. The girl moved on beds of red leaves, toward the sound of the piano, until she was met by a blond, slender woman wearing an apron, standing near the mahogany door, saying in a husky, melodious voice, *"Berceuse, berceuse!"*

The woman held a phonograph in one hand, her other hand extending to turn a key and open a door, and the girl slipped in. She made her way awkwardly among dark wood furniture and tiptoed upon those dark Persian rugs. Impressionistic oil canvases perfectly matched their carved, matted gold frames, hung solemnly around the wood-burning fireplace where fresh logs melted off their sap. The rest of the wall space was jammed with photographs of strangers — those men wearing tails, with their spiral whiskers and round spectacles falling down the bridge of their hawked nose, and those women with perfectly coifed golden or chestnut hair, their hands folding grimly over long, bouffant skirts. The room smelled of cream, butter, beaten eggs, and burnt sugar. Out on the street people hurried their steps, carrying newspapers under their arms, shapeless in their heavy coats, with smoke coming out from their breath. Inside, the girl tapped her shoe on the red rug, the braids of black hair and ebony eyes constrasting against her white chemise. When she turned around, the street sign across from the misty set of French windows met her swollen eyes, accustomed already to weeping alone at night.

The sign said St. Germain des Pres.

Fall had begun and sun-bathing Parisians had all headed home from the southern coast. Toward November Paris was chilly and grey. Outside a white shuttered window, the church of St. Germain was tolling its Sunday bell, waking her up to a house full of the pleasant scent of freshly baked baguettes and brewing coffee. A pair of dark brown eyes behind wire-rimmed glasses was looking down onto her face and into her sleepy eyes.

"Get up, *cherie, ma petite.*"

Her eyes followed the mass of dark, curly hair and the bluish grey sweater that shaped the torso of the man. He had moved toward the window, pensively looking out, the porcelain coffee cup going back and forth between the table and his tight lips. Those days, the girl had been used to life in Paris and her eyes were no longer weepy at night. *Le Monde* was in the man's other hand, and he was about to swing it across the room to the sofa. She whispered to him, "Je t'aime." He did not hear her words.

She tumbled from her schoolgirl brass bed over to the table, reached for the jar of honey, and dipped one finger into the sticky golden liquid. She wrote "Je t'aime" across the table with her honeyed finger. He did not read her words.

He turned around from the window, frowned, and for a moment she could see the blackness of his coffee almost spilling, as though his hand was trembling. His unhappiness did not concern her too much, for she had made up her mind to hold on to him, having been amused by the secret they shared. She was glad the *Tata* had left for the coast, and thought of all the places she wanted to go with him, from the castles of Loire, the forests of Fontainebleau, the vineyards of Beaune, all those fishermen's villages between Marseille and Cassis. She imagined all those wild rabbits running across potato fields and grape leaves stretching to the horizon. The Parisians regarded her slender frame as that of a twelve year-old, and she might as well benefit from that misleading notion. She could be a playful child. She rubbed her honeyed finger onto her front teeth and he caught her wrist, complaining about her lack of manners. She smeared honey onto his lips, ignoring his frown as he awkwardly turned away. She grabbed his chin and forced him to face her.

The Catholic sisters at the conservatory of St. Germain des Pres were all shocked when she locked herself in the water closet. The nuns called upon Madame Foucault, who had left for the coast. So Monsieur Foucault rushed to school in his trench coat, kneeling down before the locked door and talked to the young girl curling up on the other side of the door in a language the nuns could not understand. She felt sorry for herself. She told him for the first time how bad it had been for her in Paris. The Foucault couple had fought all the time, books and plates flying across the room, leaving the young Vietnamese girl tiptoeing alone around the living room packed with French renaissance paintings and eighteenth-century antiques. She missed the dusty alley of District Eight in Saigon and did not want to go back to the luxurious townhouse in St. Germain des Pres.

Monsieur Foucault wrapped his trench coat around the girl and took her home, a different home, an art studio converted into an apartment on *Rue* St. Jean Baptiste de la Salle, where he had lived before he got married. He had his books, manuscripts, typewriter, records, even the philosophy papers from Sorbonne and pictures of old girlfriends, together with all artifacts he had brought home from Vietnam, there, at *Rue* St. Jean Baptiste de la Salle, away from his wife. The apartment was his hideout away from his troubled marital life. Outside the apartment's window, one could see the tip of the Eiffel Tower. At *Rue* St. Jean Baptiste de la Salle, the girl calmed down and he prepared her bath and she sat in the tub for a long time, lonely and upset.

The apartment had two bedrooms and the girl stayed in the guest room, on a carved Chinese poster bed the man had brought back from the Orient, among piles of ornately embroidered pillows and blankets— traces of her Orient. In the middle of the night, the girl got up, crying, crawling into the man's bed where the mattress was plush and warm. She hung on to his side, placed one leg over his belly, and cried onto his chest. She spread her legs and climbed on top of him and pressed her face onto his heart. She was lonely. In a trance, she wanted to repeat the pony ride of childhood. She took his arms and wrapped them around her like a security blanket. And then she was frightened. She felt the tense muscle and he moaned and quirked and as the Parisian moon from the window hit his face, she saw him grimace in pain, and he was grabbing her rib cage. She thought she had hurt him irreparably. She could see nothing in the dark.

He lay still, panting, and then broke out crying. She felt the man's face and it was soaked with tears.

Sorry, sorry, I was a bad girl to make you cry, she said, panicked.

He rolled over to cover his tearful eyes. *God knows in my heart I must have known this was no accident, and I must have wanted it this way,* he anguished in between sobs.

For the first time he spoke to her of death. She knew they had shared a secret. Like a winner, she knew, too, she had a hold on him. She had turned fifteen and the game was far too exciting and she was more than ready to discover adulthood. Yet he kept crying for days and said he wanted to die for betraying her family's trust and spoiling her innocence such that she should be sent home. Her real home, earlier than he had planned.

Then he fled from her, heading down south to join his wife, leaving her with the housekeeper who prepared for her to cross the ocean.

Before her departure, he took her back to the St. Germain des Pres townhouse and then to *Le Jardin de Luxembourg*. No more pony rides. They strolled the garden, sat on a bench among the pigeons and falling leaves. He recited contemporary poems by Jacques Prevert.

Les feuilles mortes qui se ramassent a la peine...
Toi, qui m'aimais...
Moi, qui t'aimais...

The poem spoke of love. She stood barely below his chest, light like a bird. At the Luxembourg garden, inside the black iron gate that separated nature from the bubbling streets of fashionable Paris, she began to understand the fate of falling leaves like those who left their home. Leaves descending from treetops, only to reach uncertainty and then be crushed by the callous steps of humans. She told him falling leaves in autumn Paris was tragic beauty.

What does a young girl know about tragic beauty? he asked, with raised brows. *What happened between us, ma cherie, is tragic beauty,* he said mournfully.

He said loving poetry meant she was about to become a young woman, bidding farewell to childhood, like young leaves maturing for fall. If growing up meant good bye, Adieu, and good morning sadness bonjour tristesse, then let me be a child forever, she said. He still had not understood her words.

She had kicked off her shoes and tiptoed her tiny steps over the bed of leaves and imagined them crying under each step. Looking back, she caught his eyes gazing at her naked heels.

Tes pas enfants de mon silence. T'en souviens tu de mes pieds nus? Your childlike steps...My silence...Remember my naked heels?

Why do I have to move from here to there, she wondered, *only to destroy the fragility underneath my feet?* She thought of the trip back home. Her parents had written about the national literature contest, the debate team, even a teenage beauty pageant, and national scholarships, including one to Sorbonne. A plane would depart from Charles De Gaulle toward all of these splendid things. And it was just a beginning for a future so bright any young girl would have been envious.

"*O clemens; O pia; O dulcis Virgo Maria.* Oh sweet Virgin Mary have mercy, have pity on us. Our weakness, our vulnerability and fragility in the wretchedness of our life. Your sacredness, your beauty, your purity, in the holiness of your light."

The music died down. The applause began and then extinguished. The black-clad men and women of the choir turned a certain way and left the stage section by section, and Constance beamed on the conductor stand with satisfaction.

Never rush off stage. In singing, never rush anywhere, he had said.

Rush. I had turned thirty five safely in America, yet all I wanted to do was rush so that nothing good could be taken away from me again. Someone handed me a rose back stage, and a few choir members were talking about late night tea in Greenwich Village or Soho.

I said yes, yes, desperately wanting to rush, hearing again in my mind the sound of a helicopter roaring on top of a building in central Saigon decades ago.

I heard, too, the French manager of the Continental Hotel in Saigon yelling "*putains, putains,*" to those young Vietnamese women wearing miniskirts and platform shoes, with their mascara running down their blotted cheeks in the heat of April 1975.

In historic April 1975, I had gone to the Continental Hotel by myself to meet a man and beg for his help. Later on, I thought by starting a new American life with Christopher Sanders, I could accept and forget.

14. Refugees in Diamondale

The summer of 1975 was a long, drugged sleep. I woke up one day and Vietnam had been miraculously replaced with America. I had boarded one of the last flights out atop the U.S. embassy by myself and months later, reunited with my family in Ft. Chaffee, Arkansas, one of the resettlement camps. We settled in Diamondale, a small town in southern Illinois. Diamondale was no diamond, its rural sleepiness perked up only with the college football and basketball games, or weekend sales at the K-Mart on Main Street. Commerce included a Steak and Ale and a Holiday Inn near the tiny airport that provided the only airway to the major metropolitan area of Chicago, and just enough shops and restaurants to serve some 30,000 inhabitants, about 25,000 of whom were college students at Southern Illinois State University.

In the beginning, while my parents were looking for jobs, the sponsoring Lutheran Church let us live in an old house in a mixed neighborhood, on a street full of big, old pecan trees. The house, provided rent-free, was old enough to incur all kinds of heat and air-conditioning problems. Parents and children cramped into the old little house. We were just thankful for a roof over our head until we could afford our own place.

I thought then I had survived.

Yet in Diamondale, I kept recalling scenes of the Continental Hotel in downtown Saigon, the hairy arms and legs of a man I hardly knew, and the infirmaries in Guam, together with the faces of Red Cross workers, military nurses and doctors, and church volunteers. Finally, the scene of myself lying alone on the beach of Guam island on a starry night, listening to the waves of the sea, crying to myself and blaming God. Those days I was not sure whether my family had safety left Saigon, so I kept strolling the beaches of Guam by myself until my feet turned sore and my eyes blanked out. Only then would I lie down on the hot sand and stare into the sky.

One night in Guam, after strolling the beach in despair, I stabbed myself with a mess hall fork. My memory of what happened thereafter became spotty.

In Diamondale, I withdrew into my own world, stopped talking to my parents and siblings, and took a waitress job at the town's only Chinese restaurant, where greasy chow mein and ready-made sweet and sour pork were considered the house specialties. I postponed all plans to go to college until my parents could save enough money for a better life.

We had not had any snow in late November, but the roads of Diamondale were icy, and the trees had lost all their leaves, bringing back sad memories of Paris. I got home around eleven from my waitress job that night. My sister Mi-Chau opened the door, her cat eyes lit up:

"Guess who's here! *Tonton* Andre!"

So he had come to find me, but perhaps it was all too late. Perhaps he was thinner. Perhaps he had aged some. Perhaps his thick, wavy brown hair had thinned out, making his forehead higher. Perhaps more lines had appeared around his beautiful brown eyes. My palpitating state of mind rejected all details. I saw him as I had seen him those days in Paris.

"Oh, Si, you have...grown so much," Andre said, his arms hanging nervously on both sides of him as though they needed to reach out. His eyes sparkled with unspoken messages and the surreptitiousness of an accomplice. It was the first time since the incident in Paris that he faced me in the company of my parents.

It was an awkward moment. I spoke very little, fearful that my parents would detect my uneasiness.

He came up to me and wanted to embrace, the French way. The verb "embracer" meant a kiss as well as a hug. So I hugged him and kissed him on his cheeks. Since the time in Paris, my breasts had fully developed, and I blushed when his arms slightly brushed upon them.

I turned away from him, coldly told my parents I was very tired from my job and would like to go to my room. My brother Pi was dancing around Andre.

"*Tonton* Andre, would you play pony with me? Would you take me to Paris?" Pi beamed.

I went to my room and changed into a nightshirt. I heard the door moving, and pretended to bury my face into the pillow.

"What is wrong, Si?" My mother sat down by the bed.

"Nothing."

My mother's eyes were sad. They had been sad since our departure from Vietnam. She and I avoided talking about Grandma Que, who stayed behind.

"Andre and Dominique are getting a divorce," my mother sighed, pausing to test my reaction. "Dominique is talking to publishers now. She wants to write a book on Indochina. How ridiculous, the woman was barely there. Now that South Vietnam has fallen, everybody wants to write a book about us."

She stroked my hair. "Andre has talked to us. If you want a Christmas vacation in Paris, you can go with him."

"No," I said feebly.

"I have always known," my mother said gravely. "Only your father is blind. Back then, I took a chance sending you to Paris because I knew how badly you wanted to go."

I leaned against the headboard, puzzled.

"You are grown now, and he is about to be free. Go with him if you want. He is a good man. But he is twice your age."

I sat still. What exactly did my mother know?

There was one thing she could not have known: The Continental Hotel. The man there was more than twice my age.

15. That day in April

Five days before the fall of Saigon, I stood hours in the sun before I entered the hotel. For a moment I could not read the room number, two hundred and ten, engraved on the door. The room belonged to an American journalist, Christopher Sanders, a friend of my father's. When I entered, he was in his bathrobe, dictating into a tape recorder.

The man looked up from the desk and asked, "Room Service?"

I said no, I had come on my own.

He asked if I was sent by the Embasssy. I said, no.

Irritated and impatient, he asked who I was.

I stood on *escapin* high-heels, in my best *ao dai*, made for ceremonial occasions, with its dignified high collar, black satin and embroidered golden dragons. My father was at home sleeping in exhaustion. For days he had been running around town looking for a way out. From the Defense Attache's Office to various embassies. He had gone home defeated. Finally my mother said, *sleep, my dear, take a nap.* She got him a hot towel. Made him a lemon soda. I watched them. I saw despair and panic written on their face. So I said, *let me try, leave everything to me. After all I am the oldest daughter and speak fluent English.*

I introduced myself to Mr. Sanders. I was Hope's oldest daughter. Hope, the nickname this man had given to my father, was the American equivalent of *L'Espoir,* the penname my father had taken durrng his college days at Sorbonne. My father, the college professor at the Faculty of Letters, University of Saigon, had become a stringer for the Associated Press. My father who had helped build this man's reporting career in the country. The man's face softened only slightly at the mentioning of my father's nickname.

"I know," he said, "you want a way out of Vietnam. There's nothing I can do."

"Mr. Sanders," I said, "I am begging you. Those people from the North who will be coming out of the Cu Chi tunnel—they don't like us. French-educated professor. Informer for the Americans. Bourgeois. Annamese aristocrat. We stand for what the people from the North have been trying to destroy. I won't watch my father sent to a communist jail. I have teenage siblings who need a future elsewhere. My mother is a fragile woman who loves to plant flowers and faints in times of crisis!"

He pointed out the high window to Saigon harbor. His pale skin looked worn from watching the devastation mount around him. He suggested I try the sea merchants who were selling spaces on their boats, at ten gold taels or so per head. He must have known we did not have that kind of money.

I offered him the two ivory plaques, made out of elephant tusks thousands of years old, one had belonged to *nhat pham trieu dinh, hong lo tu khanh*, a mandarin of the first rank of the royal court, and the other one belonging to an admiral of the royal fleet. I offered him the luscious green jade phoenix, once held by a royal concubine of the Nguyen Dynasty.

Grandma Que had removed these items from the altar and gave them to me. I told her I had to go seek a way out of Vietnam, before the Communists came in.

"Go, child," she said, "Westerners like antiques." For her to part with these items meant we faced a matter of life and death.

The man refused the gifts, embarrassed, as I had expected he would. Sanders told me to go home and wait with my father.

I had heard the hotel manager screaming at the throngs of desperate bar girls waiting in the lobby for their American boyfriends to get them a seat on the last airlifts. They were all in bell bottoms and mini-skirts and platform shoes, with their fake eyelashes, foam enhancers inside their bras, and all that heavy makeup and broken English. *"Putains, Putains,"* the manager waved his arms, pushing them back from the stairs.

"At any moment," said Mr. Sanders, "with a signal from Washington, Voice of America will play White Christmas, and all U.S. personnel are to report immediately to the Embassy. I'm supposed to be here twenty four hours a day, around the clock, waiting for the tune of White Christmas over the radio, to cover the end of the war. My nerves are raw..."

"All you need to do is to put us on the plane," I said, cutting him off. "Tell your boss in America I am your wife. Tell them anything, anything. Take us to America and I'll be your maid. I'll sweep your floor. I'll do anything. Either I stay here with you, or I go into another room. Any room. I'll find myself another American man and make my offer to him. A GI, perhaps..."

Mr. Sanders looked down at the floor. "No please, don't do that," he said quietly.

The floor was grey marble, cold even in the April heat. His eyes traveled back up to my face, lingering along the curves of the gold dragons around my waist.

Numbly, I took off my *escapin* shoes, held them in my hands, and walked barefoot on the marble to where he was standing. The cold spread up my legs through the tendons in my ankles. I kneeled down in front of him and put down the shoes on the marble floor. I began to unbutton my *ao dai.*

"You make it very difficult for me, *Mademoiselle.* You are exquisite," he said.

16. Winter in Diamondale

I came out of my room. The old house had no separate dining room and we used an old, chipped dining set as living room furniture. Andre and my father were sitting at the table. I stood behind the door to the den and listened. Andre's voice was like a taut wire.

"Keep this check, for Si's college education."

"My daughters are smart," my father said. "They can get scholarships."

"What's wrong with getting a little more?"

"I work, and my wife works. We are not used to charity."

"It isn't charity. It's my responsibility."

"Your responsibility? If you meant the Foucault-Thuan Thanh saga and family feud, it's stale."

"Then take it from a friend. Or a former student. You were once my teacher."

"Maybe your money should go to my in-laws in Vietnam. My mother-in-law, Ms. Que."

"I can have a separate sum set up for that. But the money can't get to them now. My contacts said they can't find Ms. Que, either in Hue or Saigon."

"I fully intend for Si to go to college, no matter what," my father continued. "She'll get out, on fast track, hopefully to get a job and help us."

"I think she ought to sing," Andre said.

"Don't be a bad influence, Andre. Don't talk to her about singing. It's all over now. The country fell. What she must have is a college education that leads to a job."

"What if I bring her to France? She'll go to Sorbonne or do

whatever she wants to do, whether marketable or not. You won't have to worry about her for the rest of her life. I'll take care of everything."

I looked out from behind the door. My father was sipping a cup of tea, that same habit from the garden of the old days. Andre was staring nervously at his own hands.

"Si is no longer a child, Andre, she is a young woman now, resourceful, courageous, and she can take care of herself. She brought us out of Vietnam."

"What?" The frown on Andre's face was getting more pronounced.

"While we were still trying to contact you in Paris for help to leave Saigon, she went out and secured a list from the American Defense Attache's office from some friend of hers at the College of Law. She refused to tell us who. The list had the names of our whole immediate family and secured our access to Tan Son Nhat airport. A grandmother was not considered part of the immediate family, so the list did not include my mother-in-law. So, Si stayed on in Saigon to get her grandmother. But Ms. Que refused to leave, and Si left on one of the last helicopters."

"C'est...extraordinaire," Andre said, twisting his fingers together.

"Stop talking about me!" I yelled, jumped out of my hiding space, and ran outside.

"Si, stop!" Andre ran after me.

I heard my mother's voice: "Andre, here is a coat for her."

My father yelled: "Ignore her, she's out of line!"

I leaned against one of the tall pecan trees that bordered the street. It was freezing cold, and I was wearing only a nightshirt and socks.

A pair of arms took me in, put a coat over me. Andre turned me around and I found the same shoulders and chest, smelled the same familiar musky smell from the man I had long desired.

"I wish you would go away," I stammered.

"I know you are upset, bebe. It was hard. But many others are in a worse position than you."

"That's not it," I managed to push out a feeble protest in quiet resignation.

"I know, you lost your scholarship, your plans, going to the university of your choice."

"You don't understand! I am not Dominique, but everyone in Saigon said I was beautiful. I had nothing else to go by."

He held my hands together.

"For all these years since you left Paris I haven't been able to sleep well. My marriage is over."

"That's not what I meant. Don't worry, my parents don't know what happened in Paris. No one blamed you."

"But I'm ready to tell your parents, Si, all this happened for a reason. We can be together, get married."

White flakes began to fall from the sky. All I see here is snow, white like death, I told myself.

"I want to be left alone," I stuttered in the wind, my teeth clapping together. "I can't marry you, Andre. You abandoned me on the final days. You were in Paris with Dominique."

He let go of me. Silence ensued. The flakes were falling over my hair. I did not have shoes on, so my feet were trembling. He picked me up and walked, as on that day on the streets of Roma. He stopped at a street light next to a tall pecan tree. He sat down, leaning against the light pole and I was in his lap. Snow flakes were all over his brown hair and pale face.

"You've grown up and you don't like me any more, Si?"

Oh, how could I not like him? All the time in the Continental Hotel I kept thinking of him. America and Gerald Ford had saved some 150,000 South Vietnamese by airlift. I was among those lucky ones, but somehow they had not saved me.

"D'accord. You don't have to like me. We won't get married then. But come with me to France. For a better future. Here, you are in the middle of nowhere. It's the rural midwest. People don't understand your culture here. Your father doesn't have a real job. His fellowship at the university hardly pays enough and it will expire soon. Your mother works in a factory."

"I can't," I spoke with exhaustion.

"In Paris, you can have your own friends. I won't touch you. You'll meet some boy your age. You can sing."

"There won't be any boys. *Andre, il y a quelque chose que je dois te raconter. Avril 1975...*"

The nausea that once struck me down on the beach of Guam

returned to me temporarily, and I heard again the voice of the kind-hearted Red Cross nurse who had found me and brought me to the infirmary.

You've hurt yourself, Miss. You stabbed yourself with a mess hall fork. You can't be self-destructive, Miss. Remember, you are pregnant, Miss. Where is the father of your baby? Is he still in Saigon, Miss?

Too many questions asked of Miss. After all the things Miss had done to get her family out of the country, Miss was alone, knowing not whether her family had safely escaped. Then the nausea came, and Miss wanted to die. Why couldn't you leave her alone to die, Madame Red Cross? So I told the nurse I had no husband and wanted no baby.

My stomach must have been dancing with the snow of Diamondale when I bent over Andre's arm, like a piece of silk over a wire, and I heard myself speak. The kind Red Cross nurse had stayed with me all throughout my nightmare.

You will have more babies later, later, when you are ready...

She had stroked my hair. Despite her soothing voice, her green eyes remained blank with no real sign of empathy, and I went on with my monologue.

I'm a Buddhist who went to a French Catholic school, dear Madame Red Cross Nurse. For me, a Buddhist girl, life begins at conception and sins begin with thoughts, not action.

I wiped the snow off my face and blurted out to Andre strings of words, without breaths in between. I went on and on. But his face was blank like that Red Cross nurse. He had not understood a word. I spoke in a marathon. Completely in Vietnamese.

"Slow down, *bebe*. Tell me, in English, in French, please; my Vietnamese isn't good enough anymore..."

He picked me up and walked toward the house. It was snowing heavily and we would have died together in the cold if I had continued telling him my secret. He was carrying me like a small child, just like the old days in Rome. When I looked up, I could see the black sky and thousands of whirling flakes.

All of a sudden I realized I was in a different place. I wanted to start all over again on this land of wonders. The past could vanish with the name of a republic that had lost a war.

I looked up at him, deep into the brown eyes I had come to

love.

"Andre, there has been someone else in my life. Even my parents don't know. Five days before the fall of Saigon, I was married to an American journalist. He got most of my family out. I am indebted to him. I tried to pick up my grandmother on the way to the Embassy, but she locked herself inside the house and refused to leave, fearing she would jeopardize my chance of leaving, since she was not on the list... It's just a matter of time before I have to go to him. He's waiting for me in New York City."

In the morning, my father was to give Andre a ride to the airport. My mother was frying eggs in the kitchen for breakfast, and my father was reading the St. Louis *Post Dispatch*. I had stayed in the bathroom for a long time, putting on eyeshadow to cover up my puffy eyes. Instead of my routine outfit of jeans and sweater, I put on a pullover and a long skirt. Part of me still wanted to be pretty for him.

"What's that stuff on your eyes? You don't need makeup," my mother said. "You see what America has done to her already, Andre?"

"I don't know when I will see *mes amis* again," he replied, looking at me.

"Oh, don't be sentimental, Andre. We just lost a country, but we are still living."

My father put the newspaper down. Andre looked haggard, with dark circles under his eyes and disheveled hair.

"I stayed up writing a poem. I'll leave it with Si. It's meant to be her birthday present," he said, handing me an envelope.

"Cool," Mi-Chau said, chewing on a piece of toast.

"It's a temporary present, Si. The real one for your next birthday will be coming soon. What about an apartment in Paris, overlooking Champs Elysees? It will be yours whenever you want to visit."

"Thank you, but I'm very busy here."

Soon, it was time for Andre to go to the airport. My father had gone outside to wipe off snow from the car. Andre and I were alone, together, for a fleeting moment.

"Will you practice singing again, Si?"

I tried to smile.

"Please, think about what I've said. *Au revoir, mon Indochine.*"

And then he was gone.

17. His Black Rose

I sat at the dining table, with Andre's envelope in my hand. I opened it. The poem fell out, together with a cashier's check for twenty thousand dollars.

I looked at the poem. It was written in French, in free verse, abstract and vague. It described a maiden who sang, hoping to achieve a mythical voice. One day in singing, she turned into a black rose.

The black rose. Those three words struck a core of familiarity in my confused head, reviving images of the art studio on the eighth floor of number thirteen, *Rue* St. Jean Baptiste de la Salle. I saw the young girl sitting in a bath tub, crying. I saw Andre leaning against the door frame, turning his head away. *My black rose,* he called her to calm the young girl's black mood. When she calmed down, he explained that the black rose was a type of flower that existed only in one's imagination. There was no such thing as a black rose in life.

I was brought back to Diamondale when I heard footsteps and my mother appeared at the door. I hurriedly pretended to sip on my coffee. I skipped blocks of stanzas in Andre's poem and shifted my eyes to the last line before the piece of paper fell onto the carpeted floor. I had just caught sight of the Latin phrase.

Nec amo, nec tussi celatur. Love is like a cough. Cannot be hidden.

I stayed up that night and scrutinized myself in the mirror. My body had filled up in the right places. The curves had matured and there was no more trace of the slender teenager who wandered the streets of St. Germain des Pres and asked to be carried in Rome.

When I finally dozed off I dreamt of Andre. I felt his hot breath on my skin, and then we were both swimming in a warm ocean. I was wide open and engulfed the ocean and Andre in me.

When I woke up, I could still taste the saltiness of the ocean. The images and sensations of Paris in 1970 revived. His touch, his feel, the contours of his body, the fuzzy hair on his skin. My mind drifted to the fresh air of the South of France and the greeneries of French country roads, the vibrating sounds emanating from the grandiose churches of Roma. Finally, my wandering mind stopped upon the panoramic view of Paris with its peaking Tour Eiffel, piercing the sky, towering over the balcony of *Numero treize, Rue* St. Jean Baptiste de la Salle. Night had fallen over the balcony of the art studio. It all first happened in Paris where he mentioned to me his black rose for the first time.

I read Andre's poem, word by word.

Toward the end of the poem, the black rose was destined to wilt. So before the moment of wilting, the black rose asked the poet — the narrator— to peel off all petals and preserve them inside his poem collection. The poet agreed and began peeling. Fragrance emanated and sensations heightened at the tips of his fingers, upon his touch. Finally, the black rose disappeared. What remained of her were dried petals, nestled between pages of poetry.

I did not just read, I savored his words.

I felt feverish alongside my inner thighs. I tossed and turned on the floor of the tiny bathroom as though a pair of brown eyes were focusing on me. Every part of me was being peeled off. Every petal of his black rose corresponded with every part of me. My hands touched and felt as the pair of eyes instructed and dictated. I reached a dimension too secretive, too private, a newness of self I had never experienced. I became the silk worm my great-grandmother had become, weaving the most beautiful fabric for Annam.

I lay bare, like that silk worm ruthlessly removed from all those silk threads—product of its own creation, acknowledging the naked truth about itself.

Since those days in Paris, my mind had created a maidenform —the sacred place saved for Andre. That night in Diamondale, crawling on the bathroom floor, I let Andre's poem break the maidenform. In the tiny bathroom, I became drunk in the memory of the obsessive brown eyes affixed upon me outside the window in Saigon's District Eight, when I was tring to reach the high A note. I relived the moment of a once-in-a-lifetime passion so consumed I had to lose myself. Unable to refuse. Or resist.

With Andre's poem in my hands, I lay drowned in remembrance.

But the passion of Andre's words soon fell apart; the chill returned to me when memories of April, 1975, crept back into my head. In the Continental Hotel, I had kept my eyes to the room's grey marble floor. In the U.S military infirmary on Guam Island, I had grabbed the cold headboard of the narrow iron bed, and there was no one dear to hold my hand, except the kind Red Cross nurse.

I got out of bed and packed. I took out the business card bearing the emblem of the Associated Press, on which the man in the Continental Hotel had written down his address in New York City. I had carried the business card with me all through the exodus. Quietly I planned my life. I hardly knew him, yet he bore my shame. He owed me the secret we shared. In Guam, when I rid myself of his baby, I had sinned, since in the Buddhist faith, life began at conception. I thought that somehow by facing my shame and my crime head on, I could regain my peace. He had the jade phoenix and the ivory plaques that belonged to Grandma Que's ancestral altar — the essence of her life. I had turned them over to him that day in April. On the death bed of a city.

My sister Mi-Chau and I shared a bedroom, and I tiptoed around carefully so I would not wake her up. I wrote a long letter to my parents explaining everything that had happened in Saigon, in Guam, and the future I planned for myself in New York City. I put the letter inside an envelope, together with Andre's cashier's check, and sealed it. I went through my pocket and wallet and got all the cash together for a one-way bus ride to New York City.

Life decisions made in crisis could happen in a split second, with no real effort at rationalization or justification. I felt compelled to reunite with my accomplice, the only witness to the selling of my body in exchange for a ticket to America. I thought somehow by facing my shame head on, I could regain my peace.

Later on, that course of life was defined as my success. The achievement of my American dream. Beneath that success were the seeds of resentment.

That next morning, in the winter of 1975, I took a bus ride from Diamondale, Illinois, to New York City and reunited with Christopher Sanders, much to his surprise. He had not expected to see me show up at his door step.

During the first year of our cohabitation, I kept seeing myself standing before the Vietnamese judge in Saigon. The judge had looked at me with pleading eyes, telling me again and again that if he signed the marriage certificate without questioning, he would want me to procure a way for him and his family, somehow, to go to America, too, since as a judge, he would surely be persecuted by the Communists. The taxi driver who took Christopher and me to the precinct for the hasty marriage ceremony waited for us outside, and he, too, pleaded for me to help him leave the country. That day in Saigon, I had gotten sick during the ceremony, and Christopher had to hold me up when we exited the judge's office. I had covered my face until I entered the taxi, citing the harsh sunshine as an excuse. In fact, I thought that seeing me with Christopher that day in April outside the precinct, all Saigonese must have known what went on in the Continental Hotel—what I had to do to secure myself the ticket out of the country.

In New York, as Mrs. Sanders, I never had to take another a waitress job. A strange, unexplained bond developed between us, despite my deliberate avoidance of communication, and in so many ways, Christopher became my security blanket, and the bridge to my American dream. As Mrs. Sanders, I escaped my Vietnamese identity, in which the haunting memory of my childhood and Andre always existed. I no longer thought of Christopher as the man who shared my secret in the Continental Hotel, but rather as my husband of convenience.

Despite my denial, part of me always wanted to follow Andre's footsteps, so I made my best efforts to be admitted to Columbia University and thought of the law as a career. I succeeded, and did not stop there. After graduating from Columbia with a business degree, I went onto law school. I passed the New York Bar and became the first Vietnamese refugee hired by a Wall Street law firm. I specialized in mergers and acquisitions, and remained Christopher's wife until he succumbed to cancer in 1985. He died at age fifty-five. I was then only thirty years of age, bearing the clammed heart of a young widow unaffected by the loss of love, because she was not in love.

When Christopher's cancer had put us in separate bedrooms, part of me had silently celebrated. Yet I nursed him through long days in the hospital with the dedication of a devoted wife, frequently bringing my work to the hospital to read, watching nurses sedate him with morphine, and staying with him at the hospices during the final hours. My dedication won me the approval of his family members, who, prior to his death, had never accepted me as Christopher's Vietnamese "mail bride." That mail bride attended her husband's funeral with a tearless and stoic countenance. After the funeral, I did not eat for days, consumed with the guilt for not loving him.

Christopher's death added little to the void that already existed. In the first year after his death, I made it a habit to bring flowers to his grave and talk to him. In one of these gravesite monologues, I finally told Christopher about our baby whom I had killed, and asked both father and child for forgiveness. At some point during the following year, the flower habit and visits stopped altogether. My late thirties became the debut for a new, superficial life. I dated business acquaintances and other lawyers, all good-looking, healthy, cheerful, and successful men. Many were Christopher's age. A few were younger than I. No one looked like Andre or reminded me of him. One by one, they came and went. I went to dinners with them, lay down with them, took off my clothes, smelled toothpaste or coffee or cognac on their lustful breath and let them push themselves onto me. I gave them the language of ardor, but never of love, passion or romanticism, always conscious of the division between my heart and my flesh, painfully realizing that for years I had constructed a different kind of maidenform for myself.

I called it the perfect Americanization of a woman without a soul. I let America brainwash me with its pop culture, the yuppy lifestyle of the eighties, New York City's fashion, business hype, and fast-paced materialism. To insulate myself from the memory of my years with Christopher and his illness, I purchased a suburban house in New Jersey while keeping a small apartment in Manhattan. There were also purchases of a new luxury car for the commute, antique furniture, artwork, crystals, and china. There were all kinds of trips to make for business and pleasure, although I consciously stayed away from Paris. There were also Thanksgiving, Christmas, Fourth of July, and other American holidays. Superficial friendships and business networking. Power lunches and breakfasts and shopping sprees at Saks, Bloomingdale's, and Bergdorf. The corporate ladder to climb, the partnership track to grab, clients to please, and money to be made in the practice.

18. Rendezvous in New York City

At the beginning of 1990, the year of my thirty-fifth birthday, I heard from Andre for the first time after an absence of fifteen years since that snowy night in November of 1975. His letter was short:

"Si, for years I have never stopped thinking about you. Kept in touch with your mother occasionally, enough to know about your graduation from Columbia Law. If you are unattached, please consider going back to Vietnam for a visit with me, now that the government has opened doors to the West. Andre."

I knew realistically I could not join him. My law practice filled up my days, hours, and minutes. So I wrote him back, despondent and full of regret, asking him if he could delay the trip. I kept writing him in Paris. There was never a reply.

I heard from Andre again that same year, this time by phone, about two months before my thirty-fifth birthday in November. The phone call was made from Vietnam. He had made the trip without me.

The phone line was frequently interrupted with static, and obviously our conversation was monitored by the operator. I could hear clicking noises and even the operator's voice cutting in occasionally.

"It's probably the government," Andre said.

He sounded like a stranger, his voice feeble and nervous. Occasionally he lost his train of thought as though it were hard for him to concentrate. Words got caught in my throat and I, too, had difficulty expressing myself. Still calling me "bebe," he asked whether I was involved with anyone. No, no, no one, I said.

He asked to spend time with me, upon his return from Vietnam, assuring me that there were good reasons why he had never replied to any of my letters. On the way from Vietnam back to Paris, he would stop by New York. There would be so much to tell, and share.

So we made a date to meet in New York City. We blocked out a week. He said he would call at the beginning of that week, once he got to New York City. We would have the whole week to ourselves.

In the following days, I relived the sensations of my life in Vietnam and my teenage days in Paris. I went to my safe deposit box and retrieved Andre's poem on the black rose and cherished every single word. I recalled the moment of languor when I spread myself on the tiny bathroom floor reading about Andre's black rose. I dreamt of my hands resting in his hands, his breath on my nipples, our legs intertwined, and my long black hair falling all over his shoulder blades — all those things I had wanted to give to Andre, but never had the chance to bring to life.

In anticipation of our reunion, I looked for my copy of Baudelaire's "Fleurs du Mal" and read "Receuillement" until I fell asleep. I looked forward to Andre's arrival with the naivete and bubbling heart of a young girl falling in love for the first time, expecting to see his brown eyes, dashing smile and lean frame. I expected my angel to descend on my life again, this time, no longer with French dolls, but instead a suitcase of memories from the garden of my childhood.

Days passed in anticipation and nervousness. I dialed wrong phone numbers, made typos on documents, and forgot my keys. I even put on the wrong contact lenses and mismatched stockings. I caught myself staring at the empty space, smiling vaguely as I filled my head with thoughts about Andre. My heart palpitated from all the longing for Andre that could not be fulfilled or controlled with my daily routines. Sitting in a restaurant, a café, or walking through Saks Fifth Avenue or Central Park, I would perk up every time I saw a slim, virile-looking male with Mediterranian good looks and dark brown hair.

I existed in that high-strung state until the week of our rendezvous finally arrived, but Andre's phone call never came during the first part of the week, contrary to his promise.

For the entire week, I talked to my secretary and the building concierge constantly, leaving instructions on my whereabouts, inquiring about any unexpected visitors. At night, I listened to my answering machine over and over, hoping to hear his French accent and husky voice.

Finally by Thursday of that week, the wait wore out, and disappointment sank in. Then vibrant New York City became dead and dull like my law practice. On Thursday night, I plunged into a depression and had difficulty getting out of bed Friday morning. In sorrow, I concluded that he had decided to do without me. To make up for the void, on Friday morning I started making phone calls to route up a date for the weekend, hoping to recommence the fill-in-the-blank dating ritual with some superficial man who did not care.

By the end of business Friday, when all hopes had vanished, I gathered my strength to resume my routines. I was heading to the gym, down the hallway, when I heard my name being paged by the law firm's main receptionist.

"Ms. Sanders, please call your secretary. There is an emergency call for you," the pager said.

For a moment, I almost twisted my ankle on my high heel, as I hurriedly turned around and headed back to my office. Too anxious to finish the walk, I stopped at a secretary's station and picked up the line.

"Simone," my secretary said, "I am glad I caught you in time. There is a man on the line with some sort of a foreign accent. He sounded upset. He said you were supposed to meet him, and pleaded for me to find you. I think this must be the friend that you are anticipating."

"Will you put him through right away?" I said in one breath. "And please, don't cut him off..."

A moment passed, like an eternity, and I heard Andre's voice, too far away, too soft, too hesitant and too fragile to be real.

"Hello, Simone? Simone, Simone, Simone," he repeated my name several times as though to assure himself that I existed at the other end of the line. "Are you there, are you there at all?"

"Of course, I am here, Andre. I've been waiting all week," I paused, reproachingly. "Oh, Andre. I can't describe what it meant to wait for you." I heard myself sounding a little sullen and resentful, just like the old days, when I was still a little girl and could not get my way with him.

The past reeled through my head, our pony rides, the recitation of poetry, all such sweet time in my mother's blossoming garden of Hue and her patio in Saigon's District Eight. My hands trembled and I wanted to cry.

"Where have you been and when did you arrive in New York, Andre? Why didn't you call me sooner? I almost gave up." I shouted like a little girl.

He told me, almost incoherently, that he had been in New York all week, but had not felt well. So he had stayed in a small hotel, avoiding sunlight, and did not have the courage to call me.

"Please forgive me, Simone. Just forgive. May I see you now? I am leaving for Paris in the morning."

From his agitation I sensed that something had gone wrong. I did not know whether I should be joyous or sad. He had been here all week, and all we could have together was Friday night?

"Where are you now and where can we meet, Andre?" I tried to hide my disappointment and stay calm.

"I've been wandering around Manhattan all day thinking about what to do, Simone. About whether to see you, to tell you, all about things. All about me..." He sounded somewhat broken on the end of the line. "I am somewhere near Orchard and Delancey, right outside of Chinatown."

It was getting dark when I emerged from the subway station. My feet ached from all the running and walking in a rush. I dashed my eyes around to look for Andre. He was nowhere to be found. I stood by the subway entrance, on high heels, in a heavy cashmere coat. Another wait, just like eternity. I decided to walk around the block looking for him. Just before I started to move, a skinny old man approached me.

The man was gray and feeble, almost staggering in the cold evening hours of New York. I noticed the disheveled salt and pepper hair, and dark circles under bloodshot eyes that stared without looking, and looked without seeing. I instinctively moved away from the old man when he leaned forward, almost falling onto me with one skinny arm extending in an effort to touch. He lost the momentum and raised his eyes to meet mine. At first glance, I did not recognize him, until I backed away again and looked, from a distance, with a frown. He was holding a book in one hand.

Andre stood before me, but gone was the lean muscles of a young man. Hollow chest. Hollow cheeks. Hollow eye sockets. Tauter face. Wrinkled eyes, saddened by the realization that I had backed away.

It took a moment for me to get over the shock. I approached him and took his hand. It felt dry, trembling, and cold.

It was a time of awkward reacquaintance. I felt alien toward him. But gradually the bond of childhood somehow thickened and filled the space between us. In an instant, I realized how time could be too slow and too fast. In Hue and Saigon, I had frustratedly longed to grow inches taller so the top of my head could reach Andre's chest, and time was hatefully slow then. In adulthood, all of a sudden, when I failed to watch, the velocity of time swept away all youth, beauty, and vitality. Like Princess Mi-Nuong of the Vietnamese folklore, who had to see the man's ugly face that trapped the beautiful voice she loved, I had to see how time had damaged the beautiful image of a man.

"Andre," I babbled, "in 1975, I made a mistake. I should have gone with you to Paris."

He shook his head and put his hand over my mouth.

We spoke very little after that, just small sentences, but I could tell he was very depressed and agitated, as though a threshold had been reached and he was desperately holding on to me as an anchor. He said he had come to my building and spoken to the concierge, who told him I was at work. Like a madman, he had wandered around Manhattan for hours before he had the courage to call my office.

It was the irrational, desperate act of a dying fish gasping for air, a man wandering around Manhattan, in the early evening rush hour.

I asked him if he would want something to drink or eat, but he only wanted to walk. So we walked in the cold of a New York winter night. As we passed a row of brownstones, he stopped and held my face with his hands. People were passing by and he stood there, the lifeless eyes affixed to my face, his two hands awkwardly framing my cheekbones. He told me I was beautiful as he had always predicted, and that I would remain beautiful for a long time after he was gone.

And then he started talking as though he were reciting Baudelaire again, with such intensity it was hard to follow. He talked of those days in Paris, when, in between bouts of drinking, he had shut himself off from the world and a vibrant City of Light—in those moments, America, France and Indochina all rejected him and let him down. He talked about how his law practice had crumbled, how he had tried to get Dominique back, how manuscripts had been rejected and the motivation to work was reduced to zero, how the struggle was hard and the world and his friends all turned against him.

The book he wanted to write was never finished. He talked of how the Foucault brothers and sisters had bitterly fought over the division of property and estate, and how the Foucault empire had tumbled down, its connection to Indochina reduced to the past glory of a colonial industry.

He talked of his recent return to Vietnam, now an alien world run by the new comrades and foreign investors. He talked of how buildings were going up with Hong Kong style and semi-American luxury and comfort, and how the French architecture and charm that had persisted for a hundred years were gradually disappearing. How the greedy and poverty-stricken young women of Indochina who looked just like me had tried to get his money, how the new prostitutes of Vietnam had approached him and they were as young as I the day I descended from the Air France aircraft to rush into his arms in 1970. The new government had suspected and followed him. Vietnam was no longer a place of romantic tranquillity where, despite a devastating war in the jungles, deltas, and villages, he could sit in a garden and recite Baudelaire to a young Vietnamese girl who looked at him with adoring eyes.

He talked too of the Asian prostitutes of Pigalle with eyes that resembled the shape of a boat lying upside down on the white sand of a deserted beach, amber skin that smelled like the tropical rain over coconut palm leaves, and pointed breasts small enough to fit in his palm, smooth and taut like a sweet green mango. He talked of the rapid deterioration of health and good looks and spirits, so devastating that he no longer had the confidence to respond to my letters.

He talked of how he had composed his *Black Rose* in the longing for the smell and feel of my skin. How he had often relived the experience of number thirteen, *Rue* St. Jean Baptiste de la Salle, with the same surreal intensity, remembering always how it felt like when I spread my legs and climbed on to him in the dark. How he had smoked and drunk and wilted away, all the time dreaming of the darkness of my eyes and hair as though the image of me was but a hallucinated vision in opium smoke. He talked, too, of all of the longing for a time when I became a woman and could be his, with all the alluring darkness of the hot and humid summer nights in Indochina, where the blondness and coolness of his wife's hair and brows seemed so out of place.

"*Aimer et mourir. Au pays qui te ressemble.* Loving and dying. In a country resembling you."

He talked of the unfulfilled poet, of creativity and failure. How the emptiness was so immense and the destructiveness so terrifying they killed off the will to create. And then he kissed me, his hands lingering on my cashmere coat. I could feel he was shaking. It was first a small kiss on my cheek, and then he brought his mouth to mine, his lips nervously opened and grabbed on to mine. I could not breathe and then his darting tongue was parting my lips. It was as if he were trying to penetrate through, grasping what was left of life. The desperate neediness of someone who was close to death.

I yielded to his wish.

The moment seemed to last forever, yet I was too confused, fearful and overwhelmed by the course of events to feel anything real. The night was so cold and I was all covered up in the heavy coat, tired from walking on high heels, after the long day of hard law office work.

When he let go, he looked deep into my eyes. Terror rose in me because as I looked into his lifeless eyes I could no longer find images of the nocturnal butterflies of my mother's garden in Hue. He tumbled a little, waved to a cab and then disappeared inside it, leaving me with my own sadness of knowing the brown butterflies of my childhood, once hovering over my mother's tropical flower beds, were to be buried with the still image of an angel.

In kissing me, he had dropped his book and I picked it up, after his taxi had rolled on. It was a volume of Baudelaire's *Fleurs du Mal*.

"*Je t'aime, toujours,*" I said under my breath. "*Attends,*" my heart cried out to him, "*Ne me quitte pas. Avons nous une derniere chance?* Wait. Don't just leave me, Andre. Do we still have our last chance?"

But he could no longer hear me. Only I could hear the cry of my heart. I love you, always, Andre, no matter what.

That was the last time I saw Andre.

Again, I plunged into work and a superficial social life to make up for the loss. The nostalgia about Andre came back to me once, one early evening at the Metropolitan Museum of Art on Fifth Avenue and Eighty Second Street. I was strolling in the museum to relax after a major corporate acquisition closing, a long-drawn project that had kept me sleepless many a night.

I caught the eyes of a young man, looking at me.

For a moment, I stopped, tottered, and almost lost my balance, as though I were seeing, again, twenty six-year-old Andre walking under the magnolia tree of my childhood: dark hair, dark eyes, and an elegant, virile frame. But the young man's face did not have the romantic, melancholy touch of Andre's face. Mouth too full. Nose too long. The facial skin too coarse. The young man's countenance carried the earnest, mischievous look of a hungry animal looking to start a pursuit.

His brown eyes, however, were obsessive. He was eyeing me, his curvy mouth ready to pull into a flirtatious smile. He started a conversation, full of trite lines used a thousand times by his gender to lure a woman into a casual relationship. "My name is James. Have I met you somewhere?"

"I like art, don't you?" he continued.

"No," I told him. "I prefer dinosaurs to art," I answered, imagining stuffed dinosaurs on display among medieval paintings.

In an era of animal rights protection and activism, I was wearing a mink coat, vestige of my life as the companion of the late Christopher Sanders, part of New York City's old money. I leaned against a railing, the coat fell open and I displayed a glimpse of my naked thigh. I wore a short skirt and black stockings that stopped at mid-thigh. I looked twenty eight. The young man was staring. He wanted to buy me a cup of coffee.

At the sidewalk café, I discovered he would prefer reading reviews of books, rather than the books themselves. He would rather see action movies and thrillers than off-Broadway plays. He told me he wanted to write a sci-fi novel, a fantasy or a mystery. He claimed he could produce a novel in a month, having fully utilized his engineering background. Given twelve months of unemployment, he could produce twelve novels with no sweat.

He was everything Andre was not, but that day, I saw young Andre's face cutting against posters of Parisian scenes—the café-sitters of *Rive Gauche*. I looked into the brown eyes of a young man named James, someone I hardly knew, and found a sense of *deja vu*.

After we finished the coffee, I went home with him, some

studio apartment in some building on the west side of town. Young James was elated and proud when I lay myself down on his blue-striped bed sheet, the mink coat flung open. It had been too easy, he said sincerely, asking me again and again whether I would change my mind.

He did not know me, but we talked for a while about him, his hand travelling up my stockings. He tried but could not undo the snap of the garter belt, his fingers nervously and greedily moving away from it, up to the dark triangle above. I told him there was no hurry, and we kept on talking. He was half-Italian, had an engineering degree, and had never known a real Asian girl. He bragged about how he had travelled to Europe with a camera. And he was a fitness freak, always working out on his muscles, always watching out for his diet of vegetables and energy drinks, believing he would find himself, his fortune and beautiful girls that way.

I did not contradict him and began to undress. He wanted to watch. I took off my silk blouse and skirt, garter belt and stockings, and he asked that I leave the matching black lace bikini set on underneath the mink coat. It was an erotic fantasy of his, he said predictably. His hand fumbled underneath the black lace and I felt cold. So cold that I grabbed his wrist and told him to stop. I grabbed my purse next and ran.

I could not get the brown eyes and lashes and the Mediterranean features of this man named James out of my mind, so I called him and returned to his West Side apartment the following day, upon his promise that he would first show me his new computer system — the state of the art, one of his hobbies as well as that of the generation. This time, I had on a long, full skirt and a turtleneck sweater. When we got through with the computer, James stretched and casually laid down on his couch. I looked over and found Andre's eyes.

Beyond all control, I longed for the pony ride of childhood. I moved my leg alongside James' rib cage, although there was no desire in my heart. It was an aggressive invitation, because I was a woman and no longer a child. James grabbed the front of my turtleneck sweater with his clumsy and greedy fingers. His eyes lit up and he flashed a beautiful smile at me. A look of surprise, followed by a smile of misplaced confidence, reflecting the flirtatious knowledge that sooner or later he would be a lover.

I looked to James' square face and bluish chin, and found again the pair of beautiful, clear brown eyes under thick, curly lashes, which gave me peace. It was the same pair of cheerful eyes that had looked up at me when, in the tropical garden of Hue, I spread my legs and sat on a beautiful Western male — a man with a complex conscience and the spirit of a melancholy poet, a man who bore almost a hundred years of my history and a collective guilt upon his shoulders from the black-and-white photographs he had seen of Indochina, such that as a grown man, he had to become attached to a little Vietnamese girl. I had bent down and kissed him in the garden, before pain and anguish crept in. In that pair of eyes, I found myself — the clear, happy, compartmentalized look of innocence that dangerously approached ignorance, the selfishness of tender youth that could easily and unintendedly destroy the peaceful sanctity of childhood.

I kept going back to James' West Side apartment and making love to him because he looked like Andre, in a short-term relationship described at best as repeated one-night stands. Like most women, I closed my eyes during the act. Occasionally in the middle of love-making or the restful state of the aftermath, I would be struck with the terror of abandonment. So I opened my eyes to make sure Andre had not disappeared. I found, next to my face, those beautiful thick curly lashes, closed in contentment under languorous lids. I was peaceful again. But soon I quickly realized the lashes were James'. Sorrow swept through my limbs when I realized I had offered my body to a stranger who did not care why I did what I did.

And as I closed my eyes again, I painfully realized that with my consent, this stranger, a user of my body, was entitled to love me this way, a way I had never been able to offer to Andre.

19. The Phone Call

I was in my law office when I received my mother's letter telling me that my family had heard from Dominique. Dominique would like to talk to me about Andre. Holding my mother's letter in my hand, I looked out at Manhattan's sky from my office window. Something inside me signaled the warning that perhaps disaster had hit. Instinctively I fretted the moment I would have to call Paris. Yet, I could not understand the source of my anxiety. All of a sudden, I remembered Grandma Que's story about the Mystique Concubine's haunting anxiety. It was all about the Face of Brutality awaiting her outside her half-moon window of the ancient Violet City, the threatening power of uncontrollable fate.

In the days to come, could I, too, encounter the Face of Brutality in the daylight of New York City?

Constance announced the rehearsal schedule for the next concert series, with Haydn's "Paukenmesse" and Mozart's "Misericordias Domini KV 222." I had used the rehearsal schedule as an excuse to delay the phone call I would have to make to Paris. One Sunday night, I decided to stay in my Manhattan apartment, skip rehearsal, and order a pizza, knowing I could not go on avoiding what was evident.

I had moved the telephone from the night stand to the floor. The telephone sat on the hardwood floor, and I stared at it, twisting the cord around my wrist.

I got up to put a load of laundry in the washing machine. My heart raced and I could not concentrate. I kept sorting and resorting my dirty clothes. Folding, unfolding, and refolding bed sheets. Turning the dryer on and off. I tripped over the clothes basket. I spilled detergent on the hardwood floor. Finally, I dumped all of my clothes, dirty as well as clean ones, dry ones and wet ones, into the washer and closed the lid.

I went to my bedroom and dialed the Paris number my mother had forwarded in her letter, registered under the name Dominique Clemenceau.

"Allo, allo, qui est la?"

She sounded the same — the elegant Parisian accent and husky resonance.

"Parlez, s'il vous plait. Qui est la?"

I couldn't make a sound.

"Ecoute, toi, salaud."

She was getting impatient and vulgar. Typical Dominique. Cool, aloof, and elegant at times. Temperamental and crude at times.

"Tata Dominique," I finally uttered tiny sounds, *"C'est moi, Simone."*

I stuttered in rusty French, small courtesy sentences, carefully constructed.

A moment of silence ensued at the other end of the phone line, and then the Parisian accent sharpened:

"Simone, I knew you would call. It took longer than I thought."

I stared at the wandering patterns in the ceiling stucco.

"Aren't you going to ask, Simone? About the papers, Simone?"

She said *les papiers*. Some personal papers? If she meant the newspapers, she would have said *les journaux*.

"All those pictures of Indochina, Simone. The things he kept."

The ceiling was about to drop. I swallowed several times to keep it in place. *"Tata* Dominique, I don't know what papers you're talking about."

"I want to give you those papers. That's all."

Twenty one years ago, at times her Parisian accent could sound so sweet, when she was baking *petits beurres* or stirring her *soupe d'oignon*, forcing me to eat so I could quickly grow tall. All I ever wished then was to have a Parisian voice like her.

"He did it, Simone! Get it into your head. About a year ago," she yelled, "in November. And mind you, he was Catholic."

My head became the pillar to hold the ceiling in place. It would collapse on me, soon. Oh Simone, *poupee* Si, cutie Si, coquettish Si. Back to your laundry, Si. And then perhaps life would be normal again. My thoughts went back to my birthday last year. November of last year. My birth month; the year of my thirty fifth birthday. Where was I? What was I doing? Did I feel a stab in my gut? Did I feel anything at all? Life could have been hatefully normal over a year ago, on such a day, or a night.

Dominique was calling me a *poseur*, someone who posed, a pretender. The ceiling moved and became dozens of faces. The faces hanging over my head nodded in agreement.

"Ask, Simone. Ask how he did it. I am ready."

I felt the lump in my throat. I could not make a sound.

"Let me ask you then," she slowed down. "He went to America to see you, didn't he?"

"He was here," I said.

"I knew it. What did you do to him?"

"Nothing," I said.

"Liar! You fucked up his mind, again. You did a lot, Simone, even when you were still a child. He told me everything. What happened at Number 13 St. Jean Baptiste. I've known for so many years. Remember, I was his wife and his friend. I saw your eyes the first time in Hue. You were a child with eyes of a woman."

She was speaking all in English. I wished she would revert back to French, as I did not want to understand.

"The balcony?" I asked.

"No, Simone. There was no more balcony at *Rue* St. Jean Baptiste. Get it into your head. Come to Paris and check it out yourself. They renovated the building. And chopped off the Roman pillars."

She kept speaking, and I saw you, Andre, standing on the eighth floor balcony of number 13 *Rue* St. Jean Baptiste de la Salle, twenty one years ago. The morning after our fated night, you were climbing over the roman pillars. You were walking on the limestone railing, your arms stretching across to help you keep your balance, like an airplane. You were not looking down, although Paris must have spread herself below you, in the transparent white, gleaming sunlight. You were about to fly.

"Please don't jump, Andre," I had screamed that day in Paris. "I promise to be a good girl," I had cried out.

The "Dalida" record was playing inside. *"Les yeux battus la main triste et les joues blemes. Tu ne dors plus tu n'es que l'ombre de toi meme.* Those beaten eyes, the sad hand, and the ghastly cheeks. You don't sleep any more. You are just the shadow of yourself."

I kept yelling, but you couldn't hear me. You kept on walking, tiptoeing, balancing on the limestone railing. Away from me. The top of the Eiffel Tower was not too far away. Perhaps you were trying to catch it.

"Oh, please don't jump, Andre, please!" I could still hear my own voice shrieking.

I did not really want to know. But Dominique kept on speaking.

"Was it in the bathroom, or the bedroom, *Tata* Dominique?"

"*Oh mon Dieu*, that's what you want to know? Where it happened? Perverse. You are insane, Simone. When you came into my house," she continued, "you touched things that weren't yours. And he let you. With eyes of a woman, and poisonous hands, you touched and everything turned black."

Black, black, black, the last word duplicated itself, like a broken record.

The black rose.

20. Requiem in New York City

In my Manhattan apartment, I went to the washer and opened the lid. I looked inside the washer. Dry clothes. Wet clothes. Dirty clothes. Clean clothes. Socks and bed sheets. I kept putting more things in. Filling up the washer. My life was in it. I closed the lid. The familiar noise of the washing cycle numbed my eardrums.

I sat there, for hours. Perhaps Sunday night had passed. Slowly.

I saw it, Andre. I saw what happened.

You stood by the glass door. You were looking out at the stars and the moon. Perhaps it even snowed slightly. The lights of Paris filled the horizon, and the Eiffel Tower pierced the blackened sky. City of love. City of lights. You were watching, Andre. Simply watching the city of memory. You stood motionless. In a robe.

It was the same robe. Inside it was dark like this, Andre. Dark like my Manhattan room at this moment. There was no more balcony, she said. So you could not step outside to walk on the railings of the balcony. You were turning, Andre, toward the dark space inside. Leaving Paris to the thousand lights outside that glass door. I let you walk through that dark space. Alone.

Toward the bathroom. You kept on moving toward the bathroom.

That was where I had gone, Andre, at number thirteen *Rue* St. Jean Baptiste. I turned on the bath and I was cold. You went to the kitchen to boil water. You returned to fill the tub with warm water and scented soap.

Under the bubbles, I kept crying. I wanted to prove to you how ridiculous it was for the Parisians of *St. Germain des Pres* and the nuns at the music conservatory to mistake me for a twelve year-old child. But you had turned and walked away.

I stayed under bubbles for hours.

Finally, you came in and gave me a towel and told me there was nothing to fuss about. All it meant was the process of growing up. I threw the towel back at you. You looked away and left the bathroom in a hurry. When I cried again, you stood behind the door and told me I would have to wrap the towel around my bubbled body and stop being a child. I promised to be good and you reappeared and gave me a rose. I stopped crying. I was safe. I asked you what would happen to the rose. You said it dried up. And the rose turned black. I had something no one else had. I had a black rose.

You were inside the same bathroom.

Hold on to life, Andre, hold on and wait. For me.

I began to run. I ran toward you, Andre. To *Rue* St. Jean Baptiste de la Salle. I bumped into the concierge of my building.

I could hear him calling my name behind me. Ms. Simone. Ms. Simone.

Monday morning. Manhattan was awakening. It was no longer dark outside. The night lights were all extinguished, replaced by a gleaming sun. Thousands of New Yorkers were out on the street, beginning their hectic day all over the City. In and out of subway entrances. With their newspapers. Hot dogs. And bagels. They moved on. With life, Andre. Moving on. I kept running, in between them. I kept bumping into them. Some of them cursed. Others stared. Others did not notice.

It was dark, Andre, where you were. It was light and sunny, Andre, in Manhattan. But both places were cold. I was here and you were there. You were still rummaging in the dark.

Stop, my gorgeous Andre. Stop wrinkling. Stop aging. Stop going in there and rummaging. What were you looking for? All those black-and-white pictures of the faraway past, of a *L'Indochine* that obsessed the melancholy young boy of Paris? *L'Indochine* was gone and you were still looking.

I kept running.

I passed Bergdorf Goodman. Saks Fifth. Henri Bendel. Sixty-eighth street. The Ritz Carlton. I passed all the vibrant spots of Manhattan.

I screamed and held out my hands. I aggravated pedestrians. I antagonized busy New Yorkers. Still I could not get where I wanted to be. I couldn't reach you.

Wait, Andre, wait.

The blade.

You found the blade.

You took it and went from the bathroom into the bedroom.

In the bedroom.

You had laid still, panting, weeping, and I was still on top.

In confusion, I smiled my innocent yet deadly smile. I wanted to stand up, naked, hairless skin and raised nipples.

Precious Andre, why are you weeping?

I rolled and put a white pillow in between my legs. And I looked sideway at you, from the corner of my eyes. My eyes beamed. I rolled my childlike naked body over your weeping self. The slippery wetness made me frown. Hearing your agonizing sobs, even in sweet innocence, I was terrified to face what I had done.

But then, it was all too late.

In the dark, you were raising the blade.

I was still running. In Manhattan. Breathless. Blurred eyes. Dry mouth and empty stomach. My breath turned into smoke, Andre. It was cold here. And it was cold there.

No, Andre, No.

I stopped at the traffic light. Hurrying, impatient New Yorkers had to stop with me.

You hit the hardwood floor. You bent and curled up into a fetal position. Embracing your own wounds.

I bent, Andre, embracing my own wounds. It hurt where you hurt, Andre. I bent but it was not over for me. Somebody picked me up. The green light was on. And people around me moved.

Blood flowed and flowed, Andre. It flowed forever, until it could not flow any more. And then blood turned black. And frozen. Into the color and shape of the black rose.

There was a black rose, Andre, in the dark space where you lay.

Someone was dragging me on. A few people gathered around me. A few more. And then a circle was formed. Curious faces bent over me, separating me from New York City's sky. Curious faces, but not concerned faces. Whoever dragged me to the sidewalk must have passed by a New York hotdog stand. Or perhaps it was fresh pretzel and mustard. Smoke must have come out of the hot dog grill, or was it my breath, my sign of life? Life was all around me, and I smelled death.

Call an ambulance, someone said. Over my head.

Wait, Andre, why couldn't you wait?

21. Postcards

The package from Dominique arrived from Paris about a month later. That night, I emptied the contents onto the bed. Old black-and-white photographs and postcards, yellowish and curled at the edges and corners, cascaded down from the brown envelope. The postcard first in my hand was the picture of a costume-clad Vietnamese teenager, perhaps fourteen years of age. The Emperor boy. His brocade gown was embroidered with shapes of dragons, clouds, moons, suns, and stars. A metal belt pulled the cloth together around his waist. His boots were studded with gems. He wore a fitted crown, curved up on both sides of his head, marked in the center with a large gemstone. Swallowed in the grandeur of his clothes, the teenage boy stared uncomfortably at the camera, restricted in his armchair, lost and dazed in his environment. His gaze was defiant and stubborn, his lips tight and pouting. He did not smile.

The caption under the postcard said:

Coronation, Thuan Thanh, King of Annam

The small legend at the bottom of the postcard showed a credit line attributing the picture to the collection of Foucault Gallery, 53 Rue Jules-Ferry, Hanoi.

My hand reached for the largest postcard with gold trim, inside an intricate cover made out of silky fabric, the gathered layers of which were sewed together with red and gold thread. The ensemble of postcard and cover seemed so fragile and old as though they could immediately crumble under human touch. I raised the oversized postcard to my eyes. Surprisingly, from the feel underneath my fingers, I realized both the folded cover and the picture inside had been laminated with plastic. Someone in France who took care of the collection must have wanted to protect and preserve the special image.

The postcard consisted of two pictures of the same lovely woman. In the first picture, the woman sat sensuously in the middle of a carved lacquer divan, her naked back turning toward the camera, her hair woven into a chignon that hung low at the back of her neck. The strings of her camisole dropped down her hourglass back, accenting the smallness of her waist, which curved into the roundness of her hips like the silhouette of a cello. She turned halfway toward the camera, the corner of her eye glancing amorously at the photographer's lens. The pear shape of her perked breasts displayed alluringly underneath the soft camisole. A dozen of diminutive young men and women gathered around the divan, either kneeling or sitting on the floor. The men were dressed in traditional Vietnamese costumes at the turn of the century, the sheer organza fabric of their loose-fitting ao-dai's draping over their crisp, wide-legged pantaloons. The women, all petite and childlike, wore identical satin silk Vietnamese ao dai's, trousers, and gold pendants. Their hair was parted in the middle, sleekly combed and tied back in a bun. Their hands rested docilely in their laps, and they looked sideway, demure, shy and self-conscious before the camera.

The beautiful and stately woman who sat among her entourage had her naked feet dangling down the divan, her dainty toes almost touching the edge of an oval-shaped blue and white ceramic sink. Her two hands, bejewelled with numerous carved bracelets, grabbed the divan's edge.

In the second picture that occupied the remaining half of the oversized postcard, a closer view of the woman showed her upper body, her arms wrapping around her shoulders, covering up the shape of her breasts. Again, the strings of her camisole dangled down her naked back. As in the first photograph, she turned sideways, displaying the distinctive jawlines and elegant profile of her face.

The caption under the postcard said:
Un coup d'oeil, La Concubine Mystique du Roi Thuan Thanh —
A side glance, The Mystique Concubine of King Thuan Thanh.

I hurriedly went through the rest of the black-and-white photographs. The same woman in the postcard was featured again and again in various poses, both in long shot and in close-up. She stretched on the divan, either alone or among the group of costumed men and women who docilely gathered around her.

The next group of photographs showed scenes of various French chateaux, with their steep slate roofs and harmonious facades of pale stonework, their round corners underneath the spikes, reflecting over sparkling tranquil lakes and ponds and nestling among little poplars and willows, specimens of fine oaks, fertile meadows and striking green hills. Against those landscapes of castles, bushy trees and vast gleaming lakes, the same woman, dressed in Western attire, stood next to a stocky, whiskered Frenchman. In some of the pictures, they were holding hands. In other pictures of Paris cafés, the same woman, fashionably dressed in flapper style of the thirties,sat forlornly in an iron chair underneath café awnings. The same whiskered Frenchman stood behind her, either holding an umbrella or resting his hand on his thick waist.

I turned the scenes of France upside down and moved my shell-shocked eyes to the set of the immense lotus ponds and dainty curved roofs of the Violet City, savoring memories of my beloved Hue. Among these photographs, I found a portrait of the same woman.

I could see her face more clearly. In the portrait, the woman looked about forty years old, the trace of maturity and experience undeniably reflected in her stately gaze at the camera. Her dark hair was sleekly pulled back into a tight chignon behind the strong square jaw, which contrasted distinctly against the soft oval chin. The dainty neckline of her *ao dai*'s mandarin collar slightly opened in the middle. What was seen of her dress, around the delicate shoulder blades and over the roundness of her breasts, suggested a very fine, silky fabric. The face had become more mature and fuller, her eyes serene and sad. Gone was the amorous flirting with the camera. I scrutinized those widely opened eyes, watery and probing, too big and too deeply set to typify the slanting shapes of northern or eastern Asian eyes commonly found in the Koreans, Japanese, or Chinese.

I recognized my own eyes in those photographs. It was also the face. The woman had the same face as mine, as though I were in the portrait, only dressed a different way. I turned the picture over and read the handwriting in dark, blue ink on the back of the photograph, already smeared in several places:

Mon amour, ma reine, ma tendresse, ma douleur, torture de mon ame, crie de ma conscience, chagrin de mon coeur. SF.

My love, my queen, my tenderness, my pain, torture of my soul, cry of my conscience, chagrin of my heart, SF.

The handwriting was strong and fierce, the ascending strokes connecting together with grace and definitude, the descending strokes refusing to end, culminating in ink dots, already smeared and blurred with time.

I could not deny the reality that existed before I was born, the secrets I did not wish to know.

I pulled my strength together to overcome the shock, and browsed through the rest of the photographs. In a number of them, the same woman was seen with two identical little girls.

I picked up other photographs of the two little girls and tried to study their face. In one picture, the girls leaned cheerfully on both sides of the whiskered Frenchman, who was dressed in shorts and a khaki shirt as though he had just come back from a safari. The three of them stood in a Vietnamese garden full of tropical trees and landscaped bushes.

In another photograph, the girls wore traditional Vietnamese silk pajamas, posing demurely in a studio setting, their braided hair falling on both sides of their face, their almond eyes staring at the camera. There, I could see their facial features more clearly.

I saw, again, my own face on the two little girls. They looked just like the young me, the serene little girl who sat on the stairs in Tan Tan's photography studio in Hue.

My fingers trembled as I turned the picture over to look at the handwritings on the back:

Cong Chua An Nam: Huong Sam va Huong Que.
Ginseng and Cinnamon, the princesses of Annam

I fumbled next across a portrait photograph of a teenager, sweet and innocent, smiling with both her almond eyes and her heart-shaped lips, her long hair falling lusciously to her shoulder blade, the lapel of her pajama top accented with a strand of pearls. The back of the picture stated:

Nam Tran Cong Chua, Cong Tang Ton Nu Huong Que, 1920
The Princess of South Sea Pearl, Cinnamon Fragrance, 1920

It was a picture of Grandma Que, taken when she was fifteen.

But the face was mine, that sullen fourteen-year-old teenager who listened to Andre reciting Baudelaire in my mother's patio in Saigon.

Shivering, I turned off the light. For the rest of the night, I drifted in and out of the sceneries and images from four generations, hearing in my head the choral music of Beethoven's "Elegischer Gesang."

My lips mimed silently to the German lyric. *"Sanft wie du lebtest hast du vollendet..."* No eye weeps while your heavenly spirit returns home. Gently, gently as you lived, have you finished.

I mourned in silence for all those gentle departing souls that had made up my history.

Part Four

PART FIVE

Ombra mai fu di vegetabile
cara ed amabile, soave piu
(There never was a plant's shade
more dear, amiable and mild)
— G.F. Handel

Simone's Memoir (New Jersey, 1994)

1. House and Trees, Mother and Daughter

It was time to leave the United States.

It was a spring day in early April when I stepped to the balcony of my house in New Jersey and looked down at my front yard below with a different eye. My pink saucer magnolia tree had blossomed. The red bud tree, too, had lost its pale green leaves and had turned violet pink with its clusters of tiny flowers burdening those brown, flower-laden branches.

I no longer saw America. I knew in my heart the journey into the past would have to be made.

I left the balcony, went back inside, gathered white bed sheets and headed downstairs to the living room. Soon, the bed sheets would cover up my piano, velvet armchairs, and collection of porcelain dolls. All of the books in my study would be placed in carton boxes, all art frames and mirrors crated, rugs rolled up, and china wrapped in foam.

I had sold my New Jersey house and this was my moving day. I had my mother with me that day. She was sitting in the living room looking up at me. She had moved in to the house to help me plan my move from the East Coast. That meant cooking for me and helping me with household chores while I buried myself in folding up my Manhattan law practice.

She was sitting near the fireplace in my contemporary Italian loveseat, looking small and lost. I could see her clearly as the sunshine darted from the mini-blind to her shallow skin and painted parallel lines onto her face. She had on a pair of Vietnamese black pantaloons. In such traditional Vietnamese attire, she belonged somewhere else, in an ancient Confucian house with rosewood pillars and embroidered satin scrolls. If she had been in Hue that day, she would have rolled her hair inside a velvet turban, or worn it in a bun behind her neck. But she was in America, and her hair was cut short, styleless and chin-length, like a young girl's hairdo framing the face of an old Asian woman. Her teeth slightly protruded underneath her wrinkled lips, and her nostrils flared.

My mother rose slowly from the loveseat, her small stature edging against the Andy Warhol poster hanging on the wall, and I recognized once more she was so much out of place. She walked on small steps toward the front door, out to the front yard and I followed her. For the first time, I noticed how slow her movements were and how her back slightly stooped.

For months, she had cooked my meals in the kitchen, moving around in the smoke and mist that emanated from steamy boiling water and sizzling oil and broth, chopping Kai Lan and scallions and stirring brown sauces over the stove. In those moments, she perked up, lively and animated, and in the beginning of her stay with me, I had assumed she would always be that way. Later on, I discovered that she was only comfortable in the kitchen cooking Vietnamese food, where she came alive in the smoke and smell of Oriental spices and vegetables. The rest of the time she sat or tiptoed around the big house like a shadow, quite often escaping my notice, although occasionally, I saw her pass by my study. She was too careful moving from room to room, as though fearing my own furniture and afraid of disturbing me by making noises with her heels. So, she either sat still in her room, or passed from room to room like a ghost. I noticed, too, that in the morning it took her hours to make her bed. Yet when I casually looked into her room,

I saw that the comforter was not tucked underneath the pillows. Instead, she had folded the comforter and placed it at one end of the bed, the Vietnamese way. Perhaps self-conscious that she was not making the bed the right way, she preferred keeping her door locked. So I stopped looking in.

We stood in the front yard of my New Jersey house, mother and daughter, and when I looked over, I could see the thinning top of her salt and pepper hair. She had turned to look up at me, and I no longer saw the pair of eyes that reminded me of Grandma Que. I had assumed our eyes would remain black forever. But that day, I noticed for the first time that the pupils of my mother's eyes had faded into a greyish color, and the corners of her tired eyes looked watery.

The pink magnolias that smiled radiantly in my front yard no longer spoke to me of America, but rather, reminded me of my mother's life as a young woman in Vietnam. Back then, she loved a different type of magnolia. White flowers that grew on very tall trees in the tropical climate, giving sweet-smelling, silky white petals that curled at the edge.

"Do you miss your white magnolias, mother?"

She was walking away from me, toward the row of spiky rose stems in my front yard. She stopped to examine and caress each bloom as though gently looking for defect. Among those long stemmed roses, I saw my mother as who she really was: the quiet gardener, creating life and growth, even in transient places.

When she first moved in with me to New Jersey, she insisted on planting rows of roses in all colors along my living room windows. Since then, the roses she planted had bloomed. Initially, I tried to stop her, painfully aware of my need for a life change, and the possibility that soon, I would sell the house, and then, all her gardening efforts would be wasted. She knew this. She knew, too, that her stay with me was temporary, and when the house was sold, she would be leaving, back to Texas, where the rest of my family had settled for the warmer climate. Yet quietly she called a charity working with senior citizens, and the social worker came over to take her shopping at the nursery.

The roses came in white, yellow, deep red, and pink, among which one rose stood tall, displaying the unusual lavender touch to the edges of its petals. If Grandma Que were around that day in New Jersey, she would have said that the beautiful lavender rose represented the spirit of the Mystique Concubine in exile.

On the day of my move, among those bright colors, my mother moved silently as though saying goodbye to the roses. She was mumbling something.

"Roses are so impermanent. They wilt so quickly."

She turned and raised her voice to tell me. She said that when I settled down again in another house, I should plant a strong, tall tree that gave my life some sense of permanence and some comforting shade.

"Although nothing is permanent these days, including tall trees," she added.

I wondered if she meant that there could never be anything permanent for an old immigrant living in exile like her, including the bond between mother and daughter, houses and trees.

In America I had never owned the shade of a strong, tall tree.

On our last day together in my house, I rushed toward my mother and almost scratched myself against a tall, thorny rose stem in order to reach out and hold her hands. She looked at me in confusion and amazement, the pupils giving off a dazed look under the drooping epicanthic folds, and her shoulders automatically jerked back. My years of living away from her, my lack of time to talk to her, and the orderly coldness of my house must have caused her to feel alien toward me. Such a house and my schedule as a practicing corporate lawyer were a far cry from the disorderly comfort of my childhood in District Eight, Saigon.

"Maman."

I addressed her by the French word for mother, like in childhood.

"I am not coming with you to Texas. The Americans are officially returning to Vietnam for business. I have volunteered to return to

Vietnam to help open my law firm's office there. I'm leaving next week."

We stood for a long time in the front yard feeling the morning breeze of spring time and inhaling the scent of blooming roses. I held her hands all this time. Faintly, I felt her trembling.

"In Vietnam, will you do something for me and go find..." She had asked quietly, with no tears, but stopped in the middle of the question.

I was expecting her to tell me to go find Grandma Que's tomb.

But she said nothing about her mother. Perhaps the bond there was too sacred, and the separation at the fall of Saigon almost two decades ago was too painful to be articulated or mentioned in words. Instead, she repeated and finished the question dreamily:

"Will you go back to Hue and find the villa and the magnolia tree?"

I nodded.

2. The New Vietnam

I arrived in Ho Chi Minh City, my former Saigon, on a hot and humid summer day. But neither the tropical heat and humidity nor the familiar clipping sounds of the tonal, monosyllabic Vietnamese language spelled any welcome-home message. Instead, at the airplane exit, I found myself squinting my eyes at the blazing sun in disbelief. Gone were the bright lights and glass windows of the passenger lounge overlooking the airport runway. Gone was the elegant canary yellow compound that connected the passenger lounge to the row of office buildings that once housed American military headquarters. A bare ground and unkempt hangars had taken their place.

I was shocked by the primitive austerity of the new scenery.

The alarm in my mind started to buzz as I observed customs officials in their mustard green uniform, with their blank face, flat cheekbones, greenish skin, and yellow teeth. *The Viet Cong, the enemy, the wicked*, the buzz words and the irrational fear of childhood attributed to widespread propaganda quickly revived. I pretended to act nonchalant by adjusting my sunglasses and smoothening my linen pantsuits, although my heart pounded with anxiety. I had to apply the one Asian trait that had helped me make it through life—the ability to stay emotionless and bury my feelings deep inside.

Wait and wait patiently, even if it means eternity, I had heard the saying from my childhood.

So I waited patiently in a long line of nervous Vietnamese expatriates returning home, all looking exhausted and restless, yet still arguing about cargoes that contained gifts for relatives, representing the excess and comfort of America. A fellow traveller, a middle-aged, jovial Vietnamese woman, put her mouth to my ear:

"Put a 10-dollar-bill inside your passport, my dear, and you'll make it through the line quicker. "

I thanked her for the tip, but bribing my way into the path homeward was something the lawyer in me would not do. When it was my turn to present my American passport, I decided to address the young immigration official in mustard green uniform, who was staring at my passport picture, by the familiar pronoun "anh," and referred to myself as "em." For that moment, the young man had become my respected older brother and I was his little sister, a feeble female looking up to his fraternal power. In informal conversations, the Vietnamese always address each other by familial relationships. Nineteen years ago, he would have been my enemy, the Viet Cong. The young man flashed a smile.

"Born in Hue?"

"Yes," I said.

"A lawyer?"

"Yes."

"Make lots of money in America?"

"Not really."

"Any gift for fellow countrymen?"

"No, I'm on a commercial, business mission, not allowed to carry gifts."

He returned the passport and I headed toward the exit.

A hord of haggard people gathered behind the metal fence separating the airport from street peddlers, taxi and cyclo drivers. For a fleeting moment, I saw the crowd outside the airport gate as the same group of anxious and despairing people I had seen climbing over barricades outside the U.S. embassy, that day in April of 1975. After two decades, these same people just looked poorer. Their hollow faces, shallow skin, sunken torsoes, and chopstick arms and pantlegs all spelled the hard life of the developing world. They leaned against thin ropes and the metal fence that separated common life from the privileges of a plane taking off, away from the plague of poverty, to a better life elsewhere.

The crowd had signs with names of the foreign guests to be picked up. I, too, was welcomed with one such sign. It said, Ms. Simone Sanders. Not a Vietnamese name. I walked toward the sign, passing two women selling oranges and grapefruits at a wooden stand. I caught their stare lingering upon my linen suits and leather purse.

"Tay hay Ta?"

They were talking among themselves, wondering whether I was "foreign" or "domestic." "Tay," one of the women said definitively. She considered me foreign. The dark sunglasses helped me hide my emotions.

My driver, who held up the sign, was a typical middle-aged Vietnamese man with scrupulous eyes and balding hairline. An old polyester shirt hung loosely over his diminutive torso. Eager to please, he flashed a broad smile at me, showing his bad teeth, and crammed my luggage into the trunk of an old Toyota. The car rolled on to the crowded streets of Saigon and we made our way through the hords of cyclos and mopeds. Thousands of mopeds rushed around us from what seemed to be thousands of directions, as though at any moment a collision could have taken place, springing these cyclists into the air. The residential streets of Saigon were framed with food carts and street vendors. The display of culinary delights ranged from dried cuttlefish to boiled peanuts wrapped in newspapers, and beef noodles served in chipped bowls glazed with a thin film of yellowish oil.

Despite all that animation, the City appeared dreary. A few rare spots of green trees diversified the urban chaos, yet unable to brighten or sweep away the dust. The smoky sky of Saigon became a huge movie screen. I was the only spectator and also an actress, watching and reentering that surreal movie, back into a place once called home.

3. Looking For the Marble Floor

By 1994, the Socialist Republic of Vietnam had made the historic Continental Hotel of Saigon into a state-owned joint venture project. That meant the French owners were long gone, together with the elegance and luxury of the past, since the hotel had partially become an investment of the new government together with its non-French investors. Inside the lobby, the French touch remained only in the intricate wood beams and dark wood paneling. Outside, French architectural features remained in the structure's cheery white facade.

Earlier, I had asked the reservation clerk specifically for room 210, overlooking *Rue* Catinat, now called Dong Khoi, or Uprising Street. As soon as I opened the door, I looked down to the floor.

There was no gray marble.

Although the French owners were gone, the new management still placed French instruction booklets, greetings, and menus on the *table de nuit*, which was no longer a copy of a Louis-the-Fourteenth antique, but, rather, a Hong Kong-made nightstand. The cheap nightstand did not go well with the grandiose opera curtains covering an entire wall — the only real vestige of old French Indochina left in that drab room. I had no recollection of the curtains, either, although I remembered distinctly the moment when Christopher asked me to approach the window. There, nineteen years ago, I stood, looking out at Saigon skyline, harbor and downtown district. Perhaps back then, the curtains were drawn up and opened. Perhaps I was too confused and self-absorbed then to notice the details of the room.

I stood in the middle of the room, seeing vividly the 20 year-old girl who walked away from the tall French window that allowed her one last look at the city, before she was determined to leave it behind for good. Quietly she unbuttoned her *ao dai*. The golden embroidered dragon danced its last dance when the black satin fabric dropped to the floor. The first cold breeze of conditioned air hit her belly like a sharp blow, when the black silk pantaloons finally rolled off.

In my business suit, I knelt down on the carpeted floor, crawled toward a corner, dug my fingers under the baseboard and peeled off the carpet.

I recognized the cold grey marble floor underneath.

I drew up the deep red opera curtains and stood pensively at the window overlooking Dong Khoi, as I had done that day in April. Farther, on my right, toward the other end of the downtown district, the round clock on top of the gate to the *Ben Thanh* market still defied the passage of time.

I could see it. It was the same clock.

I craned my neck to look to my left, back at the white Opera House that landmarked Saigon. The white dome and the French colonial facade had endured. In front of it, what was once known as Saigon's miniature Champs d'Elysees had lost the glamour, yet was busy still, with pedestrians, cyclo drivers, and its four-laned traffic separated by paved medians that housed bazaar-style kiosques and souvenir shops. The City, deteriorating and impoverished, was still intact. At one end of the shopping square, the statue of a paternal Uncle Ho, grinning among a group of children at the end of Dong Khoi Street, replaced the bronze statue of a South Vietnamese soldier of pre-liberation days.

I left the Continental Hotel and walked onto the street. A little girl selling postcards had followed me all the way, her large, black eyes pleading for my cooperation. I took a one-dollar bill out of my purse, and dozens of other large, black eyes immediately appeared from nowhere, quickly forming a circle around me. Beggars, women and children with their rugged brown faces and toothpick limbs, tugged at the hem of my skirt. They uttered small pleading phrases that sounded like refrains of a mourning tune. It took me almost an hour to escape from the singing beggars of the new Saigon.

Back in room 210, standing on the balcony, I saw darkness bestowing its threatening presence over the city. There were no street lights. Suddenly, I understood why my great-grandmother, the

Mystique Concubine of the Violet City, had analogized the night to a villain and called it the Face of Brutality. Somewhere, in all that darkness, floating in the blackened sky, Andre's dreamy Indochina smiled her amorous smile, exactly the way she was portrayed in the Foucault collection, sluggish, languorous and mystical in her undying romance, awaiting a revolution or the last conquest.

She faded away, Andre's *l'Indochine*, leaving me alone with memories that would not die. I understood the place of memories. For those who quickly forgot, memories did not exist. For others, they got tucked away somewhere waiting to be uncovered.

4. The Lacquer Divan

I went back to the townhouse in the back alley of District Eight, paid a healthy lump sum to the present owner, a government cadre named Minh, and asked to spend one night in his living room. He was hostile at first, obviously concerned that I might be attempting to reclaim the house.

"The government deeded the house to us," he declared.

By the time I had doubled the size of the initial offer and placed the cash in his hand, he pretended to smoothen the corners of those dollar bills I gave him, tapping one foot lightly while dancing his eyes around to avoid my gaze. He placed the money inside his trouser pocket, a signal that he had graciously acceded to my request.

"Please feel at ease and look around," he said.

The house had been chopped into three quarters, occupied by three cadre families, as the government's reward for their contribution to the People's revolution. Cadre Minh, my host, occupied the largest quarters, a three-meter-wide claustrophobic room filled with old furniture and spider webs in all corners.

The old tile floor, stain-filled, used to be part of our living room where my piano sat. There, I had practiced the scale while Andre looked on from the window. The tiles had passed the stage of turning yellowish. A brownish shade had taken over what used to be a translucent white, each piece of tile blackened at all four corners with accumulated dirt.

My eyes drifted from the broken chair to the chipped table before I caught sight of some sparkling thing in the corner, underneath a torn, flowery cotton curtain. I stooped to look and saw the carved glistening phoenix wings made out of mother-of-pearl inlaid onto lacquer, underneath a layer of dust.

I raised the curtain and gaped.

Under a torn mosquito net, the old lacquer divan, too flashy and stoic for the meager surroundings, occupied a dark corner, as though it had been waiting for my return all this time. Despite the abundant scratches and chipping of the mother-of-pearl inlay, the enduring woodwork shone stubbornly, mocking and challenging its filthy surroundings.

For another exorbitant amount, I persuaded Minh to let me spend my night on the divan. In the beginning, he wanted to bargain for a better price, bragging to me that because the divan looked so antique and beautiful, for years, despite extreme poverty, he had been reluctant to sell or dispose of it. He knew it was an antique. I let him go on with his bragging until he detected my impatience. Only then did he voluntarily stop his song-and-dance with a wide yawn.

Nothing would have prepared me, however, for his next reaction. When I quietly told him that I was the great-granddaughter of the original owner, his face turned whiter than a sheet:

"My children, my wife, and I, even our relatives and guests, have tried to sleep on this beautiful thing. None of us could stay the whole night," he said. "We all had terrible nightmares about being drowned in a river, or caught in a fire. At times we felt someone was pulling on our legs or pushing our back so that we would fall off. The truth is, by the time word got around, no one would want to buy this divan, even if we had wanted to sell. I thought of chopping it up, but everytime I raised an ax, something stopped me and I just couldn't destroy this beautiful thing."

I stared at him speechlessly. Was he telling me the truth, or was he simply playing with my emotions, knowing of my background and reasons for returning to the house for a visit? How did he know to use the images of a river or a fire, if the story he told was not true? I tried to rationalize. The country, after all, was deceptively complex, and the city, despite its growing population, was still functioning like a small town, especially when the Ministry of Interior and the neighborhood police, the Cong An, actively controlled the flow of information, tourists and visitors, as well as the lives of its citizens.

Whatever the possibilities, Cadre Minh and I stared at each other from opposite sides of the divan, for a long time. A chill traveled down my spinal cord as I peered down at the luscious mother-of-pearl dragons and phoenixes dancing around its four legs. I wanted to ask Minh more questions, but he had conveniently left the room.

Minh came back to give me a thin blanket that smelled of mildew. The extra service cost me a dollar, or ten thousand Vietnamese piasters. The amenities did not include pillows, so I had to put my overnight bag under my head.

My back ached as it came into contact with the hard wood. Unable to sleep, I focused my eyes intensely on the flickering light coming from a kerosene lamp. Lack of electricity and blackouts had become a routine for the inhabitants of modern Saigon. A humid odor—a combination of mildew, sewage, damp soil, and kerosene — filled my nostrils.

I felt the cool and smooth wood surface underneath my back and limbs. I could still hear Grandma Que speaking to me on that same divan while tears fell down her face. It was indeed very rare that she cried.

I went back to the past and needed no sleep to relive the nightmare. It was Grandma Que's nightmare, related to me in 1972, after I had returned home from Paris.

5. The Coffins of Cinnamon

My father's townhome in District Eight of Saigon had no extra bed-room for Grandma Que, and while I was in Paris, Grandma Que had slept in my bedroom. Upon my return from France, she insisted that I was grown enough to have a private bedroom all to myself, and that she would be sleeping on the divan, which had been placed next to the family altar table, adjacent to the dining area. So, my father set up a rattan screen that separated the lacquer divan from the dining area and the altar. What was behind the screen became Grandma Que's modest quarters. She settled in to the small space quietly, never once mentioning the luxurious spaciousness of her villa in Hue.

Those days, I hid my broken heart about Andre by studying hard for the final two years of high school before the college entrance examination. Quite frequently, I stayed up very late to prepare outlines for classes. I studied at the dining table, where I could spread my papers and homework.

It was a late, quiet night in the summer of 1972. The air was stuffed with humidity, as air conditioning was not part of the lifestyle of the average Saigon household. I had dozed off from studying, my head falling on to the table, when I suddenly woke up and heard sobs from behind the rattan screen.

It took me at least a few minutes to readjust my vision. I had forgotten to blow out the kerosene lamp, which flickered on, casting shadows of the furniture onto the tiled floor. In the still night, the sobbing sounded eerie and tragic. I listened carefully. Grandma Que was crying in her sleep.

Up until then, I had never heard or seen her cry.

Terrified, I went behind the screen and found her quivering. She was awake, her eyes wide open, her trembling fingers clutching onto the edge of the pillowcase in the flickering yellow light of the kerosene lamp. Tears filled her distorted face and dropped onto her salt and pepper hair, spread on the pillow.

I took her slender frame into my arms, not knowing exactly what to do. I did not realize how grown I had become until I felt her trembling against me, delicate like a child, and I was able to embrace her fully. I, the spoiled and weepy Simone, was comforting my strong-willed grandmother, a woman in her sixties, my protector, my guardian who always made things right for me.

In tears and sobs, she told me of her nightmare. In the dream, Grandma Que was sitting alone by a riverbank, facing a tranquil river, the cooling stream of water flowing downward, its movement obvious and distinct, yet eerily silent. The silence was absolute, and although the river was moving, time had frozen in place. There were objects, flowing downstream in harmony with the flowing water. They, too, floated in silence.

"Coffins, floating coffins, so many of them, I couldn't even count," she whispered. "It was my job to catch them, but there was no use. I could not reach out."

Listening to her and holding her in my arms, I myself could feel the stuffy air over the flowing river, and see the image she painted with words: eery coffins, all floating downward, passing by me, in utmost silence.

I told her what seemed natural to me — the lacquer divan was the cause of her nightmare. It was not the most comfortable bed to sleep in. Further, the origin of the divan was mystical enough. She herself believed that the wood had come from the deep jungles of Vietnam, where trees became the sanctuary of wandering spirits. I assured her that when I finished college and started working, I would buy a luxurious new house in Saigon, with plenty of bedrooms, to replace the villa in Hue, and we would donate the divan to the national museum, where it should belong.

It was a solemn promise, I told her.

"Oh, Si, you are such a child." She held on to my arms. "It could not be the divan. It was something else. That Face of Brutality haunted my mother for so long. It must have followed me, too. I wish my mother would come and let me see her face."

"What do you mean, Grandma, seeing the Mystique Concubine's face?"

I, too, had heard of her great beauty. Yet I had never seen any picture of her.

"Oh, Si, she was destroyed. My beautiful mother. Why did everything beautiful have to be destroyed? I was never able to hold on to what was mine. All those beautiful things."

She was hanging on to me, palpitating as though in shock.

"What do you mean Grandma?"

"The way she died, Si."

"With nightingales singing outside her window, around her bed, the symphony of music, and those stars and the moon. Crystal teardrops falling into the water..." I dreamily described the same old details of the romantic fairy tale that had been told to me a thousand times as I grew up.

"No, no, Si, it was a lie. I lied. I couldn't change what I saw that day, when the fire broke out. Lying was the only way I knew how to..."

"What fire?"

"It was a summer day in 1930, the year of the revolt of *Yen Bai* near the Red River in Tonkin, led by Thai Hoc the Patriot. The revolt was unsuccessful and the French had just guillotined Thai Hoc and 12 of his fellow comrades. Later, there were isolated farmers' and laborers' uprisings of 1930, in various parts of Annam, resulting in oppression and bloodshed, all allegedly organized or instigated by the communists. To me and my mother, it was all the call of the Cach Mang—the revolt of the people. To us, at that time, we could not distinguish communists from non-communists. Couldn't even understand what the difference was. It was all about the people against the harshness of French colonialism. By then, both my sister Ginseng and my brother Forest had left home to join this call, the Cach Mang."

"My mother was still very beautiful then. There were fighting and gunshots in the villages between French legionnaires and the Cach Mang. There was a river behind the silk farm. It flowed through the hamlet of Quynh Anh and provided transport to the adjacent villages. She sent Son La, Mey Mai, and me off on a boat, up the river, to the next village where we could take refuge, while she stayed on with the silk farm and the ancestral house in Quynh Anh, waiting to meet the Cach Mang rebels. She was hoping she could be reunited with my sister and brother or at least send news to them. When I turned around the last time, from the boat, I could still see her face behind the window frame. She was looking out at us, the same way she had been looking out of her window frame at night before bedtime, her eyes sad and pensive."

My heart raced together with Grandma Que's panicky words. She had stopped for a moment to breathe, and I wiped off her tears.

She opened her mouth for air, and I held her head up.

"We got to the next village safely. That night, I couldn't sleep. I felt pained in my rib cage and my entire body was burning hot. Oh Si, I felt like I was set on fire."

"I felt like that once," I broke in, recalling the séance in Hue. "I had just turned ten and you had taken me to see Mey Mai inside the Citadel. At the end of the séance, I felt the heat around me, burning me. And I flew high above the flame, looking down at my body on a burning bed of straw."

I held her up and wiped away her tears, but Grandma Que kept crying into my palm:

"At four in the morning, the gunshots subsided, and I was determined to board the boat. I was ready to paddle home. I knew I had to come back to her, alive or dead. Mey Mai and Son La tried to stop me. Useless. So they got on the boat with me. We traveled up the river, back to the silk farm. Oh, Si, how can I ever forget what I saw during that boat trip? Green bamboo trees once bordered the riverbanks. Yet, when our boat approached the village of Quynh Anh, toward the silk farm, the bamboo trees were all gone. It was as though the whole bamboo forest had burnt down. And we began to smell that awful smell of dry heat and fire. You see, either the French or the Cach Mang rebels had set fire to our property. I don't know who. You see, people hated her. She was involved with the French, some say she was sleeping with the enemy, and she was also financing the Cach Mang at the same time. And yet no one protected her in the village. All she had was me. Son La and Mai were loyal, but they were old and powerless.

"The ancestral house in the village of Quynh Anh she built had been been burnt to the ground. The silk farm was severely damaged. I walked through the ruins and smelled the awful smell of burning flesh. I followed the smell and found her corpse by the dirt road leading to the riverbank. She lay there, blackened and stiff like an ill-smelling coal log. She must have run from the fire toward the river, the flame burning on her back and engulfing her as she made the last effort at life — trying to jump into the water."

I stroked Grandma Que's salt and pepper hair to calm her down. Yet I felt rotten inside. I had to shake my head continuously to control my own emotions. I was about to cry for those nightingales

236   Part Five

singing outside Huyen Phi's bedroom window, and for the image of Huyen Phi, beautiful in her death, which dominated my childhood. The images were forever gone. No teardrops disturbed the surface of the River Huong so the sparkling waves could harmonize with the twittering birds. No beautiful woman lay peacefully on the lacquer divan while nightingales sang in harmony with nature and music came from a thousand directions. I silently mourned the loss of the fairy tale. The twitching muscles on Grandma Que's face spoke of the excruciating pain she bore inside.

"My mother's face was gone. All that luscious beautiful hair was gone. All the soft and pink flesh on her limbs was gone. I picked her up and wrapped her in my smock, that awful smell of burning flesh sticking to my skin. I held and rocked her as though she were my child. I inhaled into my lungs and heart that awful smell. Hysterically, I started digging a hole in the ground with my hands to bury her, but Son La and Mey Mai ripped her away from me and pushed me forward. There was no time. The fighting was still going on and we had to move on to stay alive. We had to run along the river under gunshots. So I closed my smock around her and left her there, among all those ruins. Oh Si, I had left my mother burnt to death in that awful fire, her corpse unburied and rotten."

The fire did not wipe out all of Huyen Phi's silk empire, which was scattered all over Hue and Annam and did not just concentrate in the battered village of Quynh Anh. In tears, Grandma Que told me how the fighting subsided when the Cach Mang rebels withdrew back into the jungles, and French legionnaires ceased shooting into the villages. A few days later, Grandma Que and the two trusted servants returned to the village of Quynh Anh to gather the remains of her mother for cremation.

"My mother had decomposed, you see. I saw tiny white worms, maggots and beetles crawling out of her, or what was left of my beautiful mother. Mey Mai, Son La, and I cremated her in the back garden, and I saw those worms wiggle under all that fire. Her ashes were spread over the River Huong, and I began concocting the tale about my mother's death. I made Son La and Mey Mai promise they would go along with my story. Later I gave out 500 piasters to any villager who could repeat my beautiful tale with accuracy. I paid handsome rewards to have the tale drilled into people's head. So the tale continued to spread, acknowledged by even those who knew about the fire or who had helped me collect the remains of Huyen Phi. I wanted her to remain the beautiful mystery she was meant to be."

Grandma Que buried her face into my palm, and sighed:

"To start all over, I moved away from the village to the resort villa in Nam Giao, built by my mother at the suggestion of foreign merchants who were her trading partners. We were able to keep the lacquer divan and altar items intact, since they were kept at the Nam Giao villa. There, I set out to recreate what I had lost. I repurchased antiques and replaced those items lost in the fire. I rebuilt the silk farm and made it operational again. I was determined to produce the most beautiful silk in memory of my mother. A year after the fire, I commissioned a portrait artist to create a painting of the Mystique Concubine. But the man did not have anything to go by, so he painted onto silk a stereotypical image of an ancient Asian maiden."

That same year, Grandma Que went on to tell me, she began caring for the young magnolia tree her mother had planted, in the front yard of the villa at Nam Giao.

That same year, 1930, what is known today as the Vietnamese Communist Party was formed.

"Oh, Si, my child, I successfully recreated everything possible, except for the beauty of her face. All I could do was to commission a silly silk painting. Even my memory was no longer intact after that fire, and all I could remember about my mother was that blackened, ill-smelling, blistered and puss-oozing corpse. And all those little white worms that crawled through her burnt and rotten flesh."

She was leaning against me, her mouth gaping for air in between words:

"And when my sister was released from Hoa Lo, I thought I could have that notion of beauty again. Perhaps I could recall my mother's beautiful face in my beautiful sister. But my sister came home, an invalid, an imbecile."

She calmed down, and let go of my hands:

"For years, I prayed every night that God would allow me to see again my mother's beautiful face, or to hear my sister's laughter again, but never once could I dream of either one. Instead, I began having this recurring nightmare. Those floating coffins. Floating at their own pace, as though they had a life force of their own, in all that silent hot air and on that sparkling water."

"But the face isn't gone, Grandma," I told her ardently, trying to convince both of us. "Look at me, Grandma, I am here, with you. You've told me all my life that the spirit of Huyen Phi has come back in me. It has, Grandma, I know that for sure now, because that day when you took me to the séance at Mey Mai's house, the spirit spoke to me. That day, I knew nothing about the fire. No one had told me. Yet at the séance I saw fire, all over me. I was floating in and out of all that heat. I saw so many women, all strangers, dressed as the dancers of Champa, I guess, from the ancient temples and towers of some lost kingdom. The dancers came and gathered around me, revering and protecting me, lifting me up above that fire. No, Grandma, you have not been lying at all. The images just came to you and became the story you had to tell. There were indeed nightingales, Grandma, in my voice, when I sang. I saw them. Felt them. Heard them. And petals of magnolias, too, danced around me, before I finally flew to the top of the magnolia tree you had planted. And later on, after the séance, I once dreamt of a floating coffin, made out of the red brocade of her cloak. It opened like a red flower, and I saw a beautiful woman lying in it. That had to be the Mystique Concubine. Oh, Grandma, I saw everything you saw, and I felt everything you felt.

I talked non-stop, drunk in the images I created and remembered, afraid that if I slowed down, I would stop believing and then I could no longer convince myself.

"Feel my face." I took her bony fingers and placed them on my cheeks. "You see, it is still here, with you all the time. No fire can ever, ever take away the face."

"What's in the floating coffins, Grandma?" I asked her after a long pause.

She turned away, obviously not wanting to share with me the rest of her nightmare. She started crying again, softly.

"I couldn't catch the coffins. I could not keep and protect what I love. And I am afraid of dying alone."

"No, that's not true, Grandma. You have always protected me and made things right for me. And I will never let you die alone."

"If I die, bury me in silk, a nice coffin, sealed and stuffed with fragrant cinnamon. Like your mother, I am afraid of earthworms. They crawl. Put my jewelry inside my mouth and ears to keep those earthworms from crawling in." Her bony body shivered in my arms.

I heard a noise at the door. I turned around and looked. Mi-Chau was standing there, sobbing. She crawled onto the divan, and nuzzled her head against Grandma Que.

"Oh Grandma, I love you," Mi-Chau cried. "I love you even more than Simone can ever love you. She left you to go to France. I will never do that. I'll take care of you always. I hate coffins. I don't like earthworms. Please don't die."

After I blew out the kerosene lamp, both Mi-Chau and I crawled onto the divan with Grandma Que. I dozed off into my own dream. I was standing by the river with her, watching floating coffins. *"I promise, I promise,"* I yelled across the river to the beautiful old woman who sat demurely with her head cocked to one side, her stream of salt and pepper hair sparkling against the afternoon sun. I glided on that gleaming body of water, approached the coffins, and kicked one of them open. I looked inside the coffin, but it was dark. I could not see what was inside.

I woke up from the darkness inside the coffin I had kicked open, to be greeted by the morning sun spreading its gleam across the room. The day had begun. Mi-Chau and I were alone on the divan, inside the white mosquito net. I heard Grandma Que's voice in the kitchen and then out on the porch, chatting with the neighborhood women about the wet market, in the same calm voice that commanded respect. I got up and watched her continue the routines of her day with amazement. She prepared my breakfast, never once mentioning what happened the previous night.

I had just spent the whole night on that same divan after a nineteen-year absence. I had dozed off intermittently, and when I woke up, the unbearable sorrow nibbled at me, as I realized for all my years in America, I had never been able to dream of Grandma Que.

That morning, I offered Cafre Minh another healthy sum to purchase the divan, pleading to him that I needed to hold on to what was left of my family history. He readily accepted the idea, yet continued to haggle over the price. He called it "fair negotiation," citing the years he had spent taking care of it. He kept raising the figure.

"Best of luck with a divan that invokes bad dreams for whoever lies on it!" I finally gave up.

I pretended to walk away. I badly wanted the divan, but did not know how to get it within my means. I was on the verge of tears when Minh called out to me, announcing that out of kindness, he would be ready to return the precious divan to the descendant of its owner. We reached an agreement and finalized the details. He talked constantly about emotional values while counting the dollar bills.

There was the problem of shipping the divan out of Vietnam, since Vietnamese law prohibited the export of antiques. Minh emphatically reminded me. My problem alone, not his.

I decided to go see Mai Anh.

6. Mai Anh

My childhood buddy at Lycée Marie Curie of former Saigon, a beautiful girl named Mai Anh, daughter of a former South Vietnamese colonel, had transformed herself into a carefully madeup woman in her late thirties. She was still a sensual beauty with her almond-shaped eyes, swollen lips and delicate arms and legs. Yet her coarse, uneven skin, yellow teeth, and those dark circles under her eyes, bordered thickly with blue crayons, belied a former beauty queen who had stayed up too many nights, smoked too many cigarettes, drunk too much hard liquor, and made love to too many wrong men. Her complexion, once fair and pale, showed the creases of early wrinkles and too much oil from bad makeup. Her fingernails and toenails were painted orange. She bragged to me that all her makeup, skin care, clothes and shoes were imported.

She greeted me with the warmth and ardor of a long lost best friend, holding and squeezing my hand the whole time we spoke. Unlike the typical poor Saigonese receiving his or her relatives or friends from America, she expected no financial help, accepting only the Lancome makeup kit I had purchased for her at the Changi Airport in Singapore. She did not complain about her life in Saigon or the hardship she had had to endure in its dark days, right after the Russian tanks rolled in and the comrades of the north began to nationalize property and industries. Many families associated with the former regime were moved to economic zones near the jungles, mountainous areas, and on undeveloped deltas.

All for the good of the reconstruction of the country, she said. I could not tell whether it was an ironic statement.

She revealed that her father had died in a concentration camp and her mother had died, too, at sea when they tried to escape in 1977. Mai Anh survived the shipwreck, but was arrested and jailed. She emerged from jail as a new woman, she said. From that point on, Mai Anh set out to master the ropes of the new regime.

Mai Anh hired a car and a chauffeur and treated me to an outing at sea and a fresh seafood feast at Vung Tau, the former *Cap* St. Jacques of colonial days. When we got back to Saigon after the day trip, she took me to a kareoke bar and showed me how the young girls of Saigon interacted with wealthy Asian businessmen while Hong Kong music was playing in the dark. She told me of extravagant banquets held in exclusive restaurants in Saigon, where potent Chinese dishes like shark fins, birdnest soups, and tiger bone marrows were served, and young and beautiful Vietnamese hostesses spoonfed foreign businessmen all throughout the meal.

Mai-Anh was determined to show me a glimpse of what her life was like and what my life could have been had I not entered the Continental Hotel that day in April. The message she gave was clear: in the poverty-stricken, transitional Vietnam of the early nineties, Mai Anh had become a rich and savvy woman who knew the trade of femininity.

She kept an air-conditioned apartment in District Three, paid for by one of her Taiwanese clients. God knows how many wives and girlfriends the man had had in Vietnam, but the arrangement kept Mai Anh well-fed, she readily admitted. She told me the Taiwanese, who ran a new hotel in central Saigon, was about to go home. He had made arrangements to pass her on to his friend, a Korean petroleum engineer representing South Korean oil interests in Vietnam. The engineer was in Vietnam for a one-year contract of offshore drilling work. That mythical sea dragon of the Vietnamese culture, Lac Long Quan, the forefather who stretched himself along the 2500 kilometers of narrow and winding coast, must have blessed the country with rich mineral resources deep in the blue sapphire waters. Conveniently, the mystical blue dragon also blessed Mai Anh with her next meal ticket and luxurious lifestyle by giving those foreign petroleum project engineers and managers a reason to be in the developing Vietnam. All for the good of the country, Mai Anh retorted.

"But what happens when the engineer's one-year contract expires?" I asked.

Quite often, Mai Anh explained, local women in servitude concocted a fantasy—that somehow the cohabitation would lead to a marriage and a ticket out of the country. In some cases, the fantasy came true, providing the majority of the girls with more impetus to dream on. For a way out.

"Out of the country's poverty and backwardness," Mai Anh added emotionlessly, explaining to me that her deep pockets were always middle-aged Asian men.

"White men, who often stink and are far too hairy," she declared, "can be quite stingy and expect to get it for free, after a meal and a night of slow dancing."

She showed no shame, talked bluntly, almost defiantly, and considered herself lucky compared to other women. Some walked the streets. Others rode their mopeds alongside foreign shoppers who were carousing to make their Far East experience worthwhile. These butterfly-like silhouettes in their charming *ao dai's* could propose and negotiate, just as skillfully and boldly as the pimps, who could either be teenage boys or white-haired old men.

Her crude comments made me flinch. No typical Vietnamese girl, demure, indirect, and non-communicative, could be that blunt. But Mai Anh was not a typical Vietnamese girl. She was the *Lycée* Marie Curie girl who had survived jail and the tragic deaths of both parents during the dark days of Saigon.

I told Mai Anh of my desire to export the old divan. Considered an antique by the authorities, by law, the piece of furniture could not leave the country.

"Have you heard of the law of the jungle, my friend?" She asked me mockingly.

I told her I understood.

"Welcome to the Socialist Republic of Vietnam," she said.

She advised me to give up the official application procedures through Customs. She knew a kept woman in Hanoi, mistress of a powerful cadre at the Ministry of Interior, who could help. She said given sufficient time, she could get to almost everyone of power in Vietnam who had a mistress. She said she had found her place in the new Vietnam but was concentrating on leaving the country, eventually with one of her wealthy foreign hosts.

I spent the night with Mai Anh in her air-conditioned apartment and listened to her tape of Vietnamese music in the seventies, banned at one time by the communist government. The music brought us back to our old days at Marie Curie. For a split second or so, I thought she might have teared.

In the morning I left Mai Anh to go to a law firm meeting at the Century hotel, where my English and Australian law partners talked of how the government was attempting to curtail the practice of law by foreign firms to protect the new law graduates of Vietnam. Those few privileged lawyers of the new Vietnam were eager and needy to enter the international commercial world.

It was the era immediately following the lifting of the U.S. embargo. My partners warned me the office phone line could still be tapped, and documents generated from the office could still secretly be screened by the Local People's Committee or the Ministry of Interior through the network of local employees furnished to foreign enterprises by the government. The discussion at the meeting centered around the various ways international law firms could legalize their presence in Vietnam and bypass local regulations prohibiting foreign lawyers from practicing Vietnamese law. The suggestions included teaming up with the so-called "friends of the government" as co-counsel, even if they had no legal training, and disguising time sheets showing the international lawyers were practicing Vietnamese law, or international law on Vietnamese soil, against the prohibition of the Socialist Republic.

"So, we complain about the country's lawlessness. Yet, we find ways to evade or break their laws, in order to make a profit," I blurted out sacarstically.

All the lawyers sitting around the breakfast table stared as though I were a monster, incomprehensible, out of place. I felt sick in the stomach and left the meeting early.

Mai Anh's hired chauffeur took me onto the bumpy Highway One stretching between Saigon and Hanoi. The endless winding road was waiting for World Bank's infrastructure development loans to fill the bumps. I passed through the greeneries of Vietnam, the breathtaking *Col de Nuage*, or Pass of Clouds, nestling against the whiteness of flying clouds, hovering over perpendicular cliffs that soared from the sapphire sea below. I passed white sand beaches and green forests, square rice paddies with sluggish, skinny water buffalos dipping themselves in muddy water. I passed quaint bamboo tree entrances to villages that have endured for centuries, with those old yellow and low-roofed schoolhouses, their front yard filled with shoeless children who wandered toward the side dirt road, their neck craning out, their inflated bellies protruding over bony knee caps.

I arrived in Hanoi just in time for its nostalgic fall season, its breeze of cool air welcoming new foliage and buds of plum flowers, stirring tiny and peaceful waves on Hanoi's traquil lakes.

I walked through government offices in buildings that seemed a hundred years old. Their classic French architecture and facade contrasted with the neglected interior, the chipped coats of painting and baseboards, and the Oriental furniture sitting over stained tile floors. I came in and out of these buildings, frustrated with red tape and the inert bureaucracy, saddened by the Hanoians' poverty, yet bewildered and awed by the city's overwhelming air of history.

I followed the steps Mai Anh had carefully outlined for me, meeting with her contacts, one person after another, mostly in the famous fish restaurant La Vong located in the old commercial neighborhood of Hanoi, the *ba sau pho phuong*. There, grilled fish was served in a claypot of sizzling oil over a tiny coal stove, next to a clay plate full of fresh dill, lettuce and mint leaves. I followed someone into a house near the West Lake in the outskirts of Hanoi, where I was told to drop off an envelope full of U.S. currencies. I never met the mysterious mistress of the Ministry of Interior official, but when all had been said and done, the woman sent one of her runners out, promising me that my divan would be delivered at the dock of Singapore's World Trade Center within a month.

The runner said part of his job, at the instruction of the madame, was to entertain me to a night out in Hanoi. A taxi picked me up and took me to the Metropole Hotel for dinner, and then to a dance club in the outskirts of Hanoi. The darkness of the place, together with the silhouettes of slender, red-lipped women wearing black dresses, was not far from the feel of the second-class discotheques and mini-nightclubs of New York City. Under the dim light, the women all reminded me of Mai Anh.

Just when I was leaving the dance hall, I caught a glimpse of a familiar face at the door. I recognized the English partner at my law firm, his thinned-out hair and clean-shaven chin lighting up over his necktie as the neon sign outside the dance hall beamed across his balding forehead. He was getting into a cyclo with a petite Vietnamese girl who looked half his size and his age. Crowding in the narrow sedan seat of the cyclo, she sat in his lap, resting her childlike frame upon his pot belly. I knew the man's Christian wife and his three children, all living in Singapore while he set up business in Hanoi and made trips back to Singapore during the weekend. I felt nauseous. Off I fled, leaving the neon sign of the new Hanoi.

Part Five

7. O-Lan

In the following days, I managed to take a trip to Hue and looked for the old places. It was in the late afternoon when I strolled by the French villa at Nam Giao. An earlier visit to the People's Committee of Hue confirmed what I had expected to hear—the villa had been nationalized into a guesthouse for government workers. Plans were underway to evict the residents and convert the villa into a bed-and-breakfast hotel to meet the needs of foreign tourists attracted to Hue's royal tombs, vast open land, and dreamy sceneries.

I walked around the villa several times. Peeping inside the stone wall encircling the villa, I saw again scenes of my sixth birthday. I walked to the front gate, and met a man in his early thirties, who introduced himself to me as the house manager.

"I saw you circling the property. What do you need, Miss?" he asked.

"Nothing," I said. "I just want to look. It's not a crime to look, is it?"

He looked at me strangely, perhaps noticing the dampness in my eyes.

"You are from abroad, aren't you? I'll let you look, but only for a few minutes."

He opened the gate. Part of the front yard had been blocked off, and a narrow cemented walkway had been built, leading to the front door. I recognized the high ceiling and cool checkerboard marble floor, but the entire open living room had been chopped up into smaller rooms. The villa had been divided into small, filthy apartments, all facing a dark hallway. Tiny doors and windows opened to rusty iron balconies, painted in gaudy orange, where trash was not contained in bags, and dripping wet clothes were clipped to old, unused electrical wires.

I stood dazed in the dark and humid hallway. The wretched poverty of modern Vietnam had taken away all romanticism of memory.

"Someone must have lived here once, before liberation, before the nationalization of private assets. The house once belonged to some-one," I told the house manager on the way out to the gate.

"This house belongs to the people of Vietnam," he looked at me defensively.

I observed his obstinate face. He could not be more than thirty-five years old, speaking with the coastal accent of North Vietnam instead of the musical accent of Hue. I moved to the front yard and he followed me.

There was no more magnolia tree. I saw instead piles of dirt, lumber, rusty sinks, clay containers, and metal bars. Like a construction site.

I went to the spot where there once was the magnolia tree. It was difficult to make my way through the piles of dirt and metals. I finally located the spot, convinced it was the right location.

"This is the commune's patio," the man went on. "Residents come here to work, cook, and the children play after school. The water does not drain properly in this patio, so they are undertaking renovation. They are doing all this work themselves."

I was bending over to look for traces of the tree, among piles of metal bars.

"Where is the tree? You've cut down the tree!" I said.

"Excuse me?" He said.

"Where is the tree?" Tears lingered on every word I spoke.

His voice softened, his head lowered, and he almost whispered. "You used to live here, didn't you?" He asked, already knowing the answer. "I moved here from the north. I don't know the history of this house." He avoided my eyes.

"Some one died here. By hanging herself some 50 years ago."

"A woman?" he asked.

"My mother saw her die."

"I am not surprised, Miss. You must have heard the rumor. The residents kept talking about some ghost. I told them there is no ghost. Even if someone did die here, it was too long ago. Enough time has passed for all ghosts to be reincarnated. They must have started their new life already. Besides, in this country, so many people have died through the years. Good cause. Bad cause. We don't have enough room for the living, let alone ghosts."

"Wait, Miss," he called after me as I headed toward the street.

I was standing on Princess Huyen Tran Street, watching the sunset. Somewhere I could feel the unobtrusive silhouette of Grandma Que in her black silk pantaloons, standing still, looking into a dying sun. Next to her was the little girl in her pony tail, holding her bike.

In front of me, the same sun was dying. I looked toward the river across the street, muddy and full of trash. The body of water no longer had the cool, calming color of imperial jade. Trash accumulated on both banks and the green grass had turned dry and yellow.

"I heard about the princess and her silk farm. She died after liberation. She had no family," the man said after me.

I ceased my footsteps and turned to face the comrade.

"She died," I could only repeat. "Tell me how she died." I forced a smile.

"There was a housekeeper here once, I heard," the man continued, his eyes glancing downward, his hand hanging in the air in a gesture of guilt and embarrassment, perhaps, as though he were too proud to apologize for his earlier lies. "I know who you are, Miss. You're coming back to find what was once yours."

His fluttering hand seemed to tell me: I am not responsible for your loss.

"The housekeeper, they call her O-Lan," the man said slowly, pausing to wait for my reaction. "She used to live here to take care of the altar when the princess was away in Saigon. All before liberation. I heard from the people around here."

"Where can I find her? This O-Lan. In the village of Quynh Anh?"

"Do you have relatives there in the village?"

"No, I have no one," I said. "The person I cared for so much in Vietnam is dead. And I have never met this O-Lan."

"I would not go to the village if I were you. Let me find O-Lan for you."

I opened my purse and took out all of the cash I had with me.

I expected him to grab the green U.S. dollars, but he pushed my hand away.

"No, no, please don't do this," he said.

"Why are you being so nice?"

"You have something to do with this place, and I saw tears in your eyes. You are out of place here. I like you and don't want you to wander out to the villages. That would make you very sad."

"Why?"

"There is nothing in the village but sheer poverty and deterioration. Central Vietnam is the poorest part of a very poor country. The village is not sanitary like your hotel. You may get sick drinking and eating there. Further, the villagers are very poor. Children have no shoes, and they smell. Those villages just recently got electricity, and there isn't enough of that. The villagers expect you to give them cash and gifts. You are one of the lucky and wealthy Vietnamese who live overseas and return home to visit. Those poor souls will follow you, expect things from you, and make you even sadder. Are you rich enough in America to feed an entire village, and many more, for the rest of their lives?"

I shook my head.

He stopped talking and looked down at his feet.

"Why do you care?" I asked.

I sought his eyes and he looked away. He was looking at the spot where the magnolia tree once stood. His eyes shifted toward the river across the street, and he began talking again, this time non-stop as though he were hurrying through to hide his emotions.

"I may be from the north, but my family is originally from Hue. The people from overseas come back home and spread their money around. Or the people here ask for money. Coming home becomes a money transaction. Done for love, family, pride, duty, whatever, it is still a money transaction. This takes place everywhere in Vietnam nowadays. But I want to say Hue is different. There are Hue citizens who will do something for the sake of doing it, and who are not for hire. Also, we from the north got the bad reputation: mean, stupid, unreasonable, argumentative, greedy commies who blinded themselves in Ho Chi Minh's thoughts, took out their hatred and jealousy on the people of the south, and got rich because they robbed the south of its property. But there are exceptions, too. You don't have to pay me to help you, Miss."

I was speechless. A wind gushed by, and the cluster of green dollar bills in my hand flew off.

"You should hold to your money, Miss, that's negligent," he yelled at me in his northern accent, agitated to see the cash fly away, his hungry eyes following the dancing bills.

Together, we picked up the green dollar bills scattering on the street. One bill flew toward the river. He ran after it, crossing the street, breathing heavily.

"We almost lost it to the river. That's a lot of money, Miss. A U.S. twenty dollar bill. It's more than what I make in a month as a government cadre."

He went on to promise me again he would try to find O-Lan in the village of Quynh Anh. And then he would send her to my hotel. All free of charge.

My room at the Huong Giang Hotel overlooked the River Huong. Once used as housing for the Regents of Hue University in the sixties, the formerly colonial structure had been transformed into a three-story complex that resembled more a schoolhouse than a first-class hotel. It sat solemnly by the riverbank, grave yet modest in its washed-out peachy color: a thin shade of diluted limestone solution, brushed hurriedly upon the stucco walls by a careless artisan. The peachy structure looked vague as though it had no real identity against the vast, picturesque scenery of a river, a grey bridge, and green grass — all dreamy like a Monet landscape, tucked in a corner of this sleepy, sluggish ancient town. The hotel was a proud display of the Socialist Republic's economic joint venture process, where foreign capital joined forces with the state in hopes of transforming the old structure into a commercial enterprise, supposedly in the international three-or four-star standards of the hotel industry.

Earlier in the evening, at the front desk, I had encountered a young woman in her flowing polyester pink *ao dai*. She asked me whether I was a *Vietkieu*, the term used for a Vietnamese expatriate returning home. She glanced surreptitiously at my U.S. passport with my name printed in all caps, *Simone M.U. Sanders*. I could have told her M.U. stood for Mi-Uyen, a metaphoric name too Hue-like in style and spirit to suggest the simple background of a village girl. I asked her whether she was a *canbo*, one of those privileged Communist cadres, the ruling class of the country. She readily said no, as though she were denying something sinful. Her coral lipstick, coquettish smile and gentle Hue accent were all too bourgeois to constitute the trademark of the revolutionaries from the jungles or coastal regions of Vietnam. I had always imagined the *canbos* to have high cheekbones, a flat face, brown teeth, and the unique high-pitched accent that typified the rural area of north Vietnam or the coastal regions of the Gulf of Tonkin, where all r's are pronounced as l's, and all l's are pronounced as n's.

I watched her meticulously write my name down in the hotel registry. If she was not a *canbo*, I thought to myself, then she must be the relative of one of those guerrilla war participants, undercover agents, or symphathizers who had made their contributions to the revolutionary cause — a contribution substantial and well-remembered enough to have earned her this post.

I am on your side, her eyes sparked the unspoken message as she responded to my gaze with the knowing smile of an accomplice. She complimented me on my white T-shirt and black jeans and silver buckled belt, and told me it must have been really nice to live in America. Her gentle Hue accent and sweet mannerism lessened the harshness of stereotypic, class-conscious terminologies such as *Vietkieu* and *canbo*, which so far had marked my debut to the ancient city of birth.

The calm water of the River Huong put me immediately at home. The hotel had kept the riverbanks well-cared for. No trash accumulated by the riverbanks, and the water maintained its distinct shade of deep, dark bluish green like imperial jade.

Only in Hue did the night have its own fragrance.

On the balcony of my hotel room, I inhaled into my lungs the smell of fresh water shrimp and snails, mixed with the ripeness of yellow bananas and fermented coconut milk, the richness of boiled peanuts and peanut oil, and even the musky scent of blood-like betel juice and home-grown tobacco, which dyed and cracked the lips of those old, toothless country women who came to visit Grandma Que from the hamlet of Quynh Anh.

All that was lacking, I whispered to the night, was the sad folk songs on the pentatonic scale of the East, vibrating through the small waves of this calming, mysterious river, the sound of that *Nam Binh* song, which typified the spirit of Hue:

"*Nuoc non ngan dam ra di, cai tinh chi, muon mau son phan, den no O Ly, xot thay vi, duong do xuan thi. Thousands of miles an exodus from home, a heart full of sorrow, oh pity her, paying her debts with her spring days.*"

The telephone rang inside and disrupted my immersion. The voice of the receptionist in the pink *ao dai* was on the line.

"There is someone here to see you," she said.

My visitor was standing next to the elevator bank, a plump, old country woman, carrying a straw bag, dressed in black pantaloons and a polyester blouse, her gray hair pulled back, hidden under a Vietnamese cone hat.

"Mey Mai!" I cried out in shock.

I recognized the old, grey-haired woman who once danced in an incense-filled room, riveting on one foot, her head swirling underneath a satin silk cloth. Many, many years ago, she told me the tale of the Spirit of the River Huong. In a country filled with under-nourished citizens, she was rather plump. In a city full of sad inhabitants perhaps still mourning the massacres of the past, she was rather cheerful, her animated eyes dashing around from the hotel cashier's counter and the magazine stand, onto the elevator banks, where her eyes focused on the open-shut movement of the elevator door.

She stood quite a distance from me, not recognizing me immediately, her eyes lingering upon my face, probing for some familiarity, and then moving on, back to the movement of the elevator door. The curiosity in her eyes revealed her fascination and awe with the luxury of the hotel.

"Turn, Mey Mai, speak to me again, in the language of the Paddle Girl of the River Huong. I am home, at last," I cried to myself.

"Mey Mai," I called out to her again.

This time, she turned toward me, her eyes fixed upon my face, for a long time.

"Oh Heaven Buddha, you look just like the young Madame Cinnamon, dressed in Western clothes. You are Madame Cinnamon's granddaughter, aren't you?" She laughed whole-heartedly. "Oh, no, I am not Mey Mai. I couldn't be that old and still living. I am O-Lan. My mother, Mey Mai, would have been over 100 years old this year, if she were still living."

From that point on, she acted as though I was a long lost relative. I invited her to my room so we could talk, and she was getting very excited, wanting to ride the elevator.

"I have never ridden an elevator before. Will I get caught between those metal doors?"

She approached the elevator on timid steps, leaning onto my arm with obvious apprehension.

I assured her, and we slipped inside the elevator.

"All you need to do is touch it slightly."

I illustrated my point by standing right on the edge of the elevator door, expecting the closing door to bump slightly against me. But the door did not stop. Instead, it closed on me, causing me to lose my balance, pushing me toward the outer edge of the metal frame. I struggled to push myself against it. The scene of my struggling must have looked ghastly to her, because the old peasant woman was screaming.

I was not crushed, but in the moment of embarrassment, I cursed myself, concerned that she would never trust me again. I had failed my demonstration. I had forgotten that the Huong Giang hotel was once an old schoolhouse, renovated in haste. Technology had reached Vietnam, but not in the most reliable way.

The old woman had turned pale, still screaming her heart out. A couple of young men from the hotel's front desk rushed over to help.

When the ordeal was over, the old woman still stood riveted inside the elevator as though she were glued to the metal wall, with the straw bag in between her black trousered legs. She refused to get out. I had to ask the two young men to block the metal door, while I took her hand and pulled her through the narrow space. I led the panicked old woman toward the stairway.

She held the straw bag against her chest, sighing with relief, telling me she would never again enter an elevator.

There was a tea tray in my hotel room, with a thermostat of hot water. I poured a cup of tea for the old woman, who kept feeling the edge of my bed and commenting on the thickness of the foam mattress, informing me that in the village of Quynh Anh, she slept on a bamboo bed covered with a cod mat that squeaked at night.

"Your grandmother called me O-Lan; Miss Lan, that's what O-Lan means in the Hue style."

Comrade Chuyen, the house manager at the villa, had sent his men out looking for her. As usual, O-Lan, a food peddler, was busy that day selling glass noodle soup from the coal-burning stove that she put in a basket. The other basket contained bowls and chopsticks and she carried both baskets with a pole that rested on her right shoulder. She was going from door to door, village to village, the two baskets rhythmically bouncing with her footsteps, when Comrade Chuyen's errand men passed on the news to her that I had returned.

She had been waiting all these years for my return, she claimed, so when she heard the news, she immediately carried her baskets to the Huong Giang hotel. She had left the baskets outside the entrance with the cyclo drivers who congregated in front of the hotel, leisurely waiting for the next tourist to emerge from the hotel lobby. And then the fierce competition would begin. The tourist was up for grabs by the luckiest and most persistent cyclo driver, who would follow his prospect, pouring out his pleading words, refusing to leave, until the client felt guilty or exasperated enough to step on the cyclo's sedan chair.

"Comrade Chuyen is a nice man," she said. "Too nice to be a comrade."

"I never knew Mey Mai had a daughter," I said.

"A bastard."

She gulped down her tea, slipping from the edge of the bed to the floor, where she comfortably squatted. A faint smell of cut onion emanated from the flap of her blouse. She had overcome her shock about the elevator and was more at ease to talk.

"My mother had me when she was already in her forties. A shameful thing for an old maid. It was because of me that your grandmother sent my mother away. To give birth somewhere else, away from the community gossip, and to look for my father. I was born in in the foothills of the Truong Son range, which later became the Ho Chi Minh trail."

O-Lan talked about her life emotionlessly, as though she were describing someone else's life, from an opera, or a book, having nothing to do with her.

"I've lived in the village all my life. Used to take care of the silk farm. I raised the worms and took care of the threads. The farm continued to generate silk until the cadres from the north took over in 1975 and ran it to the ground. Now it is a deserted place, just the four walls, and no life.

"All these years before liberation, your grandmother helped support me. I was hidden away, since it was not a good thing for people to know that my mother, a virginal medium, had an illegitimate child. After the *Tet* Offensive, my mother disappeared, and your grandmother brought me to her villa. I lived in your house, taking care of the altar, making trips back and forth to the Quynh Anh village to attend to the silk farm. But you know, after the *Tet* Offensive, business was no longer good. From Saigon, your grandmother still sent me money every month, and the farm was still running moderately. After liberation, the cadres took over the silk farm, kicked me out of the house in Nam Giao, and I returned to the village."

"So it was not the 1945 famine or the Japanese occupation that caused Nanny Mai's departure," I said. "My grandmother never mentioned you to us, O-Lan. There were too many things hidden in my grandmother's heart. For example, my mother never knew her father. All she knew was a black-and-white photograph of an Annamese mandarin, wearing an *ao dai* imprinted with embroidered Chinese characters. "

I was talking more to myself than to her at this point.

"Ms. Que's husband supposedly passed away young during the Indochinese War. At least your mother had a photograph of her father. I have none. I might as well believe I've fallen out of the sky."

The old woman finished her tea and reached out for her straw bag.

"What happened to Mey Mai?" I asked.

"I assumed my mother died on her retreat into the jungle, when she went with the withdrawing troops of the Viet Cong, after the *Tet* Offensive."

She mentioned the death of her mother with the same nonchalant attitude she exhibited when recounting her life story.

"Why are you, daughter of a famous revolutionary, selling noodles on the street? Where is the government's reward for Mey Mai's contribution to the revolution?" I asked mournfully.

"Oh, Miss, where have you been?"

She raised her voice, exhibiting an outward expression of emotion for the first time. I could not decipher whether it was sacarsm, irony, anger, or disappointment.

"I don't know what my mother was. Revolutionary or medium. But I know she was not from the north. And the revolution, hell do I know what it was supposed to do? I just got poorer and poorer. Even the cadres from the north got on a boat and fled to America after liberation. North or south, winner or loser, the whole country had nothing to eat. And your grandmother, my supporter, owner of that silk farm and that beautiful villa, starved herself to death. All during her illness, I fed her spoons of *bobo* — the grains they fed to horses, given to us by the Russians, so I heard. We had no rice to eat, the healthy and the sick alike. So she died, Miss, without a coffin to be buried in."

8. Hue Recitativo

My face felt hot. *I promised you a nice coffin. Satin inside. Cinnamon scented. Properly sealed so no insect could invade and disturb you in your journey to the other world. I would make sure all your antique jewelry, those things you guarded all those years, including what had been returned to you by the Foucault family and presented to you by young Andre, would accompany you on that journey. But I had failed you.*

"No, no coffin," O-Lan went on. "We were all too poor. I was too poor to buy a coffin for your grandmother. We did not have a bed to sleep on, let alone a coffin to bury her in. So, I wrapped her in a cod mad, and buried her in the wet rice paddy."

"What happened to all those antiques and jewelry?" I despaired.

"I don't know anything about antiques or jewelry. Don't suspect me of taking them. If I had, I would not have been a peddler selling noodles for all these years. Perhaps you should ask the government. Comrade Chuyen and his men.

"I was with your grandmother till the last minute, about a year after liberation. That was the hardest year. I am getting old and can't remember any more." O-Lan frowned in an effort to remember details, her fingers fumbling with the hard edge of the straw bag.

"Your grandmother wanted to save this for her granddaughter to remember her by." She put her hand inside the bag. "I knew you would be coming back."

O-Lan pulled out, from the straw bag, a long salt and pepper wig. The stream of hair swept against O-Lan's hand, cascading down, alive and defying like an animal. I saw Grandma Que standing, removing her ivory comb and the velvety net that held the stream of hair in place. Set free, the stream of hair danced its way down her flank.

"I cut off your grandmother's hair and made it into a wig and saved it for you, as she wanted me to."

That night, in her monotonous voice, O-Lan told me what happened to Grandma Que after my family had left for Tan Son Nhat airport.

Communist North Vietnam celebrated its victory by tightening its iron hand on the south, cutting off the country's ties to the West, sending South Vietnamese to "reeducation camps" and newly created economic zones. The winner of the war nationalized the assets of private citizens, especially those who had fled the country. Grandma Que joined the rest of South Vietnamese in that fate.

Kicked out of the townhome in District Eight, she packed a couple of suitcases and bought a one-way bus ticket back to Hue, only to learn her French villa and what was left of her silk farm had been nationalized. So she returned to the village of Quynh Anh. Poverty plagued Vietnam and changed victory and liberation into a joke. Two decades of warfare resulted in a starved country.

Back in the village of Quynh Anh, Grandma Que and O-Lan moved into a hut and sold off Grandma Que's belongings to survive. One day Grandma Que did not feel well and went to the infirmary in the outskirts of Hue. The health care cadres told her something very bad had happened to her internal organs, but there was no firm diagnosis by any trained doctors, nor was any medicine available. O-Lan thought Grandma Que's internal organs had become rotten from too much sorrow. Maybe a bad seed had grown into a tumor and caused her pain. *Rau thui ruot*, she said, too much sorrow and sufferings could rot the gut of a warrior, let alone a fragile woman like Grandma Que.

The health cadres at the infirmary told her she might need an operation to remove the rotten part from her gut. The infirmary had no anesthesia. If she wanted to have an operation, she would have to travel to the big cities, perhaps back to Saigon, and even then there was no guarantee. She said she already knew what was wrong with her gut. *Rau thui ruot*, she told O-Lan. She needed no medical diagnosis.

She no longer wished to live.

So she went home to the hut in the village of Quynh Anh and lay down on the cod mat. She never got up again. O-Lan fed her *bobo*, the foodstuff for horses, holding her nose, forcing her to swallow to keep up her strength. She persisted for months and then she stopped eating all together, the *bobo* grains foaming around her blistered lips. All during those months, she never mourned. Never spoke. Never cried. She just wilted away. When the last moment was near, O-Lan turned her over to wash her, and found her back full of puss-oozing open wounds and nasty broken blisters, developed from lying too much, too long, under unsanitary conditions.

O-Lan was still talking about the village, the country, the revolution, her mother, my grandmother, and all the things that made up the decades to which I was not privy. I no longer had the capacity to listen. As she spoke, I fell into a trance:

I am inside the villa again, on Nam Giao slope. I am tiptoeing barefoot on the cool marble floor, and the checkerboard design dances under my feet. I am reentering the ancestral house, with my naked heels pressing onto the checkerboard marble that cools off the heat outside. I stop, concentrating on my heels while feeling on my skin pores the silence that embraces me into its enormous presence. The silence becomes a cold wind that sweeps through me. In perfect rhythmic synchronization, I move along with the wind.

I crawl inside the mosquito net that waves like a layer of mist, and find her lying still with her eyes closed so I can't see the black longan seed pupils underneath her thin, smooth eyelids, with their tiny wrinkles that hold the secrets of her life. Her mass of long hair, salt and pepper, spreads to one side of her body. I lie down next to her and talk. There is so much to tell. I have in my mind images of barren trees, skeleton branches, and red leaves that fill up the damp ground of St. Germain des Pres, Paris, or the suburbs of New York City. She has never seen red leaves. Nor has she seen the kind of magnolias grown in the West.

I find myself falling down a cliff so blackened I cannot see the bottom. It is an excruciatingly slow fall. Slowly, slowly, tumbling like those leaves departing the trees of St. Germain des Pres. In my descending path I hear every word of her whisper. She says what good does it do to go on living when all your loved ones are gone and you never know when you will be able to see them again?

And then she says the last thing that sticks to my mind, following me until I hit the bottom of the cliff. The fall makes no sound. I land and the heaviness of silence will not let go of me. She reminds me of all my promises unfulfilled. Put her on the lacquer divan in the old French villa at Nam Giao. Let her hang on to her jade and diamond earrings and gold bracelets — memory of a royal concubine, artifacts already blessed with the holy water from the bottle of Quan Yin, the Compassionate Female Buddha. Place the rings inside her mouth to keep insects away, the bracelets on her chest to protect her heart, earrings tucked inside her ears, blocking the ear canals.

My very strong grandmother wants to be safe. She once talked about the baskets of violet orchids hanging all around her French villa. She said when my grandfather— the man she loved —was still alive, the only flower he liked was mauve orchids. Orchids prefer shades and only occasional sunshine. Gentlemen grow orchids for the women they love a lifetime and for the cause they pursue.

In death, let her be with the gentle fragrance and violet shades of the flower that signifies the dignity of her womanhood and symbolizes the color of the horizon in her beloved city.

I held Grandma Que's hair in my arms. I caressed the hair that had waited for years for my touch and embrace. The presence embraced me as much as I embraced it. I felt her and saw her in her last moment on earth.

I held on to the salt and pepper wig and thought of all the losses. No more magnolia tree in front of an old villa to welcome me home with those hanging baskets of violet orchids and a chime-filled porch. No more dainty white mosquito nets hanging over a mother-of-pearl inlaid lacquer bed. She had wanted all those physical things within her upkeep to welcome me home, once I turned old and grey and tired of life in exile.

I was not yet old and gray, and I had returned home.

Grandma Que and her world were gone.

I raised the wig and pressed it to my heart. The pain revived and cut me in half, sharp like a sword piercing through. I bent along its gradual and precise path into numbness.

9. Last gifts

I had offered O-Lan money. Just like Comrade Chuyen, she refused my gift. She did not come to see me for money, she said.

"Is there anything you want or need, 0-Lan?"

She hesitated for a while and then spoke, almost too eloquently, as though she had planned the speech.

"I have grown children, and many granddaughters. They are all healthy and good. I would be pleased if you could take one of my grandchildren to America. You can just pick one among them. Any particular one you like? A little girl, perhaps?"

"*Chung toi ngheo qua, co oi!*," she said. "You see, Miss, we are poor, too poor. The parents would be grateful to give the child away to an adoptive parent like you, and no one would create any problem for you. It would be the greatest deed you could do for me..."

When she detected no overt sign of enthusiasm from me, she deflated like a flat tire.

"O-Lan, I will consider it seriously," I said, watching her mouth open again with hope. "I will just have to let you know. But I can't just pick up a child on this trip."

"Perhaps the next trip, then?"

I opened my suitcase and took out my mid-length coat.

"It gets cold in Hue, so please keep this from me."

I put the coat inside the straw bag.

"If I accept this, you will still consider adopting one of my grandchlidren, then, or will this be all? You wouldn't think you would have paid your debt to me for burying your grandmother by giving me this coat, would you, Miss?"

"No, no, no," I said. "I'll do all I can."

She jumped up to squeeze my hand.

"One more thing," she continued with her excitement. "The silk farm."

"What about the silk farm?"

"Deserted and abandoned by the government. Without silk, the village of Quynh Anh is dead. For years, I have been selling noodles instead. Nowadays, fabric is smuggled from China. But Vietnamese silk is good, darn good, so delicate, so fine, and I know all about silk worms. All my children and grandchildren and in-laws can work. The village can revitalize. Maybe you can get your friends in America to be interested in rebuilding that silk farm. That would make your grandmother's soul very happy."

She sounded sophisticated and solemn, as though she were delivering another practiced speech. My eyes searched for O-Lan's and she met me there. I found, again, the pair of animated eyes in an animated old woman, like that day at the séance, in all that incense smoke. Through these eyes, I had met the Spirit of the River Huong. I found in that pair of eyes the sincerity that gave meaning to my homecoming. I had to believe in the rare signs of goodness on this ravaged land. I had traveled on this land like a stranger, not knowing for sure whether it was indeed dear to me. I had to hold on to my own conviction that it loved me, honestly loved me, like Grandma Que had loved me, and that I could do some good to the place.

Another item, old and fragile, lay at the bottom of O-Lan's straw bag. O Lan said it was a handwritten notebook prepared and kept by the Eunuch Son La until his death in 1935. Grandma Que had kept it on the altar, behind the photographs, and managed to retrieve it from there before the North Vietnamese closed the door to her villa at Nam Giao. After she died, O-Lan became the custodian. Son La's notebook, the eunuch's recording of my great-grandmnother's life in the Violet City, was meant to be with me. So O-Lan turned it over, together with the wig.

I saw O-Lan to the door and bought the rest of her chewy tapioca noodles so she would not have to worry about her income for the day. I gave the basket to the hotel's restaurant staff.

"Everyone in town knows O-Lan, the *banh canh* peddler of Hue. She wanders around, talking to tourists and concocting stories all the time to win sympathy," one of the waiters said. "What were you doing with the *banh canh* peddlar, Miss? Be careful, and don't believe everything she said. That old, shrewd woman must be up to something."

10. River, Coffins and Memory

In the aromatic air, the River Huong sparkled under the bluish moon-light. A laminating lamp hanging from the balcony shone onto the eunuch's notebook that I held in my hands.

I began to read Son La's handwritten notes, describing the making of a royal concubine — the transformation of the poor Paddle Girl of the River Huong into the legendary Mystique Concubine of the Violet City. Written from the perspective of the lady he served, Son La's notes became the only official recording of the Mystique Concubine's memoir depicting her life in the West Palace. The loyal old servant had recorded the tale in the new Vietnamese, using the Roman alphabet, devoting to it the same intricate attention as to his calligraphy. The handwriting shone in perfect penmanship, meticulously and consistently leaning toward the right. The even strokes, blurred and stained on old notebook paper, resembled scripture from rolls of an ancient Egyptian text.

Son La's notes stopped with the Mystique Concubine's departure from the Violet City for the hamlet of Quynh Anh. Those who had knowledge of what happened thereafter were all dead. All I had to go by, as the returning child of Hue, was the notebook of the old eunuch, confirming what I had heard at a séance performed by an old medium, a former royal maid and professional guerrilla spy accustomed to deceit.

My thoughts drifted back to those old photographs and postcards that arrvived in New York City from Paris, all bearing the trademark of the Foucault gallery and containing secrets I might not wish to know.

Where was the truth?

I became the wandering soul looking for roots buried under ruin, denied forever the certainty of full knowledge.

I closed Son La's notebook and stared down at the River Huong, hoping to find, amidst those sparkling ripples, a familiar image. Through the thin film of fog, I saw the slender almond shape of a paddle boat moving slowly and silently in the tropical air of a hot autumn night. A slender, long-haired woman was paddling. The small boat appeared and disappeared. And then at the blink of my eyes it was gone for good.

I heard the eerie sound, *Mee-Ey, Mee-Ey, that noble woman of ancient Champa. Fear not death. Fear not exile. Let her soul rest on those sparkling waves. She has become part of her river and her earth.* The chorus became the promises of her eternity.

I looked to the riverbank. The hot air filled my nostrils, burdened my chest and rushed my breathing. I blinked again and saw Grandma Que, as I had remembered her for the past nineteen years of my life in America. Moonlight shone directly on her, and the stream of hair, salt and pepper, like lacquer marked with snowflakes, flowed alongside her fragile frame.

She was looking forelornly at the River Huong. Coffins. Coffins. Catching sparks of the moonlight beam above them. Coffins were floating slowly and silently, on that cool stream of water, in that hot air.

The silence seemed to last forever, until she turned to face me, with those same sad and serene eyes.

I saw her face. So closely. The wrinkles could not take away the beauty of the fine bone structure. But the face was changing, transforming into the face of a young girl. The identical twins in Andre's picture and postcard collection. The five-year-old Simone who sat on the stairway of the photography studio of Tan Tan.

The girl grew a little older and older, gradually turning into the fifteen-year-old Princess of the South Sea Pearl photographed by the Foucault gallery. The face of Cinnamon. The same face appeared on the fifteen year-old misplaced Simone who strolled the streets of Paris and sang the scale in a church in Rome. The face got older and older again, until it became the forty year-old solemn-looking woman in the portrait that bore the stamp of the Foucault gallery.

It was my face all along.

The face continued to age, older and older, until wrinkles filled it and the eyes became almost hidden behind the drooping folds. She returned to being my Grandma Que. The face I could never see in a dream.

I was facing her, again. Just her and me, with the silent river behind us.

She smiled assuringly, and the sad eyes beamed. *Mi-Uyen, my beautiful lovebird, you are the Princess of Annam; Si, poupee Si, coquettish Si, Si of the Jeanne D'Arc Institute, Si of Lycée Marie Curie, Si of South Vietnam's National Institute of Music and Drama.Mi-Uyen of Saigon's College of Law, welcome home, my child!*

11. Hope, Love and Exile

I returned to Saigon the following week and stood in front of the villa once occupied by Andre and Dominique. The name of the street, *Rue Tu Duc*, had been changed to some contemporary revolutionary's name. The villa had been converted into a French Vietnamese restaurant catering to European patrons.

I entered the restaurant and ordered a meal for my thirty-ninth birthday celebration. I ate alone.

The knowledge that in this place a long, long time ago, Andre and Dominique had lived their married life sank my mind into the mud of nostalgia. As the waiter placed my favorite French flan before me, I closed my eyes and imagined Andre and Dominique, young and serious, loving once, laughing once.

When I left the restaurant, the yellow sun ray of the end of day was still lingering on Saigon's sidewalks.

I travelled on all the streets between my former house in District Eight and what used to be the National Institute of Music and Drama, where as a young girl, I had biked and sung under the shade of those tall tropical trees.

I took a cyclo to Saigon's Notre Dame Cathedral, a miniature of Notre Dame de Paris, nestled in the heart of Saigon, amid rows of green trees — one of the few spots in Saigon that remained unchanged.

It was the early evening hours when I got off the cyclo and walked toward the cathedral. For a moment, I thought I saw Andre in between rows of trees, young and energetic, swift and extraordinarily handsome, yet reflective and wistful still. Holding a copy of "Fleurs du Mal," wearing his wire-rimmed glasses, he was walking toward me, nodding to acknowledge my presence, and when I passed him, his beautiful brown eyes obsessively followed my footsteps.

Nec amo, nec tussis celatur. Love is like a cough. Cannot be hidden.

In agitation, I closed my eyes. Sorrow sank in, as I realized perhaps in my life I had fallen in love too early. At fourteen years of age when somebody gave me yellow tea roses and read Baudelaire to me in my former Saigon.

Nec amo, nec tussis celatur.

When I opened my eyes, I thought I saw Christopher's reproaching gaze as on the date of our wedding in Las Vegas.

"You are the bride who wants no wedding or honeymoon," he had said. "Why did you come to me in New York City? You owed me no obligation. Once you landed safely in America, why not stay with your family and look for the one you truly love?"

"Because," I whispered, "I wanted to know with certainty I had boarded the plane."

Somewhere I still heard the angry roaring sound of the last helicopter atop the U.S. Embassy.

"You did board the plane," my husband seemed to say. "But you never left the place. It is always in your heart, Simone. I can never blame your heart."

My late husband, symbolic of America's largesse, had never blamed my heart. In fact, the largesse was so great that he never asked to occupy my heart, knowing that I had left my heart behind. *Allow me to say sorry,* I said to Christopher before he faded away.

Standing in the heart of the new Saigon, I began to rediscover my feelings for Andre, persistent and haunting since childhood, in a completely different light. He was the only one outside the culture who understood the bond between my soul and those of all the women in my bloodline. My love for him became the genderless, asexual love that persisted through time and space. The young boy of Paris had grown up into the young man of America, and had travelled so far to find in me images of Indochina that no longer existed. We stood at different corners of the world. To start that far from each other, loving was an impossibility, a taboo, a forbidden fruit. But we did meet in a war-torn place, bound together by the same melancholy and mysticism that housed our respective remembrance of childhood, and then off we went again, far from each other, locked in separate places, swept away by our own weaknesses and circumstances.

When the last bit of sunlight died out over the Notre Dame Cathedral of the new Saigon, I thought I saw once more Andre's soulful eyes and flutterring lashes. Those eyes told me they understood the coffins of Cinnamon. His fate was tied to mine, in ways too mystical to be expressed in words. Andre shared in the perfect world that I had lost with the fall of Saigon. Once I realized our bond, my love for him became the love I had for my own humanity, my birthplace, and generations of political immigrants— those nostalgic people, homeless in their sphere, stateless in their world. I loved him anew, beyond all manifestations. Beyond this transient existence.

The realization shook me and all of a sudden, I wanted to sing so bad, to reach those high notes on the right-hand side of my piano keyboard. Into the skyline of the new Saigon. Until night fell and darkness subsided so the evening butterflies of his eyelashes would gather and follow me into my nocturnal tune, where finally, as the young woman who practiced singing, I would reach a perfect LA.

I closed my eyes again, knowing my childhood was gone and both Christopher and Andre had departed from this world. From the point of their departure, all my fear and sorrow were mine alone to bear. Part of me had become the lonely Paddle Girl who appeared in the fog, and part of me had become Grandma Que sitting by the bank of the River Huong watching and mourning the deaths of her loved ones.

In the hot and humid air of tropical Vietnam, I heard again the choral music of Beethoven's *Elegischer Gesang*, sung for the departure of a gentle and noble spirit. The symphonic chorale filled up Saigon's sky, into a crescendo that lifted me to the top of the cathedral. Silence ensued after Beethoven ended. And then, in all that utmost silence, across the River Huong where coffins floated, I heard again the clear voice of a young woman, singing the phrase I once knew so well, in the wailing sadness of the *Nam Binh* pentatonic tune:

"Wait, and wait patiently..."

"Wait patiently, still, Simone, Mi-Uyen of the past," I said to myself.

From the muddled stream of lives crossing and recrossing, O-Lan's exlamation leapt clearly to my mind: a silk farm and a baby girl would make Grandma Que's soul very happy! The words shone on me and became a broad spray of light for the future. Alone in the country of my birth, I reminisced over all the old dreams and disappointments that seemed to have ebbed softly away, like the last note of the choral symphony before silence rushed into the hall.

　　　　　　　　　　　　　　　　　　　Part Five

In that silence, I found in me the seed for a new longing.

Somewhere in the village of Quynh Anh, there was an abandoned silk farm, almost a century old, waiting to be be rebuilt. There was a baby girl, waiting for the tender arms of a lonely woman who had loved and who had lost. I longed to touch silk wrapped around the featherly warmth of a child.

The day had ended, and I looked up to Saigon's sky, hearing my voice lingering on my high note, my question echoing in the air:

In this life, will I let go of Cinnamon's floating coffins and the garden of a place that is no more?

APPENDICES

I. Chronicle of Viet Nam as a nation

257 BC: Kingdom of Van Lang, ruled by the 13 Hung kings – the Hung or Lac era.

257-207 BC: Kingdom of Au Lac, the Thuc era

207-11 BC: The Kingdom of Nam Viet, the Trieu era

3 BC-203 AD: The district of Giao Chi, under occupation and domination by the Han dynasty [first part]

203-544: The district of Giao Chau, under occupation and domination by the Han dynasty [second part]

544-603: The Kingdom of Van Xuan, under Ly Nam De

603-939: the district of An Nam, under occupation and domination by the Tang dynasty

968-1054: The Kingdom of Dai Co Viet, the Dinh dynasty

054-1400: The Kingdom of Dai Viet, consecutively ruled under the [first] Le, Ly, and Tran dynasties

1400-1407: The Kingdom of Dai Ngu, under Ho Quy Ly

1427-1802: The Kingdom of Dai Viet, under the [second] Le dynasty, including the period of civil war between the Trinh Lord (north) and the Nguyen Lord (south)

1802: The Empire of Viet Nam, declared by a descendant of Lord Nguyen and founder of the Nguyen dynasty, Emperor Gia Long

04/1945: Ho Chi Minh declared independence; the last emperor of Vietnam, Emperor Bao Dai, abdicated

1945-1954: The Indochina War between France and the Viet Minh (joined by several nationalists)

1954: French troops surrendered at the battle of Dien Bien Phu, and the Geneva Convention was signed, dividing Vietnam into two states, awaiting a general election.

1954-1975: Era of the Vietnam War and the U.S.'s involvement

1975: Saigon fell and South Vietnam became a defunct state

1976: Reunification of Vietnam into the Socialist Republic of Vietnam

II. History of the Extinct Kingdom Champa
And the Southward Expansion of Viet Nam

982: Viet Nam force led by General Ly Thuong Kiet attacked and pushed Champa's border to south of Hoanh Son (Thanh Hoa) in what is known today as central Vietnam

1069: King Ly Thanh Tong of Vietnam invaded Champa

1307: Vietnamese princess Huyen Tran married king Jaya Sinhavarman III (Che Man), in exchange for two provinces O and Ly (part of central Vietnam today)

1402: Viet Nam invaded Champa. Ho Quy Ly forced king Campadhiraya to concede Indrapura (Quang Nam, south of Hue) and the territory of Amaravati (North Champa) to Viet Nam

1471: Vietnamese army led by King Le Thanh Tong captured and destroyed Vijaya. Viet Nam annexed the new land as provinces of Thang Hoa, Tu Nghia and Hoai Nhon

1578: Lord Nguyen Hoang annexed the Cham region of Phu Yen

1653: Lord Nguyen Phuc Tan invaded Cham's region of Kauthara and pushed Viet Nam's southern border to Cam Ranh

1692: Lord Nguyen Phuc Chu annexed the remaining Champa territory as the new prefecture of Tran Thuan Thanh. The Kingdom of Champa ceased to exist.

Daughters of the River Huong was designed by Tom Suzuki, Tom Suzuki, Inc.,
Fairfax, Virginia.
The cover design is also by Tom Suzuki.
The book was printed by Lightning Source, La Vergne, Tennessee.

The text is 11.5 on 14 Weiss; the display typeface is Trajan.

Breinigsville, PA USA
03 November 2010
248612BV00001B/144/A